Derek Farmer was brought up in a coal mining village in West Yorkshire and graduated with a degree in chemical engineering. He subsequently joined his wife, Jan, into the teaching profession where he quickly became the head of the mathematics department in a secondary school. He wanted to make mathematics more fun for students and had a series of three textbooks published, called *Getting on With Maths*, which were designed to do just that.

Derek has three children and three grandchildren and recently had his first children's book published, a fantasy novel called *Somewhere in Yorkshire*.
He loves to spend quality time with his family.

To my wonderful family. To my two lionhearted sons, Matt and Sam, who fight a daily battle to overcome the debilitating effects of cystic fibrosis. They are a true inspiration to us all. To Sam's caring wife, Joanne. To my loving wife and soulmate, Jan, and my dearest daughter, Rachel, who continues to bind us all together. To my grandchildren, James, Drew and George, who give the joy of innocence its truest meaning.

The love of family transcends all.

Derek Farmer

THE DARK SIDE OF INNOCENCE

AUSTIN MACAULEY PUBLISHERS™

LONDON * CAMBRIDGE * NEW YORK * SHARJAH

A CIP catalogue record for this title is available from the British Library.

ISBN 9781398478497 (Paperback)
ISBN 9781398478503 (ePub e-book)

www.austinmacauley.com

First Published 2023
Austin Macauley Publishers Ltd®
1 Canada Square
Canary Wharf
London
E14 5AA

This book is dedicated to my dear wife, Jan, who couldn't put it down when given the first draft. She is the one who encouraged me to share it with the world.

Table of Contents

Chapter 1

Tom Willis rubbed his eyes as he peered through the front windscreen of his car. Being a detective sergeant in the Metropolitan Police had its attractions, but today hadn't been one of them. Willis had spent a tiresome day in Oxford, where he'd been sent by his chief to interview witnesses related to a case he'd been working on for weeks. He was exhausted from a long day and was ready for home and a good night's sleep.

Willis had now become frustrated by the traffic. His sat-nav had informed him of long delays on the M40. He'd arrogantly switched it off and started to find his own way home along the many side roads. His Mondeo sped fast along the narrow country roads and the dull, featureless terrain made it more difficult for him to figure out where he was.

Another sharp bend loomed out of the darkness ahead, and as he slowed, his headlights picked out a lorry that had slithered sideways into the ditch, shedding its load of timber. The long six-wheeler was skewed at a dangerous angle with its tail reared up in the air and its hazard lights winking.

Willis instinctively pulled off the road onto a grass verge, 20 yards further on and, with unhurried indifference, ambled back to investigate. The headlights of the lorry had been extinguished in the crash and steam was gently hissing from the engine compartment. Jumping down the shallow embankment, he found the cab empty. Noticing the crazy tilt of the truck, it was apparent how lucky the driver had been, as it could so easily have rolled over. He made a circular tour of the vehicle, shouting out to anyone who might be lying injured in the grass, but all was quiet. Because there was no one there, Willis assumed that the driver hadn't been hurt and had probably gone to find help. There seemed little urgency to do anything. He decided to have a quick look around the perimeter of the wreck. If there were no problems, he'd carry on home and not bother calling in the accident.

Better to let the local plods find it and deal with all the paperwork themselves, he thought. *It's not my problem.*

It was pitch-black and Willis had brought his flashlight from the car. He grunted as he knelt on the damp, dew-covered grass and shone his light under the piles of strewn timber. His trousers knees now felt uncomfortably wet.

"Another bloody dry-cleaning bill," he cursed.

He was just about to turn away when his torch beam picked out a reflection amongst the dark shadows, arousing his curiosity. He peered closer. There appeared to be a white powder splattered over one of the planks. Reaching through the crisscross of battens, Willis stretched to his limit in an effort to reach the powder and finally managed to coat the extremity of his index finger. Withdrawing his arm, he began to examine his find. Sniffing the powder, he recognised a well-known odour. He rubbed his finger on his upper gum to confirm his suspicions. The tastebuds burst on his tongue and he nodded in appreciation.

Cocaine, maybe a whole lorry load of it.

Willis circumnavigated the rest of the wreckage. When he was satisfied that he was alone, he flopped heavily onto a pile of planks, making himself a comfortable perch. He had to clear his mind of his tiredness and think coherently. The tingling aftertaste of the cocaine was stirring his sensations and leading his mind down dark and irresistible paths.

Willis was a user. He'd been drawn in over the past few years. He thought of the free lines of coke that he could sniff that wouldn't cost him a penny of his pitiful salary. He also wouldn't have to buy it from scumbag pushers and keep favour with them, in case they blew his identity. He could even sell it on to some of his pals who shared the same habit. Like all drug users, Willis had convinced himself that he was only hooked on social drug usage and no harm would be done to anyone. The arguments for stealing the cocaine just kept stacking up until Willis had persuaded himself that he should avail himself of this free gift. He would take what he could find and leave the scene as soon as possible. He thanked his lucky stars that he hadn't called in the accident.

He knew that he would have to get filthy crawling under the debris, but what the hell. One ruined suit was well worth the effort. He went back under the timbers, grinning at his good fortune and anxious to find more of the drug.

What a coup if it turned out to be a major haul.

But, just as quickly as his euphoria had arisen, it was suddenly dashed away. A piece of timber was obstructing his view and he nudged it with his shoulder. Unwittingly, he dislodged a support that had stopped the wood from sliding downwards and tons of planking moved without warning. The network of props tumbled, taking him totally by surprise and within seconds, he found himself trapped by the heavy timbers. Panic gripped him, as he feared further movement of the load, but the night went suddenly quiet. The only sound was of his own, heavy, frightened breathing as he lay in the claustrophobic darkness.

After a few minutes, he managed to calm himself. Taking stock of the situation, he realised that although he was held fast by the weight, he wasn't actually injured. He felt badly shaken but decided that expending energy on shouting would be a waste of time. The lorry was in the middle of nowhere and his only chance of release was if another passing motorist stopped to help. He would have to wait.

Willis lay in the cold and damp for what seemed like ages. He cursed his luck so many times. He knew that when he was eventually discovered, he'd just have to give the drugs up and take credit for discovering the shipment in the first place. He found his mind wandering in all directions, but he quickly came out of his daze when he picked up the sound of an approaching engine. He clearly heard the vehicle come to a halt and his hopes were raised when several bodies came sliding down the side of the ditch.

He called out immediately, "Help! Help! I'm trapped under the load."

A voice shouted out. It was unmistakably from the east end of London. "Jesus, are you the driver of that other car?"

"Yes! That's right."

"Anyone else with you?"

"No, I'm alone. Can you get me out?"

The voices in the dark became a whisper and Willis suddenly felt uneasy.

"What's up out there? What's wrong?"

Suddenly, a bright light blinded him, as the man holding it tried to assess his predicament.

"You seem to be in the wrong place at the wrong time, matey."

"I know that. But if you ring 999, the fire brigade can have rescue equipment here in no time."

"You've missed the point altogether my friend. Now, how come you're stuck? What were you doing nosing about under there?"

Before Willis could answer, he heard the approach of another body, sliding down the banking.

His heart sank as a heavily accented Italian voice interrupted. "He's the filth. I've just checked his car."

This time a singsong Caribbean voice came out of the darkness. "Hey, Officer Dibble, you really are in the wrong place, man."

The light returned and fixed on the policeman's hand and the white, tell-tale powder.

"You have been naughty, Dibble, haven't you? Playing with our shit."

Willis groaned fearfully and his stomach churned. These were obviously the owners of the coke.

"Tell you what, man. You stay there and don't move."

The man giggled girlishly and the light moved away, but Willis could clearly hear all the voices. There were four of them.

"What do we do, boss?"

A man spoke with authority and it was clear from his tone that he was irate. "Find the rest of my fuckin' coke. It's hidden inside those oak doors. One's split already, so there are only two more. These are the codes. They're stamped on the ends. There's 20 doors to choose from, so get looking."

Willis was aware of the powerful flashlights all around him as the search began. They scrambled carelessly above him and he cringed in fear at the thought of another wood slide. Fortunately, it didn't take them long to find what they were looking for and he was able to breathe a sigh of relief.

"We're in luck, boss. I've spotted the doors. We can shift these planks to get at them more easily."

"Never mind that. Just pull the doors out, but be careful."

Willis lay silent, contemplating his fate and praying that the cars he occasionally heard approaching on the road above would stop. None of them did. He wasn't to know that his captors had cleverly placed a *police accident* sign at the side of the road to make other drivers think the law was already dealing with the problem.

All around, he could clearly hear wood being shifted. The men were working hard, examining the doors.

"Not another fuckin' useless door. You sure these codes are right boss?"

Eventually there was a relieved shout. "At bleedin' last. We've found 'em."

Willis then made out axes being wielded against the oak doors.

"Hold it there Winston. It's splitting along the edge. Siggy, you finish it off."

The sound of hacking wood resumed, but it was more controlled and soon there was a shout of triumph.

"This has split perfectly. Look, there's the stuff, in the cavity."

"There should be exactly ten bags. Siggy, you check they're all there and then take them up to the car. You two start on the second door."

Twenty minutes later, the work was complete and the conversation reconvened within earshot of Willis.

Winston called out eagerly, "What next boss?"

"This is a disaster, no thanks to your driving. You could have cost me the entire shipment."

"The lorry was overloaded, man. We should have used the big truck."

"There's nothing much more we can do tonight. Looking for the other bags of coke will take too long and they're probably split anyway. Look, it's all over the bleedin' place. What we need to do is get rid of the evidence before any other nosy coppers find it. We'll torch the whole lot. When they find the Pig's body, they'll think he was the driver."

A scream of anguish pierced the dark night. There was something quite inhuman in its pitch. Tom Willis had heard his fate. The matter-of-fact way that his future had been decided as though he was a piece of garbage had unhinged his mind.

"You can't! You can't! Please. For the sake of humanity."

A fourth voice spoke to him for the first time. The tone was condescending. "Whoops, our policeman friend's been listening. I quite forgot he was there."

Willis pleaded, "Please, fellas, I'll do anything. Give me a break."

"What you mean is, you'll get done like a steak."

There was raucous laughter. "How do you like yours, boss?"

"Well done, Siggy."

The laughter continued. They were playing a terrible black game with his mind.

"Go and get the petrol can from the car, Winston."

"Sure thing, man."

Tom Willis groaned and shuddered with fear. A dark panic swallowed him up and he thrashed about wildly in a vain struggle to get free. He achieved nothing except to bruise his flailing limbs and in the end, he lay silent, the repugnant stench of his own fear invading his nostrils.

Willis was frantic. "Hey you guys, I can help you a lot. I've got contacts everywhere. I can feed you loads of information. It could help you keep your operation clean. Listen to me, I'll do anything. Anything! I don't give a shit about the force; I'll do exactly what you want. Just give me a chance to show it."

There was a noticeable change in the tone of the man in charge. "Hey, filth, you got a family?"

Willis snivelled a reply. "A wife and three kids. For their sake, please let me out!"

"Listen, brainless, stop squealing and I might just decide to let you live."

He spoke in a low voice so that the whimpering Willis could not hear. "I've been waiting a long time for a chance like this, Siggy. We can use this copper and bring him into the fold, as it were."

"You actually mean to put him on the payroll?"

"Why not? Inside information from the Met could be very useful."

"I don't like this. I don't trust the filth. How can you keep him in line, boss?"

"Relax, Siggy. I know he'd say anything right now, but I've got a feeling about this one. We'll make threats on his family to start with, coupled with a few largish bribes. As soon as he starts taking the cash, he's ours."

The boss shone his torch at the frightened face. "I've got a proposition for you, an offer you can't refuse. You're now working for me. Got it. In return for information, you get a slice of the action and I pay some extra into your retirement funds. You double-cross me and my friend here will cut your wife and kids into little bits. How does that sound?"

Tom Willis squirmed. There was no way he could refuse. He would face prison and expulsion from the force if his involvement was ever revealed, but leading a double life was infinitely more acceptable than the alternative. He shuddered at the thought of the horrific death he now faced.

"I'll do anything to help you. Just say the word. You can rely on my total loyalty."

"I do hope so, for your family's sake."

Winston returned with the petrol tank. "Okay, boss, shall I do the business and crisp him up?"

"No. Leave it for now, I've changed my mind. I need him. Come on you big bugger, use your strength and help us get him out."

For the next ten minutes, the men gingerly lifted loose planks away. They worked quickly, shoring up any wood or panels which began to slip and slowly, they edged closer to where Willis was trapped. Eventually, they managed to identify a single plank that was the key to the problem. The boss silently watched over his team as they inserted a long lever of wood underneath it. By exerting all their strength, they managed to lift it a foot above the prostrate figure.

Willis was released.

"Come on Filth, move it. This is bleedin' heavy and we can't hold it long."

Willis pushed himself as flat as he could and squirmed backwards until at last, he reached freedom. He knelt, shaking with relief, looking up in gratitude at the man who now owned his life. In the strange glow of the torchlight, he caught sight of his face, perfectly round and grinning with self-satisfaction.

The boss spoke with authority, "Ok Copper. Start earning your keep. Take your place on the lever. Winston, I've changed my mind and I want you to see if you can find any undamaged bags of coke. Here, take the torch."

Winston began to protest uneasily. "But, man."

"Get your fuckin' arse under there and look. You don't expect me to do it, do you?"

Willis and the other two men leant on the lever again. Willis was shaking with the exertion of his ordeal, but he had to put all his remaining energy into doing as he had been instructed.

The timber began to creak loudly and the space reappeared for Winston to crawl through.

He went under on his belly.

"Come on, you great pillock, can you see anything yet?"

"Yeah, there's only two full bags that ain't bust. I've got 'em and I'm coming out."

The big man wriggled towards safety, clutching his prize. Surely, this would get him back in the boss's good books. The three men on the lever watched impassively from one side as a hand pushed the torch out from under the wood, followed by the two white plastic packets.

None of them could have foreseen what was about to happen next.

In the darkness, the unfortunate Winston had not picked up the simmering displeasure of his boss. He was never to know that he'd been blamed for the entire accident by his careless driving. As soon as the bags of coke became visible, the boss once again commanded Willis.

"Pass me those two bags of coke on the floor."

"But what about…"

"I mean now," bellowed the boss angrily.

Willis had to let go of the lever. The weight of timber was too much for the others to hold and the plank was snatched out of their hands. There was an almighty crash as the mass of wood descended, crushing the helpless victim beneath. He had little time to cry out and was killed instantly. The hand pushing the bags of cocaine twitched violently then went limp.

Willis stood aghast, realising that his actions had resulted in the death of Winston.

The boss grinned at Willis. "Welcome to my world."

Siggy spoke next, "Boss, did you mean him to do that?"

"Of course, I did. At a 100 grand a bag, that fucker cost me nearly a million. He could never earn that much in his lifetime. He was just a careless bastard."

Willis picked up the two bags lying near the dead hand, but before he could turn around to hand them over, an unseen movement in the darkness clubbed him down from behind and sent his brain spinning into unconsciousness.

"Get our friend's wallet. I want to see who he is."

Siggy rolled Willis over and felt around his inside jacket pocket. He passed a wallet over to his boss, who quickly reviewed the contents.

"There's everything we need here. Family photos, his address, police ID, everything we need. Right, Moke. Douse the lorry with petrol and torch it as fast as you can. We'll wait for you up top. Siggy, you help me with Willis. We need to get him back to his car. Christ, he stinks foul."

Ten minutes later, there was an almighty whoosh as the petrol-soaked timber was set ablaze, and three men watched in satisfaction as the flames caught hold.

"Come on, boss. We need to be away before anybody else turns up. We can't afford anybody remembering they saw your roller."

* * * * *

An hour later, Tom Willis woke up. His head throbbed unmercifully and the smell of his own body was nauseating. He found himself at the wheel of his car, parked in a dark corner of a motorway service area. He wound down the window and took in gulps of the cool night air to try and clear his mind. When he felt able, he went to the boot of his car and pulled out a holdall, which contained a spare set of clothes. He always carried clean gear because he often had to stay out overnight at short notice. He staggered across to the toilet block. The night concealed his true condition from passers-by and he was able to change and clean himself up without alarming anyone. He dare not go home in the condition he found himself, so he rang his wife and told her there was a flap on at work and he would be out all night.

The following day, he stayed away from work, giving the excuse to colleagues that he was following up leads on another case. By the time he arrived home that evening, the blow to his head had eased. He looked and felt exhausted, but had the perfect excuse to go straight to bed.

Willis managed to find time over the next few days to search the police national computer database. No contact had been made with him and he desperately wanted to find out who he was dealing with. Ironically, he found himself in the position of the countless witnesses he'd interviewed in the past. He realised it was often too difficult to identify people's faces, especially when it was dark. There was no chance that he could recognise any of the men who had changed his life. He had nothing to go on, but the leader had been adamant that they should burn the evidence; so, he felt sure he would find some record of the fire.

Eventually, he found the information he was looking for. There was a report describing the discovery of a burnt-out lorry. He felt a strange feeling of remorse as the file revealed the discovery of the charred remains of a body. It could have so easily been a report of his own death.

Forensics had examined the body. It was so badly burned that identification was impossible. The vehicle was also untraceable. Even though a death had occurred, the incident had been recorded as an accident. With a lack of evidence to the contrary, Willis knew that the investigation would be given a low priority. It was another dead end.

His only long shot was the one name he had remembered hearing in the dark. So, he tapped *Siggy* into the database and began a search for known criminals. The name was odd and could even be a nickname, but if there was any kind of match, the computer would find it. He didn't need to wait long before a message flashed on the screen.

It simply read: *No Information*.

The following morning, Willis set off for work at the usual time, but when he got into his car, he noticed a white, pristine envelope perched on the dashboard. He assumed correctly that someone had broken into his car and put it there. He looked around anxiously to see if he was being watched, but there was no one about.

Slowly, he opened the envelope and fingered the inside. A tempting wad of 20-pound notes left him in no doubt about where it had come from. He knew at some point in the future, he would need to earn this bribe.

Willis began to examine his conscience one last time. The arguments he made were in a singular direction only, designed to bring him to the same conclusion.

What had the police force ever done for him? What had the long hours done, but take him away from his family? And for what? Why shouldn't he protect the family he loved and provide for a better future? What harm could a little inside information do?

He suddenly felt undervalued and resentful that he received only scant reward for his efforts. Shaking his head, he cleared his thoughts and began counting the money—1000 pounds. He quickly put it back and slipped the package into his inside pocket.

He was hooked.

Chapter 2

The maroon Rolls Royce slid smoothly to a halt with Siggy Dexter at the wheel. His employer sat in the back, enjoying the comfort and warmth of his luxury motorcar.

Lawrence Tyburn liked the idea of being chauffeured around the Capital because it gave him an air of importance; of being somebody. A man in his mid-fifties, he'd become financially successful and he liked nothing better than to cultivate an image of sophistication and wealth. He quickly examined his appearance in the mirror before alighting from the car, drawing his fingers through a shock of thick hair, dyed dark to conceal the onset of ageing grey. After preening himself, he got out and went forward to the driver's window. He tapped on the glass and it retracted smoothly.

"Take the Roller back to the casino, Siggy, and hang about for me until I give you a bell."

"Okay, boss. See you later."

Tyburn ascended the short flight of steps to the entrance of the restaurant and disappeared from sight.

It was Tuesday night and the place was very busy, but with a quiet relaxed atmosphere; a normal evening at *Signor's*. The long room was elegantly furnished in contemporary style. It looked every bit as expensive as its designers had meant it to be and was a tribute to the craftsmen who had created such a fine setting. The quiet, ethereal strains of the American saxophonist Kenny G were piped from unseen speakers and the soulful music engendered an air of gentle serenity in which the gourmets could explore their passion for excellent food and wine. The reputation of *Signor's* had become widespread, and with it had come a class of clientele who wanted only the best and were prepared to pay for it. The place was booked up months in advance and for the past three years, had become the most popular Italian restaurant in London.

Towards the rear and slightly away from the main public area, was a large alcove. Discreetly hidden from prying eyes, there were several tables, available for a select few. On odd occasions, these tables were free all night, but this part of the restaurant was usually as busy as the rest.

Tonight, was one of those quieter times and only one table was in use. It was occupied by a small, portly man. Simon Lush was a lawyer and a close friend of Tyburn. It was he who had summoned this urgent meeting. He knew that he would have to use a great deal of diplomacy to break the news that had recently presented itself and he wasn't looking forward to Tyburn's reaction.

His companion arrived and seated himself opposite. Lush swept back the loose strands of his lank, blond hair and smiled thinly, trying to gauge Tyburn's mood, but his friend's most rewarding feature once more proved an enigma. His round face with its perpetual grin, somehow always managed to disguise his feelings. It was a well-practiced art and a constant frustration to those trying to assess what was going through his mind.

They shook hands warmly, but from the tone of the recent phone call, Tyburn was half expecting bad news. Lush looked for some chink in his facial armour, but there was nothing, just the impassive smile.

Tyburn listened intently to his friend as he blustered through the beginning of his tale. He watched in fascination as the expression on the loose, fleshy jowls became more serious. Beneath his bushy eyebrows, his eyes were clear and sharp, defining a man of quick wit and intelligence.

Lush thrust a slim document in front of him and gestured that he should read. Tyburn slowly flicked through the pages then looked up, pursing his lips.

"Come on Simon, what's the game? I can't follow a complex balance sheet like this. That's why I have an accountant. Get Henry Newsome to explain it to me. That's what I pay him for."

"But that's your problem my friend. He's shafting you. Look at the tenth line down."

Tyburn sat up sharply and he followed Lush's podgy fingertip to the bracketed figure amongst the columns of numeric data.

"But this is a loss, Simon. Even I know that. There's a five million deficit somehow." His response was one of amazement. "Are you telling me that Newsome has ripped me off for five million quid? He's supposed to be my accountant, for Christ's sake."

"I'm afraid that's the truth, Lol. This only came to light by accident. When I suspected that there was a problem, I managed to get all your files duplicated and had a full audit done by a reputable firm in the States. No questions asked."

Tyburn twitched nervously. "The bastard is going to suffer for this! I'll make him pay me back every penny he owes."

Lush shuffled edgily in his seat, "I'm afraid there's worse to come. He's spent most of it already."

Tyburn bellowed aloud, "What! Five million quid."

He looked around him in disbelief. Anxious that nobody could hear the conversation, he toned down his voice to almost a whisper.

"What's he done with it? Burned the fuckin' stuff."

Lush sighed, "More or less. He makes frequent trips to the States and I managed to find out that he's got a bad gambling problem. When the auditors' report arrived this morning, even I wasn't prepared for the scale of this rip off."

Tyburn fumed. He was speechless and his normally cheerful mask had become an indescribable picture of dark malevolence. A vein stood out on his forehead and he set his jaw as he strove to control his fury. A thousand thoughts raced through his brain as he tried to come to terms with his dilemma. He had gone through many highs and lows in his lifetime, but nothing to compare with this. To think that one of his most trusted partners was defrauding him. It was more like a work of fiction.

Lush sat and watched, but the predictable eruption never came. Tyburn sat in unexpected silence.

At last, he spoke, "How could he do this to me Simon? Weren't we good friends? Look at all the business we've put his way; all the recommendations we've made for him. Damn him. Doesn't friendship and loyalty count for anything these days?"

Simon just shrugged. "I feel like you, LOL. I couldn't believe it. I still can't."

Tyburn spoke softly but firmly, as he began to regain his self-control. "Newsome is finished. I am going to make sure that he pays for this little affair. I owe it to myself and to you. I'll get Siggy."

He glanced over his shoulder, waved a nearby waiter across and demanded two double bourbons. When the drinks had been delivered and they had sipped the smooth liquor, Tyburn pulled out his mobile phone and flicked open the lid. He hit a pre-set and within seconds, a number began to ring. There was an immediate response. Tyburn just growled, "Siggy! Get back over here and make it quick!"

There was no waiting for a reply. He flipped the lid down and clattered the phone onto the table. Tyburn looked miserable. He stared vacantly beyond his friend.

"We're up to our neck in a shit, Simon. I just hope Newsome hasn't done any lasting damage to the business that we haven't uncovered yet."

He drained his glass and immediately ordered another round of drinks.

* * * * *

A short time later as they sat examining the evening menu, a tall, well-built figure entered the restaurant. Siggy Dexter was unhappy and from the way he walked, it was easy to see that he was irritable. The phone call had been totally unexpected. He'd only just returned to the Casino, where he'd been interrupted in the opening throes of a serious poker game.

He hurried through to the rear where he knew he would find Tyburn. His hair was cropped short and as always, he was dressed in a smart suit, one of his favoured status symbols. He was arrogant, streetwise and had an air of invincibility, which made him fear no one. It was this final characteristic that made him a dangerous man and a quality for which his boss was prepared to pay well.

Lawrence Tyburn looked up from the menu and spotted Dexter striding through the restaurant. He'd calmed down a little by now and greeted his man warmly which immediately put him at ease, "Sit down, Siggy. Come and have a meal with us."

Thinking about Newsome, he grimaced. "We've had some bad news. I'll fill you in later, but we'll eat first. Then, I've got an important job I want you to do. It's something that will make people sit up and take notice."

Chapter 3

Inside the school laboratory, there was a familiar, but undefined smell. It was a mixture of waxed benches and static electricity. It was four o'clock on Friday and Matthew Morgan looked out through the window at the retreating hordes and sighed wearily. "That's right. Bugger off home and give us some peace."

It had been another stressful day and it niggled him to admit that at times he felt frustrated with his job. He'd been teaching for over 20 years and as *Head of Science,* didn't need anybody to tell him how much harder it was becoming year by year. The bureaucrats in Whitehall were forever making changes to the curriculum and it galled him. Most of them had never set foot in a school and hadn't a clue about the needs of his students. He mustered his flagging energy and set about planning for the following week.

An hour later, the work had been completed and he finally left his lab, wandering down the short corridor and trying to put school out of his mind. He pondered on what he would do for the rest of his evening. The thought of returning to an empty house with yet another frozen pizza and a night of boring television filled him with dismay.

Over the last couple of years, his existence had very gradually spiralled down into one of tedium and monotony. He'd unwittingly allowed this lifestyle to overtake him and he hated the endless domestic drudgery that complemented the lack of satisfaction with his career. He wasn't just in a rut; it was a full-blown midlife crisis and boy, did he know it. With no prospect of excitement or any direction to his life, he felt constantly irritable. The legacy of it all was a daily, lethargic struggle that weighed him down.

The suite of laboratories suddenly seemed lonely and deserted. As he approached the Prep Room, Matt picked up the sound of quiet sobbing drifting through the partially open door. He was puzzled and pushing the door open further, he peered inside. If there was some private argument going on, he didn't want to get involved. In the far corner, facing the window stood Melissa Reagan, one of his colleagues. Her head was bowed and his heart went out to the sad, forlorn figure.

Matt glanced around, sensing that she was alone. He hesitated for a while wondering what might have upset her and impulsively, he was drawn forward. He moved over to where she was huddled and quipped gently, "Hey Mel. What's up? The experiments' all gone wrong again?"

Melissa turned slightly towards him, acknowledging his presence. "No… It's nothing like that."

She spoke softly, her southern Irish lilt, soothingly magnetic. Matt could listen to it all day.

"If you want to talk. Err… if I can help in any way." Matt knew how corny it sounded. He put a hand very loosely on her shoulder, barely making contact, as though she had a *Do Not Touch* sign around her neck.

The Prep Room was not very spacious and it had a battered old settee pushed up against the wall in one corner. She allowed him to lead her over to the seat and they flopped heavily onto the worn cushions. Matt turned slightly and looked at Melissa. He had never been so close before and he began to appreciate her loose, auburn hair. It framed a quite beautiful face with large, pale green eyes and a soft, sensuous mouth.

She, in turn, appeared to enjoy his closeness and as she turned to meet his gaze, a final tear rolled down her damp cheek.

Matt's body began to stir as her intoxicating perfume began to fill his head and he found that he desperately wanted to kiss her. Thoughts flitted quickly across his mind. He was probably ten years older than she was and anyway what would an attractive female think if he took advantage of her in a situation like this? She might even accuse him of sexual harassment. If he wasn't careful, he could really make a fool of himself. He quickly backed off, failing to notice that his body language had sent a disappointing message to Melissa. She bowed her head to avoid his gaze. If only he knew.

Melissa leant back and snuffled. She blew her nose hard on a tissue and eventually composed herself.

"I've had a really bad time with one of the older boys. It was Brett Thomas in Year 11. I made him stay after the last bell because he owed me three lots of homework and he'd been a bloody nuisance all lesson."

"Yeah. I know him. Taught him a couple of years ago."

"Well, I was giving him a real telling off, but all he did was grin back at me. He said I looked sexy when I got cross. Then he put his hand up my dress and onto my thigh. It made my skin crawl."

She stopped and moaned, "The slimy bastard said he wanted to… to fuck me. I'm sorry, this is just too much." She broke down and began to weep silently again.

This time Matt put a strong arm around her and held her close to his chest.

"Why did you allow yourself to be alone with him? Couldn't you see something like this coming? All the boys fancy you. I hear them going on about you all the time."

"You know what it's like Matt. You think you're in control. Call it professional pride. I've never had an incident like this happen before. There was just no warning."

Matthew's anger rose as his protective feelings towards her grew. "That little shits got it coming to him this time."

"It's no good," she stammered. "I've already thought this through. I cracked him hard across his face, but he just continued to grin back at me. He just gloated… said if I complained then it was only my word against his. He threatened that if I reported him, he'd say that it was me that assaulted him and that I'd lose my job. He seemed to know just what to say. Damn it, there were no witnesses and no one nearby that I could turn to for help."

"You can't let him get away with it, Mel. You have to report it to the Head and then bring in your union."

"I'm not in a union. I've never seen the need for one before and as for telling the Head, you must be joking."

Matt shrugged his shoulders. He had to agree. Their Head Teacher would certainly want to hush up an incident of this kind. He was only interested in the reputation of his school in the local community.

Melissa calmed herself, "Thanks, Matt. You've been a real help."

"Not me, Mel. I haven't been able to do a thing."

"You have. Really. You've helped me to talk it through. If I'd gone home in this state and been on my own, I couldn't have faced coming to work next week."

"Listen, Melissa, I hate to think of that little toe-rag getting away with it. If you're willing, I'll come with you to the Head first thing on Monday and say that I saw him assaulting you. It's our word against Thomas. In fact, I'll ring him at home tonight and impress on him the seriousness of the situation. He'll have to act."

She looked at him directly, "Would you do that. Lie for me?"

Matt smiled. "It's not really a lie. It's only the justice you deserve. If he gets away with assaulting you, how will you feel if you have to continue teaching him? How can you live with yourself? Just look at the state you're in."

Melissa made an instinctive decision. "You're right. We'll do it. Thanks for that, Matt. I feel better already."

Matt took his arm from around her and sat up, but Melissa couldn't let the moment pass. Impulsively, she reached across and lightly touched his cheek, closed her eyes and gently kissed him on his lips. It was fleeting and as they parted, she whispered quietly, "There. At last. I've done what I've been wanting to do for months."

Matt was taken aback, but the implication of what she'd said and done was quick to dawn. She actually liked him. He felt flattered and with a few special words, she had resurrected a long-lost ego. He took her in his arms and returned her advance with a warm, tender kiss. They held each other close and Matt quickly began to feel the stirrings of forgotten emotions. She felt the satisfaction of his hardness against her and it made her feel good. He broke away breathlessly and looked at the smiling face before him. "I had no idea, no idea at all, that you felt like this."

"You're a difficult man to impress, Matthew Morgan, but if I'd thrown myself at you, it could have been a real turn off. Anyway, I'm not like that and as for you, you're so deep. You never give a girl a clue about how you feel."

Matt remained silent. He hadn't the words to tell her that she'd always seemed untouchable and beyond his reach. Over the years he'd lost his self-esteem with women and felt unable to approach her. The pain and stigma of rejection would have been too embarrassing for him to bear. He contented himself by looking into her face and grinning.

At last, he spoke, "Tell you what. How do you fancy a drink on the way home? I could certainly do with one and I bet you could. You choose a venue."

She looked pleased at his suggestion. "A glass of wine would be great. Then if you play your cards right, I might even treat you to a bar meal."

Matt visibly brightened; he could think of no better way to spend his evening.

Melissa also felt secretly elated. It would be a wonderful opportunity to get to know him better in a comfortable and relaxed atmosphere. They could put school and all its problems behind them and concentrate on one another.

Five minutes later, they had collected their bags and were out in the car park.

Chapter 4

Monique was highly delighted. The dinner party she had meticulously prepared was going very smoothly. She had been the au pair for the Newsome family for just 11 months. In that time, her reputation as an excellent cook had grown steadily and in the Newsome social circle, she was positively envied.

The party was special. It was a private, family celebration for the engagement of Robbie Newsome and his girlfriend Kirsty Morgan. Even though Monique rarely saw the couple together because they were studying at Oxford, it was evident that they were very much in love and so she set out to make the evening a memorable one. The dining room was expansive, panelled in beautiful dark oak, with a huge log fire burning in a graceful and ornate hearth. The furniture matched the walls, indicating a lavish and expensive taste. Monique loved the sheer elegance of the beautiful room.

As she cleared the remains of her strawberry crème soufflé, she took great pleasure in the carefree atmosphere amongst the family. Sir Peter, who was the most senior member of the family, had driven up from Southampton earlier in the day. He leant back in his chair and undid the bottom button of his waistcoat watched by his son.

"You're putting weight on, old chap," he quipped.

Sir Peter retorted cheerily, "Not so much old, thank you, very much. But I've got a readymade excuse, with a cook like young Monique. What else do you expect?"

Monique flushed slightly at the compliment as she removed his empty dish. At the far end of the table, Sandra Newsome and her 19-year-old daughter, Donna were deep in conversation with Kirsty. It was girl talk about wedding arrangements and their excitement was apparent to all.

Sir Peter and Henry lit up large cigars as they declared the meal ended.

Kirsty whispered to Robbie and excused herself, leaving to make use of the bathroom upstairs.

Monique continued her duties and began to serve the coffee.

In the distance, a doorbell chimed.

Henry Newsome's voice was surly as he commanded his au pair, "Quickly, girl. Answer the door. I am expecting a courier with an important document."

Monique turned to go. She had no great affection for her main employer because he had a cold, sterile manner, which she could not fathom. When he issued an order, everyone in the house was expected to respond immediately. She hurried across the hall to the main door still glowing with pride at her evening's achievement. Nothing was going to spoil her success.

* * * * *

Outside, it was a still, cold night. There had previously been several clear nights of frost, but the twilight had brought a thick, dank mist as the weather slowly began to change.

The Range Rover approached slowly and came to a halt just past the end of the long gravel drive. The headlights were extinguished and the only sound was the quiet throbbing of the 4.2 litre V8 engine. Pete Teasdale put the vehicle into reverse and then began to back into the wide entrance. It was odd that there were no reversing lights, but he'd removed the bulbs from their sockets to avoid any possible warning of the intending approach. The car continued to crawl backwards, gently crunching the surface of the gravel as the driver cautiously navigated the long curving drive. Pete stuck his head out of the window, peering into the gloom behind and looking for some landmark to guide his advance. In retrospect, he'd have been better off leaving his reversing lights in place.

"Unless one of you lot get out to help, I'm liable to back this sodding thing into the nearest tree."

A voice growled from behind in the unlit interior, "This will do okay. Just be ready to get the hell out of here when I give the word." The voice continued in a different tone. "Moke, you go round the back. Listen out for any action and watch the rear for anybody making a run for it. Make damn sure nobody gets past you. We'll collect you when it's all over. You've got five minutes to find the back door before we go in. Larry, you come with me. Remember you lot, this job is as big as it gets. I've told Mr Tyburn that we'll have no problem carrying out his wishes. Tonight, I want to show him just how good we are. I need a real professional job. Whatever you do, don't fuck it up. There could be up to ten

31

people in the house, so we need a sweep of all the rooms. Nobody gets out. You know what to do, so let's do it."

The doors of the Range Rover opened simultaneously and immediately the inner warmth of the car dissipated. Three shapes quickly disappeared into the mist. The driver shivered as he hunched over his wheel and put the heater fans up to maximum. The sound of his idling engine drowned the crunching of feet on gravel as the assailants moved stealthily onto the lawns at the edge of the house.

Two figures materialised at the front door. Siggy Dexter pulled out his automatic pistol and screwed on a silencer. The heavyweight, Larry Stafford did likewise. Their hearts thudded as they waited for Moke to find his way to the back. Dexter checked his watch. His gloved hand pushed the doorbell and they heard its nearby chime. Their short breaths rasped out streams of condensing vapour as they waited for a response.

A young woman soon appeared at the door, "Yes. What is it please? Do you have a letter?"

Monique's expression immediately changed. Her high spirits vanished as the ugly barrel of a gun was thrust under her chin and the two men emerged from the shadows, pushing her forward.

Stafford hissed into her ear, "Don't say a word or you're dead meat, sweetheart."

Dexter came forward menacingly, "Where are they all?"

She pointed to the far door and he urged her further, yanking a handful of her long blond hair.

"How many?"

She moaned fearfully, "Six. There are six people."

Monique became ashen. The sudden invasion and the ruthlessness of her attackers made her panic. The room began to swim and she fell in a deep faint, cracking her head on the gleaming wooden floor.

Dexter gave her a sharp kick in the ribs, "Bitch! We'll see to her later."

With their hands holding the guns behind their backs, the two of them silently approached the dining room door, which was slightly ajar. Dexter pushed it wide open and entered.

Henry Newsome looked up and questioned them impatiently, "Who are you? What do you want?"

Dexter spoke softly, "Henry Newsome?"

There was a look of recognition on Newsome's face. He'd met Dexter on a number of occasions, with Tyburn. He responded sharply, "You know who I am. You're one of Tyburn's thugs. You had better leave my house immediately, before I call the law."

Dexter exposed his gun in one smooth movement and fired. There was a look of puzzlement as the bullet hit Henry Newsome square between the eyes. He was dead before his torso had slumped forward onto the table before him. At the same instant, Sir Peter died, as Stafford let off a shot, which sliced through his neck and severed the nerves to his brain. He slithered heavily to the floor. The others in the room looked on with incomprehension. A scene of epic horror was unfolding in slow motion before their very eyes.

Dexter next turned the gun towards Sandra Newsome. It took her a split second to react to the situation and she began to scream hysterically. The dull thud of the gun retorted again and a shot through the heart threw her backwards over the chair. Donna looked downwards and saw the dark stain of blood through the yellow dress in the centre of her mother's chest.

She looked up pleadingly as Dexter switched his attention to her. She only managed a fleeting plea for mercy, "No! Not me! Please! Not me!"

There was no expression of remorse in his face as he pulled the trigger for a third time. The gun thudded and the bullet entered her body, passing through vital organs, smashing her spine and finally lodging in the oak panelling behind her. Donna's eyes glazed over as her body twitched in its final death throes and she slipped gently on top of her prostrate mother.

At the instant that Robbie had witnessed the first two murders, he sprang out of his chair and lurched towards Dexter. Before he could get within a yard of him, Stafford had spotted his movement and instinctively fired again. The shot was good and hit Robbie hard in the shoulder. The power of the strike spun him round viciously and he was thrown against the table knocking him senseless. Stafford then took deliberate aim at the sad, distressed figure and pumped two lethal shots into him. The once vibrant body jerked violently, then there was no more movement, just a grotesque heap with blank staring eyes.

All was silent. The massacre was over.

Dexter stood quite still, taking in the desperate scene and surveying his handiwork.

Stafford spoke first, "She said six, boss. There's another one somewhere."

Dexter looked around carefully. "Right you are, Larry. We've missed one."

Just then, Moke Saviore came bustling through the door. "No one came out the back Siggy. I heard the screams and came through the kitchen."

"There's still another one that we haven't found yet, you greasy, dago twat. I told you to wait round the back. That's all you had to do." Dexter's anger was rising. "Piss off and guard the back door, you fuckin' little shit and hope for your sake that there isn't a runner."

Saviore looked hurt. He wasn't endowed with much intelligence and he thought that he'd done his job well. It never crossed his mind that he could have made a mistake. He turned quickly and left the room.

As he passed the bottom of the staircase, he glance upwards to the landing and came to an immediate halt. He didn't take his eyes off Kirsty for a second, but shouted loudly back to Dexter, "Out here Siggy! There's a nice bit of skirt you might be interested in."

Chapter 5

Kirsty Morgan examined herself in the long mirror. The evening had filled her with such excitement. The thoughts of her future marriage with Robbie made her whole being fizz. She applied a little more lipstick, pouting wickedly to herself, and then dropping it back into her bag. Her clear-blue eyes sparkled with youthful vitality as she flicked her long, dark hair across her shoulders and adjusted the straps on the long, flowing, azure evening dress. Twisting and turning before the mirror, she smoothed it against the contours of her slim figure, admiring herself once more before she went back to join the rest. She felt both beautiful and elegant and this served to deepen her contentment. The only thing to mar her complete happiness was the absence of her dad and sister. It had been too far for Matthew Morgan to make the dinner party that Sunday evening and get back to Yorkshire in time to teach the next day. Her sister Laura was working abroad, but she contented herself that they would both be attending the official engagement party the following weekend.

Kirsty was just finishing in the bathroom when the doorbell rang. She switched the light off and strode happily along the landing to re-join the party below. She turned the corner at the top of the stairs and stopped in her tracks. Kirsty looked down in disbelief at the open door and the lonely figure of Monique's body slumped on the hall floor. Then, without warning, her world froze.

She clearly heard the dull thumping of the bullets, bodies falling and hysterical screams of anguish. Her gut knotted in fear as she tried to figure out what was happening in the room below. She began to sway and her numbed fingers grasped onto the banister as she fought to control her body and mind. After what seemed an eternity, adrenaline began to course through her veins and the danger of her predicament began to clear her mind.

Just then a small, wiry man, with a dark complexion and a shock of tight wavy hair appeared from the kitchen. He rushed into the dining room brandishing a gun. She couldn't hear the exchange of harsh words, but he reappeared almost immediately. He set off back towards the kitchen and glanced upwards to where Kirsty stood. Grinning, he stopped his forward rush, staring directly at her to make sure he was not mistaken.

He called out for *Siggy* and in a moment, two more men appeared at the door.

Saviore purred, "Just look at her. Wow! Come on Siggy! Wouldn't you just like ten minutes with her on the landing floor?"

Kirsty looked down the stairwell and into the eyes of Dexter. She became transfixed by his looks, a face so cold and expressionless. The sharpness of his features gave him a strange fascination and it made Kirsty shudder with revulsion.

Dexter growled, "Get away from me. We have a job to do." He pushed Moke aside and raised his weapon.

Kirsty instinctively knew his intention and frantically looked round for somewhere to run. She shivered and her groin felt damp, but fear paralysed her legs and she was rooted to the spot. It was Stafford who gave her the faintest of hope. He pulled Dexter's arm down and obscured his field of fire, pleading with the younger man. His tones were lewd as his head inclined in Kirsty's direction. "Come on Siggy. She's the only one left. We can all have some fun. A few minutes more won't make that much difference. Be a pal. Mr Tyburn won't mind."

Dexter stared straight into Stafford's face and with a viciousness that made Kirsty's skin creep, he howled, "No names you fuckin' cretin. No names! And don't you ever get in my way again."

Stafford instinctively moved aside. The split second that the two men had lost their concentration was just enough time for Kirsty to react. Her mind was now crystal clear as the primeval instinct of fight or flight took over. She certainly couldn't fight them, so she turned and fled, hurtling headlong back along the landing. A bullet whistled past her head shattering an ornamental mirror. It was the only shot Dexter could get off before she disappeared out of sight.

Kirsty ran straight back to the bathroom slamming the heavy oak door behind her and turning the key in the large, solid lock. She'd remembered that the bathroom could be locked, but wasn't sure about any of the bedrooms. It was her only choice. She dragged the key from its hole and threw it into the far corner of the room.

Footsteps were approaching down the long landing as the three thugs searched each bedroom in turn.

She automatically moved away from the door, looking for a window that would open, but could find none. She finally turned into a small dressing area and there, above the long marble surface, was a short, horizontal opening window, about two feet deep. As she scrambled up onto the surface, she heard the men at the bathroom door. Her hiding place had been discovered and it was only a matter of time before they would break in and finish her off.

She was now in a cold sweat and yanked at the handles of the window, but they hadn't been open for a long time. She clawed at them frantically, "Come on. Why won't you budge?"

On the landing, Dexter was directing operations. He ordered Stafford to shoulder the door open but the task was proving difficult because the old seasoned timbers of the frame refused to give.

Kirsty was at her wits end as she looked around for a tool to strike the window catches. She slipped off one of her shoes and examined the base of the heel. It was edged in steel. Using all her strength, she hammered at the catches and with a huge sob of relief, she saw them begin to move. Frantically, she renewed her efforts until at last they rotated freely. She dropped the shoe to the floor and kicked the other one off too. Without the high heels, she might still be able to make a run for it. By putting her full weight against the window, the old-hardened paint reluctantly cracked and it lifted upwards. The stiff, ancient hinges creaked open and it stayed horizontal under its own weight.

Pensively, she looked out to see what her future was to be. If it was a high window with a long drop, she had already made up her mind to chance her luck. It was better to break her neck in a fall than to be shot dead like some rabid dog or raped by a gang of mindless morons.

As she peered out into the gloom, the chill night air hit her full in the face. She gratefully drank in the smell of the thick misty swirls, which were eddying about the rooftop.

Fog! For some reason, it had always filled her with dread as a young girl. Could this unknown childhood fear, ironically be the answer to her prayers? Would it be thick enough to hide her away from the hideous thugs who were now battering at the door?

She shivered again in disgust and began to look for a way down, picking out the line of the roof as a possible escape route. She swiftly examined her clothes.

If she discarded her long dress, then she would be left wearing only tights and a pair of French knickers and the terrible cold of the night would only serve to hinder her progress. She tried to compromise by hitching up the skirts of her evening gown and stuffing them down her pants. The dress was made of silk and because it wasn't bulky, the idea seemed to work. She now had the appearance of someone wearing a huge nappy.

Kirsty climbed over the horizontal sill and could see a four-foot drop to the gently sloping roof below. The jump was easy, but she landed in a heap on the freezing tiles. Her knees had taken a solid jarring and her tights were ripped to shreds when she had hit the roof. She left the safety of the outer bathroom wall and with nothing firm to hold on to, shuffled slowly along the sloping roof. Twice, she almost lost her balance on the slippery tiles; so, she decided to crouch down and keep her centre of gravity as low as possible. She edged slowly forward until a vertical wall appeared before her. She didn't know whether it was a chimney breast or part of the structure of the rambling old house.

Oh no! Which way now?

Despite her continuing fear, she was able to rationalise her predicament. If she followed the roof upwards, she would certainly end up on the ridge tiles. The thugs would surely find her up there and finish her off with no trouble. Her mind was made up. The only way was down and into the mist, even though there was the possibility of a sudden, sheer drop.

She continued to crouch as low as she could as she made her descent. It was very dark and her feet could feel the rough surface of the tiles through her tights as they met the smooth lead flashing against the wall. Her toes were beginning to feel numb in the intense cold. She gingerly progressed downwards, feeling for the danger of free space and a possible fatal fall. She gritted her teeth. Nothing was going to stop her getting away. She spoke out in frustration, "Damn it. If only I knew how high up I was."

As she looked around in a panic, the swirling mists suddenly parted and for a brief moment, a half-moon bathed the house in gentle light. It was just enough for Kirsty to assess her position. She was precariously close to the edge. Another couple of feet and she would have been over the side.

The dark fog returned, blanking out the view. In the short time the veil had been lifted, Kirsty had spotted a drainpipe running up the side of the house and continuing above her on the outer wall. Inching forward in the darkness, she put her arm out and felt for the drainpipe. It was there. She took a deep breath and swung herself off the sloping roof and onto the vertical pipe, slithering downwards as she frantically tried to find a foothold. Her knuckles and knees grazed the rough brickwork and began to bleed, but one of her feet managed to lodge on a bracket and this halted her slide. Kirsty clung there for several seconds sobbing at the pain in her hands and wondering if the ancient pipework would hold her weight. She looked downwards into the gloom, but the thick fog stopped her from assessing the final drop.

From the house, Kirsty picked out a series of muffled crumps that sounded like gunfire. She had slipped about her own body length down the pipe and her eyes were just level with where the sloping roof ended. She could just about make out the open window from where she had escaped. It was brightly lit, surrounded by a diffused halo of mist. Her heart missed a beat as a head appeared.

Dexter had finally lost his patience with Stafford's inability to break down the door and fired into the bathroom lock. Once inside, the escape route was obvious and sticking his head out of the window, Dexter fully expected to find her on the roof. He banged the frame in anger as the filthy murk obscured any sign of his quarry. He bellowed at the top of his voice, "She's got out. She may still be on the roof or she might have fallen." A slight panic edged his voice. "She's seen us. She knows us. Come on, we've got to find her."

The voice carried across to Kirsty in the eerie darkness and she knew, all too clearly, that time was running out. In the few seconds that it took them to run down a flight of stairs and circumnavigate the house, she would have to be gone.

She began to let herself slip downwards. The thick silk padding at her waist prevented any friction burns to her thighs as she quickly dropped another 12 feet. Her senses were fully heightened as the front door slammed in the still night air. They would be upon her soon. It was now or never. Kirsty closed her eyes and let go. Almost immediately she felt the ground beneath her as she rolled over in a huddle. The final drop had only been a short one and she was able to stagger to her feet. Apart from her aching knees and agonising knuckles, she was in one frozen piece. She looked around trying to assess the best direction to follow, but the sounds of running feet were approaching rapidly as they echoed around the perimeter of the house. Kirsty turned and bolted off into the night, melting like a soft shadow into the ever-thickening gloom. She did not know her true direction. She thought it was towards the copse of dense trees, which she knew were 50 yards down the sloping garden. If so, then the fog was more likely to be thicker there and with no footwear it would be difficult to track her by sight or sound. She mustered her remaining energy and urged herself forward. Her body shuddered from exhaustion as she reached the outer rim of trees. Fortunately, she'd followed a good line. Perhaps the trees and fog would provide her with a safe haven.

Dexter and Saviore had left the front door and gone in opposite directions round the house. They met up somewhere at the back, looking up for the weak light from the bathroom window. The heavy Stafford was out of condition and followed some distance behind.

Siggy stopped and snapped impatiently, "Shut up and stand still."

They listened intently for any nearby movement, but the night was silent except for the sound of their breathing and the distant traffic, which carried through the thick autumn murk.

After a full five minutes Dexter spoke, "What a fuckin' mess. It should have been easy. The bitch could be anywhere in this fog. She could be miles away by now." He looked around in frustration at the dense, grey wall, unsure which way to look first. In the end he just shrugged angrily, "This is no bleedin' use. We could spend all night searching and get nowhere. At some point she's got to go looking for help and when she does, we have to get to her quickly, before the filth get a chance to question her." He pondered a few seconds longer, but his thoughts were interrupted by a sudden scream and continuous hysterical crying.

"It must be the maid. I'd forgotten her. All may not be lost." Dexter turned to Moke. "Go and sort out the girl, but first make sure you find out who this woman is. I want a name and an address if possible. I'll meet you back at the car."

Saviore vanished into the fog.

Dexter heard a door slam and the crying stopped abruptly. He swung round to face Larry; his voice full of malice as he rounded on his lieutenant. Looking up at the slightly taller figure, he grabbed the lapels of his coat, "You may have cost us badly tonight, you fat bastard. In fact, you could have blown everything. Mr Tyburn will not be pleased." He relaxed his grip, as Stafford recovered some composure.

"Sorry, Siggy, but we only wanted to fuck that piece. You must admit that she was asking for it."

"So true," venom tinged his voice, "but you spoilt my aim. This wasn't a simple hit tonight. It was the biggest job Mr Tyburn's ever given me and I wanted to show him how I could handle it. I needed to prove that I was the best. Now I've let him down, but it was all your fault, you fat load of shit." Dexter was seething inside, but his exterior facade remained calm. He gently removed his right hand from his pocket. There was no glint of steel, nor any hint of what was about to happen. The faces of the two men were within inches as he violently drove the long stiletto blade sharply upwards. It easily tore through Stafford's jacket and chest, parting two ribs and searing into the wall of his heart. The big man grunted. For one brief moment, there was pain in his eyes and a look of betrayal. Dexter removed the knife and there was a bland sucking, as the blade retreated from its deep incision. He stood back from Stafford as the huge man simply died on his feet. The corpse dropped heavily onto its knees and with the help of Dexter's foot, it was pushed backwards onto the frosty grass. He knelt down by the body and in an uncontrollable frenzy, he slashed Stafford's face with the razor edge of his blade. Dexter cut him over and over in a senseless act of desecration until the dead man's bloodied features were unrecognisable, "You were a nobody yesterday and you'll be a nobody tomorrow. You useless slob."

Dexter flicked through Stafford's pockets, removing his gun and any other identification.

In a final act of depravity, he undid his trousers and sprayed a stream of hot, stinking urine over the mutilated carcass, before hurrying off to find the car.

* * * * *

Saviore had found Monique in the dining room huddled over the dead body of Robbie. She was rocking backwards and forwards in severe shock, sobbing uncontrollably at the sight of the butchery. Moke approached her from behind and with one hand holding a gun at her cheek, put the other round her waist, then fondled her firm young breasts. Fear instantly lit her eyes as a new wave of terror swept over her. She fell silent and Saviore, now rubbing his hand along her thighs, whispered quietly, "That's the idea my bambino. Now tell me this, who is the girl in the blue dress?"

Monique swallowed hard. She could smell the stinking sweat of this man and it made her gorge rise. The gun was pushed hard against her temple. She started to stutter, "Kirsty. Kirsty Morgan."

He relaxed the gun a little, "That's good, babe. Now where does this woman live? I really need to know."

Monique pleaded with him, "I've no idea. She comes from the north, somewhere. Sheffield, I think. Please. I don't know any more."

Saviore turned the face of the frightened French girl towards him. He could tell that she was speaking the truth. Standing up, he beckoned her to her feet, grinning all the time. He let out a dirty chuckle, "I've got something nice for you sweetheart. Take your pants off."

Monique swooned again at the thought of this foul creature touching her. Moke saw the danger and cracked her across the face. He pushed the gun firmly under her chin, "If you don't do it, I'm going to blow your brains out here and now."

Monique sobbed as she lifted her dress and slowly dropped her knickers around her ankles.

"I bet you've never seen anything like this before?"

He removed the gun from her face and with his free hand unfastened his belt. He quickly pulled down his own pants to reveal a huge erection. He swaggered arrogantly, "What about that bambino? Are we about to have fun?"

Monique glanced down and the overwhelming revulsion of what he was about to do flipped her mind. In wild desperation. She knocked his gun arm to one side and turned to flee.

Saviore was off balance and the gun fired involuntarily, the recoil forcing it out of his hand. The bullet wasted itself harmlessly against the ceiling. He made a grab for her, missed and with his trousers round his ankles found it impossible to give chase.

Sobbing wildly, Monique rushed out of the room and seconds later, was lunging down the drive towards the road.

Dexter had found his way back to the Range Rover and sat in the front passenger seat.

Pete could see his irritation, "You seem to have been ages. Where's Larry and Moke?"

There was no answer. Dexter glanced at his watch. The whole episode had lasted only 20 minutes, but that was 15 more than he'd planned. He made out the distant thud of a gun. Even with the silencer in place, the sound carried across the misty night.

He spoke quietly, "The job's over. Sounds as though Moke should be along any time now." As he waited, contemplating their next move, the distraught French girl appeared out of the gloom. She glanced across in blind panic and seeing the two shadowy figures in the car, screamed and continued her headlong rush down the drive.

Dexter was the first to react, "The stupid bastard's let her get away. Move over Pete."

The driver slid over to the passenger side as Dexter came round the car and jumped in at the wheel. He gunned the engine and let out the clutch. The wheels spun fast and threw loose gravel into the air. The four-wheel drive hugged the ground and the Range Rover shot forward.

Monique could hear the approaching car, but could not judge its distance behind her. Her mind was lost, locked in hysteria and disorientation. Without warning, brilliant headlights lit up the path ahead. She staggered gainfully on, but the heavy car was soon upon her and she was struck down from behind. Dexter's timing was perfect and he crashed the speeding vehicle into her defenceless body. There was a resounding crack and she was smashed to one side, hitting her head on the road with a sickening thud. The car skidded to a halt and the two men got out.

Teasdale felt for her neck pulse and shook his head. He felt some sympathy for the pretty young thing strewn across the path. "This one's dead all right."

"Good. Give me a hand. We'll hide her in the bushes."

The two of them carried Monique's broken corpse behind a nearby tree and returned to the car. At that moment Saviore arrived, still redressing himself and looking very sheepish.

Dexter guessed what had happened, "Come on, let's get out of here. I've had enough tonight."

They quickly clambered aboard and a puzzled Teasdale enquired, "What about Larry?"

Dexter glared at Saviore, "He didn't make it."

As the Range Rover tore down the nearby streets, Dexter pumped Moke for information about the girl and was disappointed by the lack of anything but a name and a city.

"Looks like we need some help. I'll get in touch with our friend in the Met, Mr Willis. Since he's been taking bungs, that fuckin' pig has given us nothing. Tonight, changes everything. He's going to have to get his finger out and give us the nod as soon as the bitch resurfaces. Then we can arrange to finish this job off properly."

Chapter 6

The car dropped Matthew Morgan off at the edge of the housing estate and he waved his thanks as the car sped away. His regular Monday night lift from the squash club meant that he could have a drink afterwards and not bother about having to drive home.

The still, frosty night gave the pavements a sparkling sheen, which glittered under the bright streetlights. Up above, the heavens were radiant, peppered by the beauty of a billion pinpricks. The air temperature was very low indeed, but Matt had only a few blocks to cover, so he walked briskly to keep warm. He was in a great mood and his thoughts wandered off in all directions.

His new friendship with Melissa Reagan gave him a real tingle. He couldn't believe how quickly her influence was beginning to change his outlook. He reflected on his past and the succession of women that had tried to get close to him since the death of his wife, particularly in the early days. But that had been 20 years ago. The terrible void left by the loss of Julie had been impossible to fill, and his two young daughters had become the centre of his life. He'd taken the responsibility of single parenthood very seriously and managed to gently fend off any potential affairs. Even when the girls were teenagers, he still felt he should always be there just for them, but the past few years had proved difficult for him as first one, then the other, had reached independence and left home. The realisation that they didn't need his intense fatherly protection anymore had come as quite a jolt and it had left him feeling lonely and isolated. He'd begun to wonder if he'd find the closeness of love and companionship ever again. The uncertainty about what the future might have in store had created his progressive lethargy and sadness.

Melissa coming so suddenly into his life had turned his old existence upside down. *When did he last feel as happy?* Some of his emotions, once buried in the past, had been suddenly released with a strange teenage excitement. She seemed keen to be with him and share his interests. The fledgling relationship had already encouraged Melissa to join his squash club, even though it was a new sport to her. Tonight, he'd really missed seeing her because she was attending an evening course at the City University.

Matt quickened his pace, eager to get indoors and into the warmth. As he strode nearer home, he noticed that a police car was parked outside his house. The street lamp shining from above indicated a uniformed driver in the front and two darker silhouettes in the rear. It made him feel a little uneasy, and as he cut across the lawn, he heard a car door open. A voice called after him, "Excuse me, sir. Is it Mr Morgan?"

Matt turned to see a man standing at the rear door of the car.

"Yes," he responded easily, "is there a problem?"

A second door opened and another man emerged.

"May we come in for a moment, sir? There's something that we urgently need to talk to you about."

Matt immediately became anxious, "What is it? What's happened?"

"I'd rather we talk inside, please. If you don't mind."

He tried to allay Matt's fears, "Only keep you a few minutes, sir."

Matt unlocked the door and let them in. There was something not quite right about all this, but he couldn't figure it out. Then it came to him. The car had Metropolitan Police markings and not those of South Yorkshire. He was puzzled. *What was a London police car doing on his doorstep?*

Once inside, he invited the policemen into his lounge.

One of the officers immediately took control of the situation. "My name is Detective Inspector Tony Peterson and this is Detective Sergeant Tom Willis." He indicated Willis who nodded an acknowledgement.

"From the Met?"

"Right sir. How did you guess?"

"The car."

Peterson flicked open his ID. "Very observant of you." He went over to the adjacent bookcase and picked up a recently framed photograph of Matt and his daughters. He recognised one of the females immediately, "Are these your children, Mr Morgan? They look very much alike."

Matt was suddenly feeling uneasy. "Yes. My two daughters. There's just a year between them. What's all this about?"

Peterson hesitated momentarily. "Is Kirsty one of your daughters?"

46

Something hit Matt hard in his chest. *How did he know that? This had to be bad. What was he about to hear?*

"Yes. In the photograph. She's the younger one on the left."

"Sorry sir. Just checking. I needed your confirmation," Peterson coughed and cleared his throat. "Please sit down. I'm afraid I have some distressing news."

Matt slumped into a chair, suddenly fearing the worst.

"I'm sorry to have to tell you this, but Kirsty is in intensive care at the South Middlesex Hospital in London. She's in a coma suffering from hypothermia."

Matt looked perplexed, "You do mean my Kirsty, don't you? Are you sure it can't be somebody else?"

"No. We believe her to be Kirsty Morgan. The young woman in your photograph."

Matt put his head between his hands. "Oh! God no. Please. Not Kirsty. She only became engaged yesterday. What happened?" He looked up, but received no reply. His skin had become ashen and he was visibly shaken.

The inspector looked around and found a drinks cabinet. He poured Matt a large whisky, "Here. Drink this. It must be a big shock. I checked with the hospital, just before you arrived home and there is some better news. Her condition is now stable and she's fighting all the way."

He put a friendly hand on Matt's shoulder and continued, "Kirsty was in a critical state when she was taken in, late this afternoon, but she's made a substantial improvement. We'll drive you down to see her as soon as you feel up to it."

Matt gulped down the whisky, "I'm ready now. Please. Let's go."

Peterson put up his hand in a slightly abrupt gesture, indicating that the questioning hadn't quite finished. "Just before we set off, there is something else I'd like to ask. Does a family called Newsome mean anything to you?"

"Yes. I mentioned that Kirsty had just become engaged. It was to Robbie Newsome. They were having a celebration dinner at the Newsome house in Richmond last night." Matt paused for just a second then poured out his overriding disquiet, "What's happened? How did Kirsty get into such a mess? And what are the Metropolitan Police doing up here in Sheffield? Why would you come all the way up here just to tell me this?"

Peterson sighed wearily. Matthew had now confirmed that his daughter had been present at the massacre. That had been the main purpose of his visit. He knew he'd have to answer some of the more-tricky details of the investigation.

"We thought that she must have been involved in some way, but she was found unconscious and has been unable to tell us anything."

Matt was beginning to feel irate. Things weren't adding up and he needed answers. "Involved. Involved in what?"

Peterson grimaced, "All I'm allowed to tell you is that there was a terrible slaughter at the house last night. Five of the family and the maid were all murdered." He paused again. "I'm afraid Robbie Newsome was one of them."

Matt couldn't take in what he was hearing. It all sounded so implausible. "Are you telling me that he's dead?"

"Yes. I'm sorry. The whole family."

Matt fell silent as his mind reeled with the news of this horrendous massacre. His thoughts quickly returned to the welfare and protection of his daughter. "Poor Kirsty. How will she cope?" Then, he was struck by the finality of it all. He turned away, tears beginning to well in his eyes.

Peterson hesitated. He was finding it very difficult to explain the details. "We think, or should I say Scotland Yard thinks, that Kirsty may have been the only witness. After the murders were discovered this morning, there was a massive search of the Newsome property and Kirsty was found in a small wood at the edge of the grounds. Fog hampered the work all day and we were very lucky to find her. She'd hidden herself very well and we were about to call off the search for the night when she was discovered. Another night in sub-zero conditions would have proved fatal. Anyway, we found a purse with her driving licence in the house. That's what led us here."

Matt slowly shook his head, "I just don't believe this is happening. Please, tell me, it isn't."

The inspector spoke kindly, but firmly, "I know it has been a terrible shock, but you're going to have to face this grim reality, sir. We believe that her life may still be in danger from the gang who carried out these murders. If she really did see what happened, you can be sure that they'll try to get to her."

Willis had remained standing near the door. He'd let his superior do all the talking and his thoughts returned to the earlier phone call he'd had with Siggy Dexter. He felt deeply guilty about what he'd shared with him and couldn't look the distraught father in his face. He had to turn away.

Matt was finding it more and more difficult to comprehend the situation. His own daughter, the target for some gang of hoodlums. Peterson had been blunt and uncompromising, and he suddenly felt resentful by his lack of compassion and sympathy. His thoughts were flying everywhere and he didn't know what to make of these unthinkable revelations.

Peterson could sense his deepening distress and tried to soften his fears. "Don't worry sir. We've got the situation under control. She's got 24-hour police protection and there's a news blackout. If you're ready, then we'll go and find Kirsty."

Chapter 7

The journey to London took a little over two hours, but to Matt it seemed an eternity. The police car hurtled down the M1 with its blue lights flashing, taking him even closer to Kirsty and an uncertain future. He peered out at the silent sky which only hours before had filled him with wonder and amazement. Fear gnawed at him uncomfortably and his throat burned from indigestion caused by the whisky. Tony Peterson remained silent next to him, and Matt contemplated his total loneliness and dejection. In one instant, all the good feelings he'd had about his new life and relationship had vanished, to be replaced by the haunting spectre of Julie, all those years ago. The feelings of her loss resurfaced and no matter which way he argued in his mind, he couldn't erase the fear that he would also lose his daughter.

Eventually, the lights of Greater London interrupted his dark thoughts and the car left the M1 and joined the orbital M25. Soon, they were picking up the eastbound M4, taking them right to the fringes of Richmond. Crossing the Thames at Kew Bridge, they passed the National Rugby Stadium at Twickenham and screeched to a halt outside the accident and emergency entrance of the South Middlesex Hospital.

Flanked by Peterson and Willis, Matt was ushered forward into the hospital reception. He was immediately escorted to the intensive care unit. An armed officer from one of the Met's firearms units stood at the entrance and recognising his superior, let them pass.

Matt was shown into a small office where a white-coated female doctor looked up from her desk. She welcomed him cheerily, "Hello. I'm Dr James. You must be Kirsty's father. I had a call to say you'd arrived." She held out her hand and Matt took it, nodding grimly.

His voice was choked with emotion, "How is she? Please, tell me she's going to live?"

He found it difficult to phrase the question, afraid to hear the wrong response.

The doctor's tone changed as she suddenly became business-like. "There has been no change in Kirsty's condition over the past two hours, but the signs are optimistic. She is stable now and we have to be hopeful. When she arrived, it was touch and go, because she was in a deep coma. Fortunately, we have a number of modern techniques to help improve her chances. We are slowly removing her blood, warming it and returning it to her body. Her temperature is very gradually coming back to normal, but we can't do it quickly, otherwise it could traumatise other vital organs. I'm afraid it's now a waiting game."

"Can I see her?" he pleaded.

"Of course, but bear in mind she may look different. Her face is covered by an oxygen mask and I don't want you being alarmed when you see all the tubes and monitors. Come on, I'll take you through."

Matt was led into the private, intensive care room. Kirsty's bed was symmetrically positioned against the far wall. She was connected to an array of equipment, which continually flashed details of her vital functions. The high-tech hardware was somehow reassuring. He looked on longingly, but her features were brutally obscured by the oxygen mask. When he touched her free hand, it was cool and limp. Her face was pale and had taken on a soft waxy texture. He leant over and kissed her forehead, but when he felt her cold deathly skin against his own warm flesh, it sent a searing doubt through his mind. *How could she possibly make it?* He turned back to face the doctor, anxiety defining his features.

She spoke sympathetically, trying to give him hope, "We should see some improvement in the next few hours, but I'm afraid it's going to be a long night. Is there anything we can do for you? Perhaps ring a relative or friend. You don't have to speak to them. We'll do it for you."

Matt's speech was almost inaudible, "No. I don't think so." He was distant, his mind drifting from the conversation. His thoughts had switched to his elder daughter, Laura, but she was an air hostess and on a flight out to the Far East somewhere. There was no point in worrying her just yet. He was silent for a moment longer, then his brain clicked back to the present and as an after-thought he spoke, "Yes. There is someone. My school needs to know I won't be in."

"Certainly. Who is it?"

"She's the deputy head. Sally Baker. She's in charge of staffing and she'll pass the word around." He reeled off her number from memory and turned his attention to Kirsty.

The doctor disappeared to make the telephone call.

Matt was about to sit down by the bed when Inspector Peterson appeared at his side. One reason why the Metropolitan Police had gone to personally collect Matt was the opportunity to find out if he had any information that might be useful in the murder hunt. They'd allowed him time to see his daughter, and the medical staff had now reassured him that everything was being done to ensure her recovery. Knowing that he wouldn't leave her bedside, he was a captive audience and probably amenable to some gentle questioning.

Peterson spoke with a quiet reverence, "Sorry to disturb you, but I'd be grateful if you could spare me a minute."

There was no time to respond as Peterson hurried on, "Do you know anything about all this? It's just that we're desperate for something to go on."

Matt was phased. He pointed at Kirsty, "You mean you haven't got a clue who did this?"

"Technically, we have no proof that anyone has committed a crime against your daughter. We think she was running away from the murder scene. That's all we can guess at the moment."

"If no one has committed a crime, why the armed guard?"

"Be realistic, Mr Morgan, that's a different matter altogether. She is almost certainly our only witness, but at this time we have nothing more to go on."

Matt didn't appreciate his logic, "What you really mean to say is, the bastards who killed the Newsome family and did this to Kirsty, are going to get away with it because you can't find them." He was beginning to give the police officer the classic lines of the abused and bereaved, borne of frustration and contempt for the killers. He found it easy to focus his anger on Peterson. "Why don't you blokes get out there and do something. Find them for Christ's sake."

"We're doing all we can, but we need a concrete lead."

Matt shrugged his shoulders and turned away. "Sorry. I can't help. I'm not in the mood to think straight. I've got other things on my mind." He sighed. "Tomorrow. Tomorrow I'll fill you in on all I know, but I don't think it'll be any use."

Matt indicated Kirsty. "This is the one you need to talk to. Let's hope for everyone's sake that she makes it."

The policeman said nothing, quietly closing the door as he made his escape from the irate father.

Matt sat by Kirsty's bedside and held her hand, gently massaging the cool, dry skin. He found himself talking to her, striving to instil the will to survive by raising her sub-conscious with fond memories. He felt so helpless, but he would talk the night away and more, if only it would bring her through. The need for her to recognise him and to see her smile again, burned inside. Scenes from his daughter's childhood haunted his mind as he dredged up things to talk about throughout the long vigil.

By six o'clock, the hospital was beginning to come alive as the nurses changed shift. Matt was feeling heady and drained. His conversation with the comatose Kirsty was stilted. How many times had he repeated himself? He didn't know. He didn't care, but the fear was still there. It became sharper and focused when Kirsty's condition appeared unchanged.

Suddenly, almost imperceptibly, he felt his daughter's hand twitch, and then her head began to move slowly from side to side. Matt bounded to the door, calling for assistance. The ward sister rushed in, took one look and went out to page a doctor.

She returned immediately and Matt enquired eagerly, "What's happening? Is she coming round?"

"Possibly." The sister looked at all the monitors. "Vital signs look good." She felt Kirsty's face. "Her temperature's looking better."

Matt looked on expectantly as her eyes flickered. Her head moved again and her eyes opened, trying to focus on her surroundings. She appeared to recognise her dad and the hand he'd held all night long, lifted slightly in acknowledgement. Her eyes closed once more and suddenly bad memories began to flood back. She moaned and shook her head wildly.

At that moment, a couple of doctors bustled through the door and took control.

The sister gently ushered Matt out into the corridor and he waited silently, staring at his feet, whilst the medical team carried out their examination.

At last, one of the doctors came out. It was Dr James and she was smiling. "I think, we can safely say Kirsty is over the worst. She was quite lucid just now, but she'll still have bouts of confusion until her body temperature completely returns to normal. Now, she's out of the coma, a full recovery looks certain. However, she needs as much rest as possible, so we're going to put her under sedation. You can have a few minutes with her and there's really nothing more you can do, except get some sleep yourself. In a few hours, there should be a marked improvement, then you can chat for longer."

Matt gave a deep sigh of relief and hugged the doctor warmly. For once, he was speechless. He grinned and returned to the bedside. The oxygen mask had been removed and he could see her face. He touched his daughter and she responded by opening her eyes.

"It's Dad. It's me, darling." He kissed her cheek tenderly.

Kirsty's head rolled towards him and she spoke in a hoarse whisper, "Robbie. What happened to Robbie?"

Matt lied to her with great skill. He had already prepared himself for this, realising her recovery could depend on the credibility of his acting. He would face up to telling her the truth later. "He's safe. He's been shot, but not too seriously. They say you should be able to see him in a day or two."

The message visibly soothed her and she went on, "I have to tell you who did it."

Matt put up his hand. "No, darling. Not now. It can wait a little longer."

"I must. I must tell you now… share it."

"Okay, my love. If you have to, then take it slowly."

"There was a hideous man with a gun. Ugly. They called him Siggy. They mentioned a man called Tyburn. I think he sent them. There were two others. They wanted to rape me." Kirsty moaned, screwing up her eyes as she relived the horror.

Matt held her tightly and quickly calmed her fears. "It's no good torturing yourself any more, darling. You've shared your secret. Leave it there. Don't try to say anything else. You're safe now. I love you and I'll be here if you need me."

Kirsty took comfort from her father and his presence managed to ease her distress.

The doctor arrived to administer the sedative and Matt grudgingly left them alone.

Outside, the new ward sister was waiting to talk to him. "You're welcome to use one of our family rooms. You'll be surprised what a few hours of sleep can do. Then, when you've had something to eat, you can come back and see how Kirsty's doing."

Matt agreed. He was led down a long corridor and shown into a tiny room. It had the usual sterile decor of a modern hospital. The smell was of polish and disinfectant, and the cramped room was windowless, containing only a small bedside locker and a low, cheap metal bed.

"Not very posh, I'm afraid." The sister shrugged apologetically. "Right, I'll leave you to settle in."

Before Matt could thank her, she was gone. He flopped onto the bed and looked around at the bare and uninviting room. His mind was still in a whirl, but he was beginning to wind down, knowing that Kirsty was free from her coma. He knew he needed the rest to recharge his energy. It would help him face the remainder of the day in a clearer state of mind. Within minutes, he was drugged by the sleep of exhaustion, dreaming strange visions of fantasy and nightmare.

* * * * *

The dreams seemed to end instantly. He found himself sitting bolt upright and listening to a nearby hysterical, female scream. The sound was prolonged. It was one of anguish and terror, immediately setting him on edge. His own fear returned with a new intensity and his first thoughts were for Kirsty. He raced back along the corridor towards the intensive care unit. The screaming became louder as he approached, then it stopped abruptly. He rounded a corner and to his dismay, found a nurse leaning over the body of the police guard who had been protecting the room. Covered in blood, she was trying desperately to staunch the flow from a terrible arterial wound. Her fellow nurse was beside her, whimpering softly and clearly traumatised by the incident. Working alone, the young nurse was losing her battle.

Matt skirted the scene. He had only one thing on his mind and burst into the room, fearing what he might find. Kirsty was in bed, just as Matt had last seen her, but a deep-red stain above her chest now marred the pure white hospital linen. He surged forward, yelling at the top of his voice, "Help. We need help here. For God's sake. Please. Will somebody help?"

Looking around, he caught a glimpse of another body slumped at the other side of the bed. There was no movement. Grabbing the bedclothes, he yanked them clear to see how badly Kirsty was injured. The sight of bright blood, oozing from a hole in the hospital gown above her heart, filled him with dread.

Kirsty was still alive, but her breaths were shallow and laboured. She opened her eyes briefly and Matt responded with encouragement. "Hang in there, darling. Someone's coming to help." He bellowed again; panic etched into his voice. "For God's sake, get somebody in here. We need a doctor."

Kirsty began to cough and tried to speak, but it was almost imperceptible. Matt put his face close to hers and strained to hear the deathly whisper.

"Pony tail… pink."

The words faded away as the coughing resumed and a bright-red froth appeared at her mouth. Her head rolled to one side and she lay still.

A team of armed police and medical staff arrived, manhandling him out of the way, so the doctors could get to work.

Matt had watched Kirsty's final agony and knew she was dead. It didn't take long for the medics to reach the same conclusion. A senior consultant was directing operations. He came over to Matt, his face ashen and put a fleeting hand on his shoulder, not able to look him in the eyes.

"I'm so sorry," he mumbled. Then he left, shaking his head, unable to accept that he'd been powerless to save any of their lives.

Matt went back to Kirsty. Putting his strong arms around her body, he lifted her, holding on tightly, so that her head nestled close to his chest. He was lost in the iron grip of a mind-numbing trance as he held on for what seemed like eons. Slowly, the warmth began to seep from her youthful body and he watched in horror as the pallor of death displaced the newly returned colour in her cheeks.

Others worked around him and removed the second body. They left quietly, not wanting to interrupt his personal grief.

A short time later, he perceived that someone had entered the room.

A soft, gentle voice spoke to him. "Hi Matt."

He looked up. It was Melissa. "Mel. How did you get here?"

She didn't answer, but moved over to his chair and put a slender, comforting arm around his shoulder. He looked painfully into her beautiful face. Her huge eyes were deep wells of sadness. He swallowed hard and inclined his head towards his daughter. "Look. It's Kirsty."

Melissa whispered quietly, as she fought back her own turmoil. "I'm so sorry, my love," she almost pleaded with him, "let it go."

Something touched Matt. He buried his face into her breast and began to sob bitterly. He had locked his emotions away during those endless hours and now it was time for them to escape. The mass of sorrow, burst like a dam as he began to purge his dreadful torment.

Hot tears streamed down Melissa's own cheeks as she shared the grief of his terrible loss. She could never know what his pain was like, yet the death of his young, beautiful, Kirsty drew on her deepest emotions and she could not help but experience the intensity of his agony.

Eventually, Matt fell silent, but Melissa held him tightly and gently stroked his hair. Uncontrollable thoughts raged in her mind. What was the strange and immediate fear that gripped her, yet left her glowing? What was it about this man? Something had triggered emotions she'd never felt before. Through Matthew's pain, she had inexplicably found an intense empathy and she now had a feeling of total completeness. It was as though her life had found a new purpose. Was this what real love was like? It was something completely new, but she found this hidden emotion was one that she dearly wanted to cling on to forever.

Matt pulled himself away and wiped his eyes with the sleeve of his shirt.

She whispered hoarsely, "If you like, I'll stay."

He could have replied anything, but nothing would have dragged her away from him.

Matt looked at Melissa. He had shed his tears before a woman that he hardly knew. Yet, when he looked into her eyes, he could see something beyond mere compassion. He had a strange, new perception of her. She'd suddenly become an irresistible anchor. "Yes. I'd like that," he snuffled and Melissa pushed a tissue in to his hand. He cleared his throat noisily, "Mel, I've let Kirsty down."

"Come on, Matt. You're obviously feeling guilty. I doubt you'd have been able to do anything."

"But I should have been with her. I could have stopped it. I was asleep. If only I'd been here."

"Stop punishing yourself. There's nothing you could have done. They had guns and knives. You would only have got yourself killed too."

"I'm so sorry!"

"Don't, Matt. Don't apologise."

Their intimate privacy was interrupted by the unwelcome arrival of Inspector Peterson. He entered the room quietly, but there was no disguising the reason for his presence. Matt spotted him and stood up, breaking from Melissa's gentle embrace. His recent self-pity evaporated. Someone had to bear the blame and he immediately began to gush insults at the policeman. "You, useless bastards. This is all your fault. Call yourself police. You couldn't protect a snowman in a fuckin' blizzard."

He was as tall as the policeman and they met eyeball to eyeball. Peterson felt uneasy. He was about to offer his sympathy and excuses, but he realised he might find himself in an ugly brawl if he couldn't calm the situation. Instead, he used a different tack. "One of my best men is also dead out there. He's got a wife and two kids. How do you think I'm going to tell her that he's not coming home tonight? And the young doctor, he's dead too. He was only 25. Of, course there's been a cock up, but you're not the only one who's suffering. You haven't got a monopoly on grief."

Matt glared. He was unforgiving. "Bastard. Don't patronise me by hiding behind your failure. You should have done more."

"We thought we had everything covered."

"But you obviously didn't."

Melissa could see the danger signs and put herself between the two men as they squared up to each other.

"Anyway, what I want to know from you, Peterson is, who did it? What have you done with him?"

He gave no reply. Matt smirked at the lack of response and rounded on the inspector again. "Christ, no! He's got away, hasn't he? I can see it in your face. You useless load of wankers. I could have done better myself."

Melissa could feel Matt's anger and put both her arms about his chest to restrain him. In his present state, she feared he'd throw a punch at the policeman.

Matt thundered on. "Yeah! and suppose you do catch him. What happens next? He'll get locked up for 20 years and get out after ten for good behaviour. When he's inside, he can spend his time doing drugs, watching dirty videos and playing snooker. Great punishment that is! Imagine, if it was your family. Your daughter. How would you feel?" Matt ground out his words with cutting sarcasm, feeling a strange hatred burn up inside him. "I tell you what Inspector. I'll sort this lot out for you, but I won't put Kirsty's killers away in a holiday camp. I'll put them down permanently like the animals they are."

Peterson stiffened up. He saw something in Matt's expression that unnerved him. "Be careful what you're saying, Mr Morgan. Nobody, but nobody, can take the law in their own hands. If you try it, don't be surprised if you get yourself into serious trouble. I would strongly advise you to leave this investigation to the professionals."

"Professionals. That's rich coming from you."

It took all of Peterson's self-control not to go for Matt. Instead, he blustered on, "Whoever did this is obviously part of the gang who murdered the Newsome family. I came to offer my condolences and ask you for help. We desperately need a lead. We want to find the killer as much as you do. Now, for Kirsty's sake, did she say anything earlier when she became conscious. Anything at all?"

Matt stared icily into his face. "Nothing, pal. Not a jot."

The policeman returned his stare for a brief second, then turned and left. The whole incident left him frustrated. In many ways, he felt sympathy for the angry father he'd managed to alienate. He did feel responsible for all the deaths that had occurred at the hospital. The crippling news that the CCTV cameras were down because a new system was being installed now meant that they didn't have a single lead. Worst of all was the supposed news blackout. Someone in the force must have given inside information to the murderers. He was a very worried man.

Chapter 8

It had been an hour since the argument with Peterson. Matt was seated alone on an uncomfortable chair outside a small office that had been taken over by the police. He wanted more than anything to get away, but had agreed to make a statement before he left.

Melissa had gone to a machine to bring a couple of coffees, reluctantly leaving him alone.

He hunched forward on his seat, feeling numb and fragile, like an empty shell. He still hadn't managed to contact Laura, but when inevitably he did get through, he didn't know where he would draw the strength to tell her what had happened.

A nearby storeroom door opened and someone came out. A white-coated figure approached and passed him by. Matt looked up impassively, not taking in the features of the man who was striding away. There was nothing particularly noticeable about him. He was tall and slim and his greasy brown hair was tied back in a ponytail. It was secured with a pink elastic band. Something stirred in Matt's memory. His mind went straight back to Kirsty's last words. What had she been trying to tell him? Had she seen her killer leave? Matt shot to his feet and shouted loudly so the man couldn't fail to hear. "Oy! You! I want a word."

Pete Teasdale glanced behind and saw Matt coming after him. He'd followed Dexter's instructions to the letter and the plan had worked perfectly until now. They'd agreed to split up and remain on the premises until the heat died down. This had completely baffled the authorities, who'd unsuccessfully used stop and search tactics on everyone who'd tried to leave. Convinced that the killers had escaped in the ensuing confusion, the police blockade was being eased. He'd decided it was now safe to leave and was on his way out via the rear service entrance, where Saviore was waiting to pick him and Dexter up in a borrowed laundry van.

Teasdale turned on his pursuer and Matt found himself looking down the barrel of a semi-automatic pistol, complete with silencer. The gun was fired without hesitation, but it had been shot on the turn. The bullet thudded harmlessly into a nearby wall and before Teasdale could aim it accurately, Matt dived forward and dragged him to the floor. The thug fell awkwardly and the gun flew harmlessly from his grip. He aimed a blow at Matt's face but only succeeded in grazing his cheek. The struggle was aimless with neither landing a decent punch. The gun was lying too far along the corridor for either of them to reach, but it was closer to Matt. Teasdale glanced at the pistol, but knew he had no chance of getting it back in a straight race.

With one almighty heave, he pushed Matt away from him and made his escape in the other direction. Matt hesitated and looked back at the gun. He dismissed it and gave chase.

Teasdale burst through the double fire doors at the end of the corridor and made a right turn. Matt was ten yards behind and closing fast. The doors led onto the stairs, but Teasdale's planned escape was thwarted by repair work on the stairwell below. Instead, the chase went upwards. Matt hurtled after the other man taking the steps, two at a time. His high level of fitness started to show and he began to gain. He finally caught up with Teasdale as they reached the exit onto the roof. The door was half open, but as Matt was about to grab him, the thug swung it viciously into his face, giving him a bloody mouth and sending his mind reeling. As he staggered through the door, his adversary was racing off at high speed across the roof.

Teasdale was agile for a tall man and leapt cleanly across the low air vents littering his path. Matt grimaced, shook his head and charged after him, determined to make up the lost ground. They were heading towards a brightly painted red exit door, which would inevitably lead to a flight of steps going down. Matt strove hard to catch up but was making little impression. Just as he began to fear he might not have the staying power, Teasdale lost his footing and went down heavily. He got up immediately, but it was clear he was injured. He limped along dragging his foot in pain and Matt was soon within reach.

He launched a mighty rugby tackle bringing Teasdale down and they rolled over and over with arms flailing as each tried to gain the upper hand. The thug clawed at Matt's face, but suddenly found himself with nothing but free space under his left shoulder. He looked down and immediately ceased his struggle. He was half way over the edge of the building and ten storeys up.

Matt knelt above him, safely on the inside, with both hands tight around his collar. "Okay, shit brain, start talking." He rolled Teasdale agonisingly close to the edge. Beads of sweat appeared on the man's temples. Matt could sense his fear.

"What do you want to know?"

"Who sent you? Who pays your wages?"

Teasdale glared arrogantly and remained silent.

"Come on. Who is it? Who's this Tyburn?"

The man looked puzzled. "Are you the police? How do you know about Tyburn?"

Matt bluffed, "I'm Special Branch and I know more than you think." He grabbed Teasdale tighter and began to push him towards the edge again.

"Okay! Okay! I'll talk. You know plenty already. Tyburn's the boss."

"So? What does he do? Where can I find him?"

"South of the river at Greenwich. He owns Tybuild. It's a building firm."

"And what about Siggy. Where does he fit in?"

"Siggy Dexter. He's the boss's right arm. He'll fix you good and proper when he finds out about your meddling,"

"Piss off you piece of garbage. You're in no position to threaten me. What about downstairs? Did you pull the trigger?"

"What do you think? Do I have to spell it out?"

"Yes, you bloody well do." Matt lifted his fist in the pretence of smashing his face and Teasdale flinched.

"Okay. I got rid of the copper, but I only watched the rest. Siggy finished the bitch."

Matt relaxed his grip. At last, he had the truth. His eyes inexplicably misted over as visions of Kirsty returned. He felt a terrible lump in his throat. Then, a strange darkness descended across his mind and he carefully placed his foot on the thug's chest.

"Oy! What's your game then?"

"That bitch you just mentioned. She was my daughter."

Teasdale spoke no more. Matt effortlessly rolled him over the edge. It was only an instant before the silent, flailing body, smashed to the ground in a crazy heap of broken bones.

Matt peered over the side at the spread-eagled carcass below. He experienced a strange new feeling, a huge surge of empowerment.

"Whoops!" He turned away and sneered. "Bugger the police. I'll sort this lot myself."

Chapter 9

Matt stood silently with his head bowed. He held Laura upright by clasping a strong arm around her shoulder. Her emotions had been shredded by the tragedy of losing her younger sister and best friend, but the funeral was even worse.

The graveside was still and the weak November sun was beginning to set in a cloudless blue sky. Above them, the withered remnants of summer's canopy floated down from the almost naked trees. The vicar ended the burial service and looked across at the forlorn couple on the opposite side of the deep pit. As he did so, a light wind suddenly began to swirl and made the rustic leaves dance and tumble. They were swept forward and cascaded onto the highly polished coffin, scraping the lid in an act of indecent desecration.

Matt had decided to bury Kirsty alongside her mother. Twenty years passed by in an instant as he reflected with vivid clarity the heart-breaking recollections of that day as he'd watched the stark finality of his darling wife's coffin being lowered into that same hole. He felt the same physical pain knotting his guts again. He wanted to run away, but his leaden feet refused to move.

Matt's tragic memories were interrupted as he became aware of people slowly beginning to move. The burial service had been short and the friends and mourners of Kirsty were now starting to turn away and leave. A few threw a small handful of earth onto the casket and others dropped single flowers. Many of her young friends from university and those who had known her at school sobbed uncontrollably. They didn't seek to hide their sadness. One by one, they solemnly hugged Matt or shook his hand, kissing Laura tenderly as they filed away.

Before long, there were only the two of them left at the graveside. Melissa wasn't far away, but standing a little way back, ready to give her support when it was needed. Although she felt a terrible need to be at their side, she was also desperate not to interrupt this final act of farewell. Matt and Laura had always had a loving bond and today, it was being tested to the limit. They needed one another's strength like never before as they tried to come to terms with their loss together.

Matt tugged at Laura's arm. "Come on love, it is time to go. It's getting quite chilly."

"Dad how can we?" She looked down into the deep hole. "How can we leave Kirsty here? No. Not here, it is too cold and lonely." Her eyes were red with the harshness of a thousand tears. She shook and sobbed again; her senses numbed by her anguish.

Matt spoke softly, "It's over darling. We have to go." He had wept many times with her after he had told her about Robbie's family and Kirsty's death. For a fleeting moment, he recalled everything that had happened, but telling Laura had been the worst experience of all. Strangely, amongst all these thoughts, he was aware that his feelings were being hijacked. His heartache was slowly being replaced by a growing resentment towards the workings of the law. It seemed inconceivable, but the police were now trying to pin the death of Teasdale onto him. He'd had to take legal advice but he'd been assured there wasn't a shred of evidence that would convict him in a court of law. When he'd got rid of the killer, he'd discovered a powerful strength, a feeling that natural justice had been done. It had given him partial satisfaction as his grieving for Kirsty began. This force was now growing and feeding on his need for revenge. He was restless, consumed by a desire to do more. He argued with himself that Kirsty would still be alive, but for the thugs who'd murdered the family of his future son-in-law. They couldn't be allowed to go unpunished.

Matt's thoughts returned to Laura and he tried gently to pull her away from the graveside. It was important to break her morbid insistence that she couldn't leave Kirsty behind. He saw Melissa next to a nearby tree and the look he gave her was a clear signal for help. In an instant, she was there, supporting Laura from the other side with another comforting arm.

Matt repeated himself gently, "We have to go now Laura. It's time." He spoke softly to his daughter, "We'll say goodbye to Kirsty one last time, my love, but don't look down. Look to the sky." He pointed up to the bright evening star that was just rising over the far tree line. "Look. It's Venus, come to watch over Kirsty." Matt felt a huge lump rise in his throat. Warm tears coursed down his face again.

Together, the three of them bade a final farewell and with painful slowness, Melissa steered them along the grass border and onto the tarmac pathway. At the main gates, a black limousine was waiting to take them home. Matt gently ushered the two women into the car and closed the door. He was about to go round to the other side, when Inspector Peterson approached from behind the ancient lychgate.

"Mr Morgan, I came to offer my sympathies on behalf of the Force. I'm returning to London shortly and I thought you might like to know that you're off the hook. The Crown Prosecution Service has decided not to press charges."

Matt was impassive. "There are no charges to face. I told the truth. Teasdale tripped and fell from the hospital roof as I chased him. Didn't the post-mortem confirm that the injury to his ankle occurred before he fell?"

"Yes, it did, and that's what swung the decision in your favour. But we all really know he was pushed, don't we?"

Matt shrugged. He didn't give an answer, but instead asked one final question of his own.

"What about the ballistics report? Did Teasdale's gun kill Kirsty and the others?"

"No, only the police guard. That means there were others involved."

"I see. Then it's not over. Anyway, Teasdale got what he deserved. Goodbye, inspector."

He ducked into the car and it quietly slid away, leaving the policeman alone on the pavement. Matt's thoughts were distant, high on a hospital roof.

So, Teasdale did tell the truth after all and Siggy Dexter was the one who'd killed Kirsty.

He held Laura's hand tightly as she rested her head on his shoulder. For a moment, he closed his eyes. His head throbbed as his battered thoughts churned around in his mind. *Did he have the guts to avenge Kirsty? Could he track Dexter down? Could he finish what he'd already started?* His answer screamed through his head. *Yes! A million times Yes!*

Chapter 10

Lawrence Tyburn arrived at *Signors* in a state of high expectation. His bulldog colleague was already waiting at their usual table, a half-smoked cigar clamped between his teeth. The maître d' fussed behind Tyburn, helping him to remove his expensive overcoat and then ushering him to his seat. He handed each of them a menu, then melted away into the main restaurant, leaving them alone.

Tyburn couldn't hold his impatience any longer. "Well Simon? You got me round here pretty quick. So, what's the big deal?"

Lush grinned back across the table. "Things were looking bad a short time ago. Don't you agree? But as one door closes, another one opens."

Tyburn looked puzzled. "That's an outdated old cliche. What do you mean by that?"

"Well, I've come up with an idea that can make us a great deal of money and offset the losses from the Newsome affair."

Tyburn beamed one of his widest smiles. He was immediately intrigued.

Lush took a long draw on his cigar and continued, "Tell me, Lol. Do you ever keep abreast of politics?"

Tyburn shook his head slowly, "Not really my interest."

"Have you ever heard of Charles Rydell? He's a new junior minister at the home office."

"No. Can't say that I have."

"Well, he's a fairly new face. Keen to do well. Rumour has it that he's a high flier and probably destined for the very top."

"Go on then, Simon, make your point."

"Don't be so impatient my friend, all will be revealed shortly. First of all, I need to mention my wife, Christine. She has a wide circle of female friends and acquaintances. She meets them for coffee and gossip. You get the picture?"

Tyburn nodded at his mundane patter.

"Well, one of these women makes girl's frilly party frocks."

"For God's sake, Simon, what has this got to do with anything?"

Lush put his hand up in a calming gesture. "These dresses, my friend, are man-sized. They're made to order and sold to the kinky set. The woman who designs and makes them was having a few drinks at a recent bash and had one sherry too many. She was bragging that she sold costumes to one or two well-known celebrities and public figures."

"Surprise me!"

"Unfortunately, she realised she'd blabbed too much and clammed up. She became very cagey and wouldn't reveal any more. I don't suppose I could blame her; it was her business clientele after all and she wouldn't want to risk losing valued customers. Anyway, when Christine let this story slip in passing, I decided to dig around and see if I could discover anything interesting. It didn't take long to find out that this dressmaker has a number of outworkers and with a little bribery, I was able to get a photocopy of some of the latest deliveries. The two names of greatest significance were Lady Doreen Waterford and a certain Mrs Lynn Rydell."

"The wife of this Charles Rydell. The MP?"

"Right in one. Not only that, but there's a big connection between Charles and Sir Kenneth Waterford. He turns out to be Rydell's sponsor at Westminster and they're known to be very good friends."

"So, you think they're into this dressing-up business together then?"

"I would bet my shirt on it. What's more, I did some more detective work. The address used by Lady Waterford for the delivery of these frocks, turns out to be a flat in Kensington and it's not listed as one of their normal residences in *Who's Who*."

"And that's where you think their little parties take place?"

"I certainly do and just think, if it was made public. The government is only sitting on a tiny majority in parliament and it's trying hard to hang onto power by pushing its anti-sleaze policies and morality bandwagon. A scandal like this could easily lose them the general election next year. It would ruin Rydell's career forever"

"So, the bottom line is blackmail?"

"Of a sort. Rydell doesn't have the kind of money or resources to pay a sizeable blackmail demand."

"Then, why bother trying to get the evidence we need to nail him?"

"It's simple really. We're going to use his influence at the home office to help our cause. I've researched a scheme that's so audacious, you won't believe it's possible. All we need is some decent photographic evidence to verify Rydell's little fetish. Once we can prove that he's as bent as a nine-pound note, he's ours. I'm telling you this could make us both very rich."

"Convince me."

It took less than ten minutes to persuade Lawrence Tyburn that the inventiveness of the plan was sheer brilliance. Tyburn's eyes were wide with admiration. "However, you came up with such a convoluted, hare-brained, madcap scheme, I'll never know. It's pure genius. I'll give you ten out of ten for ingenuity." He sat back in his chair and stroked his chin, deliberating the idea and looking for potential faults, "Although the concept is superb, our timing would have to be perfect. If any government agency ever got wind of what we were intending to do, we'd end up doing some serious time."

Lush puffed arrogantly on a new Havana cigar. "I agree, but the plan effectively consists of a small number of self-contained stages. That's the beauty of it. The success of one will decide whether we can progress to the next. I would be the first to admit that there aren't any contingencies if things go belly up. If one link in the chain fails, it means we'll have to abandon the whole plan and walk away from it. We'd lose our initial investment, but… " he stopped and took another deep inhalation of his cigar, "the ultimate question is, do we think it's worth the risk?"

Tyburn was impassive. "You knew what I'd say to this, didn't you? The potential rewards are too great a temptation to turn down. What's more, we don't need to involve many people, so the risks involved are minimal." He broke into a grin. "So! Yes my friend. I'm in!"

"Good man. We can get together and thrash out the serious detail later, but to start with, we need our evidence against Rydell. It's going to be expensive because only the best technicians have the expertise to do the kind of surveillance job we need. I already have a photographer in the frame, as it were. A guy called *Flash* Gordon! Who better?"

Tyburn chuckled at his friend's corny humour. "The way our luck's gone recently, things could well be back on the up. I've a real gut feeling about your crazy plan. Now, I think it's about time we ordered dinner. A bottle of champagne wouldn't go amiss either. Let's celebrate."

Chapter 11

The van was dark and silent except for the laboured breathing of Davy Tonks. He sat contemplating his folly. He knew that he should never have accepted this job. The promise of such a large fee, for an easy night's work could have been resisted, if he'd tried hard enough.

He sighed inwardly. *Wasn't that his biggest failing, the fact that he couldn't say no? Where was his willpower?* It was the same as not being able to give up smoking, after his doctor had told him on countless occasions, it was killing him. Like most smokers, he had little time for the advice, but he now knew how bad his lungs had really become. The diagnosis of his emphysema the previous year had not been a great shock, but he had not been prepared for its swift and debilitating onset. The consequences to his lifestyle were now dire.

Besides feeling ill, he was unhappy about having to work with another man. It wasn't his style and although he'd been recruited many times to do jobs, he'd always insisted on working alone. He was uneasy about the stranger occupying the driver's seat next to him. This was the man who'd sought him out and tempted him out of his early retirement. He'd been equally adamant that the two of them had to do the job together, so there'd been no choice but to agree.

Gary Gordon glanced across at Tonks. *My God,* he thought, *you're hardly any better than a corpse. I hope I haven't dropped a 24-carat bollock bringing you along.*

He found it difficult to believe that the ancient shell of a man sitting next to him was the most renowned small-time burglar in London. He'd been assured that Tonks was a craftsman, whose vast experience would ensure that no domestic lock or security system could defeat him.

The van rocked slightly as a stream of cars passed by in the darkness. Tonks finally broke the silence with a hollow bronchial cough. He cleared his throat and spoke with a deep leathery timbre, "Okay, Waterford's been gone for 15 minutes. I'm going in. If he returns for any reason, I need to know straight away. Like yesterday. Got it. Now test the phones again."

Gordon was irritable and spoke in a derogatory manner, "Don't fuss, old man."

"It's my bloody neck on the line. Now test the bleedin' phones again or I'm goin' home."

Gordon huffed and rechecked the pair of mobiles impatiently. He couldn't help ribbing the older man. "You're not the first one I've done a job with Tonks. You don't have to go over everything 50 times. I'm not bloody stupid. Now, get lost and do what you're good at and leave me to do the rest. Don't forget, he who pays the piper calls the tune. Okay."

"What do you mean?"

"Never mind. Just go."

Tonks couldn't see the other man's face in the darkness, but wanted to lecture him on his arrogance. The reason he'd had a successful career as a burglar had been his meticulous planning. At one time, he would've told Gordon to get stuffed and left him to his own devices, but he felt jaded already and didn't have the energy for a tiresome argument. He let the insults pass.

Tonks shouldered the van door open, clutching a small, but weighty holdall in one hand and a bouquet of flowers in the other. With a bowed head, he set off diagonally across the road. The entrance to the old house was at the top of a flight of ten steps and he made heavy work of it. At the top, he stopped and panted wearily as he struggled to catch his breath.

"Damn bag," he cursed his burden. For the first time in his life, he found himself questioning his own ability. *This is a waste of time. If the alarm goes off or we need to make a run for it, I'm finished.* Past episodes from his life flashed before him as he remembered close calls when he had been a fit, young man and able to 'leg it' as well as anyone. He strove to control his feelings. This wasn't the tingling excitement he used to experience as he pitted his wits against the best security systems. No. This was the cold, cloying dread of outright failure of not being able to get away. He tried to persuade himself to turn and walk away, but in the end, his stubborn professional pride won him over. Others were relying on him and he couldn't bear to break his own myth of invincibility. He felt trapped by his own legend.

Pulling himself together, he grimaced. *Better make sure there are no mistakes this time, Tonksy boy.*

He had carefully researched the old house, which had been recently converted into a block of luxury flats. He pressed the bell for flat number four and waited for a voice over the intercom. A tense few seconds passed before someone answered.

A faraway, ill-tempered female voice demanded a response.

Tonks leant over the speaker. "Inter Flora here. I have a bouquet for Miss Wilkins."

There was some distant, static crackle, but there was no mistaking a change in the tone of the woman's voice. "Oooh. How nice. Right. It's flat number four on the ground floor."

Tonks felt relieved. His ploy had worked and there were no more immediate stairs to climb. There was a soft electrical hum and a click as the woman in the flat released the door lock. He shuffled inside and left his bag in a corner as he looked around the tastefully decorated hall. A deep pile carpet covered the floor and a pleasant smell of furniture polish filled the air. The flats were certainly well maintained and these small pointers were all tell-tale signs of the affluence of the tenants. Tonks moved along, looking for the correct door and found it at the end of the corridor. He stood upright in front of the security spy hole and rang the bell. He wore a smart jumper with an Inter Flora logo and certainly looked the part. Locks and bolts were heard sliding across and a heavy door opened a crack, held back by a huge security chain.

Tonks made a purposeful inquiry. "Miss Wilkins?"

A middle-aged woman peered through the gap. "Yes. That's me."

"I can just about push these through if you like?"

"Yes, that's fine. Provided you don't squash them."

The flowers were transferred to the woman who purred appreciably as they were handed through. She glowed excitedly like a young schoolgirl. "Thanks. I wonder who they're from?"

Davy smiled as he quipped. "They look very expensive. Anyway, I'll be off now. Cheerio."

He found his way back to the main entrance and carefully opened and closed the front door. In flat number four, a small bleep signified that the visitor had left the premises, but a very contented lady was too preoccupied with her flowers to glance through the window and verify his departure. The trick never failed.

Tonks picked up his tool bag and with trepidation began looking for the lift, which would take him up to his intended destination on the second floor. His research had indicated the presence of a lift, but if he was wrong, his physical resolve would be tested to its limit. He didn't know how many steps he'd have to climb, but just one too many would finish him for sure. He continued to look around, and at the other end of the plush hall, he spotted an odd-looking archway. His luck was in and he sidled along, entering the small, empty elevator. As the lift slowly ascended he stripped off his Inter Flora jumper to reveal a Telecom overall. Alighting on the top floor, he found his way to flat number 12.

Confidently, he stood in front of the door, glancing around for a possible CCTV. He was relieved to see nothing. Tonks rang the bell. He wasn't expecting a response, but he had to play it safe. All his precautions had been tried and tested over countless years and so far they'd kept him out of trouble. Satisfied there was no one at home, he readied himself for work.

Opening his kit bag, he withdrew a number of tools. The lock itself was standard fare and within a minute, there was a satisfactory click, indicating that entry was imminent. The simple work was done and the more difficult task of disabling the alarm system was about to start. Tonks felt uneasy. The lock had been simple and quick, but the exertions on him were already beginning to show. He was surprised at his discomfort as his breathing became noisy and rasping. *What had happened to Mr Cool?*

The urge to cough came upon him and he knew that he had to get inside the flat soon. At any time, he could be engulfed by a paroxysm of coughing and this always left him incapacitated and weak. A disturbance out in the corridor would surely attract the unwanted attention of other tenants and bring his operation to an immediate and undesirable conclusion. His heart pounded as he fought to control his breathing and concentrate on the tricky job of breaking through the security system. With the lock picked, he was able to insert a wafer-thin magnetic plate to disable the proximity switch on the door. He held it carefully in place and pushed the door open. The alarm stayed quiet and he edged inside, closing it behind. Once the lock had clicked shut, he leant heavily against the wall. The coughing spasm didn't come, but its fear had served as a warning to him and he rested for a full ten minutes, recovering his composure steadily.

He peered into the gloom trying to accustom his eyes to the dark interior, but it was pitch black and there wasn't a chink of light from anywhere. He began feeling against the wall and with a sigh of gratitude he found the light switch. The entrance hall was bathed in a subdued but warming glow. Tonks began to examine his surroundings. There were no infrared detectors in the ceiling, which meant that the control box for the alarm must be nearby. The entrance hall was exquisitely decorated and on the walls hung several expensive looking pictures. It was one of these that caught Tonk's well-trained eye. One edge of the frame appeared to be slightly off the wall. When he tugged at its corner, the hinged picture gently swung open to reveal a small recess no more than two feet square.

Inside, glowed the computerised module, which controlled the alarm system. It was a model well known to Tonks and there would be no problem in disarming it. However, this was a job unlike any other he had undertaken before. Not only did he have to disarm the system, but once Gordon had done his work, he had to rearm it and leave the flat with no trace of entry. That would be more difficult. Tonks had talked to a number of friends, including some who were knowledgeable in high tech electronics and had been given sound advice. He had tried a dummy run on some equipment he'd bought and was satisfied with his new technique.

He began by boring a small hole in the side of the control box with a cordless drill and screwing in a self-tapping adapter. The heavy bag had been a real exertion to him, but had been a necessity. The reason for his labour was a small cylinder of liquid air. Tonks lifted it out carefully and connected a reinforced flexible pipe to the adapter. He opened the valve and there was a low hiss as the escaping air passed into the control box. A thermodynamic principle called the Joule-Thompson effect took place which resulted in an immediate temperature drop. As the contents of the alarm box plummeted to sub-zero, there was a malfunction of the electronic circuit board, rendering it temporarily useless. Tonks let the freezing air do its work for several minutes and whilst he was waiting, he donned a pair of insulation gloves. By disconnecting a few wires and pressing a sequence of buttons normally reserved for maintenance engineers, he persuaded the alarm to give up its security code. Making their exit from the flat would now be simple.

Despite the cold air, he was sweating profusely and feeling weak at the knees. There was a bench seat next to the telephone table and he flopped down. His mind swam dizzily as his lungs panted for extra oxygen. Bending his head forward, he grasped his arms about himself. His distress further fuelled his anxiety and he knew that if he got away safely tonight, this would definitely be his last job. Very gradually, using all his will power and reserves, he managed to pull himself around. His mind began to function again and his heart rate slowed down. He was still breathing fast and his hands trembled weakly, but he was starting to feel a little better. A stately grandfather clock in the corner showed that it had taken him nearly 50 minutes to do something he could normally complete in ten.

In the van at the roadside, Gary Gordon had chain smoked his way through ten cigarettes. He was very agitated and his mind was flitting from one potential disaster scenario to another. Had something gone badly wrong? Had Tonks been caught? Or worse still, had the old bugger dropped dead on the job? With such an outstanding reputation, he never thought it could take the burglar so long to make the break-in.

Suddenly, his phone rang. The stillness of the van was shattered and his jangling nerves only served to heighten the noise. It was his summons. He swiftly collected his gear and approached the front door. Tonks gave him immediate access from the flat above and he bounded up the stairs two at a time to find the door waiting open for him.

Gordon grumbled angrily, "You took your time." He pushed past Tonks and into the room. Then, he noticed with some concern the ashen face and sunken eyes of the old burglar. "Fuckin' hell, you look in a bad way. Are you Okay? You're not going to snuff it?"

"I'll be all right after I've had a rest, but we need to be out of this place as soon as possible. I have to get home. I've got an oxygen cylinder there."

Gordon had a quick look round the flat and gestured to the sitting room. "Come on and sit in here. There's a massive settee. You can lie down." He helped Tonks put his feet up on the deep, comfortable three-seater, then set about his own work. He knew that he would have to fix his equipment in place as fast as possible. The two of them had already outstayed their welcome.

Just off the hall, on a short corridor, were the bedrooms. One of them was locked, which excited Gordon's interest. He cursed, "Shit. I need the silly old devil again to get me in."

He called across to the settee, "I can't get in this room. It's locked. Do you feel like giving me a hand?"

"I'm no good just yet. Give me five more minutes."

Gordon slammed his fist against the wall in frustration as he waited for the old man to recover. When Tonks appeared at his side, he gained access to the room in a matter of seconds. He shuffled back to the couch and left Gordon to it. The bedroom had been converted into two separate but identical dressing rooms. These looked promising and Gordon went inside the right-hand one. He switched on the main lights to reveal a room surrounded by full-length mirrors. Along one wall was a luxurious built-in dressing table with numerous drawers. Along another wall was a bank of integral wardrobes with mirrored sliding doors. They were locked.

Gordon tried all the drawers and found them similarly secured. There was nothing for it, he would have to ask Tonks for more help. He was just about to shout out when he noticed that one of the drawers seemed jammed rather than locked. He gave it a hard yank and it slid smoothly open. The contents revealed themselves and without touching anything he chuckled with glee. This was what he'd hoped to find. His set-up would definitely be worthwhile. He closed the drawer and began to look around.

The flat was expensively furnished and was also blessed with air-conditioning. Amidst the mirrors, Gordon spotted an inlet grill. It was high on the wall, opposite the wardrobe and adjacent to the dressing table. It would be an ideal hiding place for the first of his cameras. It took Gordon a further half an hour to conceal three miniature, high-resolution video cameras in different rooms. Each had a transmitter consuming ultra-low power and fuelled by cleverly designed long-life batteries. As his work neared completion, he stirred his accomplice into action to attend to the alarm system. By now, the temperature of the console had returned to normal and the electronics were active. Tonks rewired the circuit and then replaced the front cover, filling the hole that had been drilled with a dummy screw. He finally secured the bedroom lock. They scrutinised the flat to make sure that nothing had been disturbed and after rearming the system with the correct code, they made their exit. With bated breath, they waited for two full minutes and thankfully the alarm remained silent. It had reset correctly and they were in the clear.

Gordon was relieved and he hummed as he gently pushed Tonks forward. He almost stumbled over the ambling burglar in his impatience to usher the old man safely out of the building. He had one lingering worry. Would Tonks still be around in another couple of weeks? Gordon still couldn't do without him. Although he now had the code for the flat's security system, he still needed Tonks to help him break-in again, so he could retrieve his expensive gear. He pondered thoughtfully about the need to look after his ailing partner. "Come on, Tonks you old bugger. Let me take you home for your oxygen cylinder. Then, I'll buy you a few pints to cheer you up."

Chapter 12

Number 50, Queen Anne's Gate, is positioned just off St. James's Park in central London. This huge, impressive office block is also one of the administrative corner stones of Her Britannic Majesty's Government and is just a few minutes' walk from the Palace of Westminster. The front fascia of this imposing building announces its purpose to all who pass by with tall letters marked on the side, which clearly identify it as the *home office*.

Charles Rydell was trying to relax for five minutes. He was standing at a large picture window and could just see a corner of St James's Park above the nearby buildings. The sky looked threatening. Layers of dark grey ruffled cloud, with the texture of whipped cream, were rolling downwards. Droplets began to patter quietly against the windowpane, then the wind suddenly gusted and heavy rain was lashed against the glass, blurring his view. Turning away, the politician returned to his desk. He'd had a very busy schedule that afternoon and although he felt exhausted, he knew there was still a great deal of work to do before he could finish for the night. He sipped a piping hot cup of tea and began to unwind, letting his body sink into his deep leather chair.

The late afternoon fatigue encouraged a small lapse in concentration and his mind began to wander away from the open file in front of him. He felt a warm smugness at his new position in life. His recent elevation to the government had been a welcome, but not unexpected surprise. Some of his colleagues had been canvassing on his behalf and through the normal machinations of politics, he'd finally been recommended to the prime minister by one of her close advisers. She had given him the post of minister for prisons and warned him that it had the reputation for being a difficult portfolio. She'd also told him quite bluntly that because he had no proven pedigree and had risen from nowhere, that his appointment would be coolly received by certain sections of the party. He would need to prove himself worthy of her confidence. That didn't matter a jot. He would soon show the PM and the ancient mandarins of the civil service how capable he was. The word would soon get back to the doubters and make them envious of his success. He knew that a great deal was expected of him and he relished, with arrogance, his newfound role and the power that went with it.

Parliament had only returned from the summer recess a few weeks earlier and the forthcoming Queen's Speech would promise much in the way of penal reform, as his party strove to combat new increases in crime. Rarely had the issue of law and order been higher in the public's conscience. He'd already learnt to cope with the arduous nature of the job: the late nights, long weekends and the incessant round of meetings. He was relishing the challenge, along with the perks and privileges which went hand-in-hand with senior public life.

Just then, the telephone rang and interrupted his thoughts.

It was Miss Stephenson, his secretary. "There's a call from Sir Kenneth Waterford. Would you like to take it now, sir or are you busy?"

His mind quickly switched back into gear. "I'll take it now. This will be personal, Miss Stephenson. Please, ensure that I am not interrupted."

After her acknowledgement, he pressed the green button on the telephone and picked up the receiver to talk to his old friend Ken Waterford.

The two exchanged their usual opening pleasantries; then Ken interjected, "Doing anything on Friday evening, Charles? I thought about arranging a small party." There was a slight pause. "It's just for friends."

Rydell understood. "Mmm. Yes. It seems such a long time since we had a get together. Is the dress formal?"

"Of course, Charles. The usual sort of thing. It's six for 6:30 at the Kensington flat. Don't forget to bring the wife. Tell her to wear something special."

The pleasure of anticipation in Charles' voice said it all. "Excellent. I shall look forward to that."

Listening quietly to the ongoing conversation was Kate Stephenson. Her outer office was often busy with messengers or juniors, but it was one of those calmer moments in her normally hectic day. Although she was aware of the dangers of eavesdropping on her minister, she was an inquisitive woman and was intrigued by her new boss. Over the years, she had developed a clever strategy to cover her indiscretions and she sat with the far office door ajar, it was open just enough to see or hear anybody approaching along the adjacent corridor. The gleaming wooden parquet floor always echoed the presence of any potential intruder and gave her plenty of time to disguise any guilt, which might otherwise show on her face.

Kate Stephenson was a first-rate secretary and had been working for various government departments since her graduation from Cambridge. Although her entry into the civil service had been a result of nepotism, she was a very able woman and had made progress through her own ability. Over the past ten years, she had been the private secretary to a succession of junior ministers, none of whom had been remotely similar to the present incumbent. For once in her life, she did not like her minister. In the past, her bosses had all been attracted by her charm and been warm and friendly in their day-to-day dealings. To them, she had always been known as *Kate* and, like most private secretaries, she had been trusted implicitly and her professional opinions sought and valued. She was now addressed as Miss Stephenson and the relationship was cold and sterile. Try as she might, she could not penetrate the stern facade of Charles Rydell. She had even started looking more closely at herself in the mirror, wondering if she was losing her feminine charms. Listening in on his conversations was one way of trying to find some chink in his personal armour, but the opportunities that had come her way had so far proved unproductive.

She listened intently.

"I've so much on at the moment, Ken. I'm working late all week. This will give me an incentive to get the outstanding items out of the way so that I can finish early on Friday."

The two men talked over the phone in a very matter of fact manner. They spoke in a well-rehearsed code for the benefit of anyone who might happen to hear such a conversation. No one would get a hint of the real meaning of the call and under the present circumstances, this had proved to be a good policy.

Charles put down the phone and set to work again with renewed vigour, lifted by the thought of the weekend's excitement to come.

In the next room, Kate sighed to herself and gently replaced the telephone receiver.

* * * * *

It was Friday evening and Lynn Rydell arrived at the home office at exactly 5:30. Kate Stephenson looked up from her desk at the small vivacious blond who was married to the minister. She had a neat figure and although her mouth was slightly out of proportion to her face, Kate nevertheless considered her an attractive woman. Despite this, it was the over-pretentious swing of her hips as she walked along that gave Kate the impression that she was just a bimbo. She had judged the character perfectly. Lynn Rydell was passionate about her marriage to Charles, but it was more a love of the privileges that went with his position, rather than any true desire for her husband. He could provide her with something that her previous lovers never could, the money to enjoy a comfortable style of living, which suited her gregarious personality. She wore a grey and very expensive full-length fur. It had been unbuttoned and flapped open to reveal a smart black dress, short at the hem and with a seductive neckline. A small, solitary crucifix hung deep in her cleavage and the air was filled with Chanel Number Five. She carried a small overnight bag.

Kate mused gleefully to herself. *Cindy doll's really dressed to kill tonight. The perfect bingo dress. Eyes down and look in.*

Keeping her feelings well-hidden, she smiled and greeted the minister's wife warmly, "Hello Mrs Rydell. I believe your husband is just finishing off some papers. I'll just give him a buzz for you."

Before Lynn had any chance to acknowledge the welcome, Kate was speaking to her husband. She replaced the phone on its cradle and announced quietly, "He says it's all right for you to go through."

Lynn Rydell flicked her blond locks haughtily as she strutted into the main office where Charles was sitting at his desk. When the door had closed behind her, Charles stood up. He walked round the desk and pecked her quickly on the cheek. "Have you brought the things I asked for?"

"Yes, they're in the bag. I bought most of the things from town this afternoon."

"Good."

Charles smiled and took the bag from her. He went over to his desk and opened the two red ministerial boxes, which were waiting side by side. He proceeded to empty them, stacking the various files on the corner of his desk in a precise manner. The contents of the overnight bag were removed and delicately arranged in the two boxes, which were then carefully locked. The files were transferred to Lynn's bag, zipped up and handed back to her. Still standing by his desk, he picked up his phone. "We're ready to leave now, Miss Stephenson. Arrange to have a taxi collect us in five minutes."

It was not a request, but a command and he put the phone straight down without waiting for a reply and turned back to face Lynn.

Next door, Kate fumed. "Thank God it's the weekend. Never a please or thank you. Arrogant sod. As soon as he's gone tonight, I'm away too."

Next door, Charles spoke softly to Lynn, "Don't forget. Same arrangements as usual."

She pouted at him. "It seems a while since we had a Friday frolic. Doreen and I have been planning something new. You'll enjoy the fun, I'm sure."

"If it's new, then I can't wait. You two girls are wicked."

Lynn smiled and continued, "The only thing I don't like is this place. I wish you wouldn't insist on me coming here with your things. I hate that secretary of yours. Icy knickers outside gives me the creeps. Why do we have to go through this charade with the red boxes every time we go to Kenny's? I could take everything to the flat for you and it'd be waiting there for when you arrive?"

He reacted seductively to her chiding. "I like it the way it is. You know it gives me a thrill. Now, let's go over the details for tonight."

"You're a kinky bastard, Charles. Okay, just for your benefit. I come with you and we both go to Kenny's place. The driver drops you off and takes me on home and I lock your precious papers in the safe. Then, I wait for Doreen to pick me up and we meet you back at the flat later. Satisfied?"

Before they could exchange further words, there was a knock on the door and he called out pompously, "Enter."

It was Kate. She had her coat over her arm ready to leave. She smiled thinly and spotting his weekend work she enquired casually, "Your taxi is already at the front, sir. Shall I get the driver to help you with those boxes?"

He immediately declined, as she knew he would. He never allowed anyone to carry his government cases. He was like a small boy with a new toy. Nobody was allowed to touch.

Just then, the phone went in her office and she went back to her desk to take the call. "It's the prime minister's office."

Rydell sighed impatiently. "Right, put them through."

Two minutes later, Rydell appeared with his wife. He was obviously flustered and in a bad mood. It was clear that he didn't like having to reschedule his plans for the evening.

"There's a flap on and I have to go to Number Ten for a briefing meeting. That means my wife now needs transport home. Ring for another cab, Miss Stephenson."

Lynn smirked without turning to face Kate, enjoying the offhand way Charles treated his secretary.

Rydell closed his office door and locked it, testing the handle.

Kate was quite dismayed. He'd never locked her out of his office before.

"I'll be back for my boxes later, but I suppose you'll have gone by then." He spoke in an almost derogatory manner, as though he expected her to stay until he returned. Kate flushed. He hadn't insisted that she stay, so there was no way she would wait and guard his locked office for him.

Lynn Rydell shrugged, "I'll wait downstairs in the foyer for my cab, Miss Stephenson. Do have a good weekend."

The two of them disappeared through the outer office. Charles was in a hurry, walking quickly two or three paces in front of Lynn who was swinging her hips in a ridiculous rhythmic motion trying to keep up. He turned and spoke to his wife, "Hopefully, I won't be too late. They promised a short meeting, but you know what it's like. Tell you what, you go out for a few drinks with Doreen and we'll have dinner later. We might have to postpone the party until tomorrow."

Kate watched them reach the top of the stairs; then, grudgingly ordered a cab for the minister's wife. She glanced around her desk one last time to make sure that she hadn't left anything undone in her hurry to be off. Then she remembered. She'd taken an important document for him to sign earlier. Her friend, who was the PPS to the home secretary, had rung earlier to remind her to get it into the internal mail that evening.

"Damn it."

Kate thought about the locked door, but then remembered that a previous minister, who hadn't been so paranoid about security, had entrusted her with a spare key. She rummaged around the bottom drawer of her desk and at the back she came upon a small bunch of keys. Kate recognised the one she needed and let herself into Rydell's office.

The document she was looking for was at the top of a pile in his out-tray and it had been duly signed. As she picked it out, she inadvertently nudged the ministerial boxes, which were stacked on the edge of his desk. The upper most one was so light that she sent it crashing to the floor. Kate picked it up. It seemed empty. What was all the fuss about? Why was he taking empty boxes home? She shook it gently. Something moved inside, but it certainly wasn't a wad of papers or a file. She tried the lid, but it was locked. This was even more puzzling. *What was in the red box with the regal portcullis?* Kate felt terribly inquisitive. She had to know, but how could she get inside without damaging it? Impulsively, she returned for her bunch of keys. There were a number of smaller ones on the ring which she had never used before. Scrabbling with them in her impatience, she tried one in the lock. With a gentle click, the mechanism gave way and the secret of the box was revealed. Kate's mouth drooped open in disbelief. She poked each item with her fingertip, and then picked up the courage to empty everything onto his desk. She scattered female underwear and leather bondage equipment like an array of captured weapons at a police raid. The second box revealed similar dark secrets. She picked up a small black tasselled whip and cracked it in the air. Then, the reality of what she'd found hit her and she began to panic.

Oh, my God! I should never have done this. I should never have interfered with his boxes. What if he finds out I've been in here and seen his playthings? They're private. He'll say it's none of my business. I'll be finished.

Her guilt urged a quick response and with a secretary's eye for detail, she skilfully began to repack each item as they'd been found. The boxes were locked and repositioned on the corner of his desk.

Moments later, she was back in her office, shakily inserting into an envelope the document that had led to her distressing discovery. Grabbing her overcoat and handbag, she was ready to leave immediately. By now, she was feeling a terrible sense of anxiety and only at the last second did she remember to go back and lock his office.

Kate dropped the envelope into the internal mail as she left the building, relieved to have escaped unscathed. She caught her breath in the cold December air and turned away briskly in the direction of her tube station to join the bustling throng of fellow commuters.

The normally drab journey seemed to pass quicker than ever before, as she deliberated over the incident in Rydell's office. What was behind this kinky spectre of deception? Each time she tried to find a plausible explanation for what he was hiding in his ministerial boxes, she seemed to be haunted by the same conclusion. He'd suddenly become a dangerous liability. If the Press ever got hold of the story, it would rock the government many times more than the Profumo affair in the 1950s. It made her worry.

She arrived at her flat with her mind still in a whirl. As she stood in front of the entrance fumbling for her keys, a tall, dark shadow materialised out of the nearby hedges. A man circled behind her and advanced stealthily so that Kate could not see his approach. She froze as a pair of huge hands descended over her face and onto her neck.

"Hi, babe. Guess who?"

Kate turned sharply to face her assailant. "Joe Harker. You rotten swine. Don't you ever do that to me again." Then she threw her arms around his neck and their mouths met in a warm and sensuous kiss.

When they broke off, he gave her a youthful grin. "It's my first weekend off for three weeks. I thought we might go out for a meal somewhere."

"With you lover boy, anytime. Give me half an hour and I'll be ready to hit the town."

Arm in arm, the two of them went into her flat. Kate disappeared for a shower and to get changed, whilst Joe fixed himself a drink and sat half-watching a *soap* on her TV.

The red-hot shower began to have a relaxing effect on Kate as the needle sprays peppered her body. The events of the day resurfaced again and she couldn't get them out of her mind. Kate's intellect told her that she must act on what she'd seen, but she faced a terrible dichotomy. Ever since she'd joined the civil service, it had been instilled into her that tact, diplomacy and above all loyalty to her ministers were the paramount qualities of a Private Secretary. She remembered how she'd covered up indiscretions many times before, but they had all been for real men, ones that she had liked and admired. Charles Rydell was altogether different and there was something singularly disquieting about him that she could not fathom. Kate weighed up all the arguments in her mind and as they stacked up, one by one against Rydell, she found herself loathing the man. She resolved, if necessary, to break every confidence and code of ethics to get him removed from office.

She never talked to Joe about her work and neither did he to her, but she did know he worked for MI6. Although they were lovers, his assignments frequently took him away from her and she never knew when he would turn up next. She also knew that she could never resist his advances. Kate was a terrible romantic and it was her lasting fantasy that one day he would marry her and make her life complete. She quietly clung on to her dream, even though she silently feared that something terrible might happen in his secret world and she would never see him again. That was why she always made the most of the time they had together.

Tonight, he would wine and dine her. Some time, during the evening she'd find time to explain her dilemma. He knew people in high places and he'd know what best to do about Rydell.

Then later on, they would come home and she would take him to bed.

Chapter 13

It was another Friday night. Gary Gordon was seated behind the steering wheel of his van, impatiently smoking. As usual, it was parked in the shadows, under a row of leafless trees whose branches carelessly scraped its roof. He was watching the entrance to the block of flats. Since the joint break in with Tonks two weeks earlier, he'd spent several boring hours each Friday, Saturday and Sunday evening waiting for something to happen. Tonight, his waiting ended. Sir Kenneth Waterford had arrived 20 minutes earlier and Gordon was more than hopeful that he'd soon get some action.

The taxi purred to a halt and Rydell emerged from the back seat. He was holding a ministerial case firmly in each hand. He pushed the rear door closed with his foot and fumbled around paying his fare, whilst trying to juggle his boxes. The taxi shot off, leaving him standing in the full glare of the streetlights.

Gordon checked the photograph in front of him and confirmed that it was Rydell. *At last. I was beginning to think you'd never come.*

Rydell smartly mounted the steps to the flats and disappeared through the main entrance.

Gordon nodded his head in satisfaction. *Good. He's been let in. He's expected.*

He climbed over the front seats and into the main body of his van. Gordon began switching on an array of computer equipment, which was neatly set up around the sides. The screens began to come alive and produced high-definition pictures from his hidden cameras. The coloured images and sound from the tiny microphones were top quality. Just what he'd expect to receive from the expensive, hi-fi wireless technology.

On the second floor, Charles Rydell let himself into Waterford's flat.

A voice came from the sitting room, "Good evening, Charles. You're well, I trust?"

Charles appeared at the open door and responded eagerly, "Fine and looking forward to tonight." He placed his boxes on a small reception table and flopped into the deep, comfortable settee. Accepting a large gin from his friend, they began to plan the evening ahead.

Waterford quizzed him, "We're not going to be on our own tonight, are we? I thought the ladies were joining us."

"There was an unscheduled meeting at Number Ten and I didn't know how long it would go on for, so I told Lynn to come over later with Doreen. As you can see, I got away early."

"Well, since there are just the two of us at the moment how about we do Jasmine and Lola. We haven't done it for ages."

The reference to the names was a simple code and would dictate their actions and dress. They both knew what it meant.

"Jasmine and Lola. Sounds wonderful. We'll go for it, provided I can be first."

Sir Ken nodded and a very animated Charles Rydell quickly gulped the remains of his drink and got to his feet. He picked up his boxes and vanished through the doorway. From the hall, he entered the right-hand dressing room as usual. It was the one that contained a large collection of his personal belongings. He placed the ministerial cases on the long, plush dressing table and stretched his arms wide with a contented yawn. He pressed a hidden switch and pleasant, concealed lighting illuminated the large mirrors around the walls bathing the room in a warm and welcoming glow. A small bunch of keys jingled in his hands as he moved over to the large, built-in wardrobe. He unlocked the door and slid it noiselessly to one side. Peering in at the scores of odd costumes hanging there, he quickly made a selection and clipped it over the top edge of the door. Without hesitation he then proceeded to take off all his own clothes. He put his suit and shirt neatly on hangers and then carefully folded his underwear and stored them next to his socks and shoes on empty shelves inside the wardrobe. He was soon completely naked and began to eye himself up from various angles as he stood amidst the multiple reflections of the mirrors.

Outside in the back of the van, Gordon, a half-smoked cigarette clamped between his teeth, looked on in amusement. *At last, the fun's about to start. Come on you fuckin' little pervert, what are you going to do now?* Gordon watched Rydell's actions and it soon became clear that all his waiting had not been in vain. He eagerly checked the computers to ensure they were recording correctly, then sat back and watched the sequence of events, which would ultimately change the life of Charles Rydell forever.

Charles began by shaving his face and that was the only normal thing he did. In the next half hour, a cycle of damning scenarios were captured. Rydell shaving his chest, legs and arms. Fitting into a tight gossamer corset. Fixing a pair of false, latex rubber breasts. Removing packets from a ministerial box. Pulling up a pair of sheer black tights. Slipping into a soft, black leather leotard, covered in chains and studs. Fixing a long blond wig in place and a black leather band around his forehead. Applying mascara, black eye shadow and black lipstick. Pulling on thigh length, high-heeled leather boots and fitting studded wrist bands. Finally, he painted his finger nails with black nail varnish. When they were dry, he lifted a small leather whip from his other ministerial box.

The transformation of Charles Rydell was complete. He rose to his feet and with his hands on his hips, he thrust out one of his leather-clad legs provocatively. He was small and slim with effeminate looks and the changes had made him unrecognisable as either a man or a minister of the Crown. His feminine looks were only modestly betrayed by his excited erection, which bulged slightly at the front of his leather costume. The camera had done its work exceptionally well and showed in graphic detail his strange metamorphosis.

He eyed himself up and down, twisted and twirled before the mirrors and ran his hands over the smooth contours of his new body, admiring his female form. He squirted perfume behind his ears and around his wrists as he had seen countless women do in the past. He seemed to become heady with the smell as he cracked the small whip down by his side and left the dressing room.

As Rydell entered the large sitting room he was attacked from behind and a high falsetto voice squealed out loud, "Jasmine you bitch. I'm going to give it to you."

Charles Rydell, now Jasmine, turned slightly and was firmly slapped across the face by Waterford. He was dressed in a similar outfit, but the disguise could not hide his more rugged masculine appearance.

"Lola, you hussy," Jasmine rubbed her cheek gingerly. The game had begun.

In the van outside, Gordon had switched to a different monitor and the video stream was now recording the actions of the two 'girls.' He was almost wetting himself in his excitement. This was far and away the best action he'd ever seen. Like a true voyeur, he couldn't take his eyes off the bizarre scene that was being enacted.

They appeared to be playing to some kind of script where alternately one of them would lower their guard whilst the other lashed out with their whips trying to inflict pain and create sexual arousal without disfigurement. Circling around one another like gladiators, they flicked their whips at each other's buttocks. The two were deriving a great deal of sexual pleasure from the pain, humiliation and domination of one another.

It had been agreed that Jasmine would reach her climax first and at a predetermined moment, she allowed Lola to close in. With a practised trip, Jasmine was brought to her knees and her left arm twisted up her back. It hurt and she shouted out in pain. The whip flew out of her hand and she heard the metallic click from a pair of handcuffs, clipped around her wrist. She was pushed forward, full length onto the floor and as she wriggled to get free, her face was pushed deep into the soft-piled carpet as Lola pinned her down from behind. Her other wrist was grabbed firmly and locked into place. Jasmine moaned as she felt Lola bind her ankles together with a leather thong. The excitement of the bondage was beginning to greatly arouse her.

Lola goaded her cruelly. "You've been a naughty girl, Jasmine and now I'm going to punish you. You deserve a good spanking."

"No. Please." Jasmine pleaded with her captor as she was hauled to her feet and dragged to the armchair. Lola dropped into the chair and pulled Jasmine over her knees. She pulled a pair of black frilly knickers from down the side of a cushion and stuffed them in Jasmine's mouth, gagging her firmly. With the victim held in place, Lola began to smack Jasmine's thighs and buttocks with a riding crop. Jasmine moaned and moaned as she was thrashed over and over again. Finally, the sexual gratification that Jasmine had longed for arrived and she shuddered and squealed as the hidden ejaculation erupted into her tight-fitting pants.

Lola recognised Jasmine's orgasm and pushed her onto the floor. She was quickly unshackled. True to their agreed roles, Jasmine looked up and with malice in her voice, responded to her own treatment by hissing, "Now it's your turn, my dear."

The second camera in the flat continued to silently transmit the ritual as their roles were reversed and the whole ludicrous episode repeated itself. The audio track of the affair was similarly recording with unrivalled clarity. The entire event came over like a pornographic movie. It was just what Gordon needed.

He had watched and listened to everything from start to finish. Glowing with pride, he switched his system down.

Whoever wants to buy this is going to pay me a king's ransom after that little show. The quality of the DVD will be simply stunning. Just think, that kinky bastard could be a future prime minister. It's time to hit the town and tonight, Gary you bloody marvel, you've earned yourself a truly magnificent skin full.

An hour later, Lynn Rydell arrived with Doreen Waterford. By then, both men had showered and changed.

"From the way you boys are glowing, I'd say you've been busy without us."

Doreen couldn't hide her disappointment because she loved to participate in their sexual fantasies.

Charles grinned back at her. "Never mind, Doreen. If you fancy it, all four of us can do Little Bo-Peep after dinner."

She went over to him and ruffled his hair. "Now you're talking, Big Boy Blue."

Chapter 14

The prime minister sat at her private desk working long hours into the night. The only light was from a large, ornate table lamp, which flooded the dark green, leather-topped surface with brightness. Her spectacles perched lazily on the tip of her nose but her concentration was intense as she scrutinised the cabinet papers before her. The pretentious gold-plated fountain pen, given to her by her late husband, glistened as it flickered back and forth over the crisp parchment. Sometimes, she would grumble and curse, making copious notes on a separate pad, if she found a disagreeable item which she had not sanctioned. After a while, she paused and, removing her glasses, gently massaged the corners of her eyes with finger and thumb.

There was a quiet tap on the door and her personal secretary slipped silently into her presence.

"Yes, Jim. Is it urgent?" She was quite brusque.

"It's your appointment with Paula Ross, prime minister. She's been waiting in the outer office for 20 minutes. With you being so busy, I wondered if it might have slipped your mind."

He was diplomacy personified.

The PM glanced at her watch. It showed two o'clock. "Goodness, is it that time already? You were right to pop in Jim. Show Miss Ross in straight away."

The prime minister sat back in her comfortable, high-backed chair. She was well aware of the time of night, but she often made her underlings wait, particularly female ones. She was very possessive of the power she wielded as chief executive of the nation and because her schedule was so tight, she sometimes had to arrange meetings at odd times.

Paula Ross was one of the few women to hold high office in the normally male-dominated echelons of military intelligence. The prime minister had elevated her to the top position herself and now had a formidable ally in the new head of MI6.

Although Paula was directly responsible to the home secretary, with whom she had regular meetings, she'd made an unusual request for a private meeting with the PM, who had been immediately intrigued. Something had happened to make Miss Ross bypass the home secretary and come straight to the top. Under the circumstances, the PM had readily agreed to an out-of-hours appointment.

Paula Ross was ushered into the office and at the PM's beckoning, she moved forward. She limped slightly as she approached the proffered seat on the opposite side of the desk. This was entirely due to her false leg. She had been a renegade in her younger days and was still a keen biker. She had never been able to end her love affair with fast machines even though her left leg had been amputated below the knee two years ago. Her Harley-Davison had skidded and hit a stone wall at 105 miles an hour whilst she was tearing round the country lanes of her native Norfolk. She had made a miraculous recovery and it was this steel in the woman's character that endeared her to the PM.

Miss Ross carried nothing with her except a thin blue file and before she sat down she placed it before the prime minister. She started with an apology, "I'm sorry about this cloak and dagger stuff, but the reason for my visit is very delicate. Something unusual has been flagged up. It could be nothing, or alternatively it could become a major embarrassment to you and the government. It is about one of your junior ministers. One of the rising stars. Please read the document, prime minister. It will take only a minute because there is little to offer so far."

The PM opened the soft folder and withdrew a single sheet of paper. She had read it carefully within seconds and for once, she was speechless, dropping the paper as though it burned her fingers. She looked up and gesturing with her right hand, spoke calmly, "Can there be any truth in this? You don't think it's just another fabrication of lies to ruin another promising political career? My god, what do some people get up to in their private lives."

"I can only say that there is suspicion of… errr," she hesitated, "odd behaviour. The information was passed onto me in confidence by one of my most trusted men. His name is Commander Harker and he assures me that his source is reliable and comes from the ministry itself. Under these circumstances, I had to give you the details as soon as possible."

"You were right to do so, Paula, and I thank you for it. If what you suspect is true and the media get the slightest whiff of a story, it would be catastrophic for the government. I would face the backlash and be made to look like a fool.

Everyone would criticise my ability to appoint the right people. To be candid, our popularity right now is rock bottom and the general election isn't far away. With such a tiny majority, something like this could easily precipitate the election before we're ready. As things stand, the opposition parties would annihilate us at the polls. This couldn't be worse."

Paula continued, making her points carefully. "You have only just appointed him, so, to sack him now would look very odd. I believe that we have to consider every angle, including the possibility that somebody may already know about his sexual deviances. If so, they may be blackmailing him and if you get rid of him, then this might precipitate a leak to the press. This could also end up being a National Security issue. On the other hand, it may be that the incident is trivial and he manages to keep his little fetish a well-kept secret. If that's the case, then the whole episode can be easily hushed up until you decide what to do with him at a later date."

The PM smiled and sighed loudly. "You're quite right and your perceptions about the dangers to the state are an important factor because that allows you to act with impunity."

"What I suggest, prime minister, is that we let Commander Harker try and find out what he can, one way or the other and I'll report back to you as soon as we find out anything useful."

"Agreed."

The PM continued, speaking emphatically and with cool authority. "This situation. I don't like it at all. It's a distraction I can do without. You must keep any information updates on a strictly need to know basis. This file. I want it double red-striped, for my eyes only."

"I'll do it personally. Tonight. You have no worries on that score." She took back the file.

"Very well, Paula." The PM pulled a document from her pending tray and opened it deliberately. It was the signal that the interview was over. She started scanning the contents, giving no indication of the fury that was beginning to burn inside her mind.

Miss Ross had been dismissed in this off-handed way before and although she felt some animosity, there was nothing she could do. It was a characteristic of the PM and Paula wasn't alone in her dislike of her mannerism, having heard other colleagues whisper the same complaint. Without making further conversation she rose from her seat and made for the door.

Just as she was about to leave, a warm friendly voice called after her, "Thanks, Paula. I really appreciate your care and concern. Please keep me informed. Have a good night."

Paula Ross glowed. Gratitude at last. She called back over her shoulder, "Goodnight, prime minister."

As the door closed, the PM picked up her pen and started to write more notes. It wasn't long before she found her thoughts wandering and try as she might, she couldn't engage her mind in further meaningful concentration. The thread was broken. She knew it was useless to try and go on. Her momentum was lost. She poured herself a large cognac from a beautiful lead-crystal decanter and closed her files for the night. Sipping the warming spirit, she contemplated the future and silently cursed Charles Rydell.

Chapter 15

It was five days later and Gary Gordon was waiting anxiously for his appointment to take place. The busy, smoky, tavern in the heart of London's dockland was an ideal choice of venue. Gordon always held his meetings in the full glare of a public audience and had learnt from experience to keep his own whereabouts and domicile as secret as possible. He was known for the distinctive quality of his work as a freelance photographer, but his interest in computers and video technology had rocketed his enviable reputation into a higher league. He often accepted contracts for clients who had unusual requests, but because he feared for his own safety in some of these deals, he was fastidious in the way he set up his lines of communication. Anyone wishing to contact him had to do so by leaving messages at one or more of his favourite pubs. These numbered a dozen or so, but it was surprising how an intricate jungle telegraph managed to track him down quickly when the sniff of a fee was in the air. If an approach aroused his interest, then he would ring back and make definite arrangements for a meeting.

It was lunchtime and today, he was waiting to meet Siggy Dexter. He was trying to concentrate on the Times crossword but was too nervous about the outcome of the meeting to make any headway with the clues. He didn't have long to wait and when he spotted Dexter approaching, he put the newspaper down immediately.

The smartly dressed figure didn't wait for an invitation, but sat down at his table. He remembered the cold, impassive face of the thug from their first meeting and how he'd felt very uneasy. Today, his nervousness was even more acute, because he was going to try something he'd never done before and he wasn't sure what the reaction of Dexter would be. This was one of the reasons he'd chosen a very conspicuous place to meet. Breaking a contract was unethical and dangerous, but this time he felt that he might just get away with it. Times were hard, but the fee for this job had been enormous. That sent out a clear message that someone wanted the video badly. If that was the case, then his clients might easily be persuaded to pay even more.

Dexter spoke in a low monotone, staring fixedly at Gordon, "Okay, Flash, you got the goods?"

Gordon hissed through his teeth, his hackles immediately raised by the loathsome nickname. "The name's Gary."

"Steady on sunbeam. Don't lose your shirt."

Dexter held out his hand.

From inside his overcoat, Gordon pulled out a thick jiffy-bag and handed it over.

Dexter flipped open the padded envelope and pulled out the black opaque DVD case. He opened it up only to find it empty. His face took on a puzzled expression and his hand searched the bottom of the envelope. In frustration, he looked inside. "Is there some kind of joke here, Flash? Have I missed something? Where's the disc?"

The crunch had come and Gordon fidgeted uncomfortably.

Dexter gave him a steely look and he gushed out his reply, "I've still got it and it's gonna cost you some more cash."

For the first time in the meeting, he made eye contact with Dexter. The granite cold glare that met him sent a shudder down his spine and he became afraid.

Dexter spoke softly, but there was ruthlessness in his voice, emphasising the implied threats. "You've already been paid over the odds for this job. Twenty-five grand in advance and I've got another 25 in my pocket to pay you off. So, be a good boy, stop pissing me about and hand over the disc. If you do, we can still part like old buddies."

Gordon was clearly agitated, but at the same time, he became more lucid. He snarled almost aggressively and it took Dexter slightly aback. "Look pal, I know who's in the video and I can guess what you're gonna do. Bleed the poor sod dry. Well, I just want an extra piece of the action."

"You're missing the point, brain dead, you've already been well paid and…"

Gordon interrupted sharply, "Don't try threatening me. I've got the master disc hidden away and you can't get at it. I'm the only one who knows where it is. If you come up with another 25 biggies, then you can have it. Otherwise, I'm sure I can find another buyer. Here, take this." He slipped a disc out of his pocket and handed it to Dexter. "This is a section of the video; it'll help you see the quality of the work. It won't do you any good though because you won't recognise who it is. You need to see our friendly minister 'in preparation,' as it were." It seemed inconceivable that Dexter was sitting there taking in his little speech and doing nothing. He sensed that he'd outstayed his welcome. Before Dexter could react to his reverse blackmail threats, he was on his feet. Gordon had planned his escape carefully and within seconds, he'd ghosted through the rowdy crowd and disappeared out of sight.

By the time Dexter had followed him out into the street, Gordon was already speeding away in the back of a taxi. The cab had been waiting in a side street next to the pub with its meter running for the past half-hour. It had cost Gordon a packet, but his own safety was now assured and the cost would be incidental when he creamed off the extra cash for the master disc.

On the other side of the road sat the maroon Rolls Royce of Tyburn. Dexter crossed over and got into the rear of the car. Inside, Tyburn and Lush were waiting with anticipation for a look at the promised DVD. Tyburn had fired up a laptop computer on his knees, ready to take the disc.

"What's the matter Siggy? You don't look very pleased. Haven't you got the goods?"

"We've been double crossed, boss. By that little shit, Flash. He handed over a kind of demo disc and before I could grab him, he buggered off in a taxi. He's asking for another 25 grand, or he says he might go elsewhere."

Tyburn was initially stunned by the setback. "I don't like the way this is panning out. People don't double cross me and get away with it"

Lush intervened. "We can decide how to deal with our Mr Gordon later. Let's see what we've got for our money so far." He slipped the disc into the computer drive and they watched in fascination the episode with Rydell and Waterford thrashing one another into a frenzy.

Tyburn's sarcasm was razor sharp. "Mmmm… sissy little politician is our Mr Rydell. We've got to get our hands on the full version because the quality is superb. We'll just have to pay Gordon his dues… as it were." He wasn't about to let this hitch spoil the success of part one of their plan. He dismissed the problem cheerily and winked at Dexter. "Blackmail eh! Dirty business. Organise another meeting Siggy."

Lush nodded in agreement and replayed the DVD. "Boy have we bagged a winner with this one. That slimy effeminate retard will have to dance to our tune if he wants to get his hands on this."

Chapter 16

Davy Tonks had agreed to meet Gordon at a prearranged time and waited patiently in the tavern for his arrival. He was due to be paid the second instalment for the Kensington job. After the first break-in, he told Gordon that he wouldn't risk going back again, but he'd come back with the promise of an extra bonus. Yet again, Davy found that he couldn't refuse an easy buck. He weighed up all the odds and because he knew he could use the lift; he was persuaded to complete the job.

Two nights after the recordings, he and Gordon had returned to the flat and this time there were no delays. The cameras and equipment were dismantled with ease and they had been and gone within 20 minutes.

Gordon eventually showed up half an hour late but didn't bother to apologise for his poor time keeping. Tonks had never liked nor trusted Gordon and he wasn't at all surprised when he began making excuses that he couldn't pay the money he owed.

"Listen, old pal, I've been doing some thinking. The mob who're paying for the DVD want it really bad, so I thought I might screw 'em for some more."

"I hope you know what you're doin'."

"It's not your problem. They don't even know about you. I'm the front man."

"It's not you I'm worried about. It's my cash. My share."

"Look. It's sorted. We've already arranged a meet and they've agreed to pay up. Just hang on for a few more days and I'll slip you another 'monkey'."

Tonks had no choice but to agree to the enforced extension, although he was pleased at the offer of a further 500 pounds. Something in Gordon's demeanour suggested that he wasn't about to double-cross him. He sounded confident, which made Davy wonder what extra he'd demanded that he could afford to be so generous.

The meeting finished abruptly and Gordon left.

Tonks was in no condition to follow him and sat quietly clutching his pint. He looked across the room and nodded to a young man by the door who followed Gordon outside.

Gordon stood on the corner of the street and started to hail cabs. The young man passed behind him and went to his motorbike, which was parked along the street. He pulled his helmet on and kicked up the engine. Gordon was continuously in his view and when a cab stopped, he set off on the small bike and drifted anonymously into the traffic behind, following at a discreet distance.

Davy Tonks had survived in his profession by taking every precaution that he could. Although his own body wouldn't allow him to do the job himself, he had recruited the services of his grandson. The lad was a messenger for one of the main clearing banks, and although he was only 19, he had the 'knowledge' and would be able to follow the cab to its final destination anywhere in London.

Davy had every confidence in the boy and he knew that when he reported back, he would be able to give the exact location of Gordon's home base. If, in the unlikely event, Gordon decided to lie low without honouring his debts, then Davy would have the extra insurance of knowing where he could find his accomplice. He'd give him a couple more days; then he'd try and do something about getting the money he was owed.

* * * * *

A week later, Tonks was having a quiet pint with his son at the local pub. The newspaper boy came in as usual, selling the *Evening Standard*. He drifted over and offered one to Davy, who was one of his regular customers. He unfolded the paper and there on the front page was a picture. It had the effect of seizing his chest in a vice-like grip.

The headlines read: **Local Photographer Drowns**.

The picture wasn't recent, but there was no mistaking the face of Gordon. There wasn't much of a story. Someone had fished his body out of the Thames and it appeared he'd been drinking heavily. The police didn't suspect foul play.

Davy Tonks reeled under the shock and his breathing began to labour. He felt sure the drowning had not been an accident and Gordon had been murdered. He also knew that whoever had done for him, was now armed with the master DVD and worse still, his share of the fee.

"The careless bastard. He must have pushed them too far," he almost choked on his own words as he became more excitable. His throat began to rasp loudly as his lungs fought for air.

"Dad! Dad! Are you all right?" His son got to his feet and looked in horror as Davy clutched at his chest. His lips were already beginning to turn blue.

"Oh, hell! He's having an attack."

Davy's son knew just what to do. He stormed out to the car for the spare oxygen cylinder that they kept for such an eventuality. He'd never used it in an emergency before and as he raced back into the pub, he prayed that he wouldn't be too late.

Chapter 17

It was a good morning and Charles Rydell was in high spirits. There had been a late sitting in the House of Commons the night before. A damaging amendment to the government's new criminal justice bill had been defeated by two votes and it was all down to some last-minute work by Charles and the Whips that had persuaded a number of backbench rebels to tow the party line. He flicked through the morning papers, gloating with priggish arrogance at the lush praise of the commentaries on his part in the previous night's proceedings. *The Times* was particularly gushing and he re-read the article twice over. He could expect a call from the PM to congratulate his endeavour. There was nothing quite like the full glare of positive national press exposure to fuel his ambition and fill his mind with personal aggrandisement. The full English breakfast had never tasted so good. He was finishing the meal with masses of hot toast, marmalade and coffee, when his mail arrived.

He pushed his copy of *The Times* to one side and snorted as he picked up the pile of letters. He expertly shuffled through them and put to one side the circulars, bills and junk mail. His eyes settled on a small-padded envelope. The large ornate font and the bold type immediately attracted his attention. It stated *private and personal*. Picking it up, he felt the DVD case inside and casually wondered what it contained. He ran the silver paper knife down the edge and withdrew the hard plastic case. Turning it over in his fingers, he read the large bold print on the inside cover.

For Your Eyes Only: Charles and Kenneth at Play.

His jaw dropped and he swallowed hard as he felt a wave of trepidation gush over him. Rushing to his study, he fired up his computer. His hands were shaking and he fumbled the disc carelessly. At last, he managed to insert the DVD. The disk began to play and he gazed in disbelief at what he saw. He flushed and his heart rate quickened. The realisation of the consequences quickly began to hit him hard. His stomach slowly turned and fear grumbled in his guts. There was no mistaking his identity as the DVD showed every intimate detail of him dressing in the leather bondage outfit and carefully feminising himself. The following masochistic ritual of the female gladiators was especially well defined.

He moaned and dropped his head, closing his eyes tightly. His secret world had not just been prised open; it had been blown apart. All that he had ever worked for, all that he had ever lied, cheated and schemed for, had now come to naught. If his enemies ever leaked this to the press, he would be vilified and systematically destroyed. He would be the laughing stock of the Conservative Party. His political ambitions would be buried, his public life would end in shame and disgrace and the government would face the embarrassment of dealing with the fallout. He would surely have to go abroad to live. There would be no choice.

He suddenly felt weak at the knees and very ill. Lurching out of his study, he made for the bathroom. He didn't get as far as the washbasin, but stumbled to his knees and threw up all over the floor. He lay in a wretched heap, wrenching in spasms as the stinking bile burned his swollen throat.

Lynn Rydell was in the kitchen making some fresh coffee when she heard the unmistakable sound of her husband in the bathroom. She left everything and quickly found him knelt amidst the foul-smelling remnants of his meal. She squatted beside his pitiful body and with the vile stench filling her nostrils, she put a comforting hand on his shoulder.

"Charles. Are you all right? Whatever is the matter?"

He just moaned and made no attempt to reply.

She dragged him round and looked for some sign of illness, but all she saw was a sorrowful mask, an expression of sterile emotion. Slowly, he tottered to his feet, took her by the hand and silently, childlike, led her to his study. He gestured for her to sit before the computer screen and then, once more he selected the play button.

The garish movie replayed itself.

Her reaction was one of near hysteria. "Oh no, Charles! Not this! Oh, please not this. It'll finish you. It'll finish us. You've been set up. How could you have let it happen?"

Lynn stood up and shook her head as though she refused to believe her own eyes. "When was this taken? How long ago? Where?"

Charles leant heavily on the back of her chair and the only sound was the rasping in his throat as he tried to control the burning acidity and restore his self-control.

Lynn squealed impatiently. "Charles! Answer me. I thought you always took every precaution? How could it have happened? Oh my God, there may be some footage of me."

She flopped back into the chair and feverishly flicked through the disc menu to see if there was anything else she'd missed. She found nothing and the initial shock began to wane. The confusion in her mind started to clear as she realised it was Charles who was the target of the set up. She knew instinctively that she'd have to take charge. Standing in front of him she thundered loudly. "Move!"

Charles refused to budge.

She hissed and pushed her husband hard in the chest. "Move, damn you!"

At last, there was a response and he released his grip of the chair. Lynn pushed him back to the bathroom and ordered him to strip. She stood over him whilst he removed his messy clothes, then pushed his naked form into the shower and turned it full on. The icy cold water started to do its work and brought the mind of Charles Rydell back from the brink.

Lynn slipped out of her nightdress and got into the adjoining shower. She stayed in for a full ten minutes until she was certain that the tainting of her nostrils and hands from her husband's vomit had been cleansed from her body.

The two of them eventually towelled down together in their bedroom and sat silently waiting for one another to speak.

Charles broke the spell. "That film must have been shot about two weeks ago at Ken's flat. I don't know how they got it. There must have been a hidden camera. Someone must know about us, but I just can't figure out who it is. You know as well as I do that only a handful of close friends have ever been involved in our games and they all have as much to lose as we do."

The phone interrupted their thoughts. Charles looked across at Lynn and for the first time in his life, he hesitated in answering the call. His immediate reaction was that it had to do with the DVD. A new fear had now entered his life. It was a fear of the unknown.

The sound of the ringing filled the silent vacuum and set their pulses racing. Who could it be? What would they want?

"For God's sake, Charles, answer it, will you?"

He rubbed his lips nervously and picked up the handset. It was Sir Ken. Charles had no chance to answer. He found himself on the receiving end of an agitated monologue, as his close friend described what had arrived in his morning post.

"Ken! Ken!" He tried to interrupt the flow of the manic dialogue. "Ken. I know. I know because I've received the same package. For heaven's sake, calm down man and get a grip. Grab a cab and get round here straight away. Are you listening? Don't argue. Just do it."

He put the phone down before Ken could reply. All at once, he started to feel a semblance of control return and he began to analyse the situation. "Realistically, there are two outcomes to this."

"What do you mean Charles?"

"Firstly, someone could be out to ruin my career, in which case this DVD will find its way into the hands of the press very shortly. If so, we've had it. Surely, if somebody wanted to ruin me, then why would they bother going to all the trouble sending me this disc? It would give me the opportunity to skip the country and avoid the worst before it hits the media. That would be too easy. No, I'm starting to believe that somebody wants something. Blackmail, plain and simple. I'm sure that's the motive. If they want money, then we're lost. But, I can tell you now," he swallowed hard, "if I can make some kind of deal, I'm sure as hell going to try."

"So, what you're really hoping for is a political favour in exchange for the original disc."

"Correct. I've not worked my balls off for the past few years to throw my career away on some ethical principal. Whatever they want, whatever the game, I'm ready to play."

"That's more like the darling Charles I know, back to his ruthless best and prepared to piss on anyone. Well, I'm behind you all the way, sweetie. I certainly don't want to change my lifestyle and whatever happens, we can't get into any more shit than we are at the moment."

"Thanks, Lynn. I appreciate your support, but we'll have one hell of a problem in persuading Ken and Doreen to go along with our decision."

"I can't see they have much option. Their social circle is much bigger than ours. They'd be crucified and made social pariahs to the end of their days if this lot ever got out."

"You're right of course. Just leave Ken to me. I can handle him." He sighed wearily, "I'm afraid the next few days are going to be endless. All we can do now is wait and see what the bastards want."

Chapter 18

Charles Rydell lived through three days of misery, as he waited for someone to make contact. When another letter arrived in the morning post, it came as a great relief. It was addressed *private and confidential* and was typed in the same unmistakable font. Hurriedly, he cut into the envelope and extracted a single sheet of plain paper.

It read simply. *Take the tube to Hyde Park Corner and wait at the roadside outside the station. Bring your friend. Saturday Evening. 7 p.m.*

Charles re-read the message. It wasn't what he'd expected, but then he didn't know how they would try to manipulate him. At least, the waiting was over and he would find out what they wanted.

* * * * *

The tube train rattled along the Piccadilly line, disgorging its passengers for Hyde Park Corner at ten minutes to seven.

Charles and Sir Ken set off towards the ticket barriers, carried along by the bustling throng. London's Saturday-night revellers were beginning to permeate the Capital, ready to explore the extravagant diversity of its exciting nightlife. The two men both wore long, warm overcoats because the weather in the streets above was bitterly cold and they didn't know where they might be taken. Darkness had brought an air of trepidation to their mood.

Ken was particularly apprehensive about the forthcoming meeting. "Are you sure we're doing the right thing, Charles? You know I'd give this up and go home now. You only have to say the word."

Charles didn't answer immediately as another train hurtled out of a nearby tunnel drowning any chance of conversation. "Come on, Ken, let's make our way out of here. We have to be patient and we have to be positive. It's their game and we have to play by their rules. If we back out now and walk away, just where do you think it will leave us? We're in a mess. We've discussed this so many times during the past few days. The consequences we face if we don't at least listen to their demands are unthinkable. We have to find out what they want.

Ken hung his head in dismay and sighed. "I suppose you're right; we've got no choice, whatsoever."

They left the relative warmth of the tube station and came out into the cold night air. Charles pulled up his collar against the penetrating, icy wind and stood by the kerb as instructed, looking up and down the road at the evening traffic. A large car turned the corner from Grosvenor Crescent and glided almost silently towards them.

The Rolls Royce was totally unexpected and as it drew up, Charles and Sir Ken looked on in amazement.

Questions flashed through Rydell's mind. *What type of opposition were they facing? Where were the seedy little criminals that they expected, the petty blackmailers who wanted to earn a quick buck? This smacked of something strange and more sinister.*

Dexter had been watching out for them and emerged from the shadows behind. He ghosted past and opened the rear door, gesturing that they should enter. Charles and Sir Ken looked at one another and hesitated.

A deep voice from inside the Rolls encouraged them further. "Come along, gentlemen. It's cold outside and we have much to discuss."

Charles swallowed hard and got into the car. Sir Ken followed.

Dexter closed the door and got in the front with the driver. Before the two of them had chance to settle comfortably into the luxurious interior, the Roller moved off towards Hyde Park.

Charles stared at the two well-dressed men who sat opposite them. One was rather fat with deep jowls and light, bushy eyebrows. The other was a man with a wide smile. The smell of expensive aftershave mingled with stale cigar smoke and gave the atmosphere a heavy, pungent odour, which was immediately offensive to Charles. It filled his head and added to his general malaise. He suddenly felt very vulnerable and exposed, particularly as the opposition sat impassively, almost regally, eyeing them up.

It was the small, portly man who addressed them first. "Thank you for coming, gentlemen. Let's get straight down to business. You have received copies of our blockbuster movie and I'm sure you're amazed at the clarity and content of our presentation."

He sniggered. "By the way, I had no idea that your little red boxes were so useful. A nice touch. Budget day will never quite be the same again."

Charles groaned at the reference to his use of his ministerial cases. They were digging the knives in straight away to ensure that he fully understood who was setting the rules. Ken said nothing, but sagged in his seat feeling nauseous as they were reminded of the awful evidence stacked against them. They were not in any position to refuse to listen.

"May I say from the outset that we do not intend to strip you of any of your personal wealth. Nor, may I add, do we wish to ruin your political careers or social lives. However, there are things which you can contribute to our business activities in exchange for the original copy of the film we have so discreetly recorded."

Charles was the first to react. If they didn't want his money, then it must be his power and position in the government they wished to use. Suddenly, he felt very uneasy. *Did they want him to commit an act of treason? What was their motive?*

He spoke hoarsely. "Go on. I'm listening."

"Is it part of your brief to appoint prison governors?"

He was surprised at their odd question. He cleared his throat. "Yes. Of course."

"Good. And are you also able to transfer inmates from one prison to another without recourse to the home secretary?"

Again, another strange question. "Yes. That's no problem."

"Tell me, Mr Rydell. Do all prison contracts, maintenance, refuse collecting, that sort of thing all pass through your office?"

Rydell responded sharply. "Yes. I'm in charge of all of those things. Please, get to the point."

"Now. Now. Mr Rydell, please be patient." It was Tyburn who had interceded. "We have been doing our homework on you, but we wanted to be sure that you would give us the positive answers we require. You must never lie to us, because," Tyburn paused, "if you try to double-cross us at any point, then you will suffer the consequences immediately. Our friends in Fleet Street would have a field day and I shouldn't think your parliamentary party would feel too disposed towards you both either."

Rydell groaned, suitably chastened. "We get the drift."

Lush continued chiding them gleefully. "Yes. We have rather got you girls by the short and curlies, so to speak. Now, listen very carefully to what we want and answer all questions truthfully."

The two of them turned their attention solely to Charles Rydell.

"Firstly, we want you to identify an old Victorian Prison where you can easily replace the governor with a younger man. He must be someone who is very inexperienced, who is not yet ready for the position but who possesses credibility. Then, we want a number of prisoners from different locations transferred to the prison."

"I can do all those things, but I would need some time to organise it."

"How much time?"

"At least three months."

The opposition laughed. "You've got three weeks, four at a push."

Charles pleaded. "Come on. Be realistic, you're asking the impossible. You must give me more time than that."

"It's amazing what a little pressure can do for your organisational skills. I do hope the prime minister taught you how to keep deadlines." The sarcasm was cutting and the derogatory tone continued. "Missing deadlines can lead to serious consequences. We feel sure that if you pull your finger out, then you can make the necessary arrangements within the time scale we have so generously allowed you."

Charles fell silent and Sir Ken inquired weakly. "What happens then? Are we to be part of a huge conspiracy? Are you going to engineer the escape of those prisoners?"

"The answer to that question is on a need-to-know basis and you don't need to know."

Ken Waterford was put firmly in his place and flushed with indignation. He shrank into his seat.

"We will supply you with a list of names and the rest is up to you. An event will take place at the prison at some point and when it does, we will meet again to discuss the second part of our demands."

"How can we be sure that when this is all over, you'll give us the disc and not try further blackmail?"

"The answer to your question is quite simple. To start with, you're the one who will take all the risks. At this point, we are out of the loop, safe and sound. You must, therefore, make sure that you complete the first stage successfully.

After that your insurance kicks in, which is to ensure our involvement. For that, you'll be compelled to complete our final set of instructions, because the nature of these demands ensures our total commitment. At this juncture, we'll all be up to our necks in it together and we'll all have too much to lose. This scheme is a one-off. It cannot be repeated. We're not greedy and we know that we cannot risk further blackmail. It could have dire repercussions. Suppose, you decided that you'd had enough and go to the police, your confession would lead to our certain arrest and lengthy prison sentences for all of us, including you. As you can see, we will have a hold on one another, so once our business is concluded, the transaction will be complete and it is our intention to return the single master recording to you. We certainly wouldn't want anyone else to get their hands on it, because if you fall, we fall. That's your guarantee."

Charles pondered their reply. These men were certainly sophisticated and by their nature, dangerous. He needed to convince himself that the blackmail would end. Although he didn't trust them, there was a keen logic to their arguments and what they had asked of him could be easily accomplished. His biggest enemy was the time scale they were trying to impose. He stared out of the car window at the lights of the capital. It hadn't occurred to him that the Rolls was doing nothing but sedately circumnavigating Hyde Park. Marble Arch slid majestically back into his line of sight and with it, his visions of his own career and self-importance.

His mind was easily made up. "I'll do all you ask. I haven't come this far in my life to give everything up without a fight. I'll complete your tasks as quickly as possible. However," he paused for effect, "if you push me too fast, some little pen pushing, clever dick might start getting nosy and ruin everything. There has to be some trust on your part to let me do it my way. Quickly, yes, but carefully. If I'm not above suspicion, then I'll be out of my job before you can blink and then you can forget the whole deal."

Lawrence Tyburn was quietly satisfied with the proceedings so far. They had allowed Rydell to negotiate on a limited basis, which was good psychology. He wouldn't feel so threatened and if he felt more in control, then he was likely to co-operate fully with their demands. They knew that they could screw him down at any time if he tried to be difficult. It was important to let the victim leave feeling better about what he was being asked to do, rather than having no options at all.

Tyburn and his associate looked at each other and nodded.

Lush spoke, "Very well. We agree to your request, just as long as we don't get into a protracted situation. We will require weekly verbal reports on your progress. Every Friday evening, we will ring your flat and give you the number of a public phone box. You are to ring back immediately and answer our questions. If progress is satisfactory and we achieve success, we'll meet again to discuss the continuation of our plan."

Waterford ventured a further question, "What about me? What do you want from me?"

Lush sneered. "You are just an extra pawn in the game, I'm afraid. You may be able to bring some influence to bear on the situation and help Mr Rydell. As that appears unlikely, your main job will be to give him moral support and make sure he does as he's told. Don't forget. Your future is inextricably bound up with his', so you will need to keep closely in touch."

Tyburn spoke through an intercom to his driver and the Rolls came smoothly to a halt, stopping opposite Lancaster Gate. The interview was over.

Dexter appeared and opened the rear door.

The two friends emerged into the cold and noisy London evening.

Tyburn called out from the warm interior. "By the way, next time your wife wants you to dress up as a little girly, make sure she buys your frocks from someone out of town who doesn't know her, otherwise people may get the wrong idea about you." The door slammed closed and the sarcastic laughter was drowned away.

Charles watched dejectedly as the car drifted amongst the other traffic, its rear lights merging with the others. "So, it was one of those damn women who make our outfits. Bitches. I wish I could find out who it was."

"It's no good now, Charles. They could have got their information a dozen different ways. Come on, let's get a cab. I need a drink pretty badly."

"Not yet, Ken. We need to talk tonight's events through carefully. Let's walk for a while."

They turned and entered the park, following the edge of Long Water and the Serpentine. By the time they'd reached Hyde Park corner, Charles had persuaded Ken that they should accede fully to all the blackmail demands. He convinced his friend of his complete ability to fulfil their requirements and pleaded with him to keep his nerve and wait for their final demand. He knew that Ken's resolve would be sorely tested because he was merely a sterile onlooker who couldn't do anything but watch and wait.

By the time they had managed to stop a cab, Ken had promised to put his future in his friend's hands. There was a mood of deep depression as they drove off to their club. When they arrived, they immediately booked overnight rooms and proceeded to the bar to get quietly drunk.

Chapter 19

The journey from Hampstead to Hammersmith in central London only took Simon Lush about 40 minutes, despite the many road works and heavy lunch-hour traffic. His venue for the day was the complex of buildings comprising HM Prison Wormwood Scrubs. It stood out as a dismal eyesore on the skyline. Lush had been there many times in connection with his work as a lawyer, but he hated the old brick-built structure with its solid lines and high, foreboding walls.

He parked his car and went round to open the boot. He was dressed in a grey pinstriped business suit and although he was small, he carried himself with the assurance that reflected his professional status. His Lotus Excel had been a warm cocoon, so he was glad that he'd brought a topcoat to keep out the chilly easterly wind. Clutching a beautifully embossed leather briefcase, he slammed the lid firmly and strode up to the entrance gate.

He announced his arrival and the reason for his visit through an intercom. The arrangements had been made for one o'clock and he was a good 20 minutes early. Lush was shown into a small anteroom where he and his briefcase were thoroughly searched. He was then taken through the air-lock security gates and into the main prison. A warder accompanied him along several corridors and through numerous locked doors that barred their progress. The loud echoes of their footsteps and the stillness of it all constantly reminded him of the sterility, desolation and unhappiness of the place.

He was shown into a small interview room. The furnishings were spartan with only one table and two chairs. It was a bleak meeting place. The warder disappeared to fetch his client and Lush sat on one of the uncomfortable chairs and waited. He withdrew from the inside pocket of his jacket an expensive silver tube, from which he removed a large Havana cigar. He cut the tip of the *perfecto* and adjusted his equally expensive lighter, so that there was a large flame. He lit the cigar with precision and drew deeply on the smoke, fondling the tobacco roll between his fingers as he enjoyed the first taste of the condensing tar on his tongue. His passion for the Havana leaf was equal only to his insatiable desire for female company, which he regularly satisfied at his casino, away from the preying eyes of his priggish wife. The nicotine in the cigar eventually began to permeate his blood stream and he started to relax and contemplate the challenge ahead. He'd already formulated a strategy and after going over the details again, so that the process was firmly fixed in his mind, he spent an anxious ten minutes, smoking and reflecting on the importance of the next half hour.

His thoughts were interrupted only when the door at the far end of the room was unlocked. It swung open and a tall, well-built prisoner was ushered in.

The warder called to Lush over the inmate's shoulder, without making any attempt to follow him in. "I'll be outside if you need me. Knock when you've finished."

Lush rose to his feet and called after him. "Good. That's fine, thank you."

The door closed swiftly and the lock clicked.

Lush grinned at the man in front of him and grasped his hand warmly. "Hello Mark. How are they treating you in here?"

"I'm okay, Mr Lush. Can't grumble. It's good to see you."

They sat down simultaneously and Lush began fishing about in his jacket pocket. He pulled out a couple of packets of Dunhill cigarettes and pushed them across the table. The convict gratefully took a cigarette and helped himself to the silver lighter.

Mark Bradshaw had been one of Lawrence Tyburn's minders. Siggy Dexter had recruited him and they'd worked closely together on behalf of their boss. One evening, there had been an incident at the casino and in the ensuing brawl, a man had been seriously injured. He'd died later and Bradshaw had taken the blame. Lush had acted as his defence council, but try as he may, he was unable to get Bradshaw off. He'd been found guilty of manslaughter and sent down for five years.

Bradshaw had just completed his first two years at the *Scrubs* and if he kept his nose clean for a few more months, he could look forward to the chance of parole.

"I got the message that you wanted to see me, when Mum visited last week. So, I put the request to see you through the official channels. By the way, I've not had chance to say it before, but I'm grateful for the way Mr Tyburn has looked after my old mum. She always goes on about how good he's been to her."

Lush smiled to himself. This was a very positive start. Bradshaw was in a good mood, so, he might easily be receptive to his proposals.

He continued smoothly. "You're family, Mark. We told you that we'd take good care of her if you had to do a stretch at any time."

Bradshaw nodded. "So, what's cooking then? I don't suppose you're here on a social visit?"

The big man stared mildly back at Lush. He had a wide ugly face and very short-cropped hair, reminiscent of his days in the army. He was not very intelligent, extremely short tempered, tough and had immense physical strength.

Lush looked at him cautiously wondering how he should broach his next question. Without a positive response to his inducement, the whole plan involving Rydell was useless. He continued with his usual optimism. After all, the earlier signs had been good. He lowered his voice to almost a whisper, trying to create an atmosphere of intrigue. "How do you feel about making a great deal of money?"

"That's a bloody stupid question to start with."

Lush was momentarily thrown off course. He swallowed hard and tried again. "Okay. Let me ask you this then. What would you do to get your hands on 300 grand?"

"For that kind of money, any fuckin' thing."

This was better. "Anything? Are you sure Mark? Would you…" Lush drew his finger across his own throat.

"Yeah! Even the Prime bleedin' Minister for that kind of dosh."

"Well, I'm not suggesting we go to those extremes but if you're really keen to earn a small fortune, then have a look at this."

Lush opened his briefcase and extracted a slim document. He kept his voice at low volume and continued. "This is an outline of what we want you to do. I took a big gamble bringing it in here, but the risk would have been even bigger if I talked through every detail with you. You never know who may be listening. At least, we have the pretext that I'm going through an important legal document with you, if anyone interrupts. Anyway, read it."

He passed the file over to Bradshaw. It had been written in simplistic terms to enable him to understand what they wanted from him. He flicked it open and read the contents.

At first, there was stunned silence. "Jesus, Mr Lush this is fuckin' weird. You actually want me to organise a prison riot?"

"Correct."

"What the hell do you want me to do that for? You bustin' somebody out then?"

"Ah well," Lush hesitated, "that's only for Mr Tyburn and me to know."

Lush watched his man's features carefully, looking for a response, and he noticed Bradshaw suddenly get edgy.

"I may look stupid, Mr Lush, but I'm not really. I'll still be inside after the riot's over, won't I. Someone's sure to finger me as a trouble-maker. How do I get away with it?"

"We've figured that too, Mark. You'll need to cover your back. Whilst the riot's taking place, you might need to get rid of anyone who might grass you up. That'll be up to you, but you'll know who they are by then. In all the confusion, it should be easy."

Lush threw up his arms in encouragement. "You'll need to sit tight after the riot and wait to see what happens. There are plenty of outcomes to think about and I'll spell them all out clearly. If you're lucky, you may get clean away with it. On the other hand, if they do get evidence that you're involved in the riot, you'll be charged with the offence of prison mutiny, which will undoubtedly lengthen your sentence. The worst thing is if you do somebody in and they pin a murder on you. In that case, you're likely to go down for a very long stretch."

Bradshaw fell silent and studied the papers again. At length he spoke, keeping the level of his own voice down. "There's definitely no problem with all this." He gestured at the dossier. "If you can manage to get some head-cases from other prisons transferred to the same place, we should really be able to stir up the shit."

Bradshaw looked away, wrestling with the arguments racing through his mind. "But, I keep thinking. My parole's coming up soon. That means I'll have to forget it. I had my heart set on getting out of here soon. I'm not sure I want to do this one. Money can't buy everything."

Lush sensed he was losing the argument. He'd not considered that Bradshaw would turn him down, but he was edging close to a refusal. He was pivotal to their plan, so Lush needed to make a huge concession to get him to agree. He made his final play.

"We've thought of everything, Mark. As I said earlier, you're family. Believe me when I say we can get you out of prison under any circumstances. If you do get charged with anything that will lengthen your sentence, we can spring you.

We may need a few weeks to set it up, but we have the screws on someone high up in the government. We'll be able to arrange for your transfer from one prison to another and intercept the transport. Then, we'll provide you and your mum with false identities and get you out of the country, anywhere you like. Maybe, somewhere like the Costa Brava, where you could buy a villa and spend the rest of your life in luxury. By the way, Mr Tyburn has promised an extra 100 grand if we did have to move you abroad permanently. Think of all the lovely lolly you'll have to spend."

Bradshaw grinned. He didn't need any more convincing. He thrust his hand forward towards Lush. "It's a deal, Mr Lush. Tell Mr Tyburn that I won't let him down."

Lush spoke in a condescending tone. "Don't worry about that, Mark. We know that we can trust you to do a first-class job."

Bradshaw grinned excitedly. "So, what's to do first?"

"You'll need to pick a fight with one of the other inmates and make sure you end up in solitary. Then, you'll get hauled in front of the governor and told in no uncertain terms that you can forget your parole board hearing. That should really piss you off and you can get as stroppy as you like from then on. Kick as many arses as you like. Once you've become a high-profile liability, there'll be no eyebrows raised when we issue an order transferring you elsewhere."

"Sounds all right to me. Any ideas where I might end up?"

"Not at the moment. We're working on it, but it could be anywhere. We're on the lookout for an old prison, probably some place in the north of England where the nearest riot squads will take hours to get mobilised. By the way, there must be no word of this to your mum. When you lose your parole, we'll sweeten her up for you and make sure things are straightened out at home."

"Thanks, Mr Lush. You're right. She'll take it badly. I know she was looking forward to having me back home."

"Now. About payment. After your spell in solitary, get your mum to visit. When you see the old lady, get her to ring me and I'll arrange for half the money to be deposited into a new bank account taken out in your name. Not even your mum will be able to touch it unless you want to authorise it. The other half gets paid after the riot. Does that seem fair?"

"That's brilliant, that is. Bleedin' marvellous."

Bradshaw beamed all over his face. It was as though he'd just won the lottery.

Lush glanced at his watch. The interview had lasted over half an hour. "I must be off now, Mark. It wouldn't be good to let them think that an expensive lawyer has spare time to sit around chatting. Time is money, as they say." He carefully replaced the document in his briefcase and rose to his feet. Passing over to the far door he rapped it sharply several times. As the warder unlocked the door to escort Bradshaw back to his cell, Lush winked at him and shook his hand.

For the benefit of the prison officer, Bradshaw called back. "I'll be seeing you again sometime, Mr Lush. Thanks for sorting out that financial problem for my old mum."

Lush said nothing, but nodded in acknowledgement. He turned and sat down to await the return of the warder to show him out. The meeting had been highly satisfactory, even though it could so easily have gone wrong. Bradshaw hadn't been as naive as he'd anticipated. Only the promise of a big payday and a place in the sun had won him over. Lush couldn't suppress a tingle of excitement. With Bradshaw's acceptance, another piece of the jigsaw had fitted elegantly into place.

Ten minutes later, Lush was outside the prison walls. He sauntered back to his car in high spirits. He coughed unpleasantly and the thought of his warm Lotus made him increase his stride. Even so, he was in no real hurry to get away. His next appointment was at *Signor's* restaurant where he'd arranged to meet Tyburn, but the table had not been booked until 2:30. He'd have a leisurely drive over there and savour a large bourbon and another cigar before his friend arrived.

Chapter 20

Matthew left his house at dusk and aimlessly wandered around the local area. Eventually, he took a narrow side path with hedges on one side and a fence on the other. A short distance behind in the shadows, a figure was carefully following him. He ambled along; his shoulders hunched like an old man. He reached a point in the fence, looked around to see if anyone was watching, then pushed it aside and entered the adjacent churchyard. Matthew had done this on many occasions over the past few weeks since the funeral of Kirsty. He'd come in the dark, when he knew he'd be alone. The cemetery closed its gates at dusk, so he'd had to find a secret way in. Luckily, he'd found a partially broken piece of fence that he could open and lift back once he was through.

He melted into the darkness unaware that he was being followed. He threaded his way easily amongst the gravestones. He'd done it so many times already that it was a well-worn routine. He reached the spot where his wife and daughter were buried and sat on a damp, wooden bench next to their grave. It was cold and breezy and a drizzle began to fall.

Matthew pulled the collar of his coat tighter round his neck and sat in silence. He pondered his future for the 100th time. Since the funeral, he'd striven to control his bouts of anguish and misery, but he couldn't. His only solace was to brood, but brooding led to dark, desperate moods. Here he was again, at the grave of his daughter, reliving her brutal murder and how he'd killed one of the men responsible. At one time, killing another human being would have been abhorrent, yet the more he analysed his actions, the easier it became to convince himself that the thug's death was justified. This didn't ease his suffering, as thoughts of Kirsty and their close, loving relationship flooded back.

He got up and knelt on the wet grass, next to the grave. Visions from the past once again caught him unprepared and he wept sad lonely tears. As he knelt, hunched in anguish, a friendly arm wrapped around his shoulder.

He looked up in surprise.

It was Melissa. "So, This is where you come to every night. Matthew, you need help. I'll do anything for you. You only need to ask. I know you're in pain, but coming here in the dark won't solve anything."

Matthew looked at her face and saw only pity in her eyes.

She spoke gently, "Grieving is a long and complex process and is different for everyone. You need the help of others to get you through. Please, let that be me."

He staggered to his feet and fell into her arms.

They hugged closely and cried together.

Eventually, Matthew's sorrow subsided and he looked at Melissa's kindly face. He kissed her softly on her lips.

"Thank you for being here for me. I've been in a state, I know I have. I've blocked everyone out and I've felt nothing but self-pity and recrimination."

She touched his cheek, gazing lovingly into his face. "It's been so difficult watching you suffer. I've been so worried, that's why I decided to follow you tonight. I was scared you might do something stupid like commit suicide."

"That's not my way. I was all mixed up. I killed a man. I pushed him off the roof. Yes, I lied and although I've had a few twinges of guilt, he murdered that policeman at the hospital and deserved what he got."

"I guessed as much," whispered Melissa, "don't beat yourself up. I'd have done the same."

Matthew held her closely again. "It's over, coming here at night. I've just made some big decisions. After the funeral, I promised myself that I would get back at all those who took Kirsty away from me. Now, the time has come to act."

Melissa had a strange feeling of dread as he held her by the hand and led her away from the graveside.

* * * * *

Clearly etched in the mind of Matthew Morgan were the names supplied by Teasdale before he'd hurled him from the hospital roof. The next morning, he sat by the phone and steeled himself to the task of finding out whether Teasdale's words were true. His anxiety level was high, because now he was desperate to find the others responsible for Kirsty's murder. If the thug had been lying, the trail would be already dead. This was a prospect he could not reconcile.

Directory enquiries gave a London number. The building firm *Tybuild* did exist and he was given its address in Greenwich.

So far so good, he thought to himself, *but I have to be sure that I've found the right place.*

He dialled the numbers expectantly and a singing female voice on the other end launched into the kind of cloned, mechanical welcome characterised by those serving at a fast-food restaurant.

"Hello, this is Tybuild. How may I help you?"

"Hello. I'm trying to get hold of Siggy. Is he there?"

"Just one moment and I'll see. He's never usually around at this time of day, but I think he came in early with Mr Tyburn. Who shall I say is calling?"

Matt replaced the phone, satisfied by the response to his call.

His heart pounded and he spoke aloud. The tone was venomous. "Yes, you scumbag! I can't wait to meet."

* * * * *

Matt brought Melissa her drink and they sat, enjoying the early evening atmosphere in their local. He'd become more cheerful the past few days, but tonight he seemed distant again and Melissa felt sure he was milling over something important.

She gave him a fond smile. "Okay, Morgan, what is it?"

"What do you mean?"

"You obviously want to say something."

"How'd you come to that conclusion?"

"Call it feminine intuition if you will, so tell me I'm wrong." She waited as he tried to find the courage to express his feelings.

"I can't. I can't tell you."

"Why not? Come on. Try me."

He spoke almost embarrassingly, trying hard to find the right words, "I've become very fond of you, Mel. I thought I'd never feel like this towards another woman. That's why I can't tell you anymore. I don't want you getting involved."

Melissa prickled. She was puzzled, but at the same time felt a sense of hurt. "Involved in what? Please, don't shut me out. I feel the same way about you and if you care about me like you say, then you have to trust me." She commanded him gently, "Look at me, Matthew."

He gazed into her face and saw only her deep, soulful eyes. He was drawn into them, touched by some inner emotion. Somehow, she compelled him to share his thoughts.

"Melissa, please listen carefully. I have this terrible fixation and I can't help myself. I'm about to get involved in something you don't want to know about." He looked painfully into her face. "What I'm trying to say is… that I want you to back off. I don't want you to get hurt."

"But I am involved, Matt. To me, our lives are slowly becoming like this." Melissa held up her hand with two fingers intertwined. She sat up straight, throwing her head back, so that the thick shock of auburn hair fell softly across her shoulders. Her rich Irish accent became serious. "What's burning you up? Please, talk to me."

Matt stared into his pint, refusing to make eye contact. "Apart from finding you, my whole life has been shattered. Kirsty is gone and Laura's struggling hard to get over her sister's death. After I lost Julie all those years ago, I thought that I could never feel so low again. But second time round, it's a 100 times worse. I just can't live with myself knowing that this time, there is some bastard out there responsible for it all. I find myself dwelling on it all the time and it's destroying me. I have to do something. I'm looking for justice. You can call it revenge if you like, but I mean to have it."

He gestured aimlessly and then looked into her face once more. "You must think I'm really selfish and that I don't care about you, but you're wrong. You've been more than a friend to me and I don't think I could have got through it all without you. The trouble is, you've come along at the same time as this god-awful mess has ruined my life. I don't really know where I'm going and at the moment, I just can't give myself to you completely. I can't be what you want me to be."

"And what might that be?"

"You know what I'm trying to say. I've changed. You have to take me as you find me now. Perhaps, when it's all over, I may get back to being normal again. If there ever is such a thing."

"Never mind me, what about Laura? What if you end up behind bars… or worse still?" Melissa couldn't bring herself to mention the worst scenario.

"Laura's young. If anything happens to me, she's still got her whole life ahead of her. Luckily, she's got no responsibilities either, but it wasn't like that for me when Julie died. I had two babies to bring up. She'll get over it."

"But Matt, don't you think the odds against you succeeding are just too remote?"

"It's a chance I'm prepared to take. Can you possibly understand me? I'm in a long, dark tunnel and for me, there's only one way out."

Melissa felt deep pangs of fear as she began to comprehend. The feeling she'd repressed at the graveside resurfaced. She had read him wrong all along, realising now that he would never get over the death of Kirsty without purging his own guilt. It didn't take her a second to make her decision. She was too bound up in her feelings for the man who sat beside her.

She spoke softly, her voice full of emotion. "I can't hope to know what you're going through, but whatever it is, I want to share it with you. I love you, Matthew, and I want to help you every step of the way. I promise, I won't let you down."

"But, Melissa…"

His weak protest was cut short by a tender kiss. "So then, are you going to let me in or not?"

He gave a long sigh and took her hand, holding it tightly. "Ok."

Giving a little nervous grunt, he opened up, keeping his voice low, "I've known for some time the name of Kirsty's killer. I found out most of what I needed to know at the hospital. When she came out of her coma, she gave me two names. I told you I lied to the police about Teasdale. I had that thug by the throat on the hospital roof and I forced him to give me more information, before his unfortunate accident!"

"You've obviously told the police nothing. Don't you think it's time to give them those names?"

Suddenly, Matt became irate. "Why do you think I've kept this a secret for so long? I wouldn't trust them to organise a piss up in a brewery. Something about their organisation stinks. They had a news blackout and an armed guard, but it still didn't save Kirsty."

"Calm down, Matt. Somebody might overhear."

He looked around sheepishly and continued in a quiet, level tone. "I've come to the conclusion the killers had someone on the inside. If we did go to the police, our worries could just be starting. Firstly, if someone leaks our whereabouts, the killers may come after us. Why do you think I didn't want you to get involved? Secondly, we can't guarantee justice will be done. Besides, I don't want their justice, I want mine."

Melissa saw the logic of his argument. The possible corruption of the police, his own need for revenge and, above all, his fear for her own safety. This only served to strengthen her feelings towards him, even though she knew that she'd have to go along with whatever dangerous schemes he had in mind. Her only chance to resurrect a future together was to see him through it.

"You're going to need help, Matthew. What are you planning?"

"Well, firstly, I need a trip to London. The two men I'm looking for are called Tyburn and Dexter. Tyburn appears to be at the centre of all this and he owns a building company called *Tybuild*. Siggy Dexter is Tyburn's man. He's the thug who killed Kirsty. Teasdale confessed that to me on the hospital roof."

Matt looked sorrowful as he mentioned his daughter. "To start with, I want to make a positive identification of them both. Nothing more. Realistically, it has to be done during a working day, because the only address I have is for *Tybuild*. My intention is to sit in the car outside their premises and watch the comings and goings. If I get the chance, I'll make a few discrete enquiries. It might help me put some names to faces."

Melissa seemed receptive to his idea. "Are you sure that's all you intend to do?"

"Yes. I swear it. Before I can do anything else, I have to find out who I'm dealing with and see where they operate from."

"Well, in that case, when you're ready, I'll take a day off work. I'll phone in with a migraine and drive you down in my car."

Matt sighed to himself. His solo expedition to the Capital had been hijacked, but secretly, he would be glad of Melissa's company.

Chapter 21

Melissa picked Matt up at half past five the following Friday morning. Their intention was to get to London before the start of the working day. He'd been up an hour already, packing a mountain of sandwiches and a couple of thermos flasks in anticipation of the long day ahead.

The journey from Sheffield took several hours. Despite their early start, they became embroiled in the drag of rush hour traffic and their trek across the Capital became a monotonous drudge of stop-start driving. Their final destination was just across the Thames and not far from the southern approach to the Blackwall Tunnel.

Matt acted as navigator and guided Melissa through the early morning throng. After they had passed through the tunnel, they took a slip road leading down into Greenwich and off into a maze of small side streets. There, nestling between the main Woolwich Road and the Thames was a labyrinth of industrial units, depots and factories. The whole area consisted of one commercial estate merging anonymously with another as they crowded together on the banks of the Thames.

Darkness began to fade rapidly, giving way to a new dawn. The first shafts of sunlight appeared in the east as a dull winter sun rose in a pale, crystal blue sky.

They drove around looking for street names and eventually found the right one. It was long and wide, with high warehouses and old office blocks on both sides, interspersed with open areas where trucks and lorries were parked. Some of the businesses were already bustling with activity as the commercial world of London geared up for another busy day.

No one paid them any heed as they crawled along searching for the elusive builder's yard. They crossed innumerable intersections until at last, they came upon it on the left-hand side.

Melissa continued past the entrance and turned the car round further along the road. She drove back slowly and finally halted on the opposite side of the road to the yard, behind a battered Ford transit van. There were other cars parked nose to tail at the side of the road and theirs was only one unobtrusive vehicle among many. They were situated about 20 yards lower down from the main gates and ideally positioned to spot anyone coming in and out of the premises.

The site was extensive, bounded on either side by two high warehouses and shielded from the front street by a ten-foot high, vertical steel fence. The open railings allowed a reasonably clear view of the interior of the yard. The fence extended along the outer perimeter and was topped with barbed wire. The rear of the property was obscured from view, but looked as if it had access directly onto the Thames. A large area of the site was taken up by wood, which was being seasoned on racks, in long, high sheds. These were open to the atmosphere, but had covered roofs to protect them from excess moisture in the winter and unnatural drying in the summer. The main office block was placed centrally with concrete roadways on either side to allow the passage of forklift trucks and heavy wagons. A huge liquid petroleum gas tank sat on a raised concrete plinth in a small compound near one of the sheds. It was obviously the source of heating fuel for the offices, which looked dilapidated from the outside. Sheltering under the lee of the first drying shed was a small, weather beaten, caravan. It looked like the ideal base for a night watchman.

At first, Matt couldn't believe this was Tyburn's only precaution against thieves, but on reflection, bulky timber and bricks would be very difficult to steal, so perhaps these were commodities that didn't need much security. There was certainly no evidence of CCTV cameras. Even though there was plenty of activity taking place in the surrounding area, the business itself remained still and silent.

"Well. This is it, Mel. We've found it at long last."

"Scruffy-looking dump, isn't it?"

Matt chuckled. "Not what you'd call the nub of British industry." He half stretched in the confines of the small car and then looked at his watch. "I'm feeling knackered after that drive. Let's go for a short walk. I can't see there being any action here for a while."

Melissa agreed and they went for a brisk stroll around the block to exercise their cramped limbs. They were back 20 minutes later and were soon tucking into food and coffee before their long surveillance began.

Just after 8:30, the builders yard started to come alive. The two of them watched everything, making notes about the personnel and their routine. A couple of workmen in overalls arrived first in a small white van. One of them unlocked the gates, opening them wide, whilst the other parked up against the far warehouse wall. They went over to the caravan and hammered hard on the window. Presently, an old man appeared at the door and offered each a steaming hot drink. There was distant laughter.

By nine o'clock, another six men had arrived and the yard was quite busy. The old watchman appeared again, this time with a flea-bitten mongrel dog. He carefully closed the door of his caravan and shuffled towards the main gate with his mutt in tow.

A red Ford Fiesta, polluting the atmosphere with foul, black exhaust fumes, screeched to a halt next to the night watchman. A buxom, blond-haired girl of about 20 got out of the car, wearing a tight and very short mini skirt. She was flustered and obviously late, but she looked back at the driver as though she couldn't bear to be parted. She hesitated for only a moment, then dived across the passenger seat to smother him with a goodbye kiss. The old man stopped, having a long, lustful stare at her soft meaty thighs as they disappeared up the nick of her bum. The girl turned round and immediately knew what he'd been up to. As the car raced away in a haze of burning rubber and oil, she pulled the hem of her skirt down and turned on him.

"You're a dirty old bugger, you are, Arthur. Why don't you clear off to the pub or something?"

"Would do if they were open, Janice. Nice pair of knickers you've got on." He gave her a disgusting leer. "Marks and Spencer, are they?"

She flushed bright scarlet and lost for words, swung her shoulder bag across her back and stormed across the concrete yard towards the offices.

Matt and Melissa had been listening with the window down and grinned appreciatively at the comic situation.

Several more office staff arrived and by ten, the business appeared to have settled into its normal daily routine. There was plenty of activity amongst the drying sheds, but nothing of interest for them to note. An articulated lorry loaded with bricks arrived to break the monotony. The driver expertly navigated the narrow gates and disappeared into the bowels of the yard.

By 11, they were both very bored and Matt had to go and stretch his legs again and have a pee. When he returned, he noticed that a maroon Rolls Royce had arrived and was parked in one of the bays directly in front of the offices.

Melissa spoke excitedly. "A middle-aged man in a smart suit got out."

"Did you get a look at his face? Could you recognise him again?"

"No. He was too far away."

"We're getting nowhere with this, Melissa. Somehow, we've got to get closer without being spotted."

As they argued quietly about what to do, Melissa glanced up. A gleaming, black, BMW cruised up the road towards them and indicated a left turn into the premises.

"Look, Matt. Look at the number plate on that car."

They could easily make out the clean lettering. It read *SIG 3*.

Melissa was excited. "*SIG 3*. Siggy Dexter. It has to be him."

The car parked next to the Roller and two men got out. They were in animated conversation and argued loudly as they made their way round to the office entrance.

Matt was plainly disappointed. "This is no good. We're still not close enough to get a decent look at them. We're just wasting our time sat here. I've got to get in there."

Melissa looked horrified. "You must be joking. That's not part of the plan. You can't go in there. What if they were to turn nasty?"

"It shouldn't be that difficult to make an appointment to see Tyburn. I only need some simple pretext to get in there. I have to meet him face to face."

Melissa began to panic. "I don't like this idea one bit, Matthew. Let's go home."

Matt was having none of it. "We haven't achieved anything yet. What's the point in going home? I'm not wasting this opportunity. Both Tyburn and Dexter are in there and I want to meet them."

Melissa fell silent, trying desperately hard to think of a good argument that would put him off his crazy scheme.

Meanwhile, Matt was racking his brains for a way of getting in. He had a sudden flash of inspiration and got out of the car.

Melissa questioned him anxiously, "Where are you going?"

"I noticed a phone box round the corner, when I went for a pee. I've got a call to make. I'll be back in a bit."

He returned ten minutes later. "Right. That's sorted. I've arranged a meeting for one o'clock."

Melissa's mood became darker, but she seemed resigned to his decision. "I hope you know what you're doing. What did you say to them?"

"I said that I was from the Health and Safety Executive and needed to look at their gas tank. I figure that I know enough technical jargon to sound authentic for 20 minutes or so. I don't intend hanging around any longer."

Melissa tried one last time to persuade him not to go. "Matthew, I don't want you to do this. It could be really dangerous. What if they find out that you're not who you claim to be? How can you be certain they'll let you out in one piece?"

"Don't be daft, Melissa. This is England. It's the safest country in the world. It's broad daylight. Of course, they'll let me go. They're hardly likely to bump off every nosy stranger who turns up."

"Matthew, you're dealing with a gang of murderous thugs. Think about what they did to the whole Newsome family. Surely, you can see if they were prepared to carry out a massacre like that, you'd be small fry. If they suspect you're up to no good and a potential danger to them, they won't hesitate to shut you up."

Matt wouldn't be dissuaded and when one o'clock approached, he grinned and kissed her cheek. "See you later."

"Please be careful, Matt. Please."

He crossed the road and disappeared into the offices. The reception was smarter than the exterior of the building suggested. The young secretary, who they'd seen earlier, announced his arrival and he was taken through to meet Tyburn. If the outer office looked plush, then his private office was positively luxurious.

Lawrence Tyburn rose from his leather chair and came round to shake Matt's hand. "Mr Brown, isn't it? What can we do for you?"

Matt hadn't known what to expect and was immediately intrigued by the rotund face and smug expression of the man before him. There was something about Tyburn that made him uneasy. His glossy, perfectly polished exterior and smooth, smarmy greeting belied a different person. Knowing what he was capable of, he gave Matt a sharp reminder of his ruthless nature. Knowing he'd just shaken hands with the man who had ordered Kirsty's death, gave him a deep sense of betrayal. All he really wanted to do was smash the grinning hyena in his face. He replaced his fist in his pocket as he managed to control the urge.

"It's not a long job, Mr Tyburn. For gas tanks of your size, we just need to check for corrosion and look at the pipework and valve gear." For the next 30 seconds, he gave Tyburn a checklist of technical gobbledegook to try and impress him.

"Well, I suppose you'd better get to it. By the way, do you have some form of identification?"

Matt had prepared himself for this one and fiddled about in his pockets. "Sorry, I must have left it in the car. If you like, I'll go and fetch it?" He held his breath. If Tyburn insisted, then he would go out to the car in the pretence of collecting his ID and get Melissa to drive him away.

Tyburn put up his hand. "No, Mr Brown, that won't be necessary. I'm sure you have too much to do already this afternoon. If you'd like to wait at the reception for a few minutes, I'll get someone to show you the layout."

He buzzed for his secretary. "Take Mr Brown back to reception and make him a coffee. There's a good girl."

Matt was escorted from the office and as he looked back he saw only a bland, expressionless grin on his adversary's face.

Tyburn immediately picked up the phone. His tone of voice changed as he summoned Dexter from the next office. "Siggy. I've got a problem. This bloke, Brown, in reception, he says he's come to inspect the gas tank. He's obviously a fuckin' liar. The tank was given a clean bill of health two weeks ago by his own organisation. He tried to impress me with a whole load of crap, but even I know he was talking through his arse. He said his ID was in his car, so I don't reckon he's got any. God knows who he is or what he wants, but I'm certain he's up to no good. I need you to sort it. Stick him in Arthur's van until it gets dark, then you and the boys can play about and make him talk. If you think he's a nobody, just rough him up a bit, but if he's dodgy, take him down to Moses at the abattoir and grind him up for doggy meat."

Dexter chuckled. "Excellent. That's what I like about this job, variety."

He went straight to the reception and introduced himself. Matt found himself mesmerised by the strange caricature that was Dexter. The emotionless facial expressions gave him an odd look and he remembered with sorrow how Kirsty had described him as ugly. Matt continued to stare into his face. He would never forget it. This was the man who had killed his daughter.

Matt finished his coffee and after a minute or two of small talk, Dexter took him outside. He escorted him around the front of the offices and under the drying shed to where the old caravan was parked.

Matt was puzzled. "I thought the gas tank was round the other side?"

"Yeah. It is, but some of the pipe work goes round here."

As they passed the caravan, Dexter turned on Matt and before he knew what was happening, he found himself staring down the barrel of a gun.

Dexter leant forward and opened the caravan. "Get inside, you nosy prick or I'll blow your brains out here and now." With the gun at his back, Matt stumbled into the caravan. Dexter followed.

* * * * *

Out on the road, Melissa had been watching the sleepy premises from the safety of her Peugeot. She waited impatiently for Matt's return, glancing at her watch every few seconds.

Fifteen minutes elapsed before he reappeared, but it seemed like an eternity. She looked on anxiously, as a man she recognised from earlier, ushered him round the front of the offices. She gasped in horror at what happened next as the man pulled a gun and forced Matt into the battered caravan.

Melissa suddenly felt sick. Things had gone dreadfully wrong and her worst fears had been realised. Her first reaction was to rush across and try to get Matt out, but she quickly realised the futility of such a response. It would be a foolhardy thing to do. She was now his only hope and she must not sacrifice her own freedom by playing the heroine.

In the distance, the caravan door opened and the man stepped out. He'd been in there with Matt for about ten minutes, but he now left alone. He stood, smoothing down his suit for a few moments, then crossed over to the offices and disappeared into reception.

Melissa felt totally helpless and her persistent fear for Matt's safety called for immediate action. She tried to think what options were open. Should she go to the police? If they became involved, then any plans to avenge Kirsty's death would be gone for good and she reminded herself of Matt's nagging theory that there may be an inside informer. With that kind of uncertainty, proving Tyburn and Dexter's involvement in Kirsty's murder might become impossible. They would probably walk away free. She knew that the injustice of such a situation would finish Matthew. No. She couldn't let that happen and came to the inevitable conclusion that she had to try and get him out herself. She surmised that he'd been tied up and left unguarded in the caravan, so her best bet was to wait until it got dark before she made her move.

The next few hours were the longest of her life as she watched and waited, blanking out from her mind any possibility that he may already be dead. At long last, the light of the short December day began to pale and twilight was soon replaced by darkness. Fortunately, Tyburn's business worked seasonal hours and as soon as the light began to fade, the majority of the workforce started to leave.

Melissa watched them go, counting them out as they left. Soon, the bright lights in the offices showed the only sign of activity on the premises. She braced herself and got out of the car. Quickly crossing the road and keeping to the shadows, she managed to sneak undetected on to the site. Melissa decided to approach the caravan from behind the offices and slid into the drying sheds, dodging from row to row as she made her way to her objective. She turned past a pile of timber and there, a short distance away, was the outline of the caravan. Looking around for a weapon, she found a length of wood, which could be used as a club. Slowly, she crept up to the van and peered through a side window. It was dark inside and showed no sign of life. The pangs of fear she had managed to suppress suddenly began to resurface. She had to get in there quickly. With her back pressed against the flimsy aluminium wall, she knocked firmly on the door. All her senses were heightened. If anyone appeared, she was ready to wield the club as hard as she could. There was no reply. She tried again with the same result. Melissa breathed a sigh of relief. She wouldn't need to fight. Turning the recessed handle, she pulled the door open.

Before she had a chance to react, a skinny hand locked around her wrist. It twisted hard and forced her to drop the makeshift club.

She yelled out in pain as a gruff voice echoed in her ear. "What the hell are you doing in my caravan?"

Melissa was pushed headlong inside and a shadowy figure scrambled in after her. The figure grunted and fumbled in the dark, then there was a click and the interior was bathed in a low light from a small fluorescent tube. She quickly took in her surroundings, spotting Matt, lying bound and gagged on the far bed. The look in his eyes showed that he was fully aware of what had happened.

Melissa lay on the floor and the old night watchman hovered over her. He glanced across at Matt and quickly assessed the situation. "Ah! I see. Siggy has one trussed up and ready for the pot and his little friend turns up to try and save him. Nice, but it won't work. We'll just sit here and wait till he comes. I'll be in his good books tonight."

The atmosphere was pungent and dank. The smell of ancient dog, stale beer and unwashed clothes made Melissa's stomach turn. The wizened night watchman scratched his four-day stubble and she felt him begin to ogle her. He touched Melissa on her cheek. His skin was repulsive. It was rough and abrasive, like dried bark. He bared a row of black, rotten teeth and his breath stank with the decay. It made Melissa squirm.

"Maybe Siggy might let me shag you," he grinned,

Melissa's reaction was immediate. "Not likely, you filthy old sod." She swung a leg up from her prone position and caught him a vicious kick in the groin. He staggered back and there was a three-second delay before the agony of the blow paralysed him from the waist down and he doubled up clutching his balls. Before the old man had time to react, she scrambled to her feet. Spotting an empty beer bottle in the sink, she snatched it up and in one continuous move, smashed it against the side of his head. He crashed to the floor and lay in an untidy heap groaning in pain. He was in no condition to make further trouble.

She rushed over to Matt and tore away the broad sticky tape from around his mouth. "Matthew. Are you all right?"

"Thank God you came. When it got dark, I was beginning to feel that I wasn't going to get out of here alive. I'm okay, but my arms and legs are numb."

Melissa frantically searched the drawers and found an old bread knife to cut away his bonds. They rubbed his aching limbs furiously, but when she tried to help him stand up, the circulation was slow to return and it seemed an age before he could move.

"They'll be coming for you soon. Come on, we've got to get out of here."

He grimaced in pain and stumbled over the prostrate night watchman as they finally escaped from his stinking caravan. Matt leant heavily on Melissa's shoulder and they gingerly made their way back through the drying sheds. She was able to retrace the path along the rows of timber racks and Matt hobbled painfully by her side. The further they went, the easier it became to walk until, at last, he was able to move unaided. They made a quick dash through the gates and across to the little Peugeot.

Melissa was breathless. "That was a lucky escape."

"You were brilliant, Mel. I didn't know you could fight like a tiger."

She turned on him angrily. "This is not a pathetic little game. Admit it, you were in terrible danger."

"I'm sorry, Melissa you were right about them. I'm sure they were planning to do something pretty dreadful to me. There's something not right here and if you were to meet Tyburn and Dexter, you'd know what I mean. What a pair of 24-carat bastards they are. It's obvious they'll go to any lengths to protect this place. It must be a base for some kind of illegal racket."

Their conversation was suddenly interrupted as a number of high intensity floodlights illuminated the compound and they watched as two figures chased about the drying sheds.

"Looks like they've found you missing. Come on. It's time to go."

"No. Not yet. Let's play it cool. They'll think we're miles away by now."

Melissa exploded. "What did you just say? Play it cool. Play it bloody cool. What do you mean? I've had all I can stand for one day. Don't you realise how close you were to being shot dead. Laura would go spare if she ever found out."

Matt put his hand on hers. "I owe you my life, Melissa and for that I'll always be grateful. But think about Kirsty. I guess you didn't go to the police because you thought of her?"

Melissa fumed silently.

"I only want to do another simple thing and this is the best break we've got. They don't know we're watching, so let's sit tight and wait. When that BMW leaves, we'll just follow it and see where it goes."

"What? Just follow the car home?"

"Yes. That's all I want to do. We'll have another address and something else to work on. It couldn't be better. That personalised plate has marked Dexter out for us."

Melissa reluctantly agreed and they fell silent milling over their own thoughts and fears.

The clock in the dashboard edged slowly towards five o'clock and their patience was finally rewarded when two figures emerged from the shadowy entrance to the offices and returned to *SIG3*.

"It's them. Right, let's see where they go."

Melissa turned the keys and the engine of her little car kicked up the first time. They let the BMW get 50 yards ahead, then pulled out and followed at a safe distance. The big car seemed in no hurry and it was a relief to Melissa who found it difficult keeping up in the heavy evening traffic as they drove westwards, following the south bank of the Thames. They lost sight of the BMW on a couple of occasions and but for some friendly red lights would never have caught up in the dark. The cars eventually threaded their way northwards and over the Thames, heading towards Chelsea.

Once they had turned off the Chelsea embankment, the BMW led them down numerous side roads until they came to a very expensive looking club. Bright, colourful lights emblazoned on the wall announced, *Un Coup De Chance.*

"How's your French, Melissa?"

"I think it means something like, a slice of luck. It looks like a casino."

"I bet you're right and if I'm not mistaken, it's where our two friends are heading."

Dexter's car signalled and turned down a side street. Melissa didn't follow, but stopped the Peugeot at the head of the road. Sure enough, the BMW came to a halt at the far corner of the club. The two men got out of the car and skipped up a flight of stone steps, across a small balcony and into the rear of the building.

Matt persuaded Melissa to reverse the car and stop a little way up the street, beyond the front of the casino.

"There's something I need to know, Melissa."

"Oh! No! Not again! Not more trouble. Matthew, don't you dare! You promised."

Before she could stop him, Matt got out of the car and hurried back to the casino's ornate entrance. There was a beefy looking doorman guarding the foyer. He was wearing an expensively cut evening suit and sported a double broken nose. He was definitely not someone to have on the opposite side in a brawl.

"Hello. I wonder if you could help me?"

"What do you wish to know, sir? If it's about membership, I'm afraid you're out of luck."

Matt needed to confirm his suspicions about the place, so he'd thought up a few lines of patter.

"This is Mr Tyburn's club isn't it?"

"Yes. And Mr Lush of course. They're the joint owners, but if you want to see them, you'll have to make an appointment."

The man suddenly began to look edgy. "What exactly do you want? You're not the Old Bill are you?"

Matt continued his bluff, "For God's sake, no. I'm one of Siggy's mates. Only he told me to come round this evening and he'd show me a good time. I felt sure it was his BMW I saw at the last set of lights, but with it being dark, I can't see him parked anywhere."

"That's a relief then. I think he arrived a few minutes ago, but he always parks his car at the back. If you hang about here, I'll go and fetch him for you. Who shall I say it is?"

"Just tell him it's Freddie. Freddie Brown. He'll come back with you straight away, I can guarantee it."

The bouncer disappeared and when he was out of view, Matt turned and raced back to the car. "Come on Melissa. I think we've outstayed our welcome. We've found out all we need to know about this place and more. Let's go home."

Chapter 22

The engine of the white jaguar was a straight six with a double overhead cam. It throbbed under the bonnet, giving a feeling of immense power. Melissa knew how proud Matt was of the old car and suggested the drive, so he could show it off to her. He'd immediately agreed and offered to cook her dinner in the evening. He'd bid for the XK120 at a motor auction ten years ago and because it had been in a poor state, he'd managed to get it cheap. He'd had plenty of experience tinkering around with old cars in his youth and saw the potential to rebuild the old classic. It had been a great hobby and he'd spent many years, carefully restoring it to its former condition. His garage had been his oasis from growing teenage daughters and he nurtured the car like an old friend.

They spent a pleasurable Saturday afternoon tearing around the winding roads of the Peak District beyond Sheffield and arrived home after an exhilarating trip. Matt had demonstrated his considerable driving expertise and Melissa had enjoyed every minute. He turned the jaguar into the garage and switched off the ignition. The twin exhausts ceased their growling and fell silent.

"Wow! I hope dinner is half as good."

"It's in the oven already and should take about another hour."

Matt led her into the lounge and poured a couple of large malt whiskies. They sat on the rug in front of the gas fire and lay back against the soft cushions of the settee.

After the brush with Dexter and Tyburn, Matt was on a permanent high, fuelled by the knowledge that he'd found Kirsty's killers. He'd soon forgotten the dangers he'd recently been through and was beginning to quietly formulate a strategy to bring them to justice.

Melissa slipped her arm around his waist. Although their relationship had been fraught with tension, brought about by his grief and often silent obsession, she was deeply content. There was something about his boyish looks that made her entire being glow every time they were together. He handed her a glass and she sipped the bronze, warming spirit. Although she was in a really happy mood, she had picked up that something had been bothering Matt all afternoon. The drive had shown a certain recklessness in his nature as though he was trying to prove something. Maybe she was wrong. *Was it just a man thing? Was he just showing off to impress her?*

"You seem a bit quiet, Matt. Is there something you want to say?"

"Well. Yes, there is."

He hadn't realised that Melissa was already on his wavelength, waiting to share his thoughts. "Do you remember the Dunblane massacre?"

"Yes! Those poor schoolchildren in Scotland, murdered by a lunatic with a gun."

"It was a real tragedy, but the aftermath had severe consequences for many people."

"What do you mean?"

"Well, because of the public outrage, there was an incredible knee-jerk reaction from the government and they went on to ban all hand guns from private ownership. It was just an excuse really. A way of getting potential weapons out of the public domain."

"Good idea too."

"Well, I didn't think so at the time because I belonged to a pistol club. I could only afford baby-sitters one night a week, but it was a fantastic two-hour break, when I could concentrate solely on my shooting. I used to go to the TA range. It was well organised and very safe. Even though, I say so myself, I was a pretty good shot and won a few medals along the way. Of course, I had to give all my guns, ammo and equipment in when the government changed the law."

She smirked cheekily at him, "Go on then, what's your point 007?"

Matt stood up and went over to a nearby cupboard. He came back with a leather case which he proceeded to open.

Melissa looked on as he began to remove pieces of equipment, which were stored in soft, foam cavities. "What the hell is that?"

He started to assemble the parts and soon it became recognisable as a weapon. "What do you think? It's a crossbow."

"Yes. I can see now, but it's not what I would have expected. It looks very modern."

"It is. It's quite high-tech, none of your old twelfth-century rubbish. I really missed my shooting, so I bought this as a replacement, but I couldn't get on with the sport. That's when I packed it in and bought the jag."

"I take it you know how to handle it then?"

In 30 seconds, Matt had expertly dismantled the crossbow and stored the pieces back in their preformed slots in the case. "Pretty nifty eh?" He looked down at Melissa in earnest. "Since I can't get a gun these days, then I'll have to fight Dexter with this."

Melissa nearly choked on her whisky. "You can't be serious. That's no match for his gun."

"I do have other plans to make this more lethal than you can imagine. Can you help me get together a few chemicals and some bits of equipment?"

She was surprised by the change in direction of the conversation and became suddenly defensive. "It depends on what you want."

Matt scrabbled into his back pocket and pulled out a crumpled sheet of paper. He sat beside her and handed it over. Melissa shrugged and looked puzzled as she began to scrutinise his list. "Mmm. I can help you get all of these things. I have a list of suppliers that we use at school. Didn't know you were practising to be an alchemist. Are you sure, you're not returning to the Middle Ages?" The statement was half a question and Melissa was frustrated by his negative response to the intended humour.

"Do you know if this stuff can be ordered and delivered privately? Some wholesalers only deal with big organisations, such as schools?"

"Yes, that's easy. I've got lots of contacts and most of this stuff is just glassware anyway."

Her curiosity suddenly overflowed. "Come on Matthew, what are you up to? What's the big secret?"

Matt turned his head downwards and gazed silently into his whisky.

"Morgan… just what have you got in mind?"

He whispered softly, "Nitro-glycerine."

Her mood changed instantly and she swore loudly, "Jesus Christ and Mother of Mary. You must be mad. You're surely not considering trying to make nitro. Don't you know how dangerous that stuff is?"

"Yeah. But I've no access to firearms or explosives and that's why I need to make my own. I've been doing my homework and provided I'm careful, I'm confident that I can make some safely."

Melissa scowled angrily. "If you think I'm going to be a party to a crazy scheme like that, you have another think coming."

He looked aghast at her outburst. "Look, Melissa. It is possible to make nitro. I know I can do it."

"You're a bloody loony, that's what you are. This is madness. I won't let you blow yourself into little bits. I won't."

"Come on Mel. Don't be so melodramatic."

She pushed him away and got to her feet, glaring wildly at him. "Look buster," she fumed, "just suppose you can make nitro, that's not the problem. It's storing and transporting the damn stuff. It's so unstable. A good knock and the whole lot would go up and you with it. No! No! You selfish bastard, I won't let you do it."

She turned away from him in frustration and tears welled in her eyes. She'd recently declared her love for him and promised to help in any way, but she was horrified by his fearsome proposal.

Matt appeared at her side and placed a comforting arm around her shoulder. "I knew it would be like this. Please forgive me." Matt held her tightly. He knew he'd pushed her too far. "I should have got all this stuff from somewhere else. I should have done it on the quiet and said nothing. I'm sorry."

Her tears finally subsided and she spoke to him with a lucid, throaty growl. "I suppose you're still going to carry on with this idiotic scheme. You do realise that you may end up dead before you even get anywhere near this Dexter?"

"I know. I know. I've already been through it, repeatedly. A thousand times. But if I plan everything carefully, I'm confident that I can handle the nitro and my crossbow will be the delivery system."

She gave him a watery smile. "You keep saying I, Matt. From now on, it's we… okay. You seem to forget that I've got a damn good degree in chemistry. I might just be able to give a stubborn rat like you some useful help and advice."

He grinned at her friendly sarcasm. Suddenly and unexpectedly, she had given in and although he was happy to use her expertise, he still harboured fears for her safety. When the time came, he wouldn't put her life at risk.

He didn't voice his concerns further, but accepted her help with gratitude. "Right, the more brains on the job, the better. We're both intelligent people. We just have to be meticulous in our planning. Incidentally, I'm coming back to school on Monday. I need to start picking up the threads again."

Melissa fell silent. Her life had suddenly become an incessant roller coaster and although it was scary, there was also a tingle of excitement to temper her fear. The worst part of the ride was the knowledge that she'd lost control of events. She was about to allow the man she loved to take over her life with his haunting obsession.

Chapter 23

Matt tried to find out as much as he could about the production of nitro-glycerine. Even though his research was thorough, he soon discovered that his knowledge was little more than basic. He thought that the Internet might prove very useful, but the references always led him down blind alleys. For obvious reasons, nobody was going to publicly spell out how to make the obnoxious explosive. He came to the conclusion that in the end, any success would be down to experiment, guesswork and his own good luck.

He managed to buy the glycerine locally in small quantities until he'd accumulated a litre of the clear, greasy liquid. Melissa ordered the hardware for the manufacture of the explosive and bit by bit, it was purchased and stored in the garage. The last things to arrive were the two acids and finally, they had everything needed to begin making the volatile liquid.

As soon as all the equipment and chemicals had been assembled, Matt began to pester Melissa about the safest way they could go about making the nitro. Although she had agreed to help him, she was still worried about the dangers involved and spent numerous unhappy evenings trying to dissuade him from going ahead. When she began to suspect that he was at the point of tackling the nitro on his own, she finally gave in to his demands. She promised to come round after school one evening and answer all his questions.

* * * * *

The doorbell chimed. Matt was waiting expectantly and he quickly invited Melissa in. He greeted her with a friendly kiss, but she seemed distant and reserved. It was a side of her he'd never seen before.

Melissa took off her coat and went through to the comfortable lounge. Matt had been brewing coffee and the delicious smell made her feel less anxious.

Neatly arranged on a small table was the coffee jug, a plate of her favourite bourbon creams, a bottle of Martell and two glasses.

He sat beside her on the settee, fussing and plying her with fresh coffee and biscuits. "Do you fancy a cognac to go with the coffee, Mel?"

She responded in a deadpan matter-of-fact manner. "You don't have to be all sweetness and light, Matthew," she used his full name, "you're behaving like a little boy. I said that I would help. I haven't come round to tell you anything different, even though you know how much all this scares me."

Matt said nothing at first, but looked at her sympathetically. He became serious. "I know this is going against your better instinct, but," he sighed, "I have to have a weapon to fight with. This is the only thing I can think of. You know this gang are a desperate, well-armed bunch. I have no choice."

He gestured, spreading his hands, but Melissa could not look him in the face. She was so much in love with him and she couldn't refuse to help any longer. She swallowed hard and started to fumble about in the small attaché case she'd brought. Without further protest, she extracted a thin file and began to explain the calculations that she'd made.

"First, we have to know the precise quantity of each reagent, so I've written out the reaction equation in chemical symbols, here." She pointed to her work. "I then calculated the mass in gram-moles required for each reagent. With that done, I worked out proportionately larger amounts for our needs. It's a good job you stumbled across the percentage strengths of the acids in that old encyclopaedia, because I can't find confirmation of them anywhere. I don't know how accurate they are, but I'll have no problem mixing the required strengths. However, if those figures are wrong, we're in big trouble."

Matt followed her maths closely, noisily crunching a biscuit as he concentrated on her explanations. "Great stuff, Mel. I'm with you so far."

"Don't get too excited. That was the easy part. The greatest obstacle to our success is the reaction itself. It's exothermic, very exothermic. That's what makes it highly unstable."

He shrugged. "So, the problem is basically a simple one. A great deal of heat will be generated when the chemicals are mixed? Is that right?"

Melissa glared at him. "You just don't get it, do you? The nitro-glycerine becomes more unstable the hotter it gets and it can explode spontaneously." She shook her head and her auburn hair cascaded about her shoulders. "Damn it, Matt. I've no idea how high we can let the temperature get before it explodes on its own. I've already told you it's susceptible to go off if it's jarred violently, but that's when the temperature is kept low. When it's hot, God knows. Even the slightest knock might set it off. It's pure madness!"

"Don't worry, we'll find a way to keep the temperature down. You must have a gut feeling about what it should be?"

"Matt, I'm only guessing. I have no idea how much heat will be generated. This is chemical engineering. The commercial companies who make this stuff will know exactly what to expect and have backup systems to protect their production tanks. The only figure I've managed to glean suggests we have to keep the temperature down to about 20 degrees centigrade. That scares me, Matt. It's not very high, we could easily lose control of the reaction."

Matt tried to calm Melissa. He was determined to soldier on, no matter what the dangers were, but he knew she could see every single flaw in his madcap plan. *Would she keep her nerve for him*? He poured her a cognac.

"It shouldn't be that difficult to control the temperature, Mel. Look at it rationally. All we need is a continuous supply of cold running water. Something like a kitchen tap."

Melissa pushed the proffered drink away and flew at him angrily. "You stupid idiot, Morgan. You're not seriously thinking of making the stuff at home, are you? It's far too dangerous. Only a lunatic would consider such a scheme."

Matt had to be careful. He suddenly realised that she was close to walking away. "I didn't say I intended to make it at home, did I?"

"You're bloody daft enough to try, but unless you find some field in the middle of nowhere, then you can count me out."

Matt tried playing it cool, to diffuse the tricky situation. "Okay. I get the message. So, we find some deserted barn in the Peak District. What then?"

Despite the needling reservation that made Melissa want to quit, she continued to give Matt her best advice. "We'll need a water bath containing crushed ice. What's more, to make sure the heat of the reaction is transferred as quickly as possible to the ice, the chemicals will have to be kept thoroughly mixed. You're the physicist, you'll have to rig up a stirring device."

"Don't worry about that side of things, I can sort it out."

Melissa closed her file abruptly and handed it to Matt. "There. Have I done enough to satisfy your stupid plan?"

He could see the beginnings of tears in her damp eyes and her lips begin to tremble. Before she could react further to her nagging fears, he held her close and kissed her tenderly. She responded warmly to his affections, but quickly broke away from his arms and looked longingly into his face.

She whispered hoarsely, "Matthew. Please make love to me."

"What, right now?"

"Yes, now my darling."

He gave her a coy smile. "Wow, Melissa, you bet!"

That's all she wanted to hear. She kicked off her shoes and unzipped her jeans. Pulling them down to the floor along with her knickers, she stepped out and left an untidy heap on the floor. Matt barely had time to take in the triangular flash of auburn hair below her flat stomach before she switched off the nearby standard lamp. In the warming glow of the firelight, she found him again, but their mouths met only fleetingly before she was helping to remove his trousers in a hurried frenzy. They lay together on the soft hearthrug and their warm, naked groins came together in a breath-taking and exquisite act of copulation. It had been a long time since Matt had last made love, but he could never remember it being as good as this. She held him tightly inside her as he began to push hard, but his body was soon out of control. His feelings were on a plane far above his normal senses. His actions quickly became frantic and although he didn't want it to stop, there was nothing he could do. It ended with an explosion of ecstatic pleasure. He shuddered with delight and moaned aloud.

Melissa lay beneath him enjoying every second of their embrace. From the moment he had penetrated her, she'd been in a heaven of euphoria. At last, she had given herself completely to her man. She didn't expect their lovemaking would last very long because she could feel his urgency and excitement. That didn't matter. He had possessed her. It would be longer and more entertaining next time. She would see to that. Half an hour later, that proved to be the case as they lay in one another's arms completely satiated.

* * * * *

Matt spent most of the following weekend driving around the winding roads of North Derbyshire, looking for isolated locations with derelict barns. During his travels, he came upon a small number of properties and investigated the suitability of each. He chose three of the most promising venues and photographed the aspect, accessibility and condition of each site. He downloaded them onto his laptop computer and Melissa helped to scrutinise the details of each location. Matt favoured one in particular, but he kept it to himself.

Melissa was secretly tempted to talk to Laura about her worries and Matt's gung-ho attitude to danger, but she remained loyal, so that Laura didn't become embroiled in his plot. Even so, she still kept on trying to put stumbling blocks in his way until she could hold out no longer. She finally agreed to his timetable, little realising that it was an empty sham.

It was never Matt's intention to endanger Melissa and although he wasn't unduly worried about their planning, he knew things could go badly wrong. He was all set to make the explosive himself, the following Tuesday night, one week before his arrangement to do it with Melissa.

A problem arose when Laura returned unexpectedly on Sunday afternoon and announced that her work rota had changed, giving her four days leave. This threw Matt's schedule into confusion because she would be around when he needed the house free to make his preparations. He rang Melissa and suggested that she might like to take Laura for a girl's night out, as she'd done nothing but occupy herself with work since the tragedy of losing Kirsty. Christmas was fast approaching. Melissa thought that a visit to Meadowhall, the extensive shopping mall on the outskirts of the city, would be a good idea. It was always tastefully decorated and full of bargains to tempt the late-night shoppers. Laura seemed excited. Matt also suggested they might take in a movie at the multiplex cinema. They decided to go the following night and Matt grinned to himself with quite satisfaction. His own plans would now have to be brought forward a day, but it didn't matter because he was organised and ready to go.

Melissa picked Laura up after school the next evening. They were both in high spirits and chatted excitedly, anticipating an enjoyable shopping spree.

Matt was so happy to see Laura having some fun. She needed to forget the sadness that had burdened her for so long and Melissa was like a surrogate sister. He waved them off and started work immediately. The freezer had been packed with plastic ice cube bags. He smashed the cubes into smaller fragments and emptied them into an insulated picnic box. Within minutes, his short checklist was completed and he left with the Jaguar packed to the hilt with all his equipment.

The previous week had been unseasonably mild, but darkness preceded a subtle change in the weather. Matt drove into the High Peak expecting a calm evening, but the weather quickly deteriorated as a cold northerly breeze scudded over the hills. By the time he reached his destination, the light breeze was rising to gale force and heavy rain was whipping against his car.

Matt drove the Jaguar off the main road and down a well-worn track. He halted his car a 100 yards further along beneath a row of pine trees. The engine fell silent and the only sound was the soulful howling of the air through the trees, orchestrated by the strengthening wind. In the distance, a lonely grumble of thunder hinted at an advancing storm.

He approached the silhouette of the old barn and shone a powerful torch at the door. There was no lock and luckily, the rusty hinges still worked and kept the massive doors from jamming solid against the floor. There was a loud creak as he shouldered the left-hand one, edging it open until the gap was wide enough to get his equipment through.

Matt began looking around and noticed that a section of the roof had collapsed. There were timbers and tiles strewn everywhere. The wind outside rose further and the barn creaked and groaned sympathetically. The yawning hole above seemed to accentuate the noise, but at ground level, the air was still. Rain had swept through the gap in the high-vaulted ceiling, but he found an area of the floor which was dry and ideal for him to set up production. He went back and forth to the car several times and at last everything had been moved into the relative safety of the barn. He managed to close the door behind him.

Once he'd rigged up suitable lighting with four storm lanterns, he decided to use the fallen timbers to set up a bench, saving the inconvenience of having to work on the floor. He quickly managed to manhandle several smaller beams to make a rough and ready table. Matt began opening the boxes and set to work building the apparatus. He'd practised constructing and dismantling everything at least half a dozen times, so the procedure was familiar to him. The main reaction vessel was clamped firmly in the water bath, which was packed with crushed ice. The measured quantities of acid were then carefully added. A temperature probe was connected to a digital thermometer with a vivid, green display. A small motorised propeller to stir the mixture was inserted down the side arm of the flask and tested to make sure everything worked perfectly. Finally, a small burette with a glass tap was clamped in place over the neck of the reactor.

Melissa's calculations were based on half the glycerine Matt had purchased; so, he began to pour the agreed amount of clear, viscous liquid into the burette. The battery-driven motor was switched on. It quietly whirred in the flask and began to churn the mixture of corrosive acids. The illuminated temperature display read 5 degrees. All was ready.

The faraway storm suddenly seemed close and a crash of thunder reverberated around the barn. Matt continued to absorb himself in his work. A thin trickle of sweat prickled his collar as he began to open the burette and allowed the glycerine to drip onto the turbulent mixture below. The irreversible reaction had begun and he felt a restriction in his throat as he began to realise just what he'd started. He tried to relieve his nervousness by joking to himself that he was a latter-day Frankenstein, complete with experiment and electrical storm, but the occasional sudden clap of thunder only scared him and served to make the tension worse. He had a fearful dread that things would go wrong and he tried to clear his mind, watching transfixed, as the glycerine dribbled onto the hungry acid.

Heat was immediately generated by the reaction and recorded by the bright display. The temperature quickly climbed... 20 degrees... 30 degrees. Matt started getting uneasy at the rapid rise... 40 degrees... 50 degrees... then 55.

Jesus, what should I do? Mel said to keep it below 20!

After what seemed an endless wait, the rate of increase began to slow down. Matt ran his fingers nervously through his hair, his lips felt dry and his senses were at fever pitch. The quiet motor hummed a constant reassuring tune and he watched as if mesmerised. The reaction was still too fast for his liking, but at last, the ice was beginning to do its work.

Overhead, the storm was reaching its climax and the sound of lashing rain hammered the protective roof of the barn. Far below, Matt had his attention focused on the critical point of the reaction. He pleaded with the temperature as though it had a will of its own. "Come on you sod, level out."

All at once, a monstrous gust of wind rocked the barn, breaking the spell of his insane fixation. A single timber had been dislodged from the roof, falling to the ground not more than a dozen feet away. Clay tiles shattered and flew through the air like shrapnel from an exploding shell. One such piece screeched past his face and smashed into his delicate apparatus. The tap of the burette was snapped cleanly off and the controlled descent of the glycerine was now replaced by a continuous glug, glug, glug of free-flowing liquid. It dropped into the corrosive acid and the rate of the reaction increased apace. The large, ugly lump of tile had also hit the ice bath, cracking it into two pieces, allowing crushed ice and water to spill out over the floor. The scene was one of pure horror. It was a situation so fluky that it defied belief.

Glycerine was being devoured at a phenomenal speed and with no coolant to dissipate the heat, the core of the reaction was beginning to approach instability. Matt glanced at the thermometer, his only guide to safety. It was already reading 65 degrees… 75 degrees. The numbers seemed to go round faster and faster.

Matt gasped. "Ohhhh, my God! It's going to blow."

Gripped by sheer panic, he turned and fled, reaching the door in an instant. He pushed hard against it, but it refused to budge. He was at the very edge of despair when he remembered it didn't open outwards, but inwards. He heaved against the solid wood and managed to open a gap, just large enough to squeeze through.

He was lurching across the rain-swept track, when the nitro went off. The explosion, when it came, was a tremendous thump and the roof of the barn was lifted off its walls. The ground shook, but the thick stone walls resisted the blast and saved Matt from certain death. The force of the explosion had gone skywards, disintegrating the rest of the roof. A sheet of flames shot 20 feet into the air and jagged lumps of shattered tile whistled through the darkness. Silent splinters of wood hurtled through the air, ready to impale anything that got in their way.

Matt had thrown himself to the ground at the instant of the blast and although scores of smaller fragments rained down on him, he managed to escape unscathed. He leant on his elbow and looked back with dismay at the massive doors of the barn. They had been blown completely off their hinges. One hung at a strange angle against the outer wall and the other lay flat in the nearby grass.

Matt swallowed hard and gingerly picked himself up from the sludgy earth, reflecting ruefully that only seconds before he'd been on the other side of those very same doors. He went back and peered inside the shell of the barn. A small fire was burning fiercely where he'd set up his equipment and where nature had foiled his plot. There was nothing left to indicate he'd ever been there and a new heavy downpour was already beginning to dampen the flames. The thunder continued to crash in the distance and flashes of lightening streaked the sky.

Matt stumbled back to his Jaguar and with rain streaming down his mud-spattered face, he laughed at the irony of the situation. He knew that if any locals inspected the barn, they would put the damage and fire down to a lightning strike.

He was blameless. He sped off into the night, leaving the sad debacle to the elements.

Chapter 24

Matthew Morgan left the High Peak in a state of discomfort and irritation. He'd been badly shaken and was beginning to question his own sanity. *Why was he so obdurate and why couldn't he overcome his overriding need for revenge*? Try as he might, he couldn't shake the conviction that his cause was just, nor could he come to terms with his recent failure. The more distance he put between himself and the barn, the easier it became to blank out the disaster. He found himself determined to carry on.

He was still wrapped in his own thoughts as he arrived home. He was wet, dirty and dishevelled and barged through the door in an ill-tempered mood, little expecting the girls to be there.

Laura was the first to hear his noisy entrance and rushed forward to find him. "Dad. Are you all right? Where have you been?"

Melissa, a look of intense worry etched on her face appeared at his side. "God, you look awful? We were worried sick."

The girls flanked Matt and helped him out of his wet coat. They led him to the warm fireside and sat him down. Laura knelt before him and tried to get some sense out of him, but he remained stubbornly silent, glaring wildly into the flames. He'd intended to clean himself up before they got back and carry on as though nothing had happened, but he'd been rumbled and he knew it.

Melissa brought him a huge slug of whisky and it burned his throat as he quickly gulped it down. Any sympathy for him quickly dissipated and was replaced by an atmosphere of combined anger and resentment. Before the liquor had a chance to loosen his tongue, he found himself facing a verbal onslaught.

Melissa tore into him. "I had to tell Laura what you were planning, so don't you dare tell us a single lie, Morgan. We're not stupid, we know what you've been up to. My God, you've got a lot to answer for. Just who do you think you are?"

Matt shrugged. "I was hoping to get back before you and…"

"Well, we scuppered that little scheme, didn't we?"

Laura cut in abrasively. "We came home early because we thought you'd be feeling lonely. I couldn't believe it when Melissa told me what you were up to."

He muttered loudly, "That's because you weren't meant to know."

Melissa jabbed her finger into his shoulder. "Don't go accusing me of giving your hideous secrets away." She smouldered on without pause. "What a devious bastard you are, Morgan, quietly getting us out of the way so you could go and follow your pitiful little obsession."

"It wasn't like that."

"Well, what the hell was it like. You tell me. By the look of you, it all went wrong. You could have been killed tonight. Just what do think you're doing?"

Before he could answer, Laura rounded on him. "What's gotten into you, Dad. What a mindless thing to do. What's your game? Is it disfigurement or a death wish?"

"But that's the point, it's not a game."

"Don't be obtuse. You know what we're driving at."

"Laura's right. I thought you trusted me, but it's clear you don't. Is it because I'm only a woman? I'm not strong enough for you, is that it?"

Matt responded quietly, trying to diffuse the situation. "Look, I told you before, I didn't want you taking any chances."

Melissa suddenly loathed him for his response and exploded. "What! Don't you dare use that pathetic argument against me. We'd agreed a pact and as far as I'm concerned that means everything. You just can't see it from anybody else's side can you? Do you seriously think I could stand back and watch you taking all the risks? Unless it hasn't registered yet, I'm not an itsy-bitsy female, prepared to wait at home, ready to come running at your beck and call."

Matt stood up and threw his arms up in a defensive gesture. "Okay. Point taken."

"Don't be so damned condescending, Morgan."

His defence was blown, but they weren't finished with him yet.

Laura blustered on. "You're so selfish. What about poor Melissa? She cares. She wants to help. If I'd known what you were planning, I'd have done anything to help too. I want to get back at those shits who killed Kirsty just as much as you do. You're so wrapped up in your own little isolated world. It's no good, you have to trust us."

He had no reply. His only recourse was to accept their slating and back off gracefully.

"Right, okay. I'm sorry. I apologise, I was wrong."

"Wrong! Wrong! You certainly were, buster. But don't think that a sorry will suddenly put things right."

"Dad, you've really hurt Melissa. She told me everything. She's given you so much help and now it's all been thrown back in her face."

Matt sighed loudly, "Look, I've said, I'm sorry and I mean it. What more can I do?"

Still, he could not quell Melissa's fury and she snarled at him with her full Irish brogue. "For a start, you can learn to treat me as an equal. I thought you were different from other men, but you're just the same: selfish, sneaky and underhand. I don't know why I bother. Anyway, I'm telling you now," she threw back her auburn locks and thundered at him, "I can't stand not knowing if you're alive or dead. I need to be there to make sure you stay in one piece. If you try a trick like this again, I'm finished with you and you can get on with whatever you want on your own."

Melissa was suddenly a spent force. The complexion of her face changed and tears began to well in the corners of her eyes. She immediately grabbed her bag and rushed from the house.

Matt set off after her, but Laura caught his arm. "It's no good tonight, Dad. Let her go."

"But…"

Laura looked him in the face and saw the concern in his eyes. She saw something that touched her and suddenly her attitude softened. "You really care about her, don't you?"

He looked sheepishly at his daughter. She'd never seriously asked about their relationship before.

"Yes. She's become very special to me."

"Have you told her so?"

He hesitated. "Yes, of course, but I daren't let myself get involved too deeply. Not until this business is over."

Laura touched his cheek. "You silly old thing, Dad. You really don't understand women, do you?"

"It's been a long time since your mother died. I don't know anything anymore."

Laura put her finger to his lips and smiled. "Well then, I'm the messenger. She adores you. She's not stopped talking about you all night. You only need to tell her how you really feel about her. That's all she wants to hear. Love doesn't ask why or how; she'd do anything for you. But you have to chill out and be yourself. Don't lose her, Dad, she's made for you."

Matt grinned back. "I take it you have a soft spot for her?"

"You bet. She's a wonderful person."

"So, what about tonight? Do you think I've gone too far?"

"Don't worry. It's just her reaction to the fear of losing you. She was worried silly when we came home to find those ice cube bags stuffed in the bin. It didn't take long for her to put two and two together. She couldn't keep your secret any longer. All we could do was sit around and wait because we didn't know where you'd gone."

"I never thought of it like that. I just expected to be back."

"Well, knowing how she feels about you, I suspect there's no major harm done this time, but she's got a wild temper and a strong will and perhaps she means what she says. Anyway, you've certainly got some bridge building to do tomorrow."

* * * * *

The next day, Melissa avoided him at work, but he managed to catch up with her at lunchtime. Matt didn't have to work too hard to get her to forgive him and after patching up their quarrel, he persuaded her to go out for dinner with him in the evening. They had recently found a small bistro, which served a variety of plentiful, inexpensive dishes. It was now their favourite spot and Matt booked a table for two.

Whilst they were relaxing after the meal, he described in detail what had happened the previous night.

Melissa listened intently and finally gave her verdict. "I think you were so fortunate. Fate might have just been on your side with that storm."

"Why? I thought I was in control."

"You were running the reaction temperature far too high. I told you to keep it well below 20 for safety. I'm certain it would have gone up, even if the damage to the apparatus hadn't occurred. You'd have been duped into a waiting game, watching the numbers creep up on the thermometer until suddenly, wham! It's all over." She reached across, grasped his hand firmly and spoke softly. "At least you had the sense to make a run for it when everything got smashed up. By the way, I've already ordered everything we need for another go. But after listening to the problems you had last night, we need to alter our plan slightly."

"In what way?"

"First and foremost, I'm not prepared to let you try this stunt again without my full assistance, but what's equally important is the need for a decent supply of water. I've come to the conclusion that the reaction vessel has to be kept cool under a fast-running tap of cold water, so the heat can get away quickly. Until you can find such a source, the equipment I've ordered will be delivered to my flat and that's where it stays until you can convince me otherwise." She grinned wickedly at him and Matt knew there was nothing he could say or do to make her change her mind.

* * * * *

Fortunately, the problem resolved itself quickly. Matt was resigned to spending time during his Christmas holidays looking for further locations in the Peak District. Before he went any further, he decided to look at the other two barns he'd already earmarked. He noticed on one of the photographs there was a small building behind and it looked very much like a farmhouse.

The next night, he paid it a visit and it did indeed turn out to be an old cottage. Although the doors and windows were missing, the roof was intact and his torch light showed that the inside had not been vandalised. The huge pot sink in the kitchen was still in one piece and it didn't take him long to find an old stopcock, controlling the water supply. After some initial resistance, he eased it open and his reward was a fast-flowing stream of clear, cold water. Matt punched the air in jubilation.

* * * * *

Laura had insisted on becoming part of their team and although it had precipitated another almighty row, Matt was now resigned to the fact that she was old enough to make her own decisions. She had quickly forged a strong alliance with Melissa and he had to accept that they were all in it together. They agreed on a time when her airline schedule provided a natural break.

It was another chilly night, early in the new year, when they made another bid to manufacture the explosive. They drove in two cars to the chosen venue.

Although she didn't like her role, Laura agreed to act as back up. Once she'd helped to unload their equipment, she had agreed to sit in her car and act as look out at the entrance to the track leading up to the farm cottage.

The floor of the cottage was cleared of any debris, should they need to vacate the premises quickly. In the ancient kitchen, Melissa expertly set up the apparatus. This time everything went according to plan. There was an initial surge of ten degrees to the reaction, but the icy waters of the Derbyshire Peak District, gushing over the reaction vessel dissipated the heat. Melissa made numerous fine adjustments to the flow of the reagents and under her competent eye, the temperature stayed below the required limit. Within half an hour of the start, the brew had been concocted, the reaction was complete and the liquid cool.

Melissa looked at Matt with trepidation and then at the pale-yellow oil lying dormant at the base of the clear glass flask. She whispered almost reverently, "God, what have we done? Now we've made it, we have to get rid of it."

Matt spoke firmly and reassuringly, trying to allay her fears. "Don't worry Mel. I've already decided where to store it."

"But if you slip and drop that flask, you'll blow us both to kingdom come."

Matt put a comforting arm around her shoulder. "That's why I need you. I need another pair of hands."

He grasped the flask carefully and Melissa began to dismantle the apparatus. They worked in silence as their pulses thumped and the adrenaline flowed in their veins. There had to be zero error.

Matt spoke softly with a trace of nervousness in his voice, "Okay, bring the storage tubes."

Melissa delved into a nearby box and produced a rack containing five, brand new tubes made with reassuringly thick glass. In a gloved hand, she held each up in turn, whilst Matt meticulously divided the noxious oily explosive into smaller units.

Melissa stoppered and racked them safely. She sighed deeply and clutched his hand. "Come on outside, Matt. I need a break from this."

She led him out into the chilly night air. They were quickly reminded of the terror of the ordeal, as the hot sweat on their bodies quickly cooled, turning their skins cold and clammy.

Melissa shuddered in discomfort. "How the hell did I ever let you talk me into this?"

He chided her playfully. "Listen Reagan, as far as I can remember, you invited yourself."

"To be sure Matthew, I think you're trying to get your own back."

"Who? Not me."

He smiled in the darkness and pulled her towards him, holding her close. For a fleeting moment, Melissa felt safe as they clung to each other in silence, listening to the sounds of the winter night.

"Come on Mel, there's lots more work to do before we're finished. You carry on boxing the equipment and I'll start work on the hide for the nitro."

Melissa made a quick phone call to Laura and promised they'd be finished and in the nearest pub within the hour.

Matt went back inside the farmhouse. He collected his spade and a wooden box which he'd recently made. There was an old stone wall bordering the property on the north side. It was in perfect condition and extended continuously for a 100 yards except for a gap, wide enough to take a tractor. It gave access to a field and a small copse of trees behind the cottage.

Matt picked a spot, along the base of the wall, 20 yards from the opening and proceeded to remove a slice of turf. He dug a hole big enough to accept his box, fitting it carefully just below ground level. The box and lid had been lined with glass-fibre insulation. He removed the top to reveal the underlying space. It was now ready to take the explosive.

When he returned to the cottage, Melissa had finished and was waiting patiently for him.

"Before you say anything else, Matt, I'm helping you move this stuff." She pointed to the rack of glass tubes. "You're welcome to do the carrying, but you need someone to light the way." She held out her hand for the torch. Matt could see, in the poor light, the fear and determination in her eyes. They didn't speak and Matt did as he was told, picking up the small, light rack of tubes.

Melissa led the way outside and stopped. "Where to, darling?"

He gesticulated with his head. "Over there. There's a wall. Head for the gap. Can you see it?"

Bending forward, she bathed the ground ahead of him in a bright, yellow light. The short journey to the hole was tediously slow, but eventually the rack of nitro-glycerine was gently lowered into its prepared space. A top layer of insulation was packed round the explosive and the loose lid replaced. The box was then covered with a thin layer of soil and the slice of turf re-laid in its original position. Restoration of the site was complete and casual observers would find it difficult to spot that the ground had ever been disturbed.

Finally, Matt scattered the spare soil from the hole and marked the centre of the turf with a small lump of stone from the top of the wall. When he'd finished, he was breathing heavily.

"That's it for now. How do you feel, Mel?"

"Tense and scared, but at least that stuff is out of harm's way."

"Well, you can relax now. The worst is over. Let's finish up as quickly as possible and get to Laura. She'll be desperate to know we're safe."

* * * * *

The following night, Matt was in his garage. He was rummaging around an ancient set of drawers. Eventually, he found what he was looking for. It was a box of spent-brass cartridge cases from his shooting days. He put one of the shell cases in his lathe and cut off its base, so it became a brass sleeve. The inside of both ends were drilled a short distance in, increasing the diameter very slightly. This created two small shoulders at either end of the sleeve.

Matt picked up a crossbow bolt. It was fairly short with fletching at one end and a sharp point at the other. He proceeded to cut the shaft of the bolt into two pieces near to its tip. From the longer piece, he removed a section of shaft the same length as the shell case. The brass sleeve was then pushed over the shaft and it was held tightly against the inside shoulder. The other piece of shaft, connected to the point, was slotted into the other end of the sleeve. The crossbow bolt now contained the brass section, but was back to its original length. The work was precision engineering. The final fit had to be push perfect with only the minimum amount of pressure needed to slide the tip into position.

Matt tested the modified bolt. He set up an old cushion on a shelf at the far end of the garage. He opened the up-and-over door and took the weapon halfway down his drive so the range was acceptable. He took careful aim and was elated when he scored a direct hit in the centre of the cushion. Happy with the result, he set to work converting the rest of his bolts.

At last, the job was done and Matt felt a surge of pride. He chuckled aloud. "I just need to prime those empty shell casings with some nitro-glycerine and Bang! We're in business."

* * * * *

Matthew decided his next priority was for transport. He'd long been impressed by the use of the old-style Mini in the film *The Italian Job*. These small, versatile cars would be ideal in the Capital's traffic. Whilst restoring his Jaguar, he'd assembled a vast array of tools, including welding gear and a paint compressor. He was highly skilled in dealing with rust and engine wear, so he had no fear tackling the problems posed by old cars.

Matt decided to buy two Minis and managed to get them cheaply from a motor auction, paying for each with cash. Cars were chosen with a current tax disc and he supplied a false name and address for the logbook changes.

He rented a lock-up garage, large enough to hold both vehicles and began restoring them with great energy and enthusiasm. The challenge was enjoyable and once all the major repairs had been made, tuning the Minis proved to be a straightforward task. Matt resprayed them both in *British Racing Green* for ease of identification. The paint job was superficial and it only took him a few evenings to do the work. When the cars had been finished to his satisfaction, he filed off the engine and chassis numbers.

Whilst he was rebuilding the cars, Melissa had spent several evenings after work, approaching some of the backstreet garages and had managed to acquire some sets of fictitious number plates. Each new set could be fastened in place with double-sided tape for easy removal. Only the tax disc identified the original registration number of each car; so, the small area containing the offending detail was cut away and replaced by a slip of similarly coloured paper. The cars would still appear to have a current tax disc and from a distance, no one would spot the changes. The Minis were now anonymous and if they had to be abandoned anywhere, they were totally untraceable.

It had taken Matt less than three weeks, working late every night and at weekends to get them fully serviceable. By early February, the work was finally completed.

Chapter 25

Joe Harker had no trouble in persuading Kate Stephenson to help him spy on Charles Rydell. She would have done anything he'd asked, but equally, she now despised her boss and was completely receptive to the surveillance operation.

For the next few weeks, she watched Rydell's every move and made shorthand notes describing his moods and temperament. During this period, he behaved in his usual offhanded manner towards her, then something happened and he became perceptively more insular. Kate picked up the change immediately. He had always directed her to bring him files on a whole range of important issues, but suddenly he took to rummaging through filing cabinets on his own. On a number of occasions, she even found him alone in the records department, researching information and making photocopies of a whole batch of files. This sudden deviation from his natural authoritarian style to a more introspective one made her highly suspicious. He'd began working very late at the office and sometimes she made some flimsy excuse to stay on herself, so she could keep an eye on him. This became a real source of frustration, because he never left his paperwork unattended, making it impossible for her to get even a glimpse at the documents he was working on.

Late one afternoon, she got her first breakthrough. Rydell had been working on a small pile of old reports and the instant she approached, he'd nervously flicked shut the document he was reading. *Why was he being so secretive?*

She sat in her outer office pondering how she could get a look at the reports when the phone rang. It was from the Whip's Office at the House of Commons and he'd been summoned to cast his vote in the government lobby. His party was in trouble, trying to force through some tricky legislation and they needed every available vote. Rydell was aware that a division was imminent, but the call came much sooner than he'd anticipated. He left in a hurry, but not before he'd locked his office behind him.

Kate chuckled. "You still don't know about my key, Charlie boy."

She gave him ten minutes to get away, then let herself in. Calmly, she sat in his comfortable leather chair and began sifting through the dozen or so files which had intrigued her earlier. The contents seemed insignificant and were merely maintenance reports on some of the oldest and most overcrowded prisons in the country. Kate couldn't find any obvious reason for his interest in the documents. At the bottom of the pile lay a single sheet of A4 paper. On it, written in Rydell's own hand was a list, placing each prison in some kind of order. She decided that it might be of some use. Picking up the list, she went over to the fax machine in her office and dialled her home number. The contents of the single sheet were instantly transmitted onto her own machine.

Having left Rydell's office exactly as she found it, she returned next door, put her coat on and left.

* * * * *

Charles Rydell had worked very hard to meet the deadline imposed by Tyburn and Lush. After one of his regular weekly progress reports, he was invited to meet them again, at a small coffee shop off the Edgware Road.

When he arrived, he was shown to a secluded table where he waited impatiently for 20 minutes for the others to arrive. He was taken somewhat by surprise when they suddenly appeared from the kitchen, behind him. They sat down at the table, on either side of him.

"You're late," he blustered.

Tyburn didn't respond, but clicked his fingers and a waiter materialised to take their order for tea and cream cakes.

"Don't fret, Mr Rydell, we had to be sure you weren't being followed. It's not that we don't trust you, but these days, you can never be sure."

Lush, who had previously not spoken, rubbed his floppy jowls and got straight down to business. "Please give us a full resume of your progress to date. We need all the details that you couldn't give over the phone. Take your time and don't miss anything out. We'll decide whether it's important or not."

Just then the food arrived and when the teas had been poured, Rydell began to recount the arrangements he'd made during the previous six weeks. "I've managed to organise the details you required without raising any questions. As I mentioned a few weeks ago, the prison I chose was Hull, in the old East Riding of Yorkshire. It's a Victorian prison with very poor facilities and acts as a dispersal point for a large part of Yorkshire and North Lincolnshire.

All convicted prisoners in its catchment are initially sent there to be processed, with the majority eventually moving on to other establishments. It's also a remand prison and like many of its kind, it is insanely overcrowded. The place is always very busy with new inmates, both long and short stay, so it was ideal cover for the unsavoury characters I've sent there. Another important factor in its choice is that it acts as a training prison, so there are many new and inexperienced prison officers on the staff. Its last inspection was as little as six months ago and the report stated that morale was at an all-time low."

"Good. So, how far exactly have you got?"

"As I reported some time ago, your man Bradshaw and a number of the other men you asked me to locate were moved to Hull two weeks before Christmas. That was easy."

Tyburn interrupted, "But what about the governor?"

Rydell continued pompously, "The situation couldn't be better. The ex-governor retired a year ago. His assistant, who was an automatic choice for his replacement, suffered a heart attack six months ago after the inspection, and he's still not back at work. He's applied to take premature retirement on the grounds of ill health, so I'm under pressure to find a replacement as soon as possible. At the moment, there's a temporary governor who's a much younger, inexperienced man, taken from the ranks of the staff at Hull. For your benefit, I've been tracking his progress and initial reports indicate that he's weak and the place is beginning to get out of hand. The situation seems to be resolving itself in your favour. I'll just delay finding a replacement and say that I'm giving the new man a chance to prove himself."

Tyburn grinned appreciatively. "Excellent, Charles. So far, so good."

Chapter 26

Kate Stephenson found it very difficult to find anything of further interest about Rydell in the next few weeks. She felt sure he was doing things without trying to raise suspicion, but he was both cautious and cunning and he left no clues for her to follow.

It was late one Friday afternoon, towards the end of January that she next picked up a hint of useful information. There was a phone call from Ken Waterford. Kate recalled that he used to make frequent calls to Charles Rydell, but she couldn't remember the last time she'd put a call through from him. She'd eavesdropped their telephone conversations before, but now she was more inquisitive than ever. *Perhaps they were implicated together in some way?*

The office was quiet, so she decided to listen in again.

Rydell sounded irate. "I thought we'd agreed not to discuss this over the phone. What are you trying to do to us, Ken?"

"Listen, Charles. Doreen and I have decided we can't go through with this anymore. The Hull business could turn out to be a nightmare."

Charles groaned to himself. He wished he'd never confided his dealings with Tyburn to Ken, but he'd wanted to know everything and had threatened to expose the blackmail before, if he was kept in the dark.

"For goodness' sake, not over the phone, Ken. Someone might be listening on the line."

Kate suddenly had a feeling of foreboding. *Did Rydell know what she was doing?* There was just the slightest warning of disaster as she picked up the sound of a bump on the line.

Next door, Rydell had tried to put the receiver down carefully, but the taut flex had gently pulled the instrument against a heavy paperweight. He spun in his chair and moved swiftly across the room to the door. He threw it open with a flourish, certain that he'd find Kate Stephenson eavesdropping on his phone call. He was amazed and somehow disappointed to find his secretary missing. The far door onto the corridor was slightly ajar, but no sounds came from the polished floor beyond. He was alone.

Shrugging his shoulders, he returned to his office, speaking out wearily to himself. "My God! This business is making me paranoid."

Outside in the corridor, Kate was petrified, standing with her spine pressed hard against the wall. She held her breath, unable to move, fear pounding unmercifully in her ears. Rydell had burst into her office and her mind screamed. *Please don't let him come out and find me here.*

It seemed an age before he left her outer office. At last, she let out a long sigh to calm her frayed nerves. *What should she do now? Keep well away and out of further suspicion? Or should she gamble all and go back and try to pick up the conversation again?* She weighed up the odds and decided to risk it. Rydell had just checked her office and so, he was more likely to be off guard.

Kate crept back to her desk and picked up the phone once more.

"Look, Charles, I'm telling you straight, we want no more of this."

"But, Ken, don't be irrational. This will ruin you and Doreen, and what about the kids?"

"They're old enough to look after themselves now and if life gets too unpleasant here, then we've got more than enough money to lead a decent lifestyle somewhere abroad."

"Ken. Please, just do one thing for me. Will you give me a few days to think out my future before you say anything? We can talk about it tonight at the Constituency Dinner."

"Charles, it's over. We'll give you tonight and that's all. But tomorrow, we go to the police. I'm sorry, so very sorry."

The phone went dead.

Kate was astounded by what she'd heard. She reacted quickly and went over to the main office door, making the pretence that she'd just returned by closing it noisily. She tapped on Rydell's door and coolly went through. "You wanted to dictate a letter, Minister, after your phone call?" She looked down at the man she'd just addressed. At first, he said nothing, but merely stared into space. His face was ashen and his eyes were distant.

Eventually, he spoke, but it was from a dreamlike trance as though she didn't exist. "I don't feel well, Miss Stephenson. Cancel the rest of my engagements for today. I must go home."

* * * * *

After his conversation with Ken Waterford, Rydell had left the home office and gone for a long walk along the Thames embankment. The afternoon was mild and the breeze off the river helped to clear his mind. When his anger and frustration had finally settled, his own selfish resolve was hardened and he knew what he'd have to do.

He returned to his flat and sat by the phone waiting for Tyburn to make his weekly contact. He answered the call immediately and as usual was given the number of a public phone box to ring. When he explained to Tyburn the situation about Ken Waterford, there was a stony silence.

Tyburn was perplexed. "Get back to your flat and don't leave. We'll get back to you soon."

It was barely an hour before contact was resumed. This time the business-like voice of Simon Lush questioned Rydell. "Did you say that you were meeting Waterford at some kind of function tonight?"

"Yes. The Annual Charity Dinner."

"We need to know the time, place, Waterford's make of car and the probable route he'll take to go home. Can you give it to us?"

"Yes, all you need." He gave them clear and precise details of everything he could, then the tone of the conversation suddenly changed. "Listen, Rydell and listen good, you're up to your neck in shit and you know it. If you give Waterford any inkling tonight, that we're on to him, he's likely to blow the whole gaff there and then. Your best bet is to plead with him through the evening and make him think he's letting you down. He'll be expecting you to try, so he's more likely to hold off and not get suspicious. We intend to intercept him and his lady wife on their way home and have a long friendly chat about the future. Do you get the drift?"

Rydell sighed. "I'm afraid I do, but I don't think you'll need to rough them up. I'm sure a few threats would do. They're quite soft really."

"Don't worry yourself, we can handle that side of things."

Rydell didn't make the Charity Dinner because he was summoned in the early evening to an emergency meeting at the home office.

Early reports from the Humberside Constabulary indicated a major disturbance at Hull Jail.

* * * * *

At around two the following morning, in the depths of a mild winter's night, the foundations for a new bridge were being laid on the outskirts of West Drayton. The contractors were a company called Tybuild. The arc lights shone brightly as a team of labourers prepared part of the base in readiness for a batch of 20 cubic metres of ready-mix concrete. Three wagons were standing by, ready for the pour, their noisy drums churning the mixture to the right consistency.

Without warning, the lights were mysteriously extinguished and a loud Geordie voice echoed through the darkness. "The bleedin' generator's packed up. Away to the hut for half an hour, lads, 'til we get it fixed."

The men shuffled off without complaint. It was a good time for a fag and a sandwich.

In the darkness, two men clad in scruffy overalls lugged a heavy load to the edge of the wooden shuttering which would hold the wet concrete in place. Siggy Dexter and Moke Saviore dropped the long dark shape over the precipice and there was a dull thud as it hit the steel reinforced mesh, ten feet below. They went away and returned minutes later and disposed-off a second load in the same manner. Dexter watched indifferently as Saviore went over to the nearest ready-mix wagon and pushed over a large handle. The sloppy grey mixture was sent cascading down a chute and into the depths of the hole below. Dexter shone a torch into the foundations as the concrete continued to pour and when the load was exhausted, he flashed his beam across the roadway to the site foreman.

The generator immediately began to throb and the bright working lights again illuminated the scene. It was now possible to see the surface of the concrete and its wetness shone in the arc light. Dexter grunted his satisfaction. The bodies they'd just dumped were undetectable under the tons of concrete and would be incarcerated there for decades to come.

* * * * *

The front pages of all the daily papers on Saturday morning were saturated by the disturbing news that filtered down from Humberside. Tucked away on the inside pages in the later editions was a rather concise report about an abandoned Bentley belonging to Sir Kenneth and Lady Waterford. The couple had mysteriously disappeared and their family had expressed grave worries about their safety.

Charles Rydell was searching the paper for as much detail about the riots when he came across the short paragraph about his missing friends. He was filled with dread. He'd naively assumed they'd have been warned off, but it suddenly dawned on him that he'd never see Ken and Doreen again and it was he, who'd been responsible for sending them to their deaths.

He had to chair an early morning meeting to discuss the progress of events at Hull, but he returned home as soon as it was over and drank himself into a stupor of morbid self-pity.

Chapter 27

Hull Jail was very much like all Victorian prisons, a series of brick buildings confined within a huge rectangular compound. The perimeter walls were 20 feet high with a curved top to deter the use of grappling irons and rope ladders in the event of an attempted escape. At the centre of the compound was the main prison, designed like the spokes of a rimless wheel. At the hub was a dome-shaped structure called the citadel, manned by prison officers. Radiating outwards from this centre were the wings, a number of long buildings of a two-storey construction, housing the individual cells.

The prison workshops, library, chapel and administration blocks were built around the outer perimeter of the compound. The only entrance and exit to the prison compound was via a giant air-lock security system, which was stringently monitored. Escape was virtually impossible.

The prison system had been very harsh until recently. Temporary Governor Moore had been in charge only a few short months. His staff, many who'd worked with him as an assistant governor, already knew his philosophy and attitude to penal reform. He was content to accept a relaxed regime, but his lack of authority was already having a worsening effect on the already poor morale.

It had turned six o'clock and the sky was dark. The evening was bleak and a cold front was edging eastwards, with a chilly wind blowing flurries of snow off the North Sea.

Willie Jackson was a long-serving warden and he was chancing his luck taking Bradshaw to see the governor so close to the end of the day. He'd been unwittingly set up a couple of weeks earlier and Bradshaw had interceded on his behalf to save his face. He was anxious to get this over with because he didn't like to be seen giving favours to inmates and his debt to Bradshaw would then be repaid in full.

Bradshaw's insistence on this particular time of day was puzzling and he wouldn't give his reasons, saying they were personal and could not be discussed with anyone other than Mr Moore. Jackson was hopeful that Bradshaw was applying for a transfer. He'd been a bad influence amongst the other prisoners since his arrival a few weeks earlier, and all the warders would be glad to see the back of him.

The two of them crossed the courtyard from 'B' wing and went round to the administration block, nestling beneath the towering perimeter walls. A few lights were still blazing brightly, but most had already been extinguished as staff left for the weekend.

They entered by a side door and Bradshaw was heartened by the lack of attention paid to them. They passed three half-glazed doors, the dark interiors indicating that the offices were already empty. With Jackson giving directions, Bradshaw led the way up to the second floor where the governor's office was situated. The upper corridor terminated at a large door. Jackson leant past Bradshaw and knocking briskly, opened the door and ushered him forward.

A very prim and stern woman of indeterminate age rose from her chair. Sally Lawson was the governor's secretary. She began to interrogate the prison officer. "Yes, Mr Jackson. What do you want? I hope you realise it's very late."

"I have an inmate to see Mr Moore on a very private matter."

The tiny woman, with a prune-like complexion, barred their progress. She peered over her half-moon spectacles defiantly. "But he hasn't got an appointment. Mr Moore's diary is empty for this afternoon."

Jackson would not be put off. "I appreciate that, but I'm assured this will only take a short time. That is, if the governor isn't too busy."

Sally Lawson glared at Jackson and looked at her watch. It was Friday evening and she wanted to be away. Bradshaw saw her hesitate and clenched his fists nervously. It was imperative that she didn't leave before his business with the governor was completed.

"I'll just have to see. Wait here."

Knocking on the connecting door, the guardian of the governor disappeared, carrying a number of papers in her outstretched hand.

Two minutes later she returned. "You can go in now. But you're lucky he'll see you," she chided.

The two of them were shown into the office. Bradshaw turned and noticed that Sally Lawson had gone back to her desk. *Would she be the perfect secretary and wait to see if there were any last-minute jobs, or would she go now because it was after six?* He knew he had to work fast.

The door closed behind them and Bradshaw stood tall and erect like the ex-marine he was. He eyed the governor, who was signing some papers.

Jackson stood at ease, slightly behind and to his left.

The office was fairly small, sparsely furnished and gave visitors an overall impression of drabness. The walls were lined with wooden bookcases and grey filing cabinets and to one side was a long table with a model of the prison, set in a Perspex case. Several potted plants were placed strategically around the room to try and add an air of brightness to the place.

Bradshaw glanced around, sensing that neither of the two men were concentrating on him. This was his opportunity. He was a heavily built man and had kept himself in good condition, despite his incarceration. He turned sharply on Jackson and without a word, kneed him hard in the groin. As Jackson buckled under the intense pain of the assault, Bradshaw slugged him heavily behind his right ear. The warder was poleaxed and slumped unconscious onto the carpet with hardly a sound.

The governor looked up, his face suddenly puzzled and dismayed. Bradshaw was round the desk before Moore could either get to his feet or utter a sound of protest. His assailant punched him painfully on the jaw and as he reeled in a daze, powerful forearms locked around his throat. The defenceless governor threw up his arms, thrashing wildly as he tried to protect himself. In a deft and long practised manoeuvre, Bradshaw viciously twisted his victim's neck and there was a loud sickening click as his spinal cord was ruptured. The dead governor's body became instantly leaden after the lethal onslaught and his head rolled forward onto his desk.

Bradshaw still had work to do. Beads of perspiration broke out on his forehead and the stink of excitement clung to his armpits. Looking around for a potential weapon, his eyes fell upon a china plant pot. He moved across the room and emptied its contents onto the floor. Hiding the pot behind his back, he stealthily approached the door. He opened it a crack and peered out. Sally Lawson was still there, tidying her desk. The fact that she'd not left mollified him instantly. She was the final witness. Popping his head cheekily round the corner, he winked at her. "The governor would like you and your notepad please." He grinned and disappeared back into the office.

She murmured in a low voice, grabbing a pencil, "Cheeky devil. I hope this is not going to take too long."

The door opened and as she entered, she was struck down from behind. It was a blow intended to kill. Bradshaw leant over her frail, crumpled body and felt for the pulse in her neck. It had gone.

He stood up, mopping his brow. The carnage had taken only a matter of minutes and had given him little time to think. Now, it was all over, he felt momentarily exhausted. It was then he began to feel the fear of discovery trickle down his spine. The plan had worked perfectly and all the witnesses were dead, but he must make it back to 'B' wing as soon as possible. He looked at his watch. It was ten past six. The trouble would start soon, because the timing of the mayhem had been specifically organised to cover his return.

Bradshaw steadied himself and went over to the unlocked filing cabinets. He grabbed handfuls of paper, screwed them up loosely and filled a wastepaper basket, setting it underneath the governor's wooden desk. He also massed a huge pile of papers under the curtains, making sure that the window was left slightly ajar, so the air could circulate. He retrieved a plush, gold-plated lighter from the governor's desk and adjusted the gas so there was a long flame. Soon, there were two fires burning furiously.

Taking Jackson's keys off his body, he turned and quickly retraced his steps, returning to the safety of the dark compound without being seen.

On the top floor of the administration block, the fire was beginning to take hold. The flames were gently fanned by the sea breeze and quickly spread up the curtains and along the wooden bookcases. A thick, deadly smoke rose to the ceiling and very slowly, the choking blanket descended towards the floor.

Bradshaw moved noiselessly in the shadows towards the prison workshops. He now had a master key and was determined to fulfil the penultimate part of his plan. He let himself into the workshops and carefully felt his way in the darkness. He dared not risk a light, so his progress was slow as he headed for the paint store where he knew he would find some flammable spirits. There were several demijohns of white spirit in long metal racks against the far wall. He hauled one of them out and set about funnelling spirit into plastic squash bottles, used to bring water round when the inmates were thirsty. He filled as many as he could carry. After capping them securely, he proceeded to pour the remaining spirit over the other painting materials.

At a safe distance, he used the stolen lighter and set fire to a rag soaked in spirit. He threw the burning torch towards the paint store and it sailed through the air in a lazy arc. The heavily impregnated atmosphere was ignited with a gush and the fire began to spit and growl as it echoed in the confined space of the storeroom. It promised to be a good blaze, but Bradshaw didn't have time to stand around and watch. Picking up his armful of bottles, he left and made his way the short distance, across the compound, with his bulky load to the sole entrance of the citadel. He waited in the shadows for the fun to begin.

At exactly 6:30, fighting broke out in the meal queue on 'B' wing. It was an orchestrated brawl, but those who started it were not playing games. Half a dozen or so hand-picked men began a loud fracas to attract the warders. Once the alarm had been raised, the full complement of 15 prison officers swarmed into the dining hall to break up the trouble. They were being led into a trap and as soon as they tried to stop the fighting, more prisoners who had been standing back from the fray set upon them.

The attack was vicious, well organised and quickly repulsed the warder's assault. As the prison officers became slowly overwhelmed, their initial disciplined tactics degenerated into hand-to-hand fighting as they fought for personal survival. Many inmates, who normally wouldn't have become involved, soon found themselves drawn into the ferocious mob. Some men saw the fighting as an opportunity to get back at warders they loathed, but the majority saw it as a licence to get back at the establishment. These were the ones who began to systematically wreck everything. The first thing they did was to disable the CCTV cameras and in the citadel control room, the screens showing the internal building went blank, one by one.

By this time, klaxons were blaring everywhere as the senior officer tried in vain to get through to the governor. Almost simultaneously, the fires in the administration block and workshops were discovered. They were soon burning out of control.

Panic began to seep into the minds of the custodians as control was gradually wrenched from their grasp. Prison officers were punched, dragged to the ground and viciously kicked. One particularly despised officer was savagely beaten and his throat gouged open with a kitchen fork, but the attacks weren't all targeted at the warders and many a grudge between inmates was settled that night.

Realising that the disturbance had been cleverly coordinated, the majority of prison officers were able to fight a successful rear-guard action and managed to pull out most of their injured comrades. They retreated to the outside of the rioting block.

Eventually, an off-duty assistant governor was tracked down at his home. He immediately accepted responsibility, but with little experience and nobody else to help him make decisions, he felt compelled to order a complete withdrawal of his men.

Amidst the confusion of jeering prisoners and fleeing prison officers, one inmate made his way back inside. Bradshaw threaded his way through the melee to 'A' wing which up until that point had been unaffected. He chuckled to himself in anticipation of his actions. *Time to let the animals out.*

As he passed through 'A' wing, he was able to release some of the most hardened and vicious men in the prison. They were grateful to be set free. Then, he went to 'C' wing and released the low category inmates. Some of these men didn't want to get involved in the rioting and hid in their cells whilst the others ran amok with the rest. A few managed to force their way outside, following the warders and giving themselves up.

Bradshaw found his way to the empty control room. The staff had been ordered to safety, so he had no trouble in setting fire to the equipment, which would have recorded everything that had happened over the past few hours. Soon, any videos of his movement about the prison and his involvement in the riot would be destroyed forever.

Outside, in the prison compound, burning buildings lit up the sky, with warders racing about in panic helping the injured and maimed. Humberside Police had been informed of the state of emergency at the prison and a steady trickle of help began to appear. Fire tenders were the first to arrive, followed by a number of police in fast response vehicles. The air was suddenly filled with dozens of wailing sirens as more and more officers were rushed to the scene. In a carefully organised, but untried plan, support finally arrived at the stricken prison from North Lincolnshire and later, from the South and North Yorkshire police forces.

It took two hours before sufficient police had arrived to enable the area around the prison to be completely sealed off. By then, most of the injured officers had been moved to hospital and the fire service was successfully tackling the huge fires.

Then, in the eerie light, the roof of 'B' wing suddenly became alive. Tiles began to mysteriously slide away and crash into splintered fragments on the concrete ground below. A host of hands and arms began to appear through the gaps. More tiles were pushed aside as the heads and torsos of strong, aggressive inmates began to appear. Dozens of them finally pulled themselves out onto the rooftop. Their behaviour, once out in the open, was that of an army of lunatics as they began to dismantle the roof with a manic purpose. They took the structure to bits, slate-by-slate, brick-by-brick and with moronic deviance, began hurling lumps of masonry at the unsuspecting crews of the emergency services working below.

Bradshaw found his way onto the roof with his armful of bottles. He unscrewed the top of one and stuffed a bit of rag into its neck. Lighting the taper, he aimed his Molotov Cocktail at the nearest fire engine. The bottle hit the truck and as it burst, the liquid spirit caused an instantaneous fireball. Another explosive missile erupted near the first, with flames gushing round the base of the turntable ladder. It was fortunate that nobody was seriously injured, but the chief fire officer was suddenly placed in an impossible situation. Now that he couldn't protect his men from the insane mob, howling from the rooftop, he was forced to withdraw and let the fires run their course.

Inside the prison, the bloodletting continued and those whose anger had still not been satisfied, chose to help the others do as much damage to the fabric of the building as they could. Furniture was crushed and bedding was torn to shreds. Bonfires were lit and piled high with refuse, generated by the wild pandemonium. Every light fitting and socket was smashed with wires and cables wrenched from the walls. Showers, washbasins and urinals were ripped from their fixtures and systematically hammered until they shattered and crumbled into a thousand pieces. Anything that could be used as a tool or crowbar was pressed into service.

One of the internal barred doors was forced off its hinges and used like a mediaeval battering ram to smash through walls. Water tanks and the heating system in the upper voids of the roof were bludgeoned with bricks until they cracked open, cascading gallons of water below. Each cellblock reeked with the smoke of burning fires and water from burst pipes sprayed like rain through the ceilings, slopping about the floors. The air was filled with dust and grime. Everywhere was total desolation. Nothing was left intact.

Scores of inmates began building barriers to protect their new habitat from the anticipated police reprisal, whilst others retired to the safety of the roof, content to abuse those who had gathered to see the results of the carnage and destruction.

By nine o'clock, the national press and TV had converged on the area, as the stricken prison became the centre of national and international news. With nine people killed and dozens seriously injured, Britain's worst-ever prison riot had been written into the annals of history.

Chapter 28

At 7:30 in the evening, the rioting at Hull Jail had been confirmed and Westminster was awash with activity. Home Secretary Clive Durrant had been informed immediately and he summoned Charles Rydell and a small team of civil servants and advisers back to the home office for an emergency meeting to discuss the crisis. As news of the terrible fires, injuries and destruction filtered through, the meeting was one of sombre disbelief.

It was difficult to know how to handle the situation and until there was a clearer picture of the riot, government policy had been to let those at the scene deal with the problem. Clive Durrant had been in contact with the chief constable of Humberside who was now supervising operations. A fully trained and equipped riot squad of 500 men, drawn from a number of local forces, was being assembled and would be placed on standby outside the prison ready to be deployed. The home secretary had refused permission for the use of force to storm the prison and the riot squad was held in reserve, only to be used as a defensive shield in case of an attempted mass break out.

At the end of a weary meeting, the home secretary had decided that nothing more could be done that night. As long as the general public was safe and the prison perimeter was secure, his plan was to wait until daylight and review the situation again. He gave strict instructions that he should be informed if the situation deteriorated, then he brought the meeting to a close.

The prime minister was at Chequers for the weekend and Durrant rang her to discuss the events of the evening. She listened with her usual intensity and concurred with the actions he'd taken. When he rang off, he felt he'd done all that he could, given the knowledge and resources at his disposal, but most importantly the PM had supported him 100 percent.

* * * * *

Joe Harker rolled to one side and cradled Kate's neck under his arm, drawing her closer. He sighed appreciatively. Kate nestled up to him, feeling good from top to toe. Their lovemaking had been so sensual, she wanted to shout out her joy and tell the whole world how good she felt.

Joe yawned gently and within minutes, he was breathing regularly and had fallen into a deep sleep. Kate chatted quietly to him and when she realised that he wasn't responding to her ramblings, she pushed herself up on one elbow and looked down on his face.

"Men," she murmured. Then she smiled because he looked so peaceful and content. For the short time they would spend together, she had wanted him totally to herself and be the centre of her world. Her plan had worked so far and there had been no mention of work to distract his attention. Although the passion of their lovemaking had ended, a warm afterglow lingered. It was now a time to talk and she found herself wanting to impress him with what she'd overheard between Rydell and Waterford. She touched his face and snuggled even closer. It would have to wait until morning.

* * * * *

At eight the following day, Kate was up and making breakfast for them both. Humming happily to herself, she moved about the kitchen and switched on her portable TV to catch the news. The report of the previous night's prison riot filled the screen and held her fascination. The full horror of the fire and destruction was highlighted in graphic detail, filling her with a strange trepidation. It seemed an age before the presenter finally mentioned the name of the prison.

"It's Hull! Hull! Oh my God! That's the link."

Kate ran to the bedroom and dragged her sleepy lover to the kitchen. She pointed to the television and garbled the conversation she'd overheard between Rydell and Waterford the previous day. Suddenly, another thought occurred to her and she rushed off to her small study. Seconds later, she returned brandishing a sheet of paper in her hand.

"Look at this. It's a fax I sent myself weeks ago. It didn't mean anything to me at the time, but now it's all clear." Kate showed Joe the list of prison names and sure enough the one at the very top read... *Hull.*

"This is more serious than we could have ever imagined, Kate. There has to be a connection. There are too many coincidences. God forbid, but it looks odds-on that Rydell bears some responsibility for this riot."

"One thing's for sure, darling, someone must have a very powerful hold on him if they can persuade him to get involved in something as dreadful as this."

Joe looked at her in dismay and grimaced. "I'm sorry sweetheart, but I need to use your phone."

He dialled a number and was immediately put through to Paula Ross. Her reaction to his news was unpredictable and for once she sounded flustered and lost for words. After a few moments, she began to respond more like her old self and asked that he come to her flat immediately.

Joe put the phone down. "Sorry, baby, but I have to go. Looks like I'm going to be busy for the rest of the weekend."

The look of disappointment on Kate's face said it all.

"Never mind, I'll make it up to you next time. I promise."

Chapter 29

Events in London moved rapidly. At the luxury penthouse of Paula Ross, Joe Harker recounted every detail supplied by Kate Stephenson. It seemed more than reasonable to assume that Charles Rydell was implicated in some treasonable act. Under normal protocols, this would warrant the immediate intervention of MI6, but Paula Ross was already aware that these circumstances were different. There would be a delicate political path she would be expected to follow when she reported this in confidence to the PM.

Joe was put on standby for the next few hours. So, he went home to wait for his orders.

Paula Ross had a keen intellect and her mind quickly settled on a plan of action. She immediately accessed the MI6 database to find out who was her nearest operative to Hull. A name came up that Paula recognised and she contacted the young female agent. Within minutes, she had given her a top priority assignment.

* * * * *

It was early on Sunday evening when Paula Ross finished typing out the confidential report and as the printer was spewing out the document, she put through a personal call to the prime minister at Chequers. The PM was on the point of leaving for Downing Street and agreed to an immediate appointment on her return.

The prime minister was already working when Paula Ross arrived. She broke off from her duties and ordered coffees for them both. After they'd been served and the two of them were alone, the PM read the short report that had been prepared for her.

Her face was ashen. "This seems incredulous, almost beyond belief."

The prime minister was crestfallen. It was the only time Paula Ross had ever seen her so perturbed.

She suddenly recovered her composure and spoke gravely to Paula, "One other fact that you may not be aware of is the whereabouts of Sir Kenneth Waterford and his wife. My private secretary heard on the local radio yesterday morning that their car had been found abandoned in a country lane. That ties in with the argument between Rydell and Waterford in your report. There is something truly disturbing in all this and I'm relying on you to solve this mystery as soon as possible. Have you got any ideas?"

"No. Not yet, just too many unanswered questions. If Rydell did have something to do with this riot, then what was the motive? What purpose could it serve? Perhaps, it was to hide something else? As far as we know, there hasn't been a mass break out, but early reports indicate a number of deaths. I wondered whether the riot was a cover for some gangland executions, but that doesn't seem to make much sense. Why would they go to so much trouble?"

"You could be right, Paula. The riot may be just a red herring to throw us off the track. One thing's for sure, there must have been someone on the inside who instigated the riot."

"Yes, prime minister, and that is our one slice of luck so far."

"What do you mean?"

"Our nearest field agent was not far away and yesterday morning, I sent her to the prison to find out what she could. I managed to get in touch with the chief constable of Humberside and asked for his co-operation. He was only too happy to help. Apparently, one of the prison officers was badly burnt in the fire. He regained consciousness for a short time at the hospital and the police were able to question him. He told them he'd taken one of the inmates to the governor's office late Friday afternoon before being attacked and left for dead. The prisoner must have set fire to the place to cover his tracks because the burnt corpses of the governor and his secretary were also discovered there. Post-mortems were carried out early this morning confirming they'd both been murdered."

The prime minister looked visibly stunned. "This is terrible news."

"I'm afraid the poor man's burns were horrific and his condition was terminal, but before he died, he was able to give us a name."

"Do you have it?"

"Yes. The man's name is Bradshaw, but the information was faxed through only seconds before I set out, so I wasn't able to give you written confirmation.

We have the name of one other prisoner suspected of being involved. The second man is called Cutts and one of the warders has already made a statement to the police confirming that he witnessed this man stabbing to death one of the other inmates."

In a quiet, controlled, matter of fact voice, the PM spoke, "Paula, this is a scandal that will bring down the government and ruin my career if it is ever made public and at a time when I feel that I am doing so much for the country," she sighed, "you know I'd do anything to gloss over this mess."

The mind of Paula Ross was racing. This was surely a plea to intervene on behalf of the prime minister and it was something she had been half expecting. The very notion conflicted with her brief as the non-political and independent head of MI6. By initially excluding the home secretary from her reporting and dealing exclusively with the PM, she must have given a coded message that she was prepared to support her personally. Paula owed a great deal to the prime minister in terms of her own appointment. She had great respect for her leader and felt an overwhelming sense of loyalty towards her. The decision was easy.

"I'll do everything I can to help. I have a number of people who I can trust explicitly and I know they will get things done. Unless any other security organisation gets an inkling of what's going on, I'm confident we can sort it out for you. If things should start to go wrong, you'll be the first to know. Nothing is ever certain. The key question, prime minister, is for you alone. We don't yet know who we're dealing with. Do I have your backing to do anything, literally anything, in order to achieve your ultimate tenure?"

"Paula, my dear, do what you will. Please don't consult me about your actions and whatever I have no knowledge of, I cannot criticise. Whatever you decide, I can assure you that I will protect your back with my utmost power."

Paula nodded. She had secured her brief.

"There is one thing you can do for me straight away, prime minister. I need a swift end to the riot so that we can get hold of these two characters, Bradshaw and Cutts. They are our only lead and we need to make them talk before the police get a chance to question them."

"Very well. I'll order the riot squad in tomorrow. Is that too soon for you to set up your operation?"

"No, prime minister. Tomorrow is just fine."

* * * * *

The prime minister had a long and heated argument with Clive Durrant. He was totally opposed to using force to end the siege that had developed over the weekend. The PM successfully pointed to public opinion and persuaded him that because it was the worst prison riot ever, then a government who was prepared to crush it by force would be regarded as a strong one. This would go some way to restoring their tarnished reputation.

Early the next morning, under cover of darkness, the riot squad moved in. They had been on standby, ready for action all weekend and went forward with confidence and determination. The expected resistance failed to materialise and the majority of rioters surrendered without a fight. Amongst the inmates was one man who was gratified by the success of the task he'd been set. Bradshaw had no idea that Jackson had initially survived the fire and he merged peaceably with the others as they quietly gave themselves up to the waiting police.

Chapter 30

Joe Harker was dispatched to the north with a clear mandate from his boss. This kind of operation didn't come along very often and he would enjoy it, unfettered by protocol. At his side was his likeable subordinate, Taff Rawlings, a rock of Welsh virtues. Taff's mother, an attractive girl from the valleys had married a businessman from Hong Kong. The combination of their genes had resulted in a strange hybrid whose features and stature would have been more at home on the plains of Mongolia. Joe had first met Taff when they served together in the SAS and had immediately struck up a friendship. When Joe moved into a position of authority in MI6, after a spell in the Metropolitan Police, his diminutive comrade was the first he'd recruited to the service.

They were both dressed in the uniform of sergeants in the Metropolitan Police. Their transport was also authentic, even though the licence plates were unknown to Scotland Yard or the DVLA. Driving the powerful car at high speed, they traversed the motorway network, switching from the M1 to the M18 along the boundary of South Yorkshire, and then onto the M62 which terminated at Hull.

When they arrived at the prison, it was just before dawn and in the quiet darkness, they watched with interest as the riot squad was ordered into action. In the prison compound, there was a great deal of noise and commotion as the homemade barriers were dismantled. Within an hour, news filtered out that the overwhelming force of police had proved too much and the rioters were giving themselves up.

A team of police and warders were identifying and ticking off the names of handcuffed inmates as they began trickling through the gates, ready to be shuttled to several different prisons across the region. The numbers started to swell and groups of prisoners began queuing patiently in lines. Batches of them were then shepherded into the waiting buses and vans.

Joe spotted a senior officer and shouldered his way through a throng of reporters and general public, who were held back at the barriers surrounding the prison.

"Excuse me, sir, but Scotland Yard wants to question these two characters in a bit of a hurry." He handed over the transfer documentation for the custody of Cutts and Bradshaw. The form appeared to be signed by the home secretary. The officer fingered the document in the poor light and stared at length into Joe's face.

"Strange, it seems everybody wants to talk to these two. We've all been given orders from the chief constable to arrest them on sight. Let's see if they've come out yet." He walked over to those who were checking names and returned with some favourable information. "The men you're looking for were in the last group to be processed." He looked down at his list. "Ultimate destination is Wakefield Prison. They've already been segregated from the others. Apparently, that's them over there." He pointed to the tall prison wall. In the shadows, two men were being guarded by a couple of police dressed in riot gear. "Sorry chum, they're waiting for a separate car to take them to Wakefield for questioning. Best follow behind and try your luck there." He handed back the documentation and watched with detached interest as Joe hurriedly returned to his car.

"Come on Taff, they're over near the wall. We need to act fast, before their transport arrives."

Taff drove quickly but carefully around the busy perimeter of the prison and came to a halt not far from where Cutts, Bradshaw and their minders were stood.

Joe got out of the car and approached the two policemen. He thrust the papers in front of the nearest officer. "Here, read this. We've come directly from Scotland Yard to collect these two villains."

"We were told to hang onto them until transport arrived."

Joe grinned and spread his hands. "Well, we're it."

The two officers looked very young and Joe was banking on their inexperience. He hoped they didn't know the significance of their prisoners.

One officer passed the papers over to his mate. The documentation signed by the home secretary was most impressive. "What do you think, Tony?"

The other man nodded and passed the papers back over. "Ok by me."

"Bet you lads are ready for a cuppa."

"Wouldn't say no to a bacon buttie either."

"Well, we just need a signature and you can get over to the mobile canteen."

Joe counter-signed the transfer document and gave them the top copy, complaining bitterly about the paperwork.

Bradshaw and Cutts were quickly transferred into their custody. Taff ushered them without protest into the squad car, sitting in the back with a prisoner handcuffed on either side of him.

Thanking the officers for their co-operation, Joe gunned the powerful engine and they quickly sped off into the early morning gloom.

The two prisoners were bemused by their special treatment and demanded to know where they were going.

Taff spoke softly in his broad Welsh accent, "You'll find out soon enough. Just sit tight boyo and enjoy the ride."

The snow that had threatened all weekend finally came. As the police car headed through Hull, an icy blizzard began to blow. The weather was foul and Joe had to slow right down as his windscreen wipers found it hard to cope with the freezing conditions. Car headlights blazed through the swirling vortex and the dark city was soon enveloped in a mysterious white cloak of snow.

The traffic was down to a crawl by the time they'd threaded their way through the city towards the docks. They finally reached a long, wide pier with warehouses along the left side. The murky silhouettes of large ships and cranes were evident to the right indicating their closeness to the sea. There should have been bright lights overhead, but the intensity of the storm was throwing an opaque blanket around them, dulling their effect. As the car moved slowly through the crunching snow, the buildings became more dilapidated and the ships, less numerous.

At last, the car turned left through 90 degrees and came to a halt outside the entrance to a warehouse, sheltered by an overhanging cantilever. Joe got out of the car and slid back the huge door, revealing an empty and desolate interior. Driving inside, he turned off the engine and returned to shut out the chill winter elements. Everything was thrown into darkness.

Taffy sat quietly between the two handcuffed prisoners, who began to fidget uneasily.

Bradshaw was the first to start asking questions, "Why the hell have you brought us here?"

"Soon, my friend. You'll get to know soon."

Joe pulled the master switch at the fuse box next to the entrance and instantly, the inside of the old warehouse was illuminated. The lighting was poor, bathing the innards of the ancient warehouse in an eerie light and casting a multitude of menacing shadows.

Bradshaw looked out and shivered. The gloom hinted at a fearful unknown.

Taff unshackled himself from Cutts and handcuffed his wrists behind him. The rear door of the car was thrown open and Joe dragged him out, ordering him to sit on the floor near the wall. Taffy similarly dealt with Bradshaw.

The two prisoners huddled in silence, side by side, wondering what was about to happen.

Joe stood before them and produced a gun. It was designed to be a threatening action and when he deliberately attached a long ugly silencer, it became even more disquieting for the two prisoners.

Cutts was the first to react. "What do you want from us? Why have you brought us here?"

Joe didn't answer, but nodded to Taffy. The stocky Welshman pulled two black hoods from inside his tunic and moved over to the prisoners, who were now cowering against the wall.

Cutts began to struggle as Taffy dropped the hood over his head.

"No! Please. What are you doing? Don't shoot me? What have I done? Noooooo."

The hood was tugged over him and he began a childlike whimper, shaking with fear and anticipation of what might happen.

Bradshaw tried to look his captors straight in the face, but Joe could see and smell his fear, even though his reaction to the hood was not received with the same undignified screams as his comrade.

Joe and Taffy went back to the car and brought the rest of their equipment. The roof near the wall was ideal for their purpose with a number of strong lateral beams. Two stout, hemp ropes, with a hangman's noose already knotted at one end were thrown over a beam and tied off behind a couple of stanchions. Joe unfolded three canvas stools and placed two of them side by side. They went over to Bradshaw and pulled him to his feet.

Taffy walked him over to one of the stools and commanded fiercely through the hood. "Stand on the step."

The disorientated prisoner complied with their request. The first noose was slid over his head before he realised what was happening and Joe hitched up the slack so that the rope was taut about his neck and there was no room for movement. As soon as Bradshaw felt the jerk, he realised what had happened and remained perfectly still.

Cutts was more difficult to move. He struggled and fought all the way as they dragged him to the stool. Joe put the noose around his neck and Taffy hauled on the rope. A muffled scream of anguish came from his hooded throat as the rope bit into his windpipe.

"Okay, you motherfucker. Step up onto the stool or so help me; I'll kill you here and now."

With Taffy still pulling hard on the rope, the shaking thug complied. Only when Cutts was standing in the correct position did Taffy slacken the rope and give him temporary solace from his agony.

The MI6 men breathed heavily from their exertions as they watched the two murderous convicts wobbling on their makeshift gallows. Joe went over and standing on the third stool, reached across and pulled their hoods off. He stood down.

The two prisoners were facing each other, about six feet apart. Bradshaw wore a grave expression as he viewed the condition of Cutts. The man was in agony with a huge grey weal around his throat where the noose had dug into his flesh. The rope prevented him from bowing his head and he choked and spluttered as he fought to regain his breath and composure.

Bradshaw looked down at Harker. "Okay, game over. What do you want?"

"Who says were playing games?"

Bradshaw blustered, "We're in the custody of Her Majesty's Government. You can't touch us. You have no right to bring us here."

"But you are here," Harker replied contemptuously, "let me ask you a question, Mr Bradshaw. What do you know about the riot? Who put you up to it?"

"Don't know what you're talking about pal. He's the one who started the fighting. Why don't you ask him?"

Harker turned to Cutts. "Well, your friend over here has pointed a finger at you. No honour among thieves, as they say. What do you have to say? Did you start it?"

The other man was rattled and he garbled on in dread. "Yeah, sort of, but there were loads of us. Bradshaw was in on it. He wanted it most. He told us what time to kick the riot off. It was a lark really."

"Some bleeding lark. So, tell me, who's paying you?"

"What? I don't know what you mean. What's this about?"

"You heard Cutts. Who is paying you for the job?"

"You must have a screw loose mister. I ain't been paid for nothing. Only just been transferred from Armley Nick at Leeds. I did the Strangeways riot a few years ago, but it weren't half as good as this one."

Even in his precarious position, the simple-minded and brutal thug could not help but boast about his past exploits.

"This is getting tedious, Taffy. Now, let's see. Eeeny, Meeny, Minny, Mo."

Harker went through the ritual of the childhood nursery rhyme. Without warning, he kicked the stool from under Cutts. His body dropped so that his feet were inches from the floor. The rope bit into his neck and began the terrible and excruciating process of throttling his windpipe. Thrashing about, he strove for blessed relief from his torment. His face began to turn blue and then purple as the oxygen supply to his brain diminished. In one final, futile act of escape, he threw his body about and a loud guttural growl emanated from his blackened lips. His body twitched and his sphincter relaxed, purging his bowels of putrefied body fluids.

The stench reached the nostrils of Bradshaw who began to tremble with fear. *Was he to be the next?*

The dead body hung, twisting back and forth at the end of the rope. The grotesque face was bloated out of all proportion and the bulging eyes seemed to stare crazily across at Bradshaw.

"Now, that's what I call tax payers delight. A saving of 20,000 a year for, say, 15 years. I make it 300 grand. We could spend that on hospitals or schools. A fitting end for a bag of excrement, don't you think Taff? Now, what about this one?"

Bradshaw, the tough con and ex-marine had met his nemesis. He would say anything to avoid the fate suffered by Cutts. The execution had been a calculated gamble. Harker felt sure the dead man had known nothing and that Bradshaw held all the valuable information he was after.

"Right, my friend. Last chance saloon. Who put you up to this?"

Bradshaw blabbed. The words gushed from him. "Simon Lush. He's the flash lawyer for my old employer, a man called Tyburn."

Bradshaw quickly revealed the plot. He described his past relationship with Tyburn and the huge bribe he'd been offered to organise the riot. He gave them details of Tyburn's businesses and all that he knew about his drug trafficking operation based at the builder's yard.

"So, what's the reason for this riot? You must know?"

Bradshaw pleaded convincingly. "No! No! I've no idea. I was never told. They said they had the finger on some bloke in the government, but they never mentioned a name. I swear it."

"You'd swear anything in the position that you're in. Now, think carefully. I need a name."

"Please, mate. I've told you everything. Please. How can I tell you something I don't know? They were going to put the squeeze on this bloke to get me out, but they never said who he was. I was never told."

It all made sense to Joe. They wouldn't give a small fry like Bradshaw that kind of information. The confirmation that Rydell was involved still eluded him. He had avoided being named, by the skin of his teeth.

Harker began to relax, satisfied that he had extorted everything that Bradshaw knew. "Okay, Taff. Get him down."

Taffy went over to the stanchion and untied the knot so the rope went slack around Bradshaw's neck. He ordered him to climb down off the stool and then removed the noose.

Bradshaw suddenly felt relieved. "What are you going to do with me now? I may have helped start the riot, but I never hurt anyone."

Joe turned on him. His face was filled with hatred and disgust. "Tell that to the wife and two kids of Willie Jackson. All they've got are the charred remains of a dead husband and a loving father. You're scum, Bradshaw, pure unadulterated scum."

He kneed the thug hard in the pit of his stomach and as he fell to his knees, Joe put his gun behind his ear and pulled the trigger. There was a muffled report as the high calibre bullet smashed through the killer's brain. The body jerked forward with the force of the projectile and fell face down in a small pool of blood.

"Right, Taffy, we've got work to do."

They set about the task of clearing away the carnage. The boot of the car contained two body bags. There had never been any intention that either prisoner would be set free. The dead men were zipped into the bags and dumped in the boot of the car with the rest of their equipment. The only evidence to show they'd been present in the warehouse was a small circle of blood on the concrete floor, already coagulating in the cold morning air.

Once out on the side of the dock, Joe drove the car further along the quay. There was no sign of life or evidence of other vehicles. There was now a layer of snow, one inch deep, blanketing the ground in undisturbed splendour.

At the end of the quay was a smaller jetty where an old trawler lay waiting alongside.

Joe hailed the ship. The captain of the vessel was an ex-navy man who supplemented his income by helping out MI6 with their occasional disposal work.

He came ashore immediately.

"Two government packages for you, Captain."

"Right, you are mates. Let's get the chains on 'em."

Taffy and Joe helped the captain carry the body bags on board, then they shackled each with some old chains, so they would sink easy.

"I'm putting straight to sea. By this afternoon, your parcels will be feeding the fish off Dogger Bank."

The MI6 men left the captain in good humour and wishing him a successful trip, set off on the hazardous journey back to London.

Chapter 31

Blizzards raged across the north and eastern side of Britain, disrupting communications and making driving difficult. London and the south were more fortunate as the weather front ground to a halt, saving the capital and the surrounding counties from the harshest of the weather conditions.

When Charles Rydell woke on the Monday after the weekend riot, his wife was at his bedside.

"The home office wanted to know why you went missing yesterday, but I covered for you. I told them you were in bed all day with severe stomach pains and the doctor had forbidden you to leave."

Charles tried to lift his head, but it felt as though someone had bludgeoned him with a hammer from the inside. He protested softly. "I feel as though I have a migraine."

"Yes, but yours is self-induced. It's more like two days of alcohol poisoning."

He groaned and she thrust two paracetamol tablets into his hand. "Here, take these and here's a hot coffee."

Although the relationship between them was often strained, she still felt a great deal of sympathy for his predicament. It was also important for her own future that she gave him 100 percent support, and so, she pampered him carefully.

"The good news, Charles, is that the riot is over. The prime minister decided to end it by force and it turned out to be a pretty shrewd political move. The siege collapsed this morning with little bloodshed and the television is praising her leadership to the heavens. She, at least, has come out of this mess smelling of roses. With luck, it should also take the pressure off you. Clive Durrant was interviewed ten minutes ago and was thrilled by how easily the riot ended. Now that it won't be dragging on and saturating the media for days on end, the political spotlight can be shifted elsewhere."

Charles swallowed the pills and sipped his coffee. "It's the aftermath of all this that worries me, Lynn. I've done everything those bastards have asked me to do, but I still don't know what they really want. The stakes are higher than I ever thought possible. I've already got nine deaths in the rioting and the disappearance of poor Ken and Doreen on my conscience. God knows what they've done to them. The whole thing is getting out of hand and it's beginning to get too much, even for me to stomach."

Lynn changed her sympathetic stance in an instant and responded with an icy smile, "Come on, Charles. Grow up. This is the real world we're living in. You did what you had to do and don't forget it. If you'd refused to give them what they wanted, then you could have forgotten your career, your power, your position and wealth. Everything." She continued to argue persuasively and it began to strengthen his resolve once more, "I, for one, am not ready to go back to baked beans and bed-sits and I suspect neither are you, Charles."

He gave a grunting laugh. "You put it so eloquently, my dear. You're right, we've come too far along the road to turn back. We'll just have to sit around and wait for the next turn of events, whatever they might be."

They didn't have to wait too long. Just before midday, the phone rang and it was Lush. Rydell found himself summoned to another of their meetings.

An hour later, he was picked up by a cab and taken across the Thames to Battersea Park, where the driver told him to go and stand by the edge of the boating lake.

The afternoon was bleak, but there were still a few couples and families, enjoying the park. Rydell watched them with disinterest as he stamped up and down impatiently, trying to restore the circulation to his frozen feet.

In the distance, two figures were making a leisurely approach towards him, round the left side of the lake. As they neared, Rydell recognised his smiling antagonists.

Lush greeted him like a lost friend. "Good afternoon, Charles. We need to talk. Let's continue our stroll. It should help us keep warm."

They gently guided him along the banks of the lake.

Tyburn puffed on a newly lit cigar, his tone almost affable. "I must say, we've been impressed by your organisation so far. The first part of our plan has come to fruition according to schedule with no mishaps. I believe this is yours?"

Tyburn handed Rydell a small photograph album.

They stopped walking and Rydell flicked through the pages. A dozen pictures had been expertly mounted, showing him in uncompromising positions with Waterford or applying make-up in front of the hidden cameras.

"Amazing how you can get a quality photo from a single video frame."

"Is this some kind of sick joke?"

Lush laughed sarcastically. "Not really, more of a serious reminder. Anyway, it really doesn't matter anymore because you're in this conspiracy just about as deep as you can get."

"Okay, thanks for the lecture. Now, can you tell me what you really want? We haven't come here for an afternoon outing."

"All in good time, Charles old chap. Do you remember, we said that once we threw our hat into the ring, we would be implicated along with you? Well that time has arrived, but it's worth reminding you that it will be you, who goes down for the longest stretch if you were to chicken out and decide to go to the police. The public would crucify you for all those deaths at Hull and we would give evidence to convince them that you were fully aware of our intention to murder the prison governor."

Rydell turned to face the fat lawyer. "Look here! I know my future is on the line. All I want to do now is see this through, get the DVD back and hopefully, see the back of you two. Forever. Now, what else do you want?"

Tyburn interjected, "Well, actually, we want to make a great deal of money. Legitimately, so to speak."

"I don't follow."

"Okay, Charles. We'll lay it out for you. Shortly, Hull prison will have to be rebuilt. Am I correct?"

"Yes, of course."

"Good. It is your job to ensure that the specification for the refurbishment is extremely high; as high as you can conceivably get away with. When it is put out to tender, my own building firm, Tybuild will need to prepare a bid that will be acceptable to your department. Accordingly, we will need inside information on the form of our presentation. A couple of days before the expiry of the tendering date, we will need to see the lowest bid. This will then enable us to finalise our bid, which will be slightly more competitive than the best. Can this be done?"

"Yes. There's no problem and I expect you want me to ensure that your firm gets the contract?"

"Correct, but here's the rub. Once we have been awarded the contract, legally and above board of course, so that it doesn't arouse any suspicion within your department, then you will do us one more service."

"And what might that be?"

"You will simply replace the high-quality rebuilding specification with, how shall I put it, a rather cheaper alternative. The beauty of the scheme will be that the overall cost will remain the same. We will provide you with sufficient copies to exchange all the existing files in the home office with our replacement. At that juncture, our partnership will be dissolved."

The realisation spread across Rydell's face and he had to smile. "My God, I've got to hand it to you two. You're clever and devious bastards, aren't you? You'll be able to make millions in extra-legitimate profit."

Lush purred, "Glad you like the idea. You must admit, the concept is fool proof. Once our tender is accepted in fair competition with the others, no one will suspect a thing."

The three of them walked a little longer, discussing further details to their arrangements. Eventually, they parted company and Rydell strode off alone to look for a cab.

Tyburn and Lush ambled in the opposite direction, to where Dexter was waiting with the Rolls. "You know. LOL, I think that went rather well, don't you?"

Tyburn nodded in agreement. "Yes. Now that we've got Rydell where we want him, I just can't see what can possibly go wrong."

Chapter 32

Joe Harker arrived back in the Capital exhausted after a long and appalling drive. The police car had been stuck in a snowdrift for four hours during the afternoon, delaying their return until late on Monday night.

Taffy dropped him off home, and Joe immediately went to the bathroom. Stripping himself naked, he got into the shower and turned the temperature of the hot water jets as high as he could stand. He let the near scalding stream sting his body until it began to soothe away his tiredness and aching bones. Whilst he towelled himself, he swallowed a large whisky, which invigorated him further. The alcohol went straight to his head and he realised that he hadn't eaten for nearly 24 hours. Humming to himself, he went to the kitchen and cooked a huge plate of eggs and bacon. Only when he had stuffed himself completely did his mind begin to feel completely alert and active again.

Joe compiled a short report on the days' events and after a brief phone call, he was on his way to see Paula Ross. He arrived at her private apartment in Knightsbridge by cab and his boss welcomed his return with enthusiasm.

She scanned the report quickly, "Is this the only copy?"

Joe nodded.

"Good. I'll give this to the PM personally and when she's finished with it, she can destroy it herself."

Joe was one step ahead. "Should I put a surveillance team together, ma'am?"

"Yes, but you must keep the numbers right down. Can you arrange it?"

"Sure, but without full ops, we may miss something important."

"That's a chance we'll have to take. From your report, there doesn't seem to be anyone else involved other than Tyburn and Lush. Let's hope this is strictly a cosy little set up. If that's the case, then it's going to be easier for us to keep a lid on it. I feel sure that Rydell will blow his cover sooner or later and lead us to them."

"Yes, it was unfortunate not being able to find out how they all fitted together. Bradshaw mentioned drugs and Tyburn's woodyard, so that seems the best place to start."

Paula Ross became very serious. "Joe, I explained the need for absolute secrecy the last time we met. Nothing has changed. We play this one by our own rules. I know that I can trust your discretion completely, so you can run the show any way you like, just as long as you get me some results. To start with, I'm not prepared to go through the courts for permission to tap Rydell's phone. I can't afford to let any nosy parker get wind of what we're doing. Anybody outside the department getting a whiff of what's going on will make a fortune selling leaks to the daily papers, that's for sure. We need an independent listening post. What do you think?"

"Easy. I'll arrange for a van and some equipment to sit outside his flat. I've got a pal in the CIA who can get us all the gear we need, so we won't have to go through official channels. I've also got a hand-picked bunch of people ready for a job like this. There should be no problems. I'll put one pair on Rydell, one on Tyburn's yard and one on his casino. With two listeners, a controller and myself, that makes ten. I think we can operate safely with those numbers."

"Sounds fine to me, Joe. Right, I'll let you get off. I've arranged to see the PM later tonight with your report and I have other things to sort out before then."

Joe left feeling good and set off for Kate's flat, hoping that she would still be there. He could make a few phone calls and finalise his arrangements for the next day at her place.

Kate was at home and couldn't hide the thrill of seeing him again. She was quick to seize the opportunity to get him back to bed and had seduced him within an hour of his arrival. They cuddled up together under the warm covers, feeling happy and relaxed, shutting out the cold winter's night.

Their conversation finally got round to Rydell and Joe gave her a small insight into the junior minister's involvement with Tyburn and Lush and his theory that they were involved in some kind of drugs racket.

"Sweetheart, will you continue to act as a mole for us. Now that we have names, at least we know who to look out for. Can you find out all you can about any dealings Rydell has had with either of these two? If you could get copies of any letters or documents which pass between them, it would be of enormous help. There may be a building contractor called Tybuild involved, but we're not certain."

She slipped her hand deep into his thighs. "Sure thing, lover boy, I'll do anything you want." She smiled provocatively. "Talking about moles, now that you've had a little rest, I know something else that likes to burrow around."

* * * * *

Monty Wall and Josh Gardner had been assigned to the builder's yard. Monty walked across the fusty office, situated on the third floor of the old warehouse and peered out of the filthy windows overlooking the entrance to the woodyard. Josh followed behind and looked over his colleague's shoulder.

Monty was the first to grumble, "I thought the boss said we'd been lucky to rent this grotty dump. It's almost derelict."

"I suppose the position is good, even though the facilities are crap."

"I can see you've got the same instinct about this job that I have. I bet it's a complete rave-up from start to finish!"

He sighed. "Come on Josh, let's set up shop."

They lugged a whole load of expensive tackle up the stairs, and then spent time meticulously setting up a number of tripods for their sophisticated equipment. Their hi-tech paraphernalia consisted mainly of binoculars and cameras, which were fitted with a variety of lenses, some of which had infrared capability for night-time use.

They arranged comfortable perches at two of the windows, which gave a good field of view over the area around the yard and settled down to watch.

* * * * *

The days passed slowly and the nights even slower when, as predicted, their new job quickly descended into a very boring routine. They logged every movement in and out of the yard, but there wasn't a single suspicious incident to arouse them. Josh took dozens of photographs of Tyburn, Lush, Dexter and Saviore to pass the time, but his little gallery showed nothing untoward.

Joe Harker checked all the details against the MI6 and police databases, but the computer failed to come up with anything. None of them seemed to have a police record of any kind. The expectation that there might be some activity during the hours of darkness proved unfounded. Apart from the old night watchman taking his dog for a walk, there was no movement in the yard at all. The surveillance continued for two weeks with daily reports collated by Harker. By this time, he was beginning to get frustrated by the negative progress of his watchers.

The prime minister and Paula Ross were also beginning to get impatient for results. MI6 was spending a great deal of money, using valuable resources but getting nowhere. Paula Ross had just reached the point where she was about to scale the operation down, when things started to happen.

What confronted MI6 was something she could never have predicted.

Chapter 33

"Right. That's settled," said Matt, "we're agreed that we must have a base in London to operate from. Anyone got any ideas?"

Melissa came up with the perfect suggestion. "What about a caravan? We can't use a hotel if we're taking high explosives with us. We'd have the antiterrorist squad around our necks before we could blink."

"You're right, Mel. We need as low a profile as possible."

Laura had been listening to all the arguments and supported Melissa's idea. "Another positive thing about using a caravan is that we could come and go as we please, like normal tourists, carting baggage about wherever we went. It would be no more than everyone would expect."

"Okay. That sounds good, but we'd need to lash out a load more cash on a caravan and a towing vehicle. I could fit a tow bar to my Jag, but it would be too conspicuous."

"What about a motor home? We could rent one for a week."

"Now, that's a brilliant idea, Laura. It's the perfect solution. The suspension on them is really good, ideal for shifting the nitro without jolting it about."

The three of them continued to talk frankly about their ideas and anxieties.

Matt was very matter of fact. "The only thing we have on our side is anonymity and surprise. We'll need to out-think and out-manoeuvre them every step of the way. If we use simple hit and run tactics, they won't know who is behind the attacks or how best to defend themselves."

Gradually, they sketched out a plan. The main drawback was that they only had one week to carry it through to completion. That week was scheduled for their February half-term holiday. Matt borrowed a Caravan Club handbook from a colleague and booked a one-week stay at the Crystal Palace site in South London.

* * * * *

They broke up from school on Friday night and Melissa drove Matt into Sheffield to pick up the camper van. They took it back to the house and that evening he helped the girls pack it with the provisions they'd collected for the forthcoming week.

Melissa grumbled light-heartedly to Laura. "No wonder caravaners have a reputation for taking everything but the kitchen sink on holiday, just look what we've got to pack. This will take hours."

It had been agreed that they should retrieve the explosives under the cover of darkness. Matt wanted to do it on his own, but Melissa insisted on going with him. They left a very nervous Laura behind, but promised to keep regularly in touch, so that she would be aware of their progress.

The two of them drove off to find the old farm cottage where their store of nitro-glycerine was hidden. The night turned out to be cloudy, with no moon or stars to give them any natural light. Once at the cottage, they followed the line of the ancient wall and soon managed to locate the lump of stone, which marked their cache of explosives. They had made the decision to take three of the five phials. Matt had made separate wooden boxes for them, lining each with cushion foam. A small hollow was cut in the foam, which would snugly accept a single glass phial.

Melissa held the torch as Matt delicately exhumed the deadly liquid. He extracted the glass tubes one by one and secreted each, into its own container. The hiding place was once again carefully restored to its original condition.

With Melissa preceding him and lighting the way, Matt carried the loaded boxes, one at a time, across the field to the camper. He carefully secreted them in the freezer compartment, packing the space around with further insulation. Matt hoped that keeping the temperature as low as possible would help, but he had no real idea about the stability of the explosive and ignorance was bliss as far as he was concerned. He fastened duck-tape around the freezer door in case it should accidentally swing open as he drove. There was not much danger of this happening, because he drove the precious camper at an undertaker's pace for the whole journey home.

The windy roads with their sharp bends, hidden crests and sudden dips made him over cautious in the extreme. Melissa slumped silently at his side clutching the edges of her seat, with every oncoming headlight filling her with dread as she imagined the nightmare of a collision. Although the journey was ponderous,

Matt was grateful for the soft suspension of the camper van and at last, the uncomfortable ride ended.

* * * * *

The girls watched anxiously as the huge, cream, motor home disappeared from view. It was just before lunchtime on Saturday and Matt had calculated that he should arrive in the Capital by mid-afternoon and hopefully miss the busiest traffic of the day. He was given a two-hour start, because he intended to crawl along in the inside lane of the M1 motorway all the way to London.

When it was time for them to go, Melissa drove Laura to the lockup garage and they swapped her Peugeot for the two green Minis. Driving in convoy, they set off on the southbound journey after Matt. The girls overtook the sedately moving camper van on the outskirts of London. They were so pleased to see him, flashing their lights and hooting their horns as they passed.

Laura drove to a 24-hour car park in Wimbledon. Melissa took hers to a similar location near King's Cross Station, then took to the underground and eventually met up with Laura outside the tube station at Wimbledon. It was one of the most southerly stations of the London underground network and the nearest to Crystal Palace.

Matt had memorised the best route to the site and skilfully drove the fully laden camper van round the outskirts of central London to their prearranged meeting place.

The girls stood in silence, each with her own fears, as they waited patiently for Matt to pick them up. At last, he pulled up in the thin afternoon traffic and 20 minutes later, they were driving beneath the titanic 700-foot television mast at Crystal Palace. They turned right after the mini roundabout on Westwood Hill and into the entrance of the *Harbour* caravan site, which stands on the highest point in the capital.

The site was modern and bright with a friendly reception block. The welcoming staff expertly furnished them with all the usual tourist information, designed to enhance their stay. Matt was gratified by the electronically operated security barrier, which protected the site. He punched the current four-digit code into the keypad and edged forward. The tyres of the motor caravan crunched along the gravel driveway and the barrier dropped firmly behind, making Matt feel more relaxed. He wouldn't have to worry about the safety of the van and its hideous contents when they were away from the site. They parked the van in their allotted plot and set off to explore the site and surrounding area before it got dark. They desperately needed to break the debilitating tension that had held them prisoner for the past few hours.

A cool wind had begun to blow, so they wrapped up warmly and set off to wander through the nearby park. The hilltop had once been impressively crowned by the architectural masterpiece of the original Crystal Palace. The old foundations and ruins of the palace were scant reminder of the magnificently pristine structure, which had been destroyed by fire, back in 1936. The distant landscape of London lay before them and swept across the horizon, giving a panoramic view of the city. As darkness fell, the three of them linked arms and strolled back to the camper van. Although they were windswept, the fresh air had invigorated them and they returned in a more upbeat mood.

The evening meal was cooked with enthusiasm and they were somehow able to enjoy the simple dinner, blocking out for a few short hours the sinister, surreal reason why they had made their pilgrimage to the capital city.

* * * * *

It was Tuesday evening. Matt and Laura set off from the caravan site at Crystal Palace together. It was already dark, but they didn't have to walk far before they found Melissa waiting in one of the Minis by the side of the road. Laura carried the small case, which housed the dismantled crossbow. Matt held a light, but strongly built wooden box, about 12 inches in length. Although there was very little weight to it, Matt caressed it like a new-born baby. It held three bolts for the crossbow and the tips of each had been primed with a large charge of nitro-glycerine. The bolts had been prepared that afternoon and he was well aware of the dangers of jarring the box. He hugged it carefully.

Laura got in the back of the Mini and Matt gingerly slid into the passenger's seat beside Melissa. He was tense and scared, brooding about the possibility of a freak accident that could blow them all to bits.

"Okay, darling. Take it nice and slow and hold back, so you don't have to brake heavily."

He had no idea that everyone was feeling the same intense anxiety.

Melissa prickled indignantly. "You don't need to remind me about that, buster. I'll be crawling along. I suggest you keep your comments to yourself and leave the driving up to me."

Tension and fear were creeping into everyone's minds. Matt decided to say nothing.

The car moved off smoothly and they made their way to the multi-storey car park in Wimbledon where the other Mini had been left. The journey was torturously slow and they arrived with their nerves still jangling.

Matt and Laura took the second car and the two Minis headed in a north-easterly direction to the Thames and Tyburn's premises. Laura drove the little car with great care as Matt cradled the box of bolts on his lap, clutching it so tightly that his fingers ached.

When they reached their destination, Laura drove past the entrance to the builder's yard and turned the Mini round, stopping 20 yards short of the gates.

Melissa was acting as backup and parked at the end of a nearby side road, ready to rush to their aid if the worst happened. They had practised these manoeuvres on the previous two nights, whilst surveying the activity at the yard.

Matt and Laura sat cuddled together like a couple of lovebirds and waited. It was about half an hour later, almost on the stroke of nine o'clock, that the old night watchman appeared from his caravan. He whistled his dog and it came bounding round the corner, wagging its tail ready for their nightly ritual. He put a lead on its collar and after unlocking the gate to get out, made sure it was securely fastened behind him when they left.

The night watchman ambled along the pavement, feeling no remorse for deserting his post but anticipating with pleasure a couple of pints at his local before closing time. With his dog yapping around his ankles, the old man quickly disappeared into the gloom.

The pair was given five minutes to get well away, then Matt reached behind him for the crossbow case. Opening the lid, he expertly rebuilt the weapon. The technique had been practised a dozen times and he had it down to a fine art. He strung the bow and tested its operation. There was a sharp twang as he released the firing mechanism, which had been adjusted to give let-off with only the slightest pull. It was in perfect order. Matt rearmed the crossbow string; then, delicately removed the first of his nitro-bolts from the box. He notched the end in the synthetic string and laid it in the precision-machined channel, along the upper main frame.

"Okay, let's go. Slowly does it."

Laura started the engine and set off up the street, crawling forward past the entrance. She stopped higher up the road, but still within the boundaries of the woodyard and with a clear sight of the gates. The Mini waited in the shadows on the opposite side of the street, with its engine quietly ticking over.

Matt cautiously got out of the car, removed the other two bolts from their case and gently rested them on the roof. He then settled himself behind the crossbow, using the roof as his rest, with his spare ammo at his elbow. The car vibrated gently beneath him as Laura lightly gunned the engine ready to make their getaway.

Matt concentrated his first shot at the gatepost. He needed to bring the fence down, so he could get a clear shot at the liquid petroleum gas tank. The lighting was poor, but he handled the crossbow with ease. All the tension and apprehension drained away as he began to relax behind the weapon. Memories of his days in shooting competitions came flooding back and confidence flowed through his body.

He squeezed the trigger and there was a short rasp as the bolt hurtled forward at high velocity. The gates were only a short distance over the road and as the bolt hit the steel upright, it exploded, hurtling a mass of twisted metal and wire fencing into the yard. Matt grunted with pleasure and immediately loaded the second bolt. His next target was the valve mechanism of the LPG tank which was now directly in line with the gap in the fencing. The bolt was loosened and his aim was perfect. A split second later, the impact of a direct hit ruptured the pipework beneath the tank.

There was a rush of escaping liquid as it poured out over the concrete base below. The petroleum, once at atmospheric pressure, began to evaporate so that an invisible cloud of highly combustible gases began to eddy above the mother liquid.

Matt leant over the Mini, his third bolt already loaded and ready to fire. He counted slowly to 60. Then, he discharged the final bolt, aimed at the heart of the tangled and broken pipes. This time, the explosion of the nitro-bolt was accompanied by a loud whoosh as the inflammable gas was ignited.

A huge iridescent ball of flame chased the escaping hydrocarbon vapours under the nearest drying sheds and consumed them with a rush of intense power. Matt felt the sudden heat of the blast. The planks in the nearest shed to the tank were immediately set ablaze with curls of vivid red and orange flames, dancing in a shimmering haze around the edges of the timber. The sky was suddenly aglow with a million sparks. Tiny flaming embers were pushed skywards in the hot streams of dense smoke.

At the tip of the ruptured pipe, liquid petroleum was rapidly being vaporised. The pipe had been sheared completely away and was acting like a gigantic flamethrower as the pressure in the tank forced more liquid to its burning tip. The luminous flames gushed forward, licking the concrete floor with a roaring, 20-foot tongue.

Air was sucked through howling channels, drawing angry, restless flames under the layers of drying planks. The timber spat, crackled and creaked as the flamethrower continued to hiss and growl, burning the protesting, seasoned wood. The builder's yard was gradually and irreversibly being engulfed by a devastating inferno.

Matt looked on with satisfaction, knowing that by crippling the fuel tank in such a way, he'd inflicted irreparable damage on Tyburn's business. He ducked his head back into the car and flopped into the seat next to Laura.

"Come on love, let's get out of here before that tank blows. I wonder what will be left of Tyburn's little empire come tomorrow. I only hope we've destroyed everything else he was hiding there. Drugs or whatever."

Laura let out the clutch and the tiny car screeched forward, with Melissa swiftly following in their wake. Half a mile away, they stopped in a quiet side street to change the number plates in case anyone had spotted them at the scene of the fire. The simple task was completed within a minute, but as they stood at the roadside, there was a dull, distant rumble. Looking back, they caught sight of a huge plume of flame, which fleetingly rose out of the darkness, then quickly disappeared.

Fire tenders and police cars hurtled past the end of their road with sirens wailing.

Matt grimaced. He was feeling a little guilty, but not about the fire. "I hope nobody else got hurt there tonight."

Laura consoled him. "I shouldn't think so. It was only a builder's yard after all and there wasn't anyone else around. We checked the area for other people the past couple of nights and there was never a soul about, except for that filthy old night watchman and we made sure he got safely away to the pub. Don't worry. I'm sure Tyburn's pocket will be the only thing to suffer tonight."

Chapter 34

The watchers at the builder's yard had become weary to the point of apathy by the daily monotony. Because of the small number of personnel in Harker's team, the two of them had been on the job, 24 hours a day, for two weeks.

Josh had set up a camp bed in the outer office and they took it in turns to sleep. They agreed that every couple of days one or the other could sneak a few hours off and return home. Monty was particularly displeased because he missed seeing his wife and young baby daughter, but Josh wasn't married and was much more flexible. He'd given his partner more of the spare time, so he could visit his family regularly.

Monty was very appreciative of his friend's sacrifice and to relieve the boredom, he'd been out that lunchtime and treated his pal to an Indian takeaway. They had thoroughly enjoyed the meal, but by the time twilight arrived, both of them were beginning to feel a little queasy.

"Jesus, Monty, where did you get that curry from. I feel like shit?"

Monty was feeling decidedly ropey himself, but he knew that one of them had to keep watch.

"If you feel that bad Josh, try and sleep it off. I'll take over. Go on. Get lost."

Josh gratefully disappeared and Monty tried to concentrate on work.

Over the next two hours, he fought to control his own biological urges, but his innards were rumbling round and beginning to give him severe pain. Finally, it got out of control. "Bloody hell. I've just gotta go."

He left his seat by the window and ran to the toilet. When he'd finished, his empty bowels grumbled and his guts felt as though they'd been stripped away.

Josh appeared.

"Not you as well?"

Josh said nothing, but pushed quickly past him. Monty began to wash his hands and from inside the toilet cubicle, a familiar sound confirmed that his friend had also started with the dreaded runs.

Just then the phone rang. Returning to his post, Monty picked up his mobile. "Hello, Joe. Yeah it's me, Monty. Guess what?"

Half an hour later, Joe Harker turned up with some medicine to combat their diarrhoea.

"Fancy you two getting the shits at the same time. By the way," he laughed, "I thought you might make use of these." He tossed them a double pack of toilet rolls. "Softest on the market. I hope you're appreciative."

Josh made a sickly grin. "Gee thanks, boss. I didn't know you cared."

Once Joe had confirmed they were well enough to continue, he left and they tried to settle down for the night.

By nine, the medicine had worked on Josh and he was snoring away on the bed.

Monty remained on duty, still feeling unwell. As he looked out through the window, he noticed the Mini was there again. *That's the third night in a row.*

It had looked a little suspicious on the Sunday night, because it parked there for two hours, but it had only stayed half an hour the next night. He checked the occupants with his infrared binoculars. Sure enough, it was the same man, but this time he had his arm round a different woman. *You randy bugger, getting your leg over again with a different chick. I bet it's a bit cramped in an old Mini.* He readjusted his seat to get a better view. *Oh, what a shame, they're going. I bet he's not managed to get his end away tonight.* He chuckled, but then his guts suddenly turned to jelly as another spasm of diarrhoea gripped his body. "Aw Jesus, not again!"

Rushing away from the window and across to the old toilet, he thankfully parked himself on the seat, snatching up the dwindling roll of soft paper.

He grumbled aloud to himself, "That's the last time I buy a curry from some crappy backstreet takeaway. It was even next to the dog kennels. I should have known better."

Suddenly, he heard a distant crump. A few seconds later, there was a similar noise. A full minute elapsed, then, a third and more significant thump sounded. The last one had the definite sound of an explosion and he was gripped by a gnawing uncertainty.

Something's going down outside. I know it.

He quickly fumbled with the toilet paper and pulled up his pants. Even though the pain still nagged in the depths of his bowels, he dragged himself back across the warehouse and stared with disbelief through the window at the incredible incineration taking place in the builder's yard opposite.

"Aw no! Hells fuckin' bells!" Amidst all the chaos, he tried to think straight. *The bleedin' Mini.*

It was the only common link and he quickly remembered he hadn't actually seen it drive away, only set off. He looked up and down the street, but it was now empty. He'd only been away a matter of minutes. The occupants of the car must have had something to do with the fire. He felt well and truly duped.

The intensity of the fire momentarily mesmerised his thoughts. The whole place seemed to be alight. His immediate reaction was to ring Joe Harker. His boss took in the picture instantly and screamed back down the phone. "For God's sake, grab Josh and get yourselves out of that place. It sounds as though that gas tank could blow at any time. Get out now! I'll ring for the fire brigade."

Monty dropped the phone and moved smartly across the room to where Josh was still sleeping peacefully. He shook him vigorously. "Come on, bloody sleeping beauty. Wake up!"

Just then, the tank outside exploded and the windows in the room fragmented. Shards of glass hissed through the air, indiscriminately hunting for a target. The shock wave threw Monty on top of the bed and the two men were hurtled against the far wall. The old building shuddered from the frontal detonation. Some of the roof beams collapsed, bringing down the plastered ceiling and showering them with debris. Monty moaned painfully in a semi-conscious heap. All that he could hear was an ear-deafening roar as the fire outside continued to consume the tons of combustible timber. In the distance, he picked out the faint sound of sirens, but in the shattered room, the air seemed to be stifling and it became more difficult to breathe. There was a strange haze all around and he dreamt of being at home in a warm bed. Then, his mind gradually drifted into darkness.

* * * * *

Joe Harker made it to Tyburn's premises as fast as he could. The roads were busy and the police were stopping traffic to let the fire crews and ambulances through. When he showed his credentials to the senior officer, he learnt that his two men had already been rescued and taken to St Thomas Hospital near

Westminster. Joe wasted no time and set off to find them. His mind was in a state of trepidation as he worried about what fate had befallen his friends.

When he arrived at the accident and emergency unit, he was surprised and relieved to find Josh sitting in a cubicle with a blanket around his shoulders. He looked scruffy and was smeared with dirt and grime, but he seemed perky.

"You okay, Josh?"

"Yeah. I'm fine. Just a few bumps and bruises. I've still got gut ache and I'm suffering a bit from the smoke." He gave a dry barking cough as though he needed to emphasise his condition and solicit some sympathy from his boss. "I've been given the all clear, but they're going to keep me in overnight, just to make sure there's no reaction to the smoke."

"What about Monty? Do you know anything?"

"The nurses tell me he'll be all right. He helped to shield me from the blast, but he's had a knock on the head and he's suffering from concussion and the smoke of course."

He started to chuckle.

"What's the big joke then, Josh?"

"It's Monty. The daft bugger has made more fuss since we arrived here. They've almost had to tie him down. He got a bit indignant, because the nurses told him to lie on his belly so they could pull all the glass splinters out of his arse. Rather them than me."

The two men laughed together, then Joe became more serious, "What went wrong with the surveillance, Josh? You didn't spot anything suspicious."

"You know how sick we felt. Monty offered to watch and I went to bed, so I was well out of it. Anyway, in the ambulance on the way over here, he kept mumbling on about a Mini."

Joe pumped him for more information, "Go on then."

"Well, we first spotted it outside the yard two nights ago. It had a man and woman inside. Looked like a couple of lovebirds. I've got a good photo of the bloke. I developed it yesterday afternoon. He got out of the car the first night and disappeared for a while. Thought he must have gone for a jimmy."

"Come on, Josh. That's suspicious to start with. If you were rogering some bird, you wouldn't stop halfway through and go for a piss? Were there any movements in the yard?"

"Only the old sod that acts as a night watchman."

Something suddenly struck Josh forcibly and he pulled a tattered notebook from his back pocket. He flicked through the pages anxiously. "Oh shit! We should have picked this up earlier. Both nights, the Mini vanished not long after the old man had gone walkabout. Come to think of it," he thumbed through the pages of his book. "Yeah, it's here. The first night they appeared, the bloke got out of his car almost as soon as the watchman left with his dog. He could easily have followed him to see where he was going and how long he was likely to be away."

"And where was that? Do you know?"

"The pub, boss. I followed him one night myself, last week. He keeps to the same routine, leaves around nine and returns after closing time."

"Okay. Now, have you got the car registration?"

"Sure. It's here."

"What about it then, you must have put it through the computer by now?"

Josh looked sheepish and said nothing.

"Bloody hell, man, it's standard practice. What have you two pillocks been playing at?"

"Sorry, boss. We'd have done it for certain tomorrow, with the car showing up for the third night in a row. It just seemed so innocent."

Joe stormed off to make a phone call and was back directly in an even darker mood.

"Just as I thought. Those plates don't belong to any existing car. We're obviously dealing with professionals here. It's all beginning to make sense now. The second night they only made a short visit. I bet it was to confirm that the old fella went out at the same time. They came back tonight to do the job and as soon as he was out of the way they moved in. Whoever it was, they certainly knew what they were doing. Those responsible for tonight's fireworks certainly didn't lack finesse.

We know Tyburn is involved with drug trafficking, so he could have an army of enemies. It definitely looks like a hit to me. Maybe it's a turf war or somebody is just out to settle an old score. The problem is that now we've got another variable to deal with and it's worrying me. Tyburn's premises were a cover for his drugs operation and could have been a valuable source of evidence to link him with Rydell. Now, we have to start afresh."

He pondered for a while then got up. "I'm off. I want to alert the other teams to watch out for the Mini. If somebody's out to get Tyburn, it may show up again.

210

By the way, smoke damaged lungs or not, I want the best mug shot you've got of that bloke in the Mini. He's our only lead and he may help us indirectly get to Rydell. I want it on my desk by 8:30 sharp tomorrow morning. See you then."

Chapter 35

Joe Harker returned to the scene of the fire at first light the following morning. Most of the heavy fire-fighting equipment had already been packed up and dispersed to the various stations nearby. The blaze had been of major significance, but the appliances arriving at the scene had brought it under control by the early hours of the morning. There was one engine still operating and its crew was busy damping down the smouldering remains of the wrecked yard and surrounding buildings. A heavy odour of burnt wood, reminiscent of Guy Fawkes night, hung in the air. Smoke and steam still intermingled together and twisted skywards in elaborate corkscrews.

The firefighters looked weary and dishevelled as they plied their hoses on the few piles of half burnt timbers that had survived. The rest had been reduced to charcoal and ashes. The buildings in the centre of the woodyard and on either side of the compound were just hollow shells. The LPG tank had exploded with horrendous force, devastating several adjacent walls and starting a succession of secondary fires. These had all contributed to the inferno, which the fire crews had to deal with on their arrival.

The whole area was now cordoned off by tape and there was a small contingent of police keeping sightseers away.

Joe flashed a false ID at the nearest police officer and was immediately ushered through the small posse of TV crews and pressmen who were trying to get a newsworthy story. The scene was now quiet, with a number of top brass from the fire service strutting through the wreckage. They were deep in conversation outside the remains of Tyburn's offices.

Joe walked straight up to them and introduced himself, immediately impressing them with his role as a senior anti-terrorist officer.

"National security is possibly at stake here and that's why we're interested in this blaze. We're almost certain it was arson. Have your people had a chance to look at it yet?"

The younger of the two men held the higher rank and at the mention of the anti-terrorist unit, he almost fell over himself in his desire to help.

"No, but we have a forensic team arriving shortly."

Joe nodded amicably. "So far then, you've found nothing suspicious?"

"Not really. Unless you can call the owner of this place suspicious."

"Why do you say that?"

"Well, he was here a while ago at the crack of dawn. He demanded that we allow him to get to his safe, which is in there." He pointed to the smouldering office. "He was very anxious to get to it, even though the fire had been barely put out and there was still a danger it might flare up again. I told him in no uncertain terms that he would only be allowed back on these premises after we'd finished with our own forensics into the cause of the fire."

"You said he wanted to get to his safe? Did he give a reason?"

"Yes. He said it was vital that he retrieve some very important papers. He wanted to make sure they hadn't been burnt. I pointed out to him that if he'd installed a modern, good quality safe, there was every chance that the documents would have withstood the fire and still be intact."

"So, you sent him away then?"

"I most certainly did."

"Good. Now look here, gentlemen, I don't want to interfere with your investigation, but I need to get at the safe myself as soon as possible. When your team arrives, I'd like you to concentrate your efforts on the office area, where the safe is housed, so it can be eliminated from your inquiry as a matter of priority. If the owner, a man called Tyburn, shows up again, he must not be allowed anywhere near it. Not until I give the green light. Under no circumstances must you mention our interest. Is that clear?"

"Right. We'll get onto it straight away, in fact, it looks as though our forensic team is just arriving."

Joe handed the fire chief a card with a telephone number on it. "Please, let me know when you have the all clear on the safe."

Joe shook their hands, thanked the two men and went straight back to his car. He made a short phone call and drove back to his office to have his meeting with Josh Gardner.

* * * * *

At noon, the fire service rang, giving him the all clear. He arrived back at the woodyard and paddled through the filth and black slush into the empty shell of the offices.

Already working on the fire-scarred safe was a plump, grey haired man with a ruddy complexion. He was the MI6 master safe cracker.

"Hello, Norman. How's things?"

The man looked up and smiled. "Straight forward job, this one. Type PB75. Give me another five minutes and I'll have it open."

Joe had rung Norman earlier and arranged for him to come and do this emergency job. The locksmith, who owned his own business, had agreed to come immediately. The fees paid by the department made it worthwhile for him to be on permanent standby and they'd never yet given him a safe he'd failed to crack. True to his word, the safe door was soon open.

"Do you need me anymore, Joe?"

"No. That's great, Norman."

He pulled an envelope from his inside pocket and handed it over. "Here you are, mate. Not bad for half an hour's work."

Norman winked at him and put the envelope away. He never bothered counting the cash because he knew exactly how much there would be. He packed his tools into a leather bag and left Joe peering into the depths of the safe.

Joe put on a pair of latex surgical gloves. Using a small flashlight, he poked around and was pleased to find that the contents of the safe were only slightly scorched. There were a few bundles of money, which he estimated to be worth about 3000 pounds. There were other items including some letters and a large jiffy bag. Joe slotted everything into his brief case, leaving the safe door slightly ajar.

He drove back to headquarters in a great hurry, excited by the prospect of examining the secrets from Tyburn's safe. When he was alone in the comfort of his office, he fingered the letters, carefully prising open each envelope to reveal its contents. He quickly scanned every letter and was disappointed by any lack of correspondence with Rydell. Switching his attention to the jiffy bag, he became intrigued when the CD case slipped out onto his desk. He loaded the disc into his computer, expecting to find an accounting spreadsheet of some kind, but when the home movie started, it took him completely by surprise. Joe recognised the minister instantly and looked on aghast as the cameo of Rydell's sexual exploits unfolded on the screen.

At last! Pay dirt. So that's the blackmail angle. Not quite what Kate predicted! He let out a long whistle as the DVD continued to play.

What a masochist. What a pervert. Would you believe it? No wonder you're playing their game, Rydell. This is dynamite. Political suicide.

He picked up the phone and spoke briefly to Paula Ross. Ten minutes later, she came down from her top floor office and watched a repeat of Rydell's performance over Joe's shoulder. Her jaw dropped in disbelief.

Chapter 36

The prime minister was having a fiery disagreement with certain members of her cabinet when her personal secretary delivered the note. She paused from her scathing attack on disloyalty and read the short message.

She looked at her watch. "What appointment do I have for three o'clock today, Jim? Can it be cancelled?"

"It's a meeting with the Nigerian ambassador, prime minister, and yes, we could postpone it."

"Good. Then do it immediately and arrange for the sender of this note to meet me in my office at three on the dot."

Her secretary bowed slightly and made for the door. He had not left the room before she was back in full flow, lambasting her colleagues on the ideology and strength of her economic policies.

Paula Ross was waiting in the anteroom at three o'clock as instructed. She had been on her feet a great deal over the last few days and her false leg was chafing and causing her considerable discomfort. Although she felt that Joe had made a significant breakthrough with the DVD, she was not looking forward to confronting the prime minister with it.

She was shown in, as soon as the hour hand on the nearby clock nudged to the vertical. Paula crossed the room to where the PM was seated at her desk and pushed the slim document in front of her.

"I'm afraid this doesn't look good."

The PM said nothing but gestured for Paula Ross to take a seat. She opened the file and read the three-quarter page report on the recent revelation.

"Do you have the disc with you, Paula?"

Paula Ross removed the CD case from her briefcase and passed it over. The PM pushed the disc into her desktop computer and looked on impassively. Paula waited silently as the PM watched the DVD play. All she could hear was the sound track, whilst watching the PM's tight lipped expression. She just kept fidgeting, her ashen face a mask of incomprehension. When it finished playing, she looked up and sighed deeply, hunching her shoulders. Suddenly, she looked so very old and drained, as though all the energy and vitality that marked her strength of character had been sapped away.

At last, she spoke, "Can I really believe what I've witnessed? Is this true? Can any man reach such high office and have such a dark secret? What makes people behave like that?"

She suddenly thumped the desktop, her aggression quickly reasserting itself. "How dare he have such a secret? How can he hope to keep this skeleton locked away? The man is a fool, an imbecile!"

There was a look of fanatical hatred as she instantaneously exploded into a tirade of abuse and condemnation, which made Paula blush. The monologue was cold hearted, vicious and animated, but most of it was borne of fear and frustration for her own position of power and the damage it might cause her chances of re-election.

At last, the outburst subsided and she looked Paula directly in the eyes. "This must never, I repeat, never, be made public. How will you ensure its secrecy?"

"We are still working on the blackmail demands. Until we know what they are and how they affect Charles Rydell and your government, it's impossible to plot a course of action. This disc was taken from a safe at the big fire in Woolwich last night."

"Ah, yes! I saw the report on breakfast television this morning."

"Because it's been kept in the safe, we believe that this is the only copy. With your permission, we'll damage it beyond use and put the remains back into the safe. We can do it in such a way that it will look as though the fire did the damage. Although we are no closer to solving the mystery surrounding Rydell, at least there can be no chance of the blackmailers passing it on to a third party."

The prime minister pondered a while. "You're absolutely right, Paula. Go ahead and destroy the evidence and of course, carry on with your attempts to unravel whatever plot Rydell is mixed up in. Once you find out what he's up to, then I will most certainly expect you to take further action."

She stood up and held out her hand warmly. Paula took it, but before she could break the normally fleeting shake, the PM also gripped her with her left hand, holding on tightly like an old friend.

She smiled gratefully at the head of MI6. "I am indebted to you Paula and I won't forget your courage and personal loyalty. You can expect to be mentioned in the next New Year's Honours List, with the highest award your country can bestow."

Paula grinned appreciatively. "Prime minister, you favour me graciously."

* * * * *

A short time later, the evidence retrieved from Tyburn's safe was returned to its original place. Every item was untouched except for the DVD. It had been carefully heated in an oven so that it gently warped. It would never operate in any kind of player ever again.

Chapter 37

It was evening and the atmosphere in the casino office reeked of stale cigar smoke. Empty coffee cups and half a bottle of whisky littered the table.

Lawrence Tyburn fumed. The destruction of his timber yard had left him in a state of paranoia as he pointed an accusing finger at every mob in London. "We've been through everything and looked at every conceivable possibility. I can't figure this out at all, but one thing is for sure, that fire was no accident."

Simon Lush sat opposite sipping iced tonic water. His mind was too furred with alcohol and he needed to clear his brain. "There's no doubt that somebody wants to close us down. Someone who knows that we use the yard as a front for shifting coke. Well, whoever they are, they've done a fuckin' good job."

Tyburn thumped the desktop. "They've ruined my operation and set us back years. Their life won't be worth a jot when I find out who's behind it. Where the hell is Siggy? He should be back by now."

Just as he spoke, Dexter tapped on the door and came in. He looked harassed.

Tyburn gushed at him in expectation. "Okay, Siggy. What have you found out?"

He hoped that his trusted henchman would come up with a lead.

"Err. You're not going to believe this, boss. Nothing."

Tyburn exploded, "What! You're telling me that with all our contacts, nobody has heard a thing. You're right, I don't believe it. What the hell am I paying you for?"

"Boss, I've tried everyone I know, from the smallest low-life to that bleedin' magistrate in Mayfair. I've broken fingers, arms and legs. There's just no word on the streets."

Lush butted in. "Maybe it's just too soon, Lol. We might have to hang around awhile for a whisper. At least the message is out that we need to finger somebody. Money talks. Sooner or later, we'll get a sniff."

Tyburn refused to be pacified. "What about that fuckin' copper, Willis? What do we pay him for? Get him on the case as well, Siggy. If the police think its arson, I want to know the second they get a lead." He shrugged his shoulders. "Jesus, I feel weary. I'm out of the poker game tonight. I'm going home to bed."

Picking up the phone, he directed the doorman to bring round his Rolls. He was still bristling as he left the room. "I'm not happy, I want results, Siggy. Get your arse out there and sort it."

When he'd gone, Lush gently patted Dexter on his back. "Don't worry, Siggy. Forget it till tomorrow. There's nothing more you can do tonight. Let's enjoy the poker game later, okay."

Outside the casino, but further up the street, two of Harker's people were watching the front entrance. The maroon Rolls pulled up and a few minutes later, Tyburn appeared at the roadside and got into his car.

The watchers called in to base. "Suspect on the move. We're following."

The reply was immediate. "Affirmative. Rydell is also on the move. Follow your man. They may be heading for a rendezvous."

As they followed Tyburn out onto the Chelsea Embankment, a sharp-eyed MI6 woman, who was the co-driver, spotted a small car going in the opposite direction.

"That looks like the old mini we were told to watch out for. The passenger looked very much like that bloke in the photo Joe gave us this morning."

"How can you be sure of that, Karen? This street lighting's crap."

"I may be wrong, but after the bollocking Josh and Monty got, I'm going to report everything." She duly relayed her information, but after a short pause, they were instructed to continue after Tyburn. The controller wasn't convinced by Karen and decided to follow up his hunch that there might be a meeting with Rydell. In any case, they didn't have enough watchers to put a tail on the Mini *and* Tyburn, and he was the priority.

* * * * *

The evening business was going well at *Un Coup De Chance*. The exclusive gambling club had a unique atmosphere and was one of the most fashionable in Chelsea. Membership was strictly controlled and the waiting list was growing rapidly.

The gaming area was circular in shape, with an exquisite marble floor. Directly opposite the main entrance was a wide, ornate staircase, which curved upwards to both left and right, joining an overhanging balcony, which circumscribed the hall. At regular intervals, narrow, architectural pillars held the balcony in place and afforded an eye-catching symmetry to the room.

The busy, main area of the floor hosted the more conventional games and was brightly lit with crystal chandeliers. In the many secluded spaces under the balcony, there was a chance to play less well-known games in an atmosphere of more sobriety. The centrepiece of the main floor was a long roulette table and this always proved to be one of the most popular pastimes.

Siggy Dexter looked down from the balcony at the clientele below. They were enjoying the evening's entertainment, choosing to lose their money, hard earned or not, on the excellent range of games in the bustling arena.

There was a flurry of activity around the roulette wheel as an attentive crowd of envious punters willed a young woman to further success. There were squeals of delight from the female onlookers as the croupier announced the winning number. The audacious persistence of the lucky gambler had paid off, as she continued with her winning streak.

The members of the club circulated excitedly about the gaming tables, ordering drinks from a host of attractive young waiters and waitresses who patiently drifted amongst the guests. Dexter watched every move that one pretty young girl made. He eyed her continuously.

A tall, elegant form appeared at his side and peered over his shoulder. "I see. You fancy our new little recruit, Siggy?"

Dexter turned to face the beautiful woman at his side. "Tell me everything about her, Selina. Is she ready?"

Selina Belvedere was responsible for the welfare of all the females and young men who were employed at *Un Coup De Chance*. Although the club was private and fashionable, it was not used exclusively for gambling. There were half a dozen incredibly luxurious suites used for other kinds of entertainment. The world's oldest profession was never more adequately or sumptuously provided for, but at an exorbitant cost to any prospective client. Even so, there was a regular stream of guests, willing to sample the delights for which the club's reputation was now soaring. There was nothing that the club couldn't offer its members in terms of gay, lesbian or heterosexual experiences and Selina was the Madame who controlled it all. She had no need to sell her delectable services anymore, earning as she did, a huge salary as part of the casino's management structure. With 20 years of experience, she was able to recruit only the best young bodies. She tutored her young protégés of both sexes, in the mystical art of servicing the lustful pleasures of the flesh.

"That is Sharon. Or should I say, Mercedes. We picked her up on Kings Cross station and she apparently comes from Leeds. No mother. She fell out with her father and so she came to London. It's the usual sort of story. That was six months ago. We decided to move in on her quickly because she was such a beautiful looking girl. We played the usual tricks and gave her some free modelling work. We made it really tough for her with lots of criticism. After two weeks, I went through the normal routine and told her that she wouldn't make it. After the tears, I offered her a temporary job at the club."

"Go on then, Selina. How did you train her up?"

"It's pretty easy really. It just takes time. I offered to let her stay with me and one cold night, I managed to get her in bed with me, initially just for company and gradually I managed to gain her trust."

"You mean that you started touching her up."

"Don't be filthy. It wasn't like that at all, but I could never get you to understand. Anyway, she didn't know what to do at first, but I could tell she didn't want to upset me. After a few nights, she was positively enjoying it and as the weeks went by, I tutored her in all the kinds of pleasurable excesses that women like to do to others of their own sex."

"What you really mean, Selina is that you're good at bending the sex of young kids to whatever you want."

"That's rich coming from you, Siggy. I suppose all you want is for some woman to lie spread-eagled across a bed so that you can shag the hell out of her."

He sneered at her suggestion.

"Well, that's no good these days. Our customers want more. Because I used a soft, lesbian approach, her sexuality has not been questioned. When I told her how much she could earn by using her new talents on some of our clients, her eyes nearly popped out. One evening, I pointed out some of her potential customers, both old and young and she offered herself straight away. Since then, she's become very popular. When she's a little older, I'll introduce her to men. But for now, Siggy, she's still a virgin and as far as you're concerned, it's hands off. I know you like the young ones, but I've worked hard on her for months now. For God's sake, don't damage the merchandise."

Dexter didn't like Selina telling him what he couldn't do. He grabbed her jaw with his huge hand and squeezed until it made her wince.

"No need to be bitchy. You're only jealous because you haven't got a prick, otherwise you'd have shafted her yourself months ago."

Selina blanched. She hated his insinuation. She adored her own femininity and was completely at ease with her own bisexuality.

He pushed her away, leaving huge red marks on either side of her face. "When you've pulled yourself together, go and tell Mercedes to go to suite number three for ten o'clock. If you want to keep that pretty face of yours in one piece, you'd better not let on who she'll be entertaining. Just tell her it's somebody new. I'll have finished with her in less than an hour because I've got a game of poker lined up with the boys for 11."

Siggy turned and continued to lean against the rail, ogling the young females below.

Behind his back, Selina gave him a look of intense ferocity. Had she been any relation to Medusa, it would have turned him to stone ten times over.

* * * * *

Mercedes glanced at her watch and noticed that it was approaching ten o'clock. She was dressed as a club hostess, which was designed to stimulate the male ego, although it sometimes had the same effect on women. She wore an almost sheer black, silken blouse with long voluminous sleeves. Underneath, her pure white lace bra was tastefully cut so that her young, firm breasts were pushed forward into two tight, exciting mounds. From her waist hung a short, black, pleated skirt, made of the softest silken material. It flowed gracefully over her hips and pert little bottom, swinging provocatively from side to side as she moved between the tables. Her legs were clad in the sheerest dark nylons accentuating both her height and figure. As she moved through the room, she was aware of the admiring glances of both men and women. She disappeared up the broad, ornate staircase with a dozen pairs of lustful eyes, looking up her skirt to gain the faintest glimpse of her frothy white knickers.

Mercedes knocked gently on the door of suite number three and when there was no reply, she let herself in. It was apparent that the room was unoccupied so she made herself comfortable in one of the soft, luxurious armchairs and waited patiently for her client to come. Sitting cross-legged she admired herself in the

223

dressing table mirror, over by the huge four-poster bed. The constant attention of the men in the club, night after night, always made her feel good and gave her a happy glow. Yet, it was female company she had learnt to appreciate, revelling in the soft tenderness of her own sex. Sometimes her emotions became confused, but every time she provided her service to a client, she enjoyed the demands made of her and had earned some huge tips from a number of doting females.

She was still admiring herself through the mirror when she caught the reflection of the door as it silently opened. Expecting her guest, she rose and turned to face her, but noticed with dismay that Siggy Dexter was standing there.

"I'm sorry, Mr Dexter. I must have come to the wrong room. I was sure Selina said room three."

She hurried to the door, worried that she might be late for her client.

Dexter barred her way and turning the key in the lock behind his back, slipped it into his jacket pocket.

"Not so fast, young lady. You are in the right room."

She looked puzzled as she stared at his face, which smirked with sleazy satisfaction. A look of horror crossed her face and she slowly shook her head from side to side.

"That's right, my little beauty. I'm paying for your services tonight, not some wrinkled old bag."

He quickly stripped himself down to his bright red boxer shorts.

Mercedes eyes were wide with fear, attracted by the strange stirrings taking place in his pants. She had never seen an erection before and it grew into a ramrod, suddenly escaping from its hiding place as Dexter thrust his hips forward provocatively.

She frantically looked around for some means of escape, but there was nowhere to go. He approached her slowly and she began to scream over and over again and then, in a pitiful act of subjugation she stuffed her knuckles into her mouth and bit them hard.

Dexter savoured her reaction to his domination and it fired his groin. The more she screamed in girlish terror the more he was aroused. "Scream, little Sharon. Scream all you like. Don't forget, the walls are sound proof and the door is locked. It's just you and me here, alone."

He quickly cornered her and grabbing her shoulders, hoisted her off the floor and pinned her against the wall. He pushed his huge erection into her groin. "Feel it there a while, you little lesbian. Imagine what it'll be like when I push it right up inside you. Scream a little more you whore, because no matter what you do, tonight I'm your stag. I'm your stallion and I'm going to shag that pretty little arse of yours until you can't take any more."

Mercedes shook her head from side to side and moaned fearfully as she felt his disgusting phallus between her closed thighs. She tried to manoeuvre her hips and arms, but he was too strong and had her firmly trapped against the wall. As his mouth closed on hers, she felt consumed by a creature of depravity, sucking away her beauty and innocence. She wanted to scream her nightmare away but found that she couldn't. The fear of her predicament excited her vagina and slowly, the secretions dampened her groin as her inevitable rape came closer. Her will to resist ebbed away as she lost all hope of saving her virginity. The tension in her whole body evaporated as she decided not to fight him anymore. She would let him have his way.

Dexter immediately felt her change of mood and lack of struggle. He didn't like it. It meant she wasn't afraid of what he would do to her. He pulled his mouth away from hers. "What's the matter, you bitch? Is it too much for you? Come on, you little mother-fucker. I'm going to stick my end right up your quivering little arse and I'm going to have you now."

Dexter let go of her and she dropped to the floor. Scooping her up in his arms, he turned and tossed her effortlessly onto the king-sized bed.

The young 16-year-old looked up into his face, but the pleading was only in her eyes. She tried not to offend him and made no protest as he roughly tore at the top of her suspenders and ripped down her pristine white knickers. Dexter thrust his knee hard into her groin. It was painful and he needn't have done it because she hitched up the provocative miniskirt about her waist and opened her thighs for him to enter.

Dexter fell into a wild rage. "I'll take you, you stupid bitch, you mindless little flirt. I don't need any help. I'll take you!" He pushed her legs together and lashed out hitting her hard in the soft pit of her stomach. The pain was exquisite and she rolled to one side doubling her knees up under her chin in agony. She bit her lip and moaned softly, not daring to shout out for fear of annoying him further. *What did he want from her?*

She rolled over onto her back and opened her thighs again and this time he began to rant like a maniac. He thrashed her about the face, punching her hard and tearing her blouse and bra so they hung in tatters about her shoulders. The pathetic child closed her legs tightly, having learnt her lesson, but her head was now swimming with the pain as he continued to batter her senseless. Both her eyes were puffed up and she tasted blood in her mouth. With one half closed eye, she watched his rage finally subside. He squatted on all fours above her, his chest heaving with the exertion of his efforts.

In her stupor, she waited for the pain of his penetration and then, through a misty haze, she realised that he was getting dressed. She couldn't comprehend his sudden impotence, brought about by her capitulation and refusal to fight. It had roused the demon in him and his frustration and inability to perform had ignited a fierce retribution.

Mercedes had paid a terrible price. She lay in a semi-conscious state, a pitiable shadow of the vivacious young girl she had been only minutes earlier.

Dexter finished dressing and then came over to the bed. He took a roll, containing 200 pounds, from his pocket and stuffed it into her crutch. Then he put his hand around her throat. "Right. Listen and listen good. Nod if you can understand."

Mercedes slowly moved her head in acknowledgement.

"I've just tipped you two hundred quid for tonight's pleasure. You tell anyone what really happened and one dark night you might just disappear. Get my drift?"

She nodded her head vigorously and had her face not been such a swollen mess, he would have seen the fear in her eyes.

He picked up the bedside phone and spoke quietly into the handset.

A knock on the door followed almost immediately, and Dexter let Selina in.

She was carrying a small leather satchel. One look at Mercedes and it was clear what had happened. She rounded on Dexter with a woman's fury, tears burning her eyes. "You swine. Look what you've done to her. The poor, defenceless child. She didn't deserve that."

"She was useless. She's not old enough to appreciate my body."

"You mean she wouldn't play your sordid little game?"

"What's that supposed to mean?"

All of a sudden, Selina realised she may have said the wrong thing. She already knew of his perversions and impotence from one of the other girls. Nothing in the world would have given her greater pleasure than to confront him with it, but she dare not. It was more than her life was worth.

She backed off, trying to pacify him. "I mean that a man with your sexual prowess should let young virgins be broken in gently before trying uncouth games with them. Once they've learnt a few tricks, you can get them to do anything."

Dexter snorted and his jaw line softened appreciably. Selina felt relieved. She'd got away with it.

"You'd better get her started on something tonight. Perhaps a small shot of coke. That should settle her down."

He threw the keys to Selina and left.

She locked the door behind him and went over to the pitiful, adolescent wretch on the bed. "You poor darling. Don't worry, I'll look after you. No one will ever see you looking like this. We can stay here tonight and tomorrow, when you're feeling better, I'll take you to my flat. You can stay there until you're well again."

Selina began by bathing Mercedes' face with ice-cold water to keep down the swelling and bruising of the delicate tissues around her eyes. She carefully undressed her and then turning away to her satchel, produced a tiny hypodermic syringe and inserted the needle into a phial of colourless liquid. Lifting the bedclothes, she found Mercedes' wrist and before the young girl could protest, Selina had swabbed the skin and completed the injection. She whispered sweetly into her ear, "There, there my darling, you'll sleep well tonight. Although you've lost your innocence, you still haven't lost your virginity."

Selina switched off the lights and slid into bed beside Mercedes. She lay in the quiet and stroked the child's hair until she fell into a fitful, drug-induced sleep. Selina stayed awake, wondering what psychological damage Dexter had inflicted upon the young girl. It was probable that she might never become one of their many bisexual hostesses because of the dreadful experience he had put her through. What Selina feared most of all was the possibility that Mercedes might reject her lifestyle completely. If that proved to be the case and she tried to escape, then she would be worthless to them. Worthless that is, except for her young body.

Tyburn and his associates had invested a great deal of time and money in her and would demand a return for their outlay. She had seen it happen before. Tyburn would continue to get her more and more drug dependant, then sell her to one of the notorious underworld chain houses. He would get a good price for a beauty such as Mercedes, who would spend the rest of a shortened life as a drug-dependant slave. She would never see the light of day again, but remain a sex junky, chained to a bed in some basement hovel, oblivious to those who would use her body as a vessel for their hideous depravity.

Selina shuddered at the thought of giving Mercedes up to such a horrendous fate. She kissed the sleeping teenager softly and then, between clenched teeth, she murmured almost imperceptibly.

"Dexter. You bastard. You've got a lot to answer for."

Chapter 38

The Mini drove up the narrow one-way street and came to a halt in the shadows. The street lighting was poor and uncharacteristic for that part of town, but it was ideally suited for the occupants of the little car. Melissa had parked in a road running parallel to the back of *Un Coup De Chance*. There were a few other cars parked around them, but nothing that would stop them from making a quick getaway if they needed to. They had already driven past the rear entrance to the club and confirmed the presence of the BMW with the *SIG 3* number plates. That was their target.

Driving around the block several times, Melissa decided that this street was a convenient and safe place to wait.

Matt went to the rear of the car and opened the boot. Welded to the base was a small steel case and he gently opened its heavy lid. Securely padded inside was one of the small wooden boxes containing a phial of pale yellow, nitro-glycerine. With gloved hands, Matt pulled the cold tube from its resting place.

The driver's window wound down and Melissa called out to Matt, her voice filled with trepidation. "Good luck, darling. Please be careful."

"To say I'm looking forward to this is the understatement of the century. If there's any trouble, I'll sling this stuff and make a run for it. The least it should do is cause a bit of a diversion and help us make a getaway." He gave her a sickly grin. "If you hear any kind of commotion, bring the car round as fast as you can. Don't forget, you must keep the engine going. A few seconds could make all the difference."

Melissa had a lump in her throat and said nothing more. She just nodded, unable to face him in case she showed all the fear she had bottled up inside.

Leaning through the window, Matt kissed her lightly on the cheek and set off up the street. He walked slowly, drifting in and out of the shadows until at last she saw him disappear round the far corner. Apart from the nitro, which he was holding tightly in one hand, he carried a small bundle of tools in the other.

He rounded the next corner and proceeded towards the rear entrance of the casino. The road surface had been recently renovated with smart block paving, so there were no kerbs and pot holes to trip him up. Even in the darkness, it looked smooth and safe. As he approached the shining black target, he found himself breathing heavily, his head prickling with fear. Halfway down the road, he stopped and listened, invisible in the shadows of the high walls. The only sound was that of distant traffic and a faraway aircraft. He was about to move forward again when a woman appeared at the back entrance of the club. She hesitated for just a second, looking up and down the street, then quickly made her way to the BMW.

* * * * *

Selina Belvedere was intent on exacting revenge on Siggy Dexter. She left the peacefully sleeping Mercedes and locked the room behind her. She had to find some kind of retribution that couldn't be blamed on her or the young girl. She'd hit on a great idea.

Dexter was in a poker game in one of the back rooms. She often spent time looking on, so her presence wouldn't seem unusual. Quietly she slipped into the room, almost choking in the smoke-filled atmosphere. There were five men playing and three women looking on. One was a waitress ready to bring drinks at an instant's notice. Selina looked around and immediately spotted what she was looking for. Dexter's car keys had been carelessly thrown onto a small side table next to his discarded jacket. It was his usual habit. She edged round the room and stood next to the table. Everyone was enthralled by the game and she easily palmed the keys from the tabletop. She watched the game for another five minutes and when the waitress was sent for more drinks, she left at the same time. Selina hugged the keys tightly to her breast as she made her way to the kitchens. In the steamy heat, nobody noticed anything odd as she passed through. She unobtrusively picked up a razor-sharp meat knife and disappeared through a side door.

She was now a woman fired with a mission. Dexter's BMW was his status symbol. She was intent on making him suffer by vandalising it and would derive a great deal of pleasure from performing this act. She would also make sure she was around to see his reaction when he discovered the state of his car. It would worsen his frustration and impotence because he wouldn't be able to do anything about it other than curse and rage.

Selina approached the darkened car and ran the knife blade carelessly down the side. She systematically went round and damaged every individual panel. Then, she used the key to access the car. In five frantic minutes of madness, she devastated the inside, slashing the leather seats, dashboard and trim. She finally regained her composure and closed the car door. As she looked at the destruction she'd caused, she felt oddly calm. It had been a cathartic experience and she felt so good. She threw her head back, stood up straight and made her way back into the casino. Minutes later, she had replaced the knife and Dexter's keys.

* * * * *

Matt watched the vandalisation of the BMW from the shadows. What was the crazy woman up to? At first, she seemed to have foiled his plan but he realised, as she walked away, that she hadn't locked the car. What luck, now he didn't need to break in.

A block away, the idling Mini engine rattled, bumped and hissed. Melissa strained every fibre of her body listening, but it was no good, the old car drowned out every noise. She reluctantly switched off and waited anxiously for any sound.

Matt crossed over to the BMW and gently rested the phial of high explosive on the brick road. Removing a roll of masking tape from his tool kit, he cut several long strips, attaching one end of each piece to the rear bumper, ready for use. He opened the car door and found the catch to open the boot lid. There was a satisfying metallic clunk as the mechanism released the lock. Just as the massive boot lid swung open, the peace was shattered, as the car's integrated alarm system became active. The horn gave off a loud staccato blast and all the lights flashed on simultaneously. Matt suddenly became afraid as the loud, blaring din continued unabated. *What had that manic woman done to the electrics on the alarm?*

It took him all his courage not to race away, because he knew he only had seconds before the noise attracted the attention of someone close by.

He snatched up the nitro, peeled the ready cut lengths of tape from the bumper and secured the glass container out of sight, under the lip of the boot compartment. He pushed the lid down carefully until he heard it click and just as he did, the rear door to the casino was thrown open.

231

* * * * *

Dexter was in the middle of a poor hand when a message was delivered demanding that he take a call from Tyburn. He ditched his cards and disappeared into the casino to the phone.

Just as the others were finishing the hand, the sound of a nearby car alarm went off.

Lush was the first to react. "Sounds as though that could be Siggy's car."

He pushed himself away from the table and went outside to investigate. As he opened the outer door, onto the rear balcony, he could see the lights of the BMW flashing and the outline of a man next to it.

Lush called after him, "Hey, you. What do you think you're doing with that car?"

Matt glanced up and caught sight of a portly man framed in the doorway. Turning away, he raced off up the road.

Dashing down the stairs, Lush intended catching the intruder, but by the time he'd got to ground level he was already panting for breath. Moke Saviore had heard the shouting and followed Lush out onto the balcony to see what the commotion was. "What's up, Simon?"

"Some slimy little rat's been trying to nick Siggy's car." Lush had a flash of inspiration. "Hey, Moke. Have you got his keys?"

Saviore disappeared inside and returned immediately. "They were on the side table. Are we going after that bastard?"

"Why not. It's about time we taught some of these thieving sods a lesson. If we're quick, we might be able to run him down before he gets to the end of the road."

Saviore followed behind and by the time he'd got to the car, Lush was already in the driver's seat waiting for the keys.

"Look at the damage he's done in here, the mindless yob. Come on, Moke. Let's make him pay for it."

In the nearby street, Melissa had heard the alarm go off and sensed the danger. It was time to find Matt. She switched the ignition on, but to her dismay, the Mini refused to start. She turned the engine over, again and again and her frustration slowly began to turn to cold panic as the old car stubbornly rejected her attempts to get it going.

Matt had put plenty of distance between himself and the nightclub, when he heard the engine of the big BMW burst into life. The screech of spinning tyres told him they were in pursuit. He was sprinting as fast as he could, but quickly beginning to tire.

The BMW gained ground rapidly, its headlights blazing and throwing his silhouette into sharp relief.

Matt called out frantically, "Come on, Mel! Where the hell are you?"

The fierce lights of the approaching car bore into the back of his head and from the sound of the engine, it was accelerating fast.

"Oh, my God. They're going to run me down!"

At the last second before impact, Matt made a sudden lurch to his right and bounced into the wall. The car brushed past him and screeched to a halt in front, diagonally across his path and with its front bumper only a foot from the wall.

Lush flung the door open, ready to rush out and cut off the escape route, but Matt was quick to see the trap. Before the cumbersome driver could get out and block his retreat, Matt had squeezed between the bumper of the car and the wall.

He hurtled past the road end, heading towards the street where Melissa was parked.

Saviore now posed the biggest threat. He'd got out of the BMW and quickly given chase. He was gaining ground swiftly. He was only yards behind Matt when the Mini came careering round the corner. The wheels were spinning hard as Melissa threw the little car right across the road. It slid sideways in a four-wheel skid, before the traction of the tyres gripped the tarmac and it shot forward in a straight line.

As soon as she spotted her man, Melissa jammed on the brakes, but they locked, causing the car to veer from side to side as it came to a stop. She threw the passenger door wide open and Matt half-dived, half fell through the gap. At that precise instant, she changed pedal, clubbing her foot hard on the accelerator. The tyres of the Mini groaned as they were forced into a new manoeuvre. There was a heady smell of tortured rubber as they spun hard to regain their grip, finally throwing the car into forward momentum.

Saviore, who had been on the point of grabbing Matt, was clattered by the open door and knocked onto the ground.

As they surged away, Matt managed to pull himself into his seat and drag the door closed behind him. "What kept you, Mel?"

There was no reply as she concentrated hard on steering the Mini away from trouble.

Behind them, Saviore had picked himself up and was limping back to the BMW.

Lush threw the car into reverse and waited in the centre of the road for him to climb in.

"Are you all right Moke? Fit enough to get after them?"

The swarthy Italian looked down at the tattered knees of his trousers. "Ready when you are, boss. We need to teach them a lesson. They've just ruined my 500 quid suit and I'm not going to let them get away with that."

Back at *Un Coup De Chance*, Dexter returned to the poker game to find only two remaining players and the rear door wide open.

"I think someone's tried to nick your car."

Dexter looked puzzled. Stepping outside onto the balcony, he watched in dismay as his new car raced away from the club. He could only play the part of a distant onlooker as he witnessed the strange scene unfolding at the end of the street. He knew it was Saviore, limping back to the car and guessed that Lush was in the driver's seat, but he was puzzled as to what had happened.

He ambled down the steps expecting them to reverse back to the club, but as soon as Saviore was aboard, Lush accelerated away, chasing after another car.

Dexter broke into a sprint, waving his arms above his head and yelling wildly, trying to attract their attention. It was a futile gesture and the BMW disappeared round the top of the road leaving him to stop and throw down his arms in defeat.

He shouted lamely, "You bastards! Where have you taken my bleedin' car?"

The Mini had a good half-minute start on its illustrious big brother and Melissa quickly navigated the side streets and turned left, onto the Chelsea Embankment.

Neither of them feared a pursuit, not on the streets of London, but as the Mini purred along towards Vauxhall Bridge, Matt glanced over his shoulder and recognised the powerful headlights closing fast. "Oh shit! They're coming after us. Put your foot down and go."

Melissa did as she was told and the small car shot forward.

Matt urged her on, "Come on Mel. You've got to get past that car in front."

"I can't do that, there's no room."

"This is only a Mini, for Christ's sake. It's not a bloody double-decker bus. Go for it, Mel or we're sunk."

She held her breath and put her foot down further. The Mini drew up behind the car in front, which was already breaking the speed limit at 40. At the last second, she stamped the gas pedal to the floor and swung out to pass. The car coming in the opposite direction only had time to flash his lights and swerve before they were past.

"There you are. Wasn't too bad was it?"

"Shut your mouth, Morgan or I swear I'll stop this car and throw you out."

Matt could see that she was rattled, but he kept on jibing her. He knew that sooner or later her Irish temper would flare. He just hoped that it would be a controlled explosion. "Come on! I thought you women were good drivers. Get past some more."

The trick finally worked and she became fired up. She'd had enough of his sarcasm. "All right, you bloody clever Dick, I'll show you."

Throwing all caution aside, she sped past half a dozen cars, leaving oncoming traffic spewing all over the road. The pandemonium left in her wake caused the following BMW to greatly moderate its speed in order to negotiate a safe passage through.

Melissa jumped two sets of red lights and there was a close call when a large delivery van just managed to avoid a collision. They raced south over Vauxhall Bridge and looking through her rear mirror for what seemed the 100th time, she exclaimed, "Oh shit! They're still after us and catching up fast."

As they approached the next lights, they were already on red. The stream of traffic across their path was continuous and it would have been suicide to drive straight on. There was no alternative but to slow right down and Melissa crashed through the gears to help her braking. Behind them and only a couple of cars away, their pursuers seemed ready to pounce.

Just as it looked as though they would have to stop, the lights changed and Melissa revved the willing little engine and it sped forward once again. They crossed over into Camberwell New Road and were soon tearing past endless warning triangles indicating major road works ahead.

"That's it now, Morgan, we're finished."

Melissa had spotted the layout of the road and could see a gang of labourers working on the resurfacing of the carriageway. It was a 24-hour operation to get the road serviceable again, as soon as possible. A nine-inch-deep layer of tarmac had been scraped from most of the surface, leaving only uneven ruts and gullies and as they approached, there were signs warning of ramps and raised manhole covers. A set of lights showed green in the distance and a series of large, bright arrows indicated the flow of traffic onto the temporary surface. The Mini was a long way off when the lights changed to red.

"You've got to go for it, Mel. There's probably a long cut out before it changes to green at the other end. We should make it through."

Melissa gritted her teeth and put her foot hard to the floor. The Mini groaned in response, jerking from side to side as it bounced onto the uneven road. They heard the loud horn of the BMW as it swung past the other cars that had braked to a halt at the lights.

They were not giving up the chase.

Skidding sideways and losing some of its momentum, the powerful car zigzagged between the lights and the cones. There was now a 300-yard stretch of straight bumpy road between the two vehicles. The Mini was almost leaping into the air as it hit ridge after ridge. Its undercarriage scraped and sparked as it hit the unseen raised edges of the ramps. In the BMW, the ride wasn't nearly as uncomfortable, its more sophisticated suspension absorbing the irregularities of the road.

Things were different in the boot. Although the road shocks were not individually savage, the continuous vibration had caused the masking tape, holding the tube of explosive to begin peeling away from the lid of the boot.

The chase continued with both cars hurtling down the track of unmade road. An ugly, sharp ramp ran across their path and the Mini shot two feet into the air before crashing back to earth with a jolting thud.

Five seconds later, the BMW hit the same ramp, but this time with more catastrophic results. The phial of nitro-glycerine suddenly dropped away and as it shattered, there was a hideous explosion. The rear of the car was rocketed forwards and upwards, so the car rotated about its front bumper. It bounced end over end like a giant domino until finally the momentum of the forward force was lost and it skidded on its roof along the road. Both occupants were crushed beyond recognition long before the petrol from the ruptured fuel tank ignited and engulfed the car in a huge fireball. The burning wreck continued to bounce and slew as it crashed along the badly grooved tarmac. It jolted over raised manholes, spinning and sliding as it performed a bizarre pirouette, until it finally lurched to a halt.

Matt had been watching the approach of the BMW behind them and saw everything.

Melissa heard the explosion and caught sight of the flames in her mirror.

"For God's sake, don't look, Mel. The nitro's gone off. Just get us out of here."

An impatient driver began flashing his headlights at them because the traffic lights had turned green and he'd been made to wait. He looked in horror at the burning wreck as it chased the Mini and slithered to a halt across his path.

Frantic workmen raced forward and tried in vain to get close to the trapped victims, but the terrifying heat forced them back. Lush and Saviore had both been killed on the first impact and it was just as well because their bodies burned and crackled fiercely like two incandescent roman candles in the heat of the inferno.

When they were at a safe distance from the accident, Melissa stopped the car and threw her arms round Matt, holding him tight. "We've really done it now, my love. The men in that car must surely be dead."

"There's no doubt about it, Mel, but do you know something. I don't give a damn. They were evil men, like Dexter and deserved everything they got. I only wish, he'd been one of them."

He paused and held her close, whispering tenderly, "I thought you were brilliant tonight. Can I ask you something? I've been meaning to ask it for ages?"

"What's that Morgan?"

He looked directly into her eyes. "If we get through all this, will you marry me?"

Melissa's face lit up with a radiance that filled him with joy. "I thought you were never going to ask me," she grinned wickedly, "you pick your moment, don't you? But the answer is yes, my darling. Nothing in the world could make me happier."

Chapter 39

Paula Ross stood at the front of the private briefing. Joe Harker's small team sat in silence as the head of MI6 catalogued their failings with a vitriolic tirade.

"Forensic have come up with something conclusive at the builder's yard. They have discovered traces of nitro-glycerine making it certain that some kind of explosive device was used to sheer the valve off that gas tank. Ladies and gentlemen, we have bombers. We have suspects in a dark-coloured Mini. A male and two different females. We have only one photograph of the man and none of the women. The male is unknown to us. So, what about the women?"

There was a cutting edge of sarcasm to her voice. "Sorry, no photographs were taken. The licence plates of the Mini were known for three days. Three bloody days, but they were never checked. They were false of course, as we later found out. Jesus, just what have you lot being doing on company time? Due to incompetent surveillance, we have precisely… Nothing!"

Joe flushed with embarrassment as she spat out the last word.

Ross thumped the file hard on the desk and continued to rant at them. "Now, we have last night's little episode. Despite any concrete evidence to back it up and based solely on a hunch, we ended up using our over-stretched manpower in a cat and mouse drive around London. Why, in God's name, should we expect Tyburn and Rydell to meet each other, just because they happened to set off in their cars at about the same time. We've been listening in on Rydell's telephone and there was no evidence to suggest a meeting was about to take place. Well, would you believe it, Tyburn was followed home and Rydell spent most of his evening at his club. Now isn't that a surprise!"

The tone of her voice changed and she bellowed, "What the hell were you playing at? The most concrete lead we had last night was that damn Mini turning up again. I'd like to commend Karen, who reported it heading to the casino. That was first rate observation." Paula Ross looked heavenwards and continued with her caustic attack. "And what about the outcome of that little oversight?

Something must have gone down at the casino, because what happens next? Oh! Yes, there's a high-speed car chase through the centre of London. All eyewitness reports confirm that a powerful car, driven by two men was chasing a green Mini, when the second car exploded. Simon Lush, one of our chief suspects was driving that car. Both occupants were burnt to a frazzle and the Mini did its usual vanishing trick. So, we've drawn yet another blank. I don't know how it's happening, but somebody is screwing our investigation and I want it stopped. What I want to know is, who the fuck are these people?"

She threw the file onto the tabletop. "Sort it, or I'll have you all off the case. Joe, I want to see you in my office in five minutes."

With that she stormed out of the room.

* * * * *

Paula Ross was waiting for Joe.

He only needed to take one look at her to see that she'd not yet calmed down.

Even so, he spoke his mind. "You didn't have to go on at them like that. They're a loyal bunch. Don't forget, we're more than overstretched, working with only a tiny team."

"Joe, I admit I'm in a foul mood, but I'm sick of passing excuses on to the PM. You've no idea what she's like. I know you're feeling as frustrated as I am, but somehow we need to make a breakthrough."

"Well, apart from the video of Rydell, we've still got nothing to go on."

"That's the problem, unless we can turn up some viable evidence linking Rydell with Tyburn, we have nothing to use against him. That's why it's getting to the PM. From the DVD, we know he must be being blackmailed, but we don't know if they're after him for personal reasons or whether it's his position in government. She's only just appointed him and can't be seen to sack him so soon, without some almighty reaction from his supporters. Another big split in the party, just before the election would be catastrophic to her chances of success. It's also worrying that one of our key suspects has been eliminated. If this continues, it'll spell disaster for this investigation."

Joe laughed. "Come on Paula, you can't be serious. The death of Lush and the fire are just a coincidence. I'm convinced it's got nothing to do with Rydell. Leave it with me and I'll go through every detail again and try to come up with some new leads."

239

He left her office, mulling over what she'd just said. He had to concede that this gang of bombers were seriously interfering with their case. They were becoming more than just a nuisance.

Chapter 40

It had been a very cold night and patches of dense fog had formed in many areas along the Thames Valley. Up on the hill at Crystal Palace, the swirling vapours were beginning to melt away as the strengthening late winter sun burst through.

Melissa walked away from the motor home alone. She was the first to leave and was on her way to collect one of the Minis from the car park at King's Cross.

A harsh, penetrating cold hung with silent stillness. Although she was well wrapped up against the weather, there was no danger of feeling the chill, as she had a permanent inner glow. It was a happiness she had never known before. She tingled with excitement as she reflected the joy she'd felt when Matt had asked her to marry him the night before.

* * * * *

The listeners were a specialist team. All Rydell's telephone calls at his flat had been monitored and recorded, yet despite 24-hour surveillance, there had been no communication with Tyburn. The listeners had been foiled, not because Tyburn suspected a phone tap, but because he saw no point in unnecessary contact with Rydell.

As soon as Rydell had secured the home office tender for Tyburn, he rang a prearranged number from a phone booth and agreed to meet him on the Thames embankment the following week to make their final exchange.

Two days later, Rydell was taken aback when a courier delivered a letter from Tyburn. It was terse and to the point, demanding a meeting at noon that same day to conclude their business. The venue was to be the ruins of Lesnes Abbey, adjacent to the woods in Bexley, along the Thames from Woolwich. Rydell was unaware of the destruction of Tyburn's premises, the death of Lush and the trauma that Tyburn was now experiencing. He was angered by the suddenness of the request because it meant he had to rearrange a number of important appointments in order that he could get away. He had no choice but to comply.

* * * * *

Tyburn puffed slowly on the remnants of the fat cigar. Spirals of smoke floated upwards and merged with the rest of the smog in his office. He downed the dregs of his glass and threw the empty bottle across the room. It shattered against his prized antique bookcase causing an ugly, damaging scar to the ornate wooden inlays.

He snarled, "Get me another bottle."

Siggy Dexter stood silently beside the door. Tyburn's state of mind was morose, almost moribund. It was new ground for Dexter; he'd never seen his boss in this frame of mind before.

"Don't you think you've had enough for now?" he ventured quietly, "don't forget your meeting with Rydell. If you carry on like this, you'll be pissed out of your mind."

Tyburn gave him an icy stare. "When I want your advice, I'll ask for it. Now fetch me another fuckin' bottle."

Dexter went out to the bar.

Tyburn sighed. He wrung his hands and slumped in the chair; his shoulders hunched over in sadness. He'd lost his partner and best friend and more significantly, the brains behind his organisation. Without the lawyer's sharp, incisive intellect, he felt confused and exposed. Without his mentor, decision-making had become a terrible chore.

Dexter returned and thumped the bottle of bourbon down in front of his boss. He wanted to speak his mind, but thought better of it.

Tyburn eyed him up and inexplicably swiped the bottle off his desk. The deep carpet saved it from breaking and it rolled harmlessly into one corner.

"You're right, Siggy, I've had too much already. I've been milling things over for far too long and now I need some answers. I'll tell you what I think, then you can have your say. Agreed?"

Dexter nodded.

"I'm undecided who's to blame for all this shit. Either we've upset one of the other mobs or it's a government plot to get Rydell off the hook. We've got no evidence either way, but in any case I deeply mistrust Rydell. That's why I organised a meeting at short notice, out in the open. If he's up to something, then we'll be able to spot if he's not alone. Also, if he's got a phone tap on him, it'll be too difficult to bug our conversation up in the woods."

"Good thinking, boss, but this smells all wrong to me. Don't you think we're being a bit paranoid? I'm sure he's nothing to do with our bomber. He's in it too deep. Hasn't he already agreed to exchange the contract for his DVD? What would he hope to gain by a double-cross? Surely, he only wants us to get off his back?"

Dexter had made a valid point and Tyburn seemed persuaded by his argument.

"You're right about the video. If everything seems above board with the contracts, I'll give it back today when the deal's finalised. I don't want anything more to do with him."

Dexter sneered. "Good. Then we can concentrate on finding out who's got it in for us. If it's not Rydell, then it's gotta be a turf war. But don't worry, boss; we'll sort it."

Tyburn suddenly felt more relaxed. Talking things over with Dexter had been good for him and he had a clear plan of action in his mind.

* * * * *

About an hour before noon, Dexter went out to collect Tyburn's Rolls from the back entrance of *Un Coup de Chance*.

At the very bottom of the narrow road, Melissa Reagan had been watching from the safety of her car. She immediately rang Matt on her mobile. He was waiting in the second Mini with Laura, on the south side of the Thames.

"I think *I've spotted Dexter and he's on the move. He's taken the Rolls and I'm going to follow.*"

"Take care, darling, and make sure you keep the line open."

Matt silently reviewed their successes. The week was slipping by quickly and it was now Friday. So far they had managed to burn down the builder's yard and inadvertently kill two others in the car bomb, but Dexter and Tyburn still eluded them. Today's plan was to find out where Tyburn lived, so their intention was to follow him everywhere he went. Melissa would cover north of the river in one Mini, whilst Matt and Laura watched the south in the other.

243

Melissa had hit on the idea of describing her progress using her mobile phone and had agreed to start tailing Tyburn. If he headed over the river and she lost him on the congested approaches to the bridges, then Matt might be able to pick him up on the south side.

The phone line crackled. "I've followed the Roller to the front of the casino and an older man has just got in. From your description, it has to be Tyburn. Right, here we go."

Parked lower down the next street, a short distance away, was a pair of MI6 watchers.

"Bloody hell, Karen, look what's just come up that side street. It's that chuffing Mini. Come on girl, don't let it get away."

Karen started the engine, but in her haste, she released the clutch too quickly and the Ford Focus stalled. Precious seconds were lost, but soon they were on the tail of the other two cars.

Her companion radioed the controller, who became immediately excited by the prospect of a successful tail. At last, they had a break through.

A voice came back loud and clear. "Jerry, stick with the Mini at all costs and for God's sake, don't lose it."

As she was driving along, Melissa relayed to Matt a precise account of her progress. Laura had a detailed street map on her knee, plotting her course as Matt described it out loud.

"She's at this point Dad, so it looks as though they're not coming across the river at Chelsea. We need to move on."

Matt started the car and they drove eastwards along Battersea Park Road and Nine Elms Lane towards Vauxhall Bridge, ready to make an interception if it was required.

In the Focus, Karen was being less than cautious in her pursuit of the Mini. On several occasions, Melissa spotted the enthusiastic blue Ford and began to get nagging fears about being followed. The Rolls was keeping up a sedate pace and provided that it didn't get too far ahead, Melissa felt sure she could catch up if she fell behind. She tried to alleviate her doubts about the car trailing in her rear, by experimenting with a few manoeuvres.

Firstly, she slowed right down when there was a stretch of clear road. Lots of other cars slid by her, but the Ford hung back. She then accelerated rapidly, recklessly overtaking some of the cars in front. The nippy little Mini responded positively and she was soon back in the wake of the Rolls. Without the need to look behind, she caught the sound of irate drivers blasting their horns as the other car dangerously tried to follow suit.

She repeated the same tactics twice more and on the last occasion she almost had an accident in her efforts to overtake a number of cars and pull clear of the Ford. The near miss frightened her and left her shaky. Beads of perspiration escaped uncomfortably on to her forehead and she wiped them away with her hand. Melissa looked anxiously back through the rear-view mirror to confirm that the Ford had stayed with her. Sure enough, it was still there and she was now convinced she was in trouble. She began to fret, wondering just who it was in the car behind. "Matt, I'm being followed."

"Impossible! How can that be? You must be imagining it?"

"I'm telling you; someone is following me. I've tried to throw them off, but they're still there. When I go fast, they do too. If I slow right down, they won't overtake. I've just done some idiotic manoeuvres to try and get away, but they're still there. I'm positive, darling. What should I do?"

Matt thought quickly. "It has to be either one of Tyburn's men or the police, but it's more likely to be the police. Perhaps, someone saw the Mini at the woodyard and tied it in with the chase the other night. If it's the police, they're probably checking your number plates right now, which means they're certain to pull you in. You have no alternative, Mel. You have to ditch the car. Remember the plan we worked out. Do it!"

"But what about Dexter and Tyburn? I'll lose them."

"Never mind that, it's you I'm worried about. We can pick up their trail again later."

Just then, the Rolls, which was not far ahead, indicated a right turn.

"Hang on a second, Matt. I'm approaching Lambeth Bridge. They're signalling right, so they must be coming over the river."

"Thanks, love. We're not far from the southern approach now. I think we may be able to pick them up at this end. Now, for God's sake, get rid of the car and give me a call as soon as you're safe. If you need us, we'll come and collect you straight away. Be careful!"

Chapter 41

When Melissa had given Matt the final direction of Tyburn's Rolls Royce, she slipped the handset into her bag. Her mind was clear and she could concentrate solely on the car behind. Staying in the left-hand lane, she passed the Rolls on the inside as it waited to turn right across the bridge. She stepped on the gas and headed into the busy, central London traffic.

In the car behind, exchanges were being made with control. "The Mini's stopped following Tyburn and has moved off at speed towards Westminster. I've a feeling we've been rumbled. Looks like there's only one female occupant in the car. Please instruct."

There was a slight pause.

"Follow the Mini. We need to find out who she is. I'll get you some back up. Keep tight on her and as soon as it's convenient, let's bring her in."

Monty Wall and Josh Gardner were on station outside the home office. They had now recovered from their ordeal at the builder's yard and it was their first morning back at work. They joked and poked fun at each other as they whiled away the hours of boredom. Josh nudged Monty as he recognised the figure of Rydell at the entrance to the home office. Their banter ceased and they became fully alert. A black cab was waiting and he went straight over to it.

"Right, Josh, there goes our man. Don't let him get away."

Monty's sore backside was still giving him pain and he shuffled uncomfortably in his seat. He noted on his pad the time and the registration number of the taxi. Then, he contacted control to confirm their intention to follow Rydell. They hadn't gone far in their leisurely pursuit of the cab when a message came through.

"Leave Rydell and help Karen and Jerry. They're tracking our old friend, the green Mini with one female occupant. She was following Tyburn away from the casino, but it seems pretty certain we've been rumbled because she's stopped following the Roller and shot off into town. Joe says we should bring her in. The

246

Mini's heading along Mill Bank towards Westminster Bridge, so you might be able to intercept it there."

"At last, a bit of action. This is more like it, Josh. Get your arse in gear."

Josh grinned and jammed his foot down hard on the gas. The tyres squealed and the car responded aggressively. They began weaving in and out of the traffic as they tried to get to the bridge before the Mini.

Melissa, unaware of the impending trap, had no intention of going as far as Westminster Bridge and took the next left heading in the general direction of Oxford Street.

Several cars behind, Karen spotted the move. "She's going left along Great Peter Street. Report our position."

Melissa managed to keep up a reasonable speed and maintain a gap of several cars between herself and the Ford. She skirted the rear of Buckingham Palace along Grosvenor Place and then shot up Park Lane. At Marble Arch, she turned right into Oxford Street where the traffic was reduced to a long, slow crawl in the busy shopping centre of the Capital. She found herself in a bottleneck of cars, buses and vans with little prospect of rapid movement. Pangs of uncertainty began to resurface and she began to panic. She'd managed to get ahead of a large delivery van, but now she couldn't see how far back her pursuers were and imagined someone getting out of the Ford and running up the street to apprehend her. She decided to chance her luck. The Mini was almost opposite Marks and Spencer and this seemed like as good a place as any to ditch it. The traffic was stationary, so she flicked the hazard warning lights on, grabbed her bag and slid out of the car.

With a few deft body swerves, that would have done a rugby player proud, she glided across the pavement and into the store.

The driver of the van behind was exasperated by her actions and honked his horn loudly. She didn't look back, as he frantically waved his arms and flagged her angrily.

Once inside the store, she mingled easily with the crowd, hurrying through the busy shoppers towards the rear. Wasting no time, she returned to the street via the back entrance and made a fast get away, heading through the hurly-burly, towards the nearest tube station.

The delivery van, six vehicles in front of the MI6 car, was hiding the Mini from view, but there was no indication they'd got problems until the driver started to blast his horn continuously. The watchers could hear the commotion up ahead and it gave them cause for concern.

Jerry suddenly cursed, "There's something wrong up there."

Jumping out of the car, he tore along the pavement to find the empty Mini. "Oh Shit! She's gone!"

He turned to the van driver, who was now trying to edge into the outer lane of traffic. Jerry banged on his window. "Did you see who got out of that car?"

"Yeah! A bleedin' red-haired bitch. She went in there."

He pointed to the department store and Jerry darted across and went inside. He was met by a seething mass of shoppers and apart from the terse description of Melissa, he had no idea how he could identify her. Scanning the heads of the crowd, he quickly realised the futility of his search. She had got clean away.

Jerry returned to the street to find Karen waiting expectantly. He didn't need to say anything, his look of dejection said it all.

The back-up team arrived and Monty Wall crawled all over the inside of the Mini looking for possible clues as to its ownership.

He got out and shrugged his shoulders. "Looks clean to me, but you'll need to drive it over to number 33 and let the forensic mob go over it."

Jerry became sheepish and tried to cover the embarrassment of their loss. "At least we've got the car to go on, and we know that the woman is a red head."

Karen cut in sarcastically. "Big deal, Jerry. We're working with professionals here. Have you never heard of wigs? Come on. Let's go, I've had enough. You can drive the Mini. God only knows what Harker will say this time."

Jerry sighed disapprovingly, "I hope you've got your fireproof knickers on, Karen, because your driving was just a teeny bit of a giveaway."

Karen flushed at his criticism. "Piss off, Jerry, you sexist prick"

"Oh dear, we are having a little paddy, aren't we?"

Josh butted in. "Come on, knobhead, she's your partner and we're all supposed to be working as a team. How do you think me and Monty felt the other night at the fire? We'll catch up with our mystery lady sooner or later, so don't take it out on Karen. Now do us all a big favour and bugger off with this pile of scrap to number 33 and see if they can find any clues."

Chapter 42

Tyburn's Rolls purred along, crossing the Thames by the Lambeth Bridge.

Matt and Laura were in position across the river and ready to continue the pursuit. For the next 20 minutes, they followed the luxury motorcar eastwards, following the line of the river. The fog still hung in patches, some of it dense in places, making driving quite difficult. Matt was tense as he tried to keep up with the Rolls in all the murk. At the same time, he was worrying about what had happened to Melissa.

At last, the Rolls pulled in at the side of the road and stopped.

The Mini halted 100 yards behind, well away from the Rolls. Its engine fell silent.

"Where the hell are we, Laura? This seems an odd place to stop."

"According to the map, we're on Abbey Road," she indicated with her finger, "and up there to the right are the ruins of Lesnes Abbey."

The morning weather was poor and only a few other vehicles were parked along the road. A small number of sightseers wandered up the pathways, milling aimlessly around the dilapidated ruins in the murky distance.

Matt was fraught, "I wonder where Melissa is? Do you think I should ring her?"

"It's no use, Dad. You could jeopardise her getaway if you ring now. Have a little more patience, I'm sure she'll be all right. Even if they pull her in, they can't prove a thing. Don't worry, let's concentrate on Dexter and Tyburn."

Matt squeezed Laura's arm. "I'm sorry, sweetheart, it's just that I've been thinking a great deal about what you said the other week. About how I ought to tell Melissa my true feelings. Well… I really do love her and last night I asked her to marry me. What do you think?"

Laura threw her arms around Matt's neck and hugged him tight, "I bet she said, yes."

"You're right, she did. No hesitation."

"Oh, Dad. I'm so pleased for you both. I think she's wonderful and she's already a good friend to me. You've needed someone like Melissa for such a long time. I know you'll be happy together. This is such cool news."

"It suddenly makes what we're doing kinda crazy, doesn't it? Anyway, I'm scared for her. I just want this to be over."

She hugged her dad some more and held his hand tightly. The two of them fell silent as they waited expectantly for Melissa to call.

Their interest was suddenly diverted to a black taxi, which pulled in, not far from the Rolls. The slim figure of a well-dressed man emerged, and from his gesticulations, it was obvious that he was instructing the driver of the cab to wait for his return. He looked around and pulled his coat tight around his neck, against the damp morning air.

The man walked up to the stationary Rolls Royce.

Tyburn and Dexter saw Rydell approach and got out of the car to meet him. They didn't shake hands, but Tyburn pointed towards the nearby woods, which was still shrouded by a mask of grey mist. They set off along the path and then cut across towards the trees.

"Why are they meeting at a place like this? There's something weird going on here. They obviously want to talk in private, so I suppose the trees make a good screen from prying eyes."

Suddenly Matt had an idea. "I'm going after them. This could be our best chance yet, maybe our only chance. If I can get near, under cover of this fog, I might get an opportunity for a clear shot with the crossbow. You stay here and get ready to drive away fast, if I come running."

He went round to the boot of the car and retrieved the crossbow container and the box of special bolts. As Matt carefully collected his equipment, Laura came out and argued vehemently against his latest scheme. "This is not good enough, Dad. You promised that we would plan every move carefully. It could be another disaster. Remember last time at the woodyard. You're not being fair."

Matt smiled at her grimly and refused to be dissuaded. "I said we needed to use hit and run tactics. If I can get the bastards now, then the job's finished. We can go home. Kirsty's death will have been avenged."

He slammed the boot lid and ignored her continuing protests. Striding quickly away, he headed in the direction of the woods to where he'd seen the three men disappear into the tree line.

* * * * *

In a busy Oxford Street, Monty Wall and Josh Gardner watched their colleagues drive away then got back into their own car.

"Where to, Monty. Rydell could be miles away by now."

Wall had a flash of inspiration. "Hang about! We still have his taxi number plate? It's standard practice these days for the driver to keep in touch with base. Perhaps, Joe Harker can pull a few strings and find out where they've gone."

Monty contacted the controller with the taxi registration number and explained what they wanted. As they waited, numerous phone calls were made and eventually, Joe Harker came on the line.

"Josh, the cab is on its way to the ruins at Lesnes Abbey. It's an odd place for a government minister to visit at this time of day, don't you think? This sounds like a good break. Get out there straight away and try not to botch things up this time."

* * * * *

Tyburn and Rydell walked side by side through the woods, with Dexter a little way behind watching to ensure there was nobody eavesdropping on their conversation.

The two antagonists stopped in a small clearing and Tyburn perched uncomfortably on a huge, horizontal tree trunk.

Rydell was irascible. "Why the hell have you brought me all the way out here at such short notice? I've had to cancel two appointments and I've got another meeting with the home secretary in an hour. It's one that I can't afford to miss."

"Don't be tiresome, Mr Rydell. Things have happened in the past few days that have upset me beyond belief. Someone burned down my premises the other night and now my best friend, Simon Lush has been killed."

Rydell looked genuinely shocked. "What happened?"

"The police said it was probably a car bomb."

"Ah, yes, I read about it in the *Evening Standard*. That was your friend, Lush?"

"Indeed, and I thought you might be able to shed some light on the subject?"

"I don't follow. My God, you don't believe that I had anything to do with it?"

251

"The thought had crossed my mind, perhaps a plot by MI5 to save your bacon."

"You must be paranoid if you think I'd go to anyone else. There's no way out for me, don't you understand that by now. I engineered a prison riot for you, a riot in which people were murdered. I'll be the first against the wall if this gets out. Come on man, think logically."

"You would say that, wouldn't you, but some governments would go to any length to protect their image with the electorate. This could be the ultimate cover up."

"That may be true, but if I'd made a deal in the hope of immunity from prosecution, I'd have been removed from office already. What's more, you'd have mysteriously disappeared by now and not be stood here talking to me in this damned freezing fog. I want to get on with my career, not end up in some crappy, two-bit job in some faraway banana republic."

Tyburn seemed convinced by Rydell's powerful argument and nodded amicably. "In that case, do you have the contract for me?"

Rydell patted his breast pocket in response, then countered with his own question, "And what about the master disc? I would like to see it now."

Tyburn was somewhat hesitant as he pulled out the jiffy bag from inside his overcoat. "You're not going to like this."

Rydell's face became a mask of displeasure as he grabbed the proffered package.

He growled furiously. "What's this. A deal is a deal."

"I'm sorry, my friend, but the DVD was locked in the safe in my office during the fire. Although it was supposed to be flame proof, the fire investigators told me the heat was particularly intense. What you have there is what remains of your property."

Rydell dug his hand hungrily into the packet and withdrew the plastic CD case. It was slightly twisted, having been distorted by the heat. He flicked the lid open and pulled out a similarly warped disc. He fingered it angrily. "This is useless. It'll never play."

"Exactly. So, you'll never need to worry that anyone else can play it. You're free."

"But how do I know it's the original?"

"Because I'm telling you. We've been over all this before. I've no further use for it, or you. I'm quite relieved it's been destroyed myself. Nobody can point a finger at me and say I blackmailed you into giving us the government contract. The evidence simply doesn't exist anymore."

From the sudden fear that he'd felt, at being double-crossed, Rydell slowly began to relax. He really was back in the clear. Dropping the disc into the bag, he reached into his inside pocket for the refurbishment contract. But before he had the chance to hand it over, the unmistakable ring of a nearby phone disturbed them.

* * * * *

Matt hurried along, clutching his two boxes carefully. He skirted the ancient ruins and made for the trees, where the mist provided a protective screen. Once amongst the wooded enclave, he stopped and listened for the sound of voices. His disappointment was acute. The only sound was his own breathing and a nervous pounding in his ears.

Convinced he'd entered the woods at the right spot, he looked around for clues as to which direction they may have gone. There was nothing. He edged forward cautiously, threading his way through the trees. Progress was slow, but then he picked up the faintest sound of distant voices. It had to be them.

He halted and began to rebuild the crossbow, spreading the components carefully on the ground. As soon as the assembly was complete, he fitted a nitro-bolt. Cradling it across his arms, he started to move forward once more.

The sounds in the mist ahead gradually grew louder and clearer. Matt's senses were working overtime. There was a clear impression that the men had stopped and were having some kind of meeting. The voices became audible. Although, they were seemingly within a short distance of his position, Matt still couldn't make out their form. He had to be certain where they were in the distorted, misty conditions in order to get a clear shot. He propped the crossbow safely against a nearby tree and edged forward, crouching low to keep his balance.

He'd only gone a few yards, when the fog above him began swirling away, melted by a strengthening sun. The clinging mist released its hold and at once, the hidden figures became clearly defined.

Tyburn and the man from the taxi were in deep conversation, arguing about the contents of a large packet and Dexter was prowling beyond them, on the lookout for possible intruders.

Matt sneered smugly and turned away. It was time to bring up the crossbow. Dexter would be his first target, a mere dozen yards away.

Just then the mobile phone in his back pocket started to ring. He looked around in disbelief, and then cursed his own stupidity for not switching it off.

* * * * *

Tyburn turned to the direction of the phone. "Find it, Siggy! It's over there."

Matt fumbled with his mobile and wasted precious seconds switching the bleeper off. He retreated into the woods, trying to find a safe haven amongst the mist. A patch of vivid green moss proved his undoing and he slipped, sprawling full length onto his stomach. By the time he'd staggered onto his knees, Dexter was standing over him, with the blue steel of a gun pressed hard against his temple. "Not so fast, pal. We'd like to talk to you."

Grabbing a handful of hair, Dexter pulled his captive painfully to his feet. With the gun barrel wedged uncomfortably in the small of his back, Matt was urged to walk.

Dexter thrust him before Tyburn, forcing him onto his knees in supplication.

There was a look of recognition on Tyburn's face. "Well, well, look who we have here. If it's not our old friend, Mr Brown. What might you be doing listening in on our conversation?"

Matt remained silent, totally lost for words.

"You may have escaped from us last time, but we won't make the same mistake twice. I'm a very curious man, Mr Brown. I'm also compassionate. So, I'll give you one chance to live. Spill it! Who's paying your wages? Whose patch are you from? Or, are you one of our old pals from Special Branch or the Drugs Squad?"

Matt was bemused. "I don't know what you mean. I don't work for anyone."

He'd given the wrong answer and the terrible fear of his predicament suddenly struck home.

"We can't take any chances with him, Siggy. Fit the silencer."

Matt looked round in horror as Dexter removed the long cylinder of metal from his pocket and began to screw it onto the end of his gun. He wanted to get up and run, but his fear had frozen his limbs and he sat on his haunches unable to move.

Tyburn put his hand out to Dexter. "Give the gun to me, Siggy. If he's responsible for Simon's death, I'll take great pleasure in pulling the trigger myself."

Rydell protested, "What the hell are you doing? You can't just murder a man in cold blood."

"Stay out of it, Rydell. This piece of shit was sticking his nose into my business a few weeks ago and since then everything's gone downhill."

Matt listened to Tyburn's words and suddenly found himself gushing insults at him. In a final act of defiance, he needed the satisfaction of letting Tyburn know that he was the one responsible for his troubles.

"You're right, you stinking toe-rag. I did for your bloody premises and there was nothing that you or that freak over there could do to stop me from burning it down. As for the BMW, the bomb was meant for him, shame that he wasn't driving."

Tyburn looked puzzled. "Just who the hell are you? Do I know you?"

Matt sneered and pointed at Dexter. "That bastard murdered my daughter at the hospital."

A look of understanding quickly swept Dexter's face. "Aha! The girl from Newsome's house. I see it all now. Let me kill him, boss. Let me finish the job."

"No chance, Siggy. I'll do it. He killed Simon."

Matt looked up at Tyburn as his enemy lifted the gun and aimed it at his face. He gulped and his mind flashed with untold, useless images. One such image was a vivid yellow and red cloudburst, accompanied by a thunderous roar, which deafened his ears. Three feet away from his face, something flashed across his vision and struck Tyburn below the centre of his chest. There was deep penetration, and then the deadly tip of a nitro-bolt exploded, rupturing his vital organs. Chunks of flesh, bone and gore were splattered around and his upper body was severed at the base of his spine. The tattered torso cannoned sideways into the static figure of Dexter, knocking him to the ground.

Matt touched his own cheeks and fingered the spots of fresh blood that spattered his face. He looked bemused at the sight of the carnage, unable to believe that he'd been reprieved.

Rydell was the first to react and he scuttled off into the woods as fast as he could run.

Matt shook his head and looked woefully at Dexter. He was struggling to recover from the macabre position he shared with the ghastly corpse of Tyburn. The heavy, disfigured torso lay on top of him, staring blankly into his eyes.

Suddenly, someone grasped Matt's hand and tried to pull him up.

"Come on, Dad, quick. For God's sake, get up."

Laura stared down at him with a worried frown, trying to shake him from his lethargy.

He managed a watery smile and did as he was told, scrambling quickly to his feet.

By now, Dexter had spotted the gun. It was only an arms-length away. He pushed the mass of Tyburn's remains to one side and began to crawl towards the weapon.

Matt spotted the new danger and frantically began to look round for something to fight with. His eyes fell on the crossbow, hanging limply in Laura's hand. Grabbing it from her, he hurtled it towards Dexter. The throw was good and as the thug's hand was about to close on the handle of the gun, the crossbow landed on his wrist. There was a shriek of pain as it thudded into the back of his hand.

Laura clung to Matt and pointed at Dexter. There was confusion in her voice. "I had him in my sights and I thought about Kirsty, but then he gave the gun away. Oh! Dad, I thought you were finished. I had no option. I had to shoot Tyburn instead."

Matt felt her body tremble. He looked at Dexter and the nearby gun and realised that he'd stand no chance of getting to it first. They had to get away quickly before he could react. From some untapped source, he found the energy and composure to drag Laura away from the terrible scene of bloodshed. By the time he'd tugged her through the nearby trees, his mind was razor sharp and he began to make a number of important decisions.

"We'll have to leave the car. That other man has disappeared. He's probably gone back to his taxi. Lots of people must have heard the explosion and the police are probably already on their way. We can't risk going back. We should go this way, through the woods and away from Dexter."

He held her hand firmly and guided her in a new direction. They charged headlong through the crackling undergrowth and as they ran, he mocked her with gentle sarcasm. "It's a good job you were such an obedient daughter and stayed with the car like we'd agreed."

"I'm just like you, Dad, I always stick to our agreement."

* * * * *

Monty Wall and Josh Gardner arrived at the Abbey and screeched to a halt behind Laura's car.

"Jesus, Monty there's something weird happening here. Look, there's another bleeding green Mini. They've got two of the sods. We've been chasing our own arses all morning. You can bet the action's been here all along."

As they got out of their car, they heard a loud crump coming from the woods.

"Something's just gone off up there, Josh. I bet you a tenner we're too damn late again. Let's go."

The two of them raced up the road passing the waiting black cab and Tyburn's silent Roller. They ran diagonally across, from the path entrance towards the tree line.

A small group of quizzical onlookers watched as they sped past.

At the edge of the woods, they slowed down as the discipline of their training had taught them. Working carefully through the woods, it was not long before they came upon the devastation in the clearing. All that remained at the eerie scene were the two gruesome halves of Tyburn's mutilated body.

Josh turned away in disgust and it took him all his will power not to throw up.

Amongst the pink, smouldering entrails nestled the powerful crossbow, its presence a conundrum to both men.

Monty was the first to speak. He could see the discomfort of his friend. "I'll give the body a quick search and see if there's anything in the way of evidence. You go back and call control and give them the low down. Tell them Tyburn's dead. Then we need to clear off straight away, because we don't want to get involved. The lads from the Met are welcome to this one."

Josh returned to the roadside and noted with some dismay that the black cab and the Rolls had both disappeared. The green Mini sat there, as if abandoned. They'd been outmanoeuvred yet again.

* * * * *

When Matt and Laura reached the eastern extremes of the woods, they managed to get a call through to Melissa. She'd found her way back to Crystal Palace and it was from there, she'd tried to get through earlier.

The conversation was intense, but the decision about what to do next had already been made for them. Since all the explosives had been used up and the crossbow and both Minis lost, there was nothing else they could do, so they agreed to leave for home immediately.

Melissa stowed any loose items in the camper and picked them up on the Woolwich Road an hour later. By late afternoon, they had safely made the return journey back to Sheffield.

Chapter 43

Later that afternoon, there was another debriefing. It was a second torrid affair, taking place in an atmosphere of absolute silence.

This time it was Joe Harker who was handing out the criticism and his team had no choice but to sit there as he aimed his barbed comments with pointed accuracy. At the end of his long, scathing, monologue he'd mauled their self-esteem and professionalism to the extent that they smarted with indignation.

"To recap. In a matter of days, we've presided over one major arson attack, one car bomb and one assassination in broad daylight. In each case, we've seen the same suspects come and go as they please and every time we've tried to close the net, they've given us the slip. To be candid, we've been humiliated. It's not just that we haven't a clue what ball park we're playing in, we don't even know who's holding the bleeding ball."

Monty Wall made the sole gesture of an excuse, in a vain attempt to placate Harker.

"But, boss. You've got to admit it, they were unorthodox, using two crappy identical Minis. We weren't to know."

"You can call it unorthodox, but I call it smart. Brilliant even. There's no doubt about it, we're up against the very best."

He looked around their expressionless faces, wondering what hurt, resentment or anger they harboured. At last, he paid them a grudging complement, designed more than anything, to try and boost flagging morale.

"Before this mess started, I'd have said that you lot were the best. Putting that into context tells me how bloody good this gang of assassins really is... they'd have to be, to outwit you lot." He shrugged. "This has been a delicate process from the start, trying to connect Tyburn and Lush to Rydell. Now that both our potential links to Rydell are dead, then where do we go from here? The case may already be over. For the time being, I want you all to stand down. I'll keep you posted."

There was a murmur of disapproval from the ranks. They felt ashamed. It was the first time they'd failed to complete an assignment without some degree of success.

As he left, Joe began mulling over something that had been puzzling him for a while. It had resurfaced again because of the comments made by Monty Wall. The people they were after were certainly unorthodox, but were they really clever or just lucky? Surely, they were an intelligent gang. The twin Minis were an ingenious idea and the forensic garage had quickly confirmed that both cars were untraceable. There was still something about the whole episode that made him feel uneasy. Something didn't quite fit, but he couldn't for the life of him, figure it out. In any case, his team had been neutralised and if he couldn't get to the bottom of the mystery fairly quickly, his own reputation would be soured for good.

* * * * *

That evening, Joe arrived punctually at his favourite pub. He had arranged to meet an old pal from Scotland Yard. He didn't want to involve the Met, but he was now down to asking favours.

Tony Peterson and Tom Willis were propping up the bar and had already downed their first pint. The place was crowded and noisy with a heavy, smoky atmosphere.

Joe greeted his friend Tony with a handshake, who then introduced Willis as his colleague. He ordered himself a beer and another two for the off-duty detectives. A table became free in the corner and they managed to edge their way to the seats, shouldering past the nodding evening socialites.

They exchanged a few pleasantries, and then Joe got straight to the point. He pulled a photo out of his inside pocket and pushed it over to Tony. "Do you think you could ask around discreetly and see if anyone has any information on this guy. We're getting nowhere. He's a new face to us, but he may be familiar to somebody at the Yard."

Tony grinned and passed the photo to Willis. They both recognised the face instantly.

"Well now, there's a turn up for the book. We can definitely fill you in on this character, but it'll cost you a double whisky… each."

Joe smiled ruefully and went over to order the drinks. *Could this be his big break*? He would need to be very careful of what he said, because he didn't want to link the man in the photograph to the recent attacks in the capital and arouse the suspicious minds of his friends.

"So, what's he been up to?" inquired Peterson casually.

"Early days yet," replied Harker cautiously, "but we think he may have links with a terrorist organisation."

Willis grunted. "I doubt that very much and I'll tell you why." He threw back the whisky in one and started to recount their dealings with the subject in the photo. "The bloke's name is Matthew Morgan and he's a physics teacher. Lives in Sheffield."

"What! A bloody school teacher. Did I hear you right?"

Peterson confirmed it. "Yes. He's an academic, my friend and if you're interested, I'll tell you the story of how we come to know him."

Joe nodded. His face showed a mask of calm serenity, which belied his inner thoughts. He was already seething with indignation.

"Do you remember the Newsome massacre back in November? Well, Morgan's daughter was the fiancée of Robbie Newsome and she was the only surviving witness. We put a protective screen around the hospital, but there was a security leak and a couple of the gang managed to get in and kill her under our very noses."

Willis remained impassive. His treachery had caused Kirsty Morgan's death and suddenly, he felt very guilty as the memories returned. If either of the other men had looked carefully at his expression, they would have noticed the tell-tale flush that tinged his face.

Peterson continued. "I remember coming close to a bust up with Morgan. He was in a real state and threatened he'd do away with the killers if he could ever find them."

"Was this the incident which ended up with one of the gunmen falling to his death from the hospital roof?"

"That's right. I always suspected that Morgan pushed him, but there was no real evidence and the coroner's report confirmed his side of the story. The last time I saw him was at his daughter's funeral. He was a tragic, bitter man."

Joe casually probed some more. "Sad story. Sounds as though he was pretty uptight about it all. Didn't he have anybody to help him get through it?"

"Well, he didn't have a wife if that's what you mean, but he did have another daughter who seemed very close to him."

Willis butted in quickly, "And don't forget his Irish girlfriend. The redhead, she was a really sexy piece."

Peterson grunted, "Thought you might remember her, Tom. She was another teacher. She calmed Morgan down at the hospital when he started getting aggressive. Anyway, he was totally uncooperative and wouldn't help the investigation at all."

Joe had been totally confused when Morgan's identity was revealed. He was expecting the police to give him the name of some thug. No wonder his details weren't on their database. Out of the blue, he'd unwittingly been given the link he was looking for. These people were surely his protagonists, a man and two women with one of them being a redhead. They had to be the ones behind the explosions and murders. Something else had been bugging him for a long time and it immediately slotted into place. None of them had used any firearms. It suddenly became crystal clear. They didn't have any. That would explain the crossbow Monty had found. They must have been using homemade explosives too. He suddenly felt relieved at what he'd found, but more than that, he felt suckered. His team of highly trained, specialised field operatives had been outwitted at every stage by nothing more than a well-organised bunch of amateurs.

Peterson had been surprised by Joe's attention to the case and was quick to question him back, "So, what's Morgan done to attract the attention of MI6? I have to say I'm very surprised. Apart from suffering obvious grief over his daughter's murder, I would say he leads a pretty normal existence."

Joe needed a plausible reply that would put an end to any further questions. Then he thought about Morgan's relationship with the Irish teacher.

"Bit of a co-incidence really. Can't say much at this stage, but we're looking at a possible link with a Republican group over the water. Knowing he's got an Irish girlfriend is a real bonus." He lied smoothly, "Anyway, at the moment we only have suspicions, so I can't say any more."

Peterson nodded responsively. He knew not to take it any further.

"Here fellas. Let me get you both another double, you've been a real help."

He was intent on keeping his metropolitan colleagues as talkative as he could. His mind was flying off on every conceivable tangent as he tried to piece together the background to the past few days.

"Tony, as a matter of interest, when you mentioned the Newsome murders earlier, who was this Newsome? What did he do for a living?"

"He was a smart-arse accountant, which meant he had some very rich clients."

"I suppose the case has been substantially wound down by now?"

"True. It went cold very quickly. Because we had no witnesses or motive, we got nowhere with it. Now it's in the hands of that pillock, Higgins at Fraud Squad who's tinkering with the case. He's trying to find out if Newsome was cooking the books and got caught with his fingers in the till. That might explain the murders."

Tom Willis began to slur his words as the alcohol took effect. "Anyway, you're asking an awful lot of questions, Joe. Is there something that the Met should know?"

Joe threw up his arms in mock supplication, continuing to blag his way through. "Not me, mate. Just interested. You know very well if there's any way I could help your mob, then I would."

* * * * *

After the drinking session, Joe went back to his flat. His mind was buzzing as huge chunks of his puzzle began to fit into place. He needed one final piece of information, but he'd have to wait until morning before he could test his theory.

He was at his office early the next day and immediately rang Higgins at the Fraud squad and made one or two discreet inquiries about the Newsome case. Within the hour, he had the positive response he was seeking.

An underling of Higgins spoke to Joe, "The two names you asked us to run a check on were Lush and Tyburn. Is that correct?"

"Yes. Go on please."

"Well, we know that Newsome had dealings with both of them. Apparently, Lush and Tyburn were fairly close friends of his and Tyburn had been one of his biggest clients for a very long time. Is that all you need to know?"

"That's about it, thanks."

Joe put the phone down and punched the air. He now had a connection between Newsome, Tyburn, Lush and Morgan. There was a clear-cut motive for all the mayhem and killings and luckily, it had nothing to do with Rydell whatsoever.

* * * * *

The following morning Joe returned to his office. He seated himself in front of the computer screen and began to analyse the data again, looking for the link between Rydell and Tyburn. Just then the phone rang and it was Kate. She seemed agitated, but at the same time excited and demanded to see him after work that evening. Joe tried to get her to elaborate, but she was obdurate and flatly refused to discuss anything over the phone. He was intrigued and agreed a time to meet, at her favourite wine bar, within walking distance of the Palace of Westminster.

Joe arrived before Kate and had supped half a bottle of claret before she appeared.

She grinned impishly at him as she threw off her outer coat and slid along the bench seat beside him.

Kate gave him a fleeting peck on his cheek. "Hi, 007. Don't talk. Just listen."

She beamed and opened her deep leather shoulder bag and pulled out a neat pile of papers. Each was headed with the official home office logo.

She shrugged her shoulders and chuckled. "This is the evidence you have been looking for, lover boy."

Glowing with anticipation of his praise, she began to ply Joe with documents.

"Here, let me explain. This one is the specification for the refurbishment of Hull prison after the riot. And this one is a list of the companies who tendered for the work. Notice that Tybuild is one of them. These are photocopies of each of the tenders." Kate kept on passing over sheets of paper from the wad she held in her hand.

Joe encouraged her further. "Go on, sweetheart."

"Look at the dates on the tenders. Never mind, hold on a second." She ruffled through the pile of paper. "I've typed out a separate sheet from the information gathered so far and summarised everything. It's here." She handed over the single, summary sheet. "Notice whose tender was the last to arrive, just one day before applications closed. Now, look at column two and see whose tender was marginally the lowest."

"Tybuild. So that's the plan. Rydell feeds Tybuild with the lowest tender price and they beat it with a better offer. I take it that Tybuild's price has been accepted?"

"Yes. I typed a letter accepting their tender yesterday morning."

"So, at last we have him. Rydell is guilty of providing insider information on government contracts. The man's corruption is beginning to stink."

Kate wasn't finished. "I'm afraid it's worse than that, Joe. This is only the tip of the iceberg."

Joe shrugged. "I don't get you. What more can there be?"

"When I was at work yesterday, I was looking through the pile of tenders again to double check on the details. I wanted to make sure that I was feeding you the correct information. Guess what? I couldn't find a single copy of the original specification to refurbish the prison. I was quite puzzled, but efficient secretary that I am, I'd taken a photocopy. Anyway, the final piece of Rydell's deception revealed itself this morning. When I looked again, I found this document in the file instead. It's a different specification for the same tender."

She handed over the final sheet, beaming with excitement. "Compare this new specification with the photocopy of the original I gave you."

Joe spent five minutes going through both documents. "Wow, you really struck gold with this one. The government is going to be out of pocket to the tune of about ten million pounds if this second one is substituted for the original. Tybuild will still get paid the agreed contract price, but the taxpayer is getting far less value for money. You have to give them credit for audacity. It's a masterly scheme and but for you, my treasure, they might easily have got away with it."

Kate blushed as the compliments flowed. "You started this ball rolling, sweetheart, when you first reported his fetish toys. And it was your detective work and persistence that uncovered these documents. You are a little gem and even though I'm dying to show your findings to Paula Ross, nothing is going to stop me from treating you to the biggest slap-up meal you've ever had."

He poured her a huge glass of red wine then passed her the menu. "Ready to order when you are."

Chapter 44

By late that same evening, Joe Harker had written a long and detailed report outlining the weeks' events and the links with Morgan and the Newsome massacre. He was convinced that Morgan and his female gang had carried out the Mafia style killings of Tyburn and Lush. He constructed a convincing scenario to show how everything fitted into place. The document procured by Kate Stephenson showed that the contract to rebuild Hull Jail had been awarded to Tyburn. Since both he and Lush were now dead, it was probable that Rydell was the only one left who knew about the riots. If that was true and all the blackmail evidence against him had been destroyed, then Rydell's new position seemed unassailable.

The following morning Harker went to see Paula Ross and gave her the report. She read it carefully and as she put it down, she gave a curious laugh. "Joe, this reads like a cartoon strip, but on the other hand, why not. I've a feeling your logic is sound and what seems implausible is in fact reality. What worries me is that by some insane fluke, Rydell appears to have been let off the hook. I've already had a quiet word with the Commissioner at the Met and they're completely baffled by the fire and the murders. Without any new leads, our amateur bombers are unlikely to be found out. In retrospect, they've done us a thousand favours. I see you have speculated on Rydell's next move and I think you may be right. Continue to stand your team down and we'll wait to see if your prediction comes true."

* * * * *

By six o'clock the following evening, Kate Stephenson had returned to her flat.

She rang Joe immediately. "Hello, darling, guess what?"

"Don't tell me, Rydell has been tampering with the home office files."

"Right, just like you forecast would happen. He's not wasted any time in exchanging Tyburn's substandard specification for the genuine one. He's replaced every bogus copy, which means he must have kept all the originals."

"What do you think his next move will be, Kate?"

"It's obvious. All he has to do is wait for a few weeks and when the deadline for acceptance of the tender is not received from Tybuild, he'll offer it to the next lowest bidder on his list. It's standard government practice."

"The clever bastard. He's found a perfect escape route, engineered a clean slate and is now free to continue his political career."

Later that evening, Joe had given Paula Ross an updated report, with one final recommendation. It was ready to be presented to the prime minister.

* * * * *

Paula Ross was invited to Number Ten for a midnight appointment.

The PM had been waiting expectantly and for once, the Head of MI6 was shown in as soon as she arrived.

"I believe there have been some important developments, Paula?"

"Yes, prime minister. It's all in the report and apart from one issue everything has been resolved."

The prime minister pushed her glasses to the end of her nose and looked over the top at Paula. She looked exhausted. Continuing criticism of her economic policies from within her own ranks had left her in poor spirits. Living with the Charles Rydell affair was also beginning to exact its price. It had become a worrying millstone around her neck.

"All I want is a satisfactory conclusion, so I can put this business behind me. I've enough troubles of my own with the cabinet without pariahs like Rydell making it worse. The Secretary of State for Northern Ireland has now resigned. He says it's for personal reasons, but I know he's found the job too much to handle. What a wimp! I seem to be surrounded by incompetent fools."

She held out her hand and Paula passed over the file.

"Please take a few minutes to reflect on this report, because some of the things you're about to read may seem difficult to believe. I assure you we are convinced of the authenticity of everything. The last piece of this bizarre theatre fell into place only this afternoon." She shrugged. "I'm afraid Rydell may be in the clear."

The prime minister read quickly, then totally out of character, flicked back to the beginning and re-read the whole document. She flopped back into her chair and scratched her head. "Well! Well! Would you believe it?" A broad smile burst across her face. "This, I like. The days of Bonny and Clyde seem far from over. You have to admire this Morgan fellow; he's got rid of a real nest of vipers. It would have cost the taxpayer millions to put on trial and incarcerate this little lot. But more importantly, he's done me a wonderful service into the bargain. Private enterprise, so to speak. I'd love to give him a medal."

Paula was taken aback when the PM suddenly chuckled aloud, "This is the best news I've had for weeks." She read the conclusion to the report for a third time, and then thumped her fist on the desktop angrily. "No matter what, I will not allow Rydell to get away with his scheming little plan. He's an absolute liability. He's been responsible for the deaths of many innocent people, not to mention the millions of pounds of government money required to rebuild Hull prison. Somehow, I have to get him out of office, permanently."

"May I make a suggestion that would fit in well with the recommendation made by Commander Harker? Why not promote him to the newly vacant cabinet post, the secretary of state for Northern Ireland. It will make it easier to deal with your problem. Here's the scenario."

Paula outlined her plan and it didn't take long before the prime minister had solemnly nodded her agreement. "Let it be done. Paula, I need to know the instant your team achieves its objective, before it's made public."

As soon as Paula Ross had left Number Ten, the PM carefully began planning her approach to Charles Rydell. She had to ensure he would accept the key post in her cabinet, when she offered it to him the following morning.

Chapter 45

The doorbell rang and Charles Rydell opened it to find two men standing on the threshold. There was a broad grin from the taller man, who stepped forward beyond the armed police officer, who had been assigned to stand guard at the entrance.

"Congratulations on your new position, sir. Can I introduce myself? My name is Commander Joe Harker and this is my assistant, Monty Wall. We are your new security team. We also do all the driving, in fact everything."

They thrust their ID cards forward so the new Secretary of State to Northern Ireland could check their details.

There was no need for the formalities. Rydell had been briefed on his security team and given pictures of the two men prior to this meeting. He had immediately memorised their faces. Although he was quickly coming to terms with the need for greater personal security, he hadn't yet become paranoid about the possibility of an assassination attempt. After all, the IRA had now called a permanent truce and had theoretically decommissioned all its arms.

Rydell shook hands with both of the men and then he turned and called out to his wife.

"Are you ready, Lynn? It's time to go."

The buxom blond appeared through the doorway and immediately gave Monty Wall the eye. He coughed into his hand and retreated to the car, slipping into the driver's seat.

Harker showed Rydell and his wife to the new ministerial Jaguar and opened the rear door for them to get in. A uniformed officer, who'd brought out their luggage, followed them from the flat.

Joe quickly stashed the two suitcases inside the car boot and they were on their way.

The fast car was soon clear of central London and heading west along the M4 towards Wales. The Rydells were due to fly by helicopter from RAF Valley in Anglesey and across the Irish Sea to Stormont Castle. Their itinerary was to spend an initial weekend being hosted at a number of receptions to help familiarise them with the political scene in the province. There was no disguising their excitement and they chattered amicably on the journey up to North Wales.

Joe was in contact with control on a regular basis, giving updates on their position and estimating an arrival time. As they approached the Menai Bridge, connecting Anglesey to mainland Wales, there was an emergency call to the car.

Joe spoke with apprehensive, theatrical tones to his controller and was told to follow a new procedure.

"I'm afraid there has been a slight change of plan, sir."

Rydell had picked up Harker's anxiety, as expected.

"What's happened? What do you mean?"

"There has been an accident on the runway at RAF Valley and there's a big fire. We've been told not to go there. Another helicopter has been diverted to an emergency airfield not far from here, so it shouldn't affect your flight plan."

Rydell sat back.

Lynn put a comforting hand on his knee. "Relax, Charles. There's nothing to worry about. I bet there are contingencies in place all the time for such eventualities. Isn't that right, Commander Harker?"

Joe grinned then turned round to face the politician and his wife. "Too true, Mrs Rydell. It's not much of an inconvenience. Don't worry, sir, we'll get you airborne safely."

The car crossed the bridge and followed the road to Holyhead for a few more miles. At a fork in the road, the Jaguar went right, then turned off down a minor road, which finally petered out into an unmade track. They bumped along past a number of old cottages and barns, turned through a gateway and then across a deserted piece of worn tarmac towards a disused aircraft hangar. As they approached, Rydell was relieved to see a helicopter ready and waiting in the lee of the building.

He protested pompously, "It's rather a small thing, isn't it?"

"Sorry, sir. You were due to fly in an RAF Lynx, but with the present flap, we had to take what was available in reserve. I've flown in these many times, they're a marvellous little machine."

Joe unloaded the boot and waved to Monty, who acknowledged his gesture and drove the car away from the old airfield.

Lynn Rydell questioned Harker further, "Isn't he coming with us?"

"No, ma'am. He has to take the car back to London. Most of the time you'll have both of us with you, but occasionally it's just one detective, I'm afraid. When we get over to Stormont Castle, I'll introduce you to another team of my colleagues. You'll find you have the protection of four bodyguards whilst you're over there."

This news seemed to please both of them.

Joe smiled reassuringly, picked up their bags and led the way to the helicopter. The only thing it had in common with any RAF machine, were the roundels that had been painted on the sides the night before.

Opening the side door, Joe carefully packed the suitcases into a compartment at the back. He then gave a helping hand to the new minister and his wife, ushering them into the rear seats of the helicopter. He clambered into the co-pilot's seat and clipped the waiting backpack around his shoulders. Then he fastened his safety harness ready for take-off.

"Can I introduce your pilot for this trip? He's a Welshman from the valleys, Lieutenant Taff Rawlings."

Rydell could not suppress his surprise at the Mongolian features of the pilot, who grinned round at him.

"Pleased to be flying you, I'm sure." He spoke with his broad Welsh twang, calling out aloud the checks to Joe, as he began the start-up procedure to get the helicopter airborne.

The giant blades slowly began to rotate. As their speed began to increase, there was a deafening roar. It reached a crescendo as the flailing rotors battered the air. The helicopter shook mercilessly. Taff gently pulled the joystick back and it slowly began to rise above the ground. Once in the air, the vibrations died away and it rose higher and higher. Turning away from the base, it headed out towards the sea.

Normal cruising altitude was soon reached as it scudded through the clear, cold skies above the rugged north-western coastline of Anglesey. The cloud base was high, so visibility was good and it didn't take long before land was well behind them.

Harker searched the waters below them and eventually spied the wash of a huge powerboat, now trailing in their wake. It was about two miles astern.

"Looks like Josh is on time for a change. How about it, Taff? Ready?"

The pilot said nothing, but looked across to Harker and winked. The two of them unclipped their safety harnesses.

Rydell noticed their quick, concerted actions and suddenly sensed danger. "What are you doing? What's happening?"

Joe turned round to face them for one last time. "Enjoy the rest of your trip."

With that, the two pilots simultaneously opened their side doors and jumped clear of the helicopter. They dropped away from the clattering rotor blades and at a preset height, their parachutes fluttered open to break their fall. Guiding themselves expertly, they glided into the path of the oncoming motor launch where Josh Gardner was ready to pick them up.

Cold sea air thundered into the tiny cockpit of the helicopter as the swinging front doors clattered against the fuselage. Lynn Rydell was beside herself with panic. She held her head and began to scream hysterically.

The once stable aircraft was now being buffeted about and without a pilot to trim the machine, it began to lurch and rock crazily.

Charles Rydell hunched in his seat. His sense of balance was poor at the best of times and the insane switch back, he now found himself riding was more than he could handle. He went green as a bout of nausea shook his body.

"Do something, Charles. For God's sake, do something." Lynn Rydell looked at the pitiful wretch at her side and realised that she had to act. She gathered her remaining composure and leaning forward into the pilot's seat, did the only thing she could think of and yanked the joystick over.

As Joe and Taff floated safely downwards, they watched the ailing helicopter. It rose and dipped, twisted and trembled, bumping about on the unpredictable air currents. Its direction shifted left and then right as it continued to plough a desperate furrow through the air. Suddenly, the helicopter went totally out of control and began to corkscrew towards the sea. It dropped very fast and as it spiralled downwards, they heard the screeching of its engine as terrible, unnatural forces tried to tear it apart.

In its final death throes, it hit the sea with a mighty thump. The light aluminium body and Perspex canopy disintegrated on impact. There was a small detonation of spilled fuel on the surface of the sea, but any fragments of the wreck soon sank below the surface. There could have been no survivors and it would take months of salvage work before either of the bodies or any remnants of the helicopter would be recovered, if at all. The MI6 team had at last, done a first-rate job.

* * * * *

The prime minister was seated at her desk in Number Ten. Her mind was not on the task she had set herself that morning. For some reason, she was luxuriating in the creativity of a daydream.

There was an irate knock and she automatically shook herself out of her lethargy. The door opened without invitation and her private secretary poked his head round the corner.

"Come in, Jim. What's the big hurry?"

"I'm afraid it's bad news, prime minister. This report has just come in."

He handed over a single sheet that had been faxed to her office.

"Oh dear! No! But this is a terrible tragedy. What a loss! Charles Rydell and his wife are both missing and the two pilots as well. I can't believe it's happened." She shook her head in sorrow as she read the sheet, then stared in disbelief at her secretary.

"I'm sorry, prime minister. I've already been in touch with the police to confirm these details. There's a search and rescue operation taking place now, but hopes of finding them alive are receding fast."

The prime minister shed a few tears. She'd been fed all this information an hour earlier by Paula Ross and had been waiting for the report to come through. Her show of emotion was well rehearsed. "Please, leave me now, Jim. I'd like to be alone."

He slipped quietly away and as soon as he'd gone, she unlocked the bottom drawer of her desk and took out a number of files.

Sauntering over to the machine in the corner, she set it going. The files were gently pushed through the shredder. The blades hummed quietly as they did their work, destroying forever all the evidence of the conspiracy involving Charles Rydell.

She rubbed her hands with quiet satisfaction and returned to her work.

Nobody makes a fool of me and gets away with it.

Chapter 46

The phone rang loudly, but in the busy police operations room, it took a long time to answer. A WPC finally responded and looking round, summoned Tom Willis over. "It's for you, but they wouldn't say who it was."

Willis grabbed the phone and gave his name.

"Listen, Willis. Get out to a public phone and ring this number. Do it now or you're finished."

The caller read out the number and rang off.

Willis recognised the voice instantly and knew there was no messing with this man. It was Dexter and he seemed upset. That was worrying.

Without drawing attention to himself, he quickly left the building to find the nearest outside phone. When he rang the number, he was immediately met by a barrage of questions.

"Do you remember the woman who got away from us at Newsome's house? You tipped us off about finding her at the hospital."

"Yeah! So, what."

"I need to know where she came from. I need an address. Do I make myself clear?"

Willis didn't like the tone of his voice and the implied threats, but he managed an inner sigh. He had the required information and could supply it easily.

"No problem! It's a place in Sheffield and I have the address in my office. She lived there with her father, Matthew Morgan. It's not him you're after, by any chance?"

The voice on the other end of the phone sounded wary, "What fuckin' business is it of yours?"

"Nothing, except to warn you that MI6 has suddenly taken an interest in him. I don't know what it's all about, but if they move in on him, you'd better watch your step."

"Thanks for the tip, but by the time I've finished with him, they'll only have the satisfaction of picking up the pieces. Now, get back over to your office and dig me out the address. I'll ring you at the station in exactly 30 minutes. Don't let me down."

Dexter put the phone down and grimaced. He'd kill Morgan if it was the last thing he did.

* * * * *

The Jaguar's engine beat a satisfying rhythm as Matt powered it homewards. He'd only been back at work a couple of days, but his adventure in the capital was still fresh in his mind and he couldn't help replaying each incident over and over. The girls had appeared satisfied with the outcome and to some extent he felt the same. Yet when he analysed his true feelings, he knew it wasn't over. Dexter was still at large. He was the one who pulled the trigger and the thought of letting Kirsty's killer escape, fired the rage inside him once more. He hadn't said anything, but in five weeks it would be the Easter holidays and he was determined to make another trip to London to try and trace Dexter.

Matt turned into his road and drew up on the driveway. As he was getting out of the car, his neighbour from across the street called him over. It was Mrs Pickin, a kindly old widow who organised the local neighbourhood watch.

She handed him a new telephone directory and yellow pages. "Hello, Matthew, these were delivered today and as there was no one in, I said I'd take them in for you."

"Thanks, Irene. That's very good of you."

"By the way, there's been an odd-looking stranger around all day. He called at your house twice this morning. The second time I came outside and asked him straight, *Who are you looking for?* He told me such a tale about being an old school friend of yours, but I didn't believe him. He was a southerner with a horrible, stony face. Anyway, he came back five minutes ago, in that great thing." She pointed to a white Range Rover, which was parked at the bottom of the cul-de-sac.

Matt became terribly uneasy. She'd given a perfectly, potted description of Dexter.

Mrs Pickin rambled on, "Do you know, he's had the nerve to go round the back of your house. I was just about to phone the police when you arrived."

Matt instinctively put his arm round his kindly neighbour and ushered her back to the safety of her own home. "Don't worry Irene. It's all right. I have been expecting an old mate to pop round, but I didn't think he'd come today. Thanks for keeping an eye on the house. It's much appreciated."

He made sure that her door was closed, then sprinted across to his car.

If it was Dexter, then he could use this opportunity to his advantage. He could park in one of the side streets further down the road and follow him when he eventually got fed up of waiting for Matt.

He'd barely opened the car door when Dexter ambled round to the front of the house.

Matt grimaced. "You. I knew it."

Dexter recognised him instantly and rushed forward. "Your luck's run out this time, Mr Morgan."

But he was wrong. Matt had inadvertently left his key in the ignition. He dropped into the seat and pulled out the starter knob. The engine was still warm and it fired up first time.

Dexter made a grab for the half open door, just as Matt threw his machine into reverse. He was instantly left groping in thin air and before he could react, Matt had thrust his car into forward gear. The Jaguar thundered away towards the end of the road.

Dexter raced back to his own car and started the engine. As he let out the clutch, the tyres squealed and he launched the Range Rover in pursuit. Matt was deeply troubled and he racked his brain for a way out of the mess. Dexter would most certainly be armed and ready to finish him off at the first opportunity. There was only his old car between him and certain death. They hurtled crazily along the side roads, breaking all speed restrictions and jumping red lights with impunity. Morgan tried everything he could to shake off his pursuer, but Dexter was good and he gradually began gaining ground.

It was then Matt remembered the two phials of nitro still hidden at the cottage. An idea was born of desperation. If he could arm himself with the explosive, at least he would have a chance. Darkness was falling and that would also help his cause. It seemed his only hope. Without further consideration, he turned his car away from the city suburbs and headed towards the Peak District.

Once in the countryside, he wound up the revs on the old car. The Range Rover would not be left in his wake and followed a couple of hundred yards behind. Matt was a skilful driver and threw his jaguar into the tightest bends at extreme speed. He continually crossed over the centre line of the road, chancing his luck against oncoming traffic, intoxicated by the fear of failure. Knowledge of the local roads enabled him to anticipate the hazards ahead and the gap between him and Dexter gradually began to widen. The chase continued to eat up the miles as they tore through the craggy scenery with its hidden brows and sharply twisting bends. They were not far from the cottage when Matt faced a new anxiety. The water temperature gauge on his dashboard was showing a steep increase. He'd been pushing the old Jaguar too hard. He had no option but to throttle back the engine and let the revs drop. He knew that the Rover would soon gain its lost ground, but he daren't chance seizing up his engine.

Luckily, he was nearing the cottage track and had one last trick to try and gain some precious time. He left it until the very last second and then jammed his foot down hard on the brake pedal, turning the wheel sharply. The move was that of an expert and the rear of his car whipped round so that he was in a direct line with the entrance to the track. Switching pedals, he hit the accelerator. The rear wheels spun viciously, but the powerful engine was soon pulling the heavy car forward. The Jaguar bumped and rocked mercilessly on the uneven ground, but then catastrophe struck. It had managed to get barely half way to the cottage before one of the front wheels dropped into a deep, muddy rut. The car refused to respond to the controls and the boot slewed back and forth as the rear wheels spun and began to dig themselves into ruts of their own.

Matt had no time to waste. The Jaguar was well and truly stuck, so he abandoned it and set off towards the distant wall where the explosives were hidden.

Dexter had been only yards behind the Jaguar when Matt made his sudden turn. The thug reacted fast, but the Range Rover was a heavy car with a higher centre of gravity. When Dexter braked and turned to follow, he found himself in a sideways, four-wheel skid. The big motor continued to slide off the road, coming to a halt in a grassy ditch. It was keeled over at an angle of 45 degrees and would have rolled on its side, but for a large bush that stopped it from falling over. The engine stalled and Dexter wasted precious seconds trying to get it restarted.

Matt raced across the track in the rapidly approaching dusk and reached the gap in the old stone wall. He rested for a moment, regaining some composure and taking air into his tortured lungs. In the distance, he could hear the repeated shriek of the Rover's starter motor.

At last, the powerful car roared back into life. Setting it into four-wheel drive, Dexter slowly edged forward and manoeuvred the Rover out of the ditch. Staying in low gear, he turned the car round and found the entrance to the track. He followed the unmade road and bumped along past the deserted jaguar. He headed towards the distant wall.

By now, Matt had reached the spot where the nitro was buried. He peered over the top of the wall to see where Dexter was and in the gathering gloom, saw the Range Rover, bouncing across the uneven ground towards his position.

He frantically began to burrow amongst the grass with his bare hands, looking for the edge of the turf that covered the buried box.

Dexter scanned from side to side looking for Matt, but couldn't see him. At the last minute, as he approached the gap in the wall, he realised that the Rover wouldn't get through. He braked quickly and the car lurched to a halt with its front end jutting diagonally across the gap. He thrust the driver's door wide open and jumped up onto the wall to get a better view. In the half-light, he spotted Matt squatting in the shadows of the wall.

He pulled his gun out and aimed.

Matt had finally managed to yank away the slice of turf to expose the explosive cache.

Sliding the loose wooden lid to one side, he fumbled through the insulation and aching, grateful fingers closed around one of the glass phials.

He glanced back and saw his predicament. The Range Rover was half jammed across the entrance to the field with the driver's door wide open, but where was Dexter? He looked all around.

In the fading light, he suddenly caught sight of him looking down from the wall. He was little more than 50 feet away and his image was more of a silhouette. Matt seemed transfixed, and there was no mistaking the flash and the loud report as the gun went off.

Matt felt an agonising pain rip across the top of his arm and he slipped to one knee. His hand felt weak as a dull numbness began seeping down his arm, causing him to lose his tenuous grip on the nitro. He gritted his teeth and put the nitro down. He had to make a run for it. Knowing that the Range Rover couldn't get through the gap, Dexter would have to come after him on foot. His only chance of escape was to try and hide in the gathering darkness. Bolting across the grass, he headed for the copse of trees beyond the edge of the field.

Suddenly, the Rover's headlights lit up on full beam and Matt hesitated, slipping on the damp grass. Glancing behind in fear, he had to shield his eyes from the blinding light. He was now completely at Dexter's mercy.

Just then, a voice drifted from an unseen body, somewhere near the car. "I'm really going to enjoy killing you, Morgan."

Matt detected the shadowy movement of Dexter moving along the top of the wall. The figure jumped down into the field and immediately there was a strange muffled crump. Matt watched in amazement as Dexter's body was flung high into the air. Smoke and a cascade of sparks gave the twilight a bizarre aura. All kinds of human debris, followed by a dark crimson mist, descended through the headlights illuminating the macabre scene.

Dexter had inadvertently jumped down into the hole, smashing the last tubes of nitro and causing a terrible upward detonation.

Matt turned his head and caught the grisly sight of a severed leg, lying next to him. Gingerly, he pulled himself to his feet and examined his painful wound. He'd been lucky and the bullet had only seared the outer flesh. There appeared to be no serious damage.

It took time before his eyes recovered from the dazzle of the headlights. As they gradually became adjusted to the light, he began to search for the thug. Dexter lay next to a small smoking crater. Standing over him, Matt looked down at the tortured face. Blood oozed thickly from the ruptured vessels of his severed limb. Despite his desperate situation, Dexter struggled to reach his gun, lying nearby in the grass. Matt watched his pitiful attempt to drag himself towards the weapon, but before he could get anywhere near, he kicked it away, far beyond his reach.

"Haven't you done enough, you bastard? Give it up!"

Dexter looked up and tried to speak, but nothing came from his mouth except a choking, inaudible whisper. His eyes finally rolled upwards, his jaw dropped open and his body went limp.

Matt stared into the dead man's face. "At last, it's over."

Inexplicably, a lump came to his throat and warm tears filled his eyes. "Kirsty! Oh, Kirsty, what have I become?" He stood up. Revenge was complete, but the sweetness of victory somehow eluded him. He felt numb and very weary.

After staring at the pathetic corpse for what seemed an age, he managed to shake himself from his apathy and began to put his mind to his own self-preservation. His only priority now was to cover up the incident.

He immediately rang Melissa. In guarded tones, he gave her a short account of what had happened and within the hour she'd arrived to help.

In the darkness, they set about cleaning up the site. She'd brought a couple of spades and they began by digging a deep grave amidst the copse of trees. The body of Dexter, his gun and the debris from the cache were all buried together and the location cleverly concealed.

The Range Rover had escaped the explosion unscathed and they used it to pull the Jaguar out of the deep ruts. Despite its harsh treatment, Matt's car started up first time. They took Melissa's Peugeot to the safety of a nearby pub car park, ready for collection later and returned to the cottage. She clambered aboard the Range Rover and sedately followed Matt back to Sheffield. Driving to one of the less salubrious areas of the city, they left it with its keys in the ignition and when they checked on it the following morning, were relieved to see it had disappeared.

The police found it the next night, burnt out on a patch of waste ground, after a group of adolescent joy riders had finished their midnight fun.

Chapter 47

Matt and Melissa were married at the beginning of the Easter holidays. The wedding was a registry office affair and Melissa looked radiant in an elegant, white suit. They hired a hotel and held a small reception for 50 close friends and relatives. The afternoon was a splendid occasion and the party was in full swing when it was time for the newlyweds to leave.

Tenerife was their destination, for a two-week honeymoon in the sun.

It was a tearful farewell as Laura hugged and kissed them both.

Waving frantically to everyone, they drove away from the reception and soon joined the M1 for the hour-long journey to the East Midlands Airport.

They'd only driven a few miles before a police motorway patrol car approached along the middle lane and tucked in behind them.

"Damn it, Mel, we've got cops on our tail."

"You're not speeding are you, Matt?"

"No. I'm only doing 60. Perhaps, they fancy a look at the Jag."

The police car seemed to hang back, checking them over. Without warning the driver started his siren and flashing blue light. It pulled out and drove parallel to them.

An odd-looking oriental policeman pointed to Matt and indicated that he should pull over to the hard shoulder.

"Jesus. What next? I hope they don't make us late for the plane."

Matt stopped the car and got out. The police vehicle halted slightly ahead and its co-driver came back to meet him.

"Mr Morgan, I believe?"

Matt stammered, "Yes, that's right. But how do you know? What can I do for you, officer?"

"I'd like you to follow us to the next motorway services area, it's only a couple of miles away."

"What for? What have I done?"

"Let's say that your recent past has just caught up with you and someone would like a quiet word. By the way, it's no use trying to make a run for it. You'll never get away."

Turning back to the Jaguar, Matt got in beside Melissa, a look of utter dejection haunting his face. When he'd explained the gravity of the situation, she broke down and wept. All their beautiful plans were in ruins.

Matt tried to console her, but he had no time. The police were hooting impatiently for him to follow.

The motorway service area loomed up quickly and Matt sped up the slip road, wondering what fate had in store for them. The police vehicle in front flagged him to a halt in the outer lorry park. The officer came back and beckoned him out. He pointed to a sleek, black limousine parked 50 yards up the road.

"This way, Mr Morgan."

Melissa tried to follow, but the police officer put up his hand. "Not you, Madam. He's wanted alone."

Matt approached the limousine with Joe Harker at his shoulder. The windows were darkly tinted and the occupants impossible to discern.

When he reached the rear passenger door, Harker tapped on the glass and the electric window slid noiselessly down. Matt stared in disbelief at the woman who was peering out into the strong sunlight. His mouth gaped open.

"Yes, Mr Morgan. It may seem incredible to you, but I can assure you, you certainly have not seen a ghost."

The woman had a twinkle in her eye and a friendly smile parted her lips. "I've been wanting to meet you for some time."

"But I don't understand."

"Well, let's say you've been of great service to your country. Since your recent little escapades in London, my political standing has taken on a new lease of life. You'll never understand the implication of how your actions have helped me. I fully understand your philosophy on life and I wanted to thank you personally. Please don't worry about a thing. Your little vendetta will forever remain a secret. May I offer you this small gesture as a mark of my gratitude?"

She handed Matt a small packet neatly wrapped.

"But, prime minister! I don't know what to say, except, thank you."

"Goodbye, Mr Morgan. You never know, I might need your services again sometime." She shook his hand and the smoked glass window glided closed. The engine came to life immediately and the PM's limousine slipped smoothly away.

Looking round as though he was in a dream, Matt sought confirmation of what he'd just witnessed, but there was no one else around. The surly police officer had already melted away. He gave a friendly wave as his powerful patrol car slid past and headed after the prime minister, eager to escort her on the journey back to the capital.

Melissa came racing out of the jaguar to question her smiling, bemused husband. He threw his arms around her and held her so tightly he nearly crushed her. He explained everything in a garble of emotion. "It's all right, everything's fine. Look, what I've just been given."

When he opened the package, he found a beautifully bound copy of the Holy Bible, inscribed with the PMs own signature and the simple reference.

Exodus 21: 23 – 27

Melissa eagerly looked up the quotation and read it out aloud, "*An eye for an eye and a tooth for a tooth.* Somebody's got you spot on there."

* * * * *

The old burglar, Davy Tonks died on Good Friday. After the fright, he suffered when he read about the drowning of Gary Gordon, his health spiralled slowly downwards.

All his family was at his hospital bedside during the final hours and even before he died there was a feeling of great loss. No one was more grief stricken than his wife, Mamma Tonks. She'd been a beautiful Italian teenager when he'd first met her. Her family had been refugees from the corrupt dictatorship of Mussolini and had settled in England after the war.

Bringing up three strapping sons had sapped her good looks and she was now a plain, matronly figure. She had nursed Davy through the final months and weeks of his illness and wasn't in the best of health herself. Having been married for 40 years, she was fully aware of his unlawful profession. But, like many good Italian wives, she had asked no questions. Davy had always provided for her and the boys and had never let them down. Now that he was gone, she knew her sons would take care of her in her old age. Nevertheless, she was disappointed he hadn't mentioned the existence of a little nest egg, which might have given her some luxury in her years as a widow.

Instead, just before he died, Davy pushed a small key wrapped in a sheet of paper into her palm. Kissing her gently, he finally slipped away.

Mamma Tonks was intrigued by what he'd passed on to her, but as a devout Catholic, went straight to the hospital Chapel to pray.

Later that night, she showed the key to her eldest son.

"It's a safe deposit key, Mamma. Look, this is the name of the bank and here is the box number. If you like, I'll take you round after the holiday weekend and we can see what's in it."

They were at the bank as soon as it opened on the Tuesday morning and were shown into the vaults. After all the formalities had been completed, they were left alone to examine the contents of the box. Mamma was quite excited, imagining that Davy had squirrelled away a treasure trove of priceless gems. She sighed with disappointment when she opened the lid, only to find two plain envelopes. One was small and white, addressed personally to her, in Davy's scrawling style. The other was a large, brown one, which had not been sealed.

She opened the letter that bore her name and read aloud the simple message.

To my one and only love,

I fear that I must now be gone if you are reading this note. I would have liked to provide more for you in your old age, but alas the work I have done has never provided a pension. Lady luck did smile a few months ago, and I feel I may have left you something worthwhile. A man owed me a great deal of money for a job we did together, but he was reluctant to pay. I found out where he lived and broke into his flat and took what I thought was rightfully mine. It was a good job too because he was killed soon afterwards. The brown envelope contains not money, but a DVD I copied. It's what the man was killed for! Take it to the daily newspapers. I have a feeling they will offer you a small fortune. We'll meet again in heaven,

Love Davy.

That same afternoon, her son drove Mamma Tonks to the offices of the *Daily Mirror*. They were immediately shown into the editor's office. He'd been intrigued by their earlier phone call claiming they had a startling political revelation that would rock the government.

The editor loaded the disc into his computer and watched enthralled at the content of the DVD, exposing the secret life of Charles Rydell. He whistled through his teeth at what he'd seen.

When he'd finished watching, he grinned excitedly. "I'm prepared to offer you 100,000 pounds for this. Do you think we can make a deal?"

Mamma looked at her son, and then nodded an affirmative.

The editor made two swift phone calls. The first was to his legal department, demanding an immediate meeting, and the second was to the print room.

He bawled the old Fleet Street adage down the mouthpiece:

"Stop the press!"